DEAD CELEB

DEAD CELEB SERIES — BOOK ONE

MICHELE SCOTT

DEDICATION

For you Debbie Rosen because you get it!

CHAPTER ONE

MY NAME IS EVIE PRESTON and I hang out with dead rock stars. Oh, and the occasional dead movie star or two. I've learned quite a bit about those who live on the other side over the past few months. For instance, they aren't all ghostly and transparent. Oh no. The ones I see are almost always in full- color and 3-D except when they exert, ah ... certain energies. Then they go a bit hazy. Oh, and they prefer to be called spirits.

Yeah, I know ... I sound completely insane. Like, "commit me" insane. But honestly, I am not crazy. Believe me, the first time I saw Bob Marley in my place (well, technically not my place, but I'll get to that) in the Hollywood Hills, getting high and singing "Buffalo Soldier," I thought I was either dreaming, hallucinating, or, yes, completely nuts. Thankfully, it was none of the above. In fact, Bob is a very real, very dead guy who likes to hang out with me, along with a handful of other deceased, famous rock musicians (and a few who never quite made the charts, one of whom I've recently developed feelings for—more about him later). So, not only do I hang out with dead rock stars, I also think I am in love with one, or at least in lust... which makes me totally screwed up. But I am not crazy. I swear.

Before I go any further, though, I need to take you back a few months to the day after my twenty-eighth birthday. Welcome to Brady, Texas—population 5,500 —and, according to the sign on the main road into town, "The Heart of Texas." Truth be told, the signs were everywhere. Signs, that is, telling me to get the hell out of Brady.

I was at Mrs. Betty LaRue's place. Her house smelled of Tide, home cooking, and mothballs. Betty was comforting me over the dismal turnout of my Mary Kay presentation—my latest attempt at becoming an entrepreneur—which she'd kindly hosted.

We were drinking apple-cranberry tea, with her Lhasa Apso, Princess, curled in a ball under Betty's chair, and my dog (of indeterminate breed ... possibly part-coyote and part-lab, with a dash of border collie in there), Mama Cass, across my feet. I loved how Betty always let me bring Cass in the house. My dog went everywhere with me, but not everyone was as gracious about her presence as Betty.

"I really thought this would go much better," I said, bringing the warm cup of tea to my lips.

Betty smiled sympathetically, the fine lines in her eighty- something face creasing deeper into her skin, "Oh, honey, I don't know what happened to my girls today. I am so sorry. I thought there'd be at least ten of us. They all love my snickerdoodles. But you know how some of us old gals are; we forget things." She twirled a yellow-white wisp of curled hair around her finger. The rest of it was pulled up into a loose bun (or chignon as Mama calls it). She'd obviously been in to see my mother that morning for her weekly hair appointment.

I nodded. "It's okay, Betty. Thanks for hosting anyway, and the cookies were delicious. Three isn't such a bad turnout." Thing was, only Betty bought anything. Her friends, Margaret and Hazel, came for the cookies and samples. "And I made about ten dollars, so that will buy me a couple of meals. You'll love that anti-wrinkle cream, by the way."

Betty ran a hand over her face and laughed sweetly. "Child, ain't nothing gonna work on this face now. And I'm proud of these lines. I earned them."

I laughed back. "So you only bought the cream because you felt sorry for me?" Cass's ears perked up and she lifted her head to peer at me.

Betty sighed. "Evie Preston, I have known you since you started kicking up a fuss in your mama's belly." She winked at me. "I've watched you try so hard to be exactly what your mama and daddy wanted, especially after all that bad business. And there was that unfortunate situation with—" She paused. "What was his name?"

She brought her cup to her lips, her hand shaking ever so slightly. I sighed, knowing exactly what bad business she was referring to. As for the unfortunate situation, he was the star quarterback my senior year and the lucky recipient of my virginity. Sadly, he was also the jerk who then decided to share the news with the entire town. Thank God my mother was able to intercept that little tidbit before it reached my father's ears.

Betty waved her free hand in the air as if to brush the painful thoughts away. "I know you were hoping to be a good Texas girl and marry a good Texas boy and have babies and run a family like your folks did, not because you really wanted it," she said, shaking a finger at me. "But because your parents wanted it for you. And now, my dear," Betty leaned over and gave me one of her rare, stern looks. "It's high time you stopped pretending and started living!"

"What do you mean?"

"You got a God-given talent. You need to get out there and do something with it."

She tried to set the tea cup down on the side table and almost missed. I grabbed it and set it down for her. Betty beamed at me. "Thank you, honey! Always so polite."

I looked down at my dog, licking the unpolished toes peeking out of the only pair of high-heeled sandals I owned. "Fact is, Betty, I know I'm good, but there are a lot of good musicians out there." I dejectedly twirled the ends of my long, baby-fine hair. Mama always said God hadn't been paying close attention when it came time to give me hair. It was stick straight, dark brown, and silky. I couldn't do a darn thing with it, except put it into ponytails.

Betty waved her hand again. "Nonsense!" Placing her hands on the sides of her chair, she slowly pushed herself up to a stand and ambled over to the white brick mantle. She grabbed an envelope and handed it to me.

"What's this?" I asked.

"Your birthday was yesterday, wasn't it?"

"You remembered?"

She frowned. "I may be old, Evie, but I don't forget birthdays. Especially when they're for people I care about."

"That is so sweet of you." I was flattered and grateful someone seemed happy to have me around.

"Oh honey, you know you're one of my favorite people. You got spunk! Had it since you came out ass-backward, showing the world what you thought of it."

"Thank you, I think." I couldn't help smiling. Betty was the only one I knew who spoke the truth without holding back. Betty was authenticity at it's finest. She didn't tiptoe around stuff like my family. Tiptoeing was what we did best.

"Open it! I don't have all day. It's about time for my nap."

I tore open the envelope and found a check inside for five thousand dollars, made out to me. I gasped.

"Betty! What..." Cass jumped up, her huge ears pricked forward, tail wagging, watching me like a hawk. "It's okay, girl." She lay back down but still alert.

"I was twenty-eight once too, you know, and I had dreams ... big dreams." Betty's blue eyes glazed over for a moment. "I wanted to be a movie star, and I could have, too. I was damn good, like you are at what you do, and, believe it or not, I used to be good looking." She winked at me again, but there were tears in her eyes. I knew about Betty's dreams from long ago. I also knew there was a part of her life that hadn't been so good.

"But then my folks, like yours, had other ideas and I decided to play by their rules. I don't regret it ... well, maybe I do a little. Thing is, young lady, you can sing like a nightingale and you can play the guitar like nobody's business. You need to get the hell out of this town before you wind up like every other girl here—knocked up, changing dirty diapers, and cleaning up after some idiot male who spends his nights with a beer in one hand and a TV remote in the other."

I frowned. I'd already seen almost every girl from my high school graduating class living the life Betty had just described. The lucky ones skipped town and went to college. I hadn't been quite that lucky for a variety of reasons. I had the grades and the desire, but life had other ideas. On the positive side, which is where I like to go, I'd at least not had the misfortune of marrying some guy who didn't appreciate me, expected his dinner on the table when he got home from his shift at Walmart, and wanted his wife and children to obey, just because he said so.

"Betty, I really do appreciate your vote of confidence but still, I can't accept this." I held the check towards her.

"Yes, you can, and you will. Go live your life, Evie Preston. Pack up that van of yours, your guitar, and Mama Cass, and head west. You sing your heart out in every bar, every café, every church—I don't care where you go, but go and sing. I know one thing: you have what it takes to be a star. Forget all about them cosmetics you're trying to pawn..."

"Mary Kay," I interrupted. "It is a really good line. Mama swears by it."

She frowned and waved that hand at me. "Just forget all that, because you and I both know it won't get you nowhere. That kind of thing is for people like Shirley Swan up the road trying to make an extra buck to take care of those four kids of hers. Take the money, cut your losses, and run. You gotta stop living for your mama and daddy. You didn't cause what happened and you can't never change it." She shook her head vehemently. "Go on and live life. Do it for me. Humor an old woman, please?" Her blue eyes watered, the creases crinkling as she choked back emotion.

How could I refuse after a plea like that? I tried one last time, for the sake of courtesy. "But my daddy—"

Betty dabbed at her eyes with a kerchief. "He'll get over it. And your mama is gonna secretly be cheering you on. It'll be hard on them, but this'll be the best thing for all of you." She sighed heavily. "Especially you, Evie. Trust me."

So I did. I trusted Betty LaRue.

The next day I packed up my 1974 VW bus, a suitcase of clothes, my Rosewood Gibson acoustic guitar, and Mama Cass. I pulled out of my parents' driveway while Daddy waved his arms wildly in the air, yelling, "You're gonna ruin your life out there, Evangeline!" (He's the only one who ever calls me by my full name.) "Los Angeles isn't the city of angels. It's a city of heathens and devils!"

I knew he was just scared. I'm pretty sure if I looked closer, I'd see tears in his eyes. But Betty was right. This was something I had to do.

I could see tears for sure in my mother's big hazel eyes, the same color as my own, as she mouthed, "I love you."

I rolled down the window, choking back my own sobs. "I love you, too! I'll call. Don't worry. I'll be fine."

With blurred eyes, Mama Cass's head in my lap, a Patsy Cline cassette in the tape deck (thank God for eBay—you have no idea how hard it is to find cassette tapes these days), I headed west to the City of Angels. For the first time in sixteen years, I felt like I could finally breathe again. I was leaving behind the only two people I knew who I had never been able to heal even a little bit, and I didn't think I ever could.

CHAPTER TWO

I AM NOT A REBEL by nature. Or who knows ... maybe I am. Regardless, it's never really been an option for me. Not after what my parents went through. I could never yell, lie, sneak out of the house, or talk back. None of that. And those weren't their rules; they were my own. So leaving my mother and father behind on that late April afternoon was by far the most rebellious thing I had ever done in my twenty-eight years, and honestly, it left me feeling cold.

Poor Cass with her thick coat must have hated me on that fifteen hundred mile trip, because I was freezing the whole way and cranked up the heater in my van, even as we drove through Arizona's hot, desert climate. It was the kind of cold you can feel on the inside—that only a real hot bath combined with a hot drink and a tuck between the covers can cure.

I wasn't sick. No sore throat. No aching body. Nothing like that. I was just cold.

And then, after three days of driving and staying in cheap motels, I took the 10 West all the way to L.A., and the chill left as suddenly and mysteriously as it had arrived.

The first thing I did was head to the ocean—Venice Beach to be exact. Yes, Los Angeles has plenty of tan, beautiful people and then some, but let me just say for the record, there are also a ton of freaks here, especially in Venice Beach. I saw one guy with hair the color of mashed peas that hung down to his rear in twisted, greasy ropes. He wasn't wearing a shirt and the waistband of his shorts sat well beneath his boxers. Not an attractive look, especially considering the live iguana wrapped around his neck. Never seen that before.

Cass went totally berserk, yapping at him and the lizard. I had to yank pretty hard on her leash to get her to move while the guy snarled, "Get your mangy piece of shit mutt outta my face, dude!"

Um, excuse me? At least my dog takes regular baths, which is certainly more than I could say about Mr. Mange and his lizard sidekick. I decided to keep my mouth shut and move along, tugging on Cass the entire way. I made an effort to give him as wide a berth as possible, not wanting to accidentally brush against him and deal with the onslaught of negative emotions that would happen as a result.

Okay. I guess it's probably time I let this particular cat out of the bag. See the thing is, when I turned twelve, my parents and I went through some tough times. And ever since, I've been able to get information about people through touch. But not just any information—traumatic, painful information. Caught your husband of thirty years sleeping with your best friend? Lost your mom in a car accident when you were a teen? Well, if you and I have come into contact before, chances are, I already know all about it. But that's not all. I can also help ease the pain ... give people a permanent Band-Aid to slap on that painful memory. I can't make the pain disappear, but I sure can help you to cope with it, minus years of therapy or self-medication.

Sounds great, right? Well, have you ever paid attention to just how many times a day you touch someone? At the supermarket, at the salon, at a restaurant ... it happens all the time, and you're mostly not aware of it at all.

I've had to train myself to be extra focused on where I am and who's around me in order to cope. Truth be told, I'm pretty cautious who I touch these days, and I also make a conscious effort to put some kind of barrier in place (gloves, mittens, napkins, whatever's handy) if I know there's a chance my hands might brush up against another person, because it is my hands that tend to be the main conductor of this gift. If my hands touch someone else, particularly their hands, that is when I get the clearest visions. I'd receive some information if someone were to bump against me, but the touching of hands is what I am most aware of.

Betty LaRue was one of the first people I "read." It happened at Easter, sixteen years ago, when I took her hand to show her the new kitten Mama brought home for me (another gift meant to help me deal with our recent loss). All I got were glimpses— of a much younger Betty and the baby she lost when she was only seventeen, courtesy of a pregnancy caused by a boyfriend who didn't take no for an answer one night—and they scared the hell out of me.

In any case, touching people like Cranky Dreadlock Man was simply not an option for me. No telling what sorts of nasty images I'd pick up from him.

Once we got past him, we reached the ocean. Color—silvery blue. Smell—fresh and salty—minus the cigarette smoke and sickly sweet scent of tanning oil that occasionally wafted its way toward us. The crashing waves and sandy beach were like something from a postcard. Cass and I people-watched for some time. Cheapest entertainment in the world. Bring a lawn chair, a bag of Tostitos, and a six-pack of soda, and you'll find the movies have nothing on Venice Beach. When I need to get away from anyone famous—dead or alive—I head there. And I figure, the best way to beat crazy is to go and see even more crazy.

Cass and I shared a couple slices of pizza and a Coke (yes, Cass drinks Coke, too, but none of that diet stuff), and I decided we needed to find a place to stay for the night. And then I needed to find a job. I knew five thousand dollars was probably not going to get us very far in the land of glitz and glamour. I mean, sure it's a lot of money, and I may have been born but I wasn't born last Tuesday. I'm not dumb. LA was a far cry from Grady where I'd already noticed gas prices had jumped significantly the further west I'd traveled.

I found a motel a few blocks from the beach. It was fifty-five bucks for the night, which seemed like a lot, for what the place looked like—definitely a bit worn and torn. But we were tired, and I thought being close to the ocean might be cool, because I could take Cass for a walk in the morning. Problem was, they had a "no pets" policy.

"You gotta stay in the bus, girl," I told her. She thumped her tail slightly and looked at me with her big, dark eyes. I whispered in her ear, "Only for a little bit. Soon as the coast is clear, I'll come get you." She thumped her tail even harder. I may sound a bit biased here, but Cass is the smartest dog ever. "You be a good girl, and I'll be back."

And I was, after a shower and a change of clothes. I snuck my half-coyote, half-lab, possibly some border collie pooch into the dingy motel room that smelled of stale cigarettes, bug spray, and mildew. She jumped on the bed with me and we fell fast asleep.

CHAPTER THREE

A WEEK LATER, and Cass and I were still at Motel Hell without any future prospects. We had driven around the city a few hundred times, only to find that fifty-five bucks for a motel room was cheap, and we were lucky no one had caught me sneaking Cass in and out. I had applied for a variety of jobs, from Subway to Gag in the Bag (take your pick as to which fast food joint I am referring to), to a receptionist at a variety of nail salons. I even went out on a limb and applied for a position at Nordstrom in the cosmetics department. I figured, what the heck— Mama is a beautician—and I did sell Mary Kay for two weeks.

We were in the VW driving around the city in search of inspiration and a Help Wanted sign. I reached over to pat Cass on the head—for the record, I don't read animals, but I know for sure Cass has had a good life. I've raised her since she was a pup.

"What should we do, Cass?" I'd already gone through almost a grand between the gas, food for the two of us, and the motel. Time was running out.

"I need a singing gig," I said.

Cass lifted her head and studied me. We came to a red light cruising north on La Cienega. The cross street was Fairfax, close to The Beverly Center where I'd applied for the Nordstrom job. It seemed like a decent area.

Cass whined. I looked over at her. Her head was tucked under her paws. And suddenly, clear as day, I had an image of someone bowed in prayer.

"Um, you think I should pray?" Thanks to my Southern Baptist minister dad, my home was prayer central. My parents raised me to believe in the power of prayer and miracles and trusting that God knew best.

But when you're twelve and your fifteen-year-old sister sneaks out one night and vanishes into thin air, and you prayed and prayed for months for God to bring her home and He didn't, well, it's kind of hard to get behind the idea of prayer. It had been some time since I'd bothered with praying.

Cass kept her head tucked under her paws and whined again.

"You're serious? You have been listening to Daddy way too much." She lifted her head and gave me a long look, then tucked it once more under her paws. "Okay. Fine. I get it." I took a deep breath, staring at the road in front of me, and feeling a bit silly.

"Hi, God, Evie Preston here..."

"Yeah, so anyway ... you must know what's going on with me. You know everything, right? At least Daddy says you do. So, the singing thing ... I could really use a break right about now. I don't want to disappoint Betty LaRue, and I honestly don't think you would either because, well, you know Betty, so could you help me out a little? Thanks. Amen." I know. Lame, right? But it had been a long time since I'd prayed and, well, I was a little rusty.

Cass sat up, and as we rolled up to the next light at La Brea, she let out a yelp.

"What now?"

She was looking out the window. A chalkboard sign on the sidewalk read, Two-dollar tacos and beer!! My stomach growled in response. The place didn't look like much. A big green neon sign in the tinted window on the building read Nick's.

"Lunch time," I announced. I found a meter and parked the van, cracking the windows and rolling back the sunroof. "Stay put, girl. Doubt dogs are allowed." Cass shot me an offended look, ears pinned back and head cocked to the side. "I know. It's stupid. I'll bring you back a taco and a Coke."

The atmosphere inside Nick's was, needless to say, lacking. The place was a dive, which didn't bother me because as a Texan, I knew a little something about dive bars (only at home, they usually served up some mighty fine barbecue and let folks walk around with guns). God forbid my father ever found out. He'd probably disown me.

Mick Jagger was belting out "Waiting On a Friend" from a corner jukebox. The carpet was a muddy-reddish color with black smudges here and there. I'm sure at some point it had been true red. The bar itself was long and narrow, with a row of stools covered in cracked, brown vinyl facing a mirror lit up by dim lights across the top (with a few burnt-out bulbs) covering the back wall. Liquor bottles sat displayed on the back counter. A handful of patrons, looking as if they'd been glued to those chairs for a number of years, sat in silence nursing their woes. On the other side of me were four rows of booths with the same cracked, brown vinyl seating. A younger couple sat in one of the booths playing grab-ass and giggling while downing a couple of beers.

A middle-aged guy—tall and skinny—who looked older than he probably was, walked towards me. He had longish, graying blonde hair that skimmed his shoulders, and wore a worn pair of too-big jeans and a red polo. The name Nick was stitched in black across the right side of his shirt. He semi-smiled and his green eyes, although sad, cast a little light in them through wire-rimmed glasses. "Welcome to Nick's."

"Thanks."

"Here for lunch?"

I nodded. "Two-dollar tacos and beer sound awesome, but I think I'll have a Coke instead."

He laughed. "Sit anywhere. Take your pick," he replied, his voice surprisingly deep and guttural.

I chose the back booth far from the couple and settled in to think a little more about my predicament. I noticed photos of various celebrities lining the walls, many of them autographed personally to Nick.

Five minutes passed since I'd last seen Nick. It seemed he was a man of all trades and acting host, owner, cook, and bartender of this place. Finally, he appeared and sat three tacos and a beer down in front of me.

"Oh no. I haven't ordered yet. And I wanted a Coke, please." I smiled up at him, remembering my manners.

He sat down across from me. "You're not from here."

I shrugged. "It shows that much?"

He laughed warmly. "Look, I serve two-dollar tacos every Tuesday and hands down, I know I make the best in town." He pointed at my plate. "You got chicken, steak, and my specialty— fish—there. You have to have a beer with them. Tacos without beer is, like, sacrilegious."

Now I laughed. I don't think my daddy would've agreed with Nick, but to each his own. "You must be Nick."

"That obvious?"

"The name on the shirt sort of gives you away." I decided to walk on the wild side for a moment and try the fish taco. I'd never had one before (we didn't get a lot of fresh seafood in landlocked Brady). It was mouthwatering.

"Oh, my gosh. This is amazing!" I looked at Nick, and then back at the taco, and took another bite.

"Told you," he said, winking. "I am actually planning to open a taco bar. Two, in fact. One in Santa Monica and one in Hollywood."

"No kidding? Well, I'll be your number one customer," I said.

"It's not fair for me to keep a world-class fish taco from everyone. That's my secret recipe right there." He pointed at the taco, smiling.

From the other side of the room, a slurred voice called, "Wonder what your buddy George thinks of that. He has a different story." A peroxide-blonde woman seated at the bar spun her bar stool around to look at Nick and me. Her brown eyes were glassy and hazy with drink.

"Ah, come on, Candace. You know George is full of shit. I don't even know why you listen to that guy," Nick said.

"I thought you two were partners," the middle-aged woman, replied.

Nick waved a hand at her. "Honey, you believe what they print in The Enquirer, for God's sake. Go back to your Candace Special. I'm visiting a new customer here."

Candace gave me a little wiggle with her fingers and spun herself back around. She shouldered the guy next to her. He wore an eye patch covering one eye. She whispered something in his ear and they both started laughing.

Nick cleared his throat, grabbing my attention. "Don't mind her. She loves to stir the pot. Where you from?"

I set down the taco and wiped my hands. "Sorry. I'm Evie Preston. I'm from Brady, Texas."

Nick tilted his head to the side, looking, oddly enough, like Cass when she was puzzling over something. "You don't have much of an accent."

I shrugged. "My father is from the Midwest. He's never had a Texas accent, and my mother, well, she definitely has a drawl, but I guess I take after my dad."

"I can hear it a little. Not much, though. What brings you west, Evie Preston? Let me guess—actress or singer?"

I took a sip of the beer. He was right. Tacos and beer were a perfect match. Especially the fish taco. "You're good. Singer and guitar player."

"Really?" He pointed to the lime on my plate. "Squeeze that into the beer and sprinkle a little salt in there."

"Okay." I did the lime-salt thing and continued to be impressed. "Yes, really. Why the surprise?"

"I dunno. I thought actress for sure. Woulda put money on it, actually."

"Nope. Have no desire to act."

"What kind of music do you play? Sing?" He stood and went behind the bar, grabbed himself a beer, and sat back down.

"I like it all. I'm partial to the blues … I like folksy, kind of, I don't know, I think Sheryl Crow is great. I love Stevie Nicks if you're going for some old school rock, and Heart is awesome, too. Um, Adele, Amy Winehouse, and Ellie Goulding definitely inspire me." I realized he was older and might not even know who the last few singers were.

"Love 'Rumor Has It.' Reminds me of old-school jazz in a way. I know it's a few years old now, and she's got a lot of new stuff out now, but I'm still partial to that song as my favorite one by her." He was up on his music. Of course, this was L.A. where people of all ages were surrounded by famous musicians. "Evie Preston wants to be a singing star, huh?"

I nodded, feeling heat rise to my cheeks. "Yeah. I guess I do."

"Okay. You got your guitar?"

"With me?"

"That's what I was thinking."

"I do."

"Great." He turned and pointed behind him. "See that spot over there in the corner next to the jukebox? The little step up? That's our stage."

"Yeah."

"Grab your guitar and sing some songs. I know a few show business types, and I wouldn't mind having live entertainment to bring some people in. That is, if you're good."

"Really?!"

"Really."

"Wow. Okay." I stood. "Can I get another taco?"

"You're hungry, huh? Usually three fill my customers up."

"It's for my dog. She's out in my van."

"Bring her in. She doesn't bite, does she?"

"Oh no. Not even."

"I love dogs. Go get her and the guitar. I'll make her up some tacos." He glanced over at the two barflies. "Hey, Mumbles, Candace, we're gonna get some live entertainment in here!"

Candace turned back to us and said in her scratchy voice, "Good. The kid looks like she might bring this place some much-needed class."

The patched-eye guy mumbled something completely indecipherable.

"You two are always busting my balls." Nick laughed, shaking his head.

I hurried out to the VW and slid open the door. Cass was curled up in the back. She lifted her head and I blew her a kiss. "Hungry?"

She perked right up and leapt out of the van. I grabbed my guitar, and we headed into Nick's, me wondering if playing music at a dive bar might just be the answer to my prayers.

CHAPTER FOUR

TWO WEEKS PLAYING and singing at Nick's taught me quite a bit, including how to make his famous tacos (except for the fish, his top secret recipe). I'd also learned how to pour a stiff drink or two. When my mama and daddy called every other day, I found myself telling little white lies about eighty percent of the time. I told them a story about a fancy resort I was playing at out in Malibu and how Cass and I were doing just fine.

I guess in some ways we were. The hours at Nick's were great—six to midnight every night but Monday (bar was closed ... Nick said he needed a day off, but I had a sneaking suspicion there was more to it than that). The pay wasn't great, however. I made eight bucks an hour plus tips, and the tips were, well, on the meager side, considering patrons like Candace and her sidekick Mumbles.

Speaking of Mumbles, it didn't take a rocket scientist to figure out how he got his nickname. He was a stout old guy with deep lines across his forehead and around his visible eye. Nearly bald, he never took off the eye patch. He was a character. Don't know how he got the patch, but one day, I'm sure I'll get the backstory. If I can understand it, that is. I think his accent is Irish—hard to say, though.

One warm evening I slapped him on the shoulder as I came in, guitar strung on my back, Cass tailing me. I hadn't thought about it before I did it—it was a light pat but he was wearing a tank top so the shoulder was bare, which meant no barriers. Now, I realized pretty much anyone who sat at that bar day after day probably had some significant trauma in their life, but what came rushing at me in a wave was pretty intense. There was no vision of anything, but I could hear something awful— black, loud, and scary as ... well, you know. It was only two seconds worth, but I yanked my hand off his shoulder like I'd burned it and brought both my hands up to cover my ears. I began shaking my head frantically, trying to rid myself of the pain and confusion. That had never happened before. I had only seen traumas before, never heard them.

Mumbles was staring at me with his one eye, a look of concern spreading across his face. I quickly pulled myself together and shot him a weak smile.

"Hey, Mumbles. How's it going?"

It's hard to tell but I think his answer was something like, "Good. Yep. Okay ... don't know, really. You? Your ears covered! Okay?"

I decided to mumble back, "Good. Okay. Think so anyway. Ears are fine." And that was the beginning of my strange and unexpected friendship with Mumbles.

Candy—who preferred to be called Candace even though she revealed to me one night her name was really Barbara— always sat two seats away from Mumbles. I think she'd once been beautiful. She had deep-set brown eyes, long, white-blonde hair, and a terrific smile, but time, a hard life, and booze had taken a toll on her. It's funny what people will reveal after they've had a few drinks. It didn't take long before I knew all about Candace's four husbands, her hopes of being an actress, her daughter who hadn't spoken to her in eight years, and her cat, Goldy. I didn't have to touch Candace to quickly understand the traumas in her life.

I also learned a bit about Nick himself. He didn't exactly have as many show-biz contacts as he'd initially indicated. Turns out, he was the child star of a seventies show called Next Door Neighbors. He didn't talk much about it, but I know he played the precocious kid named Jeff.

I didn't know much about actors or actresses. We were not allowed to have a TV in the house growing up. The only exposure I ever really had to television was the one in my mama's beauty shop.

One Tuesday night, not too long after I started at Nick's, things were a bit busier than usual. Some of the college kids from USC liked to pop in on occasion. I had just finished playing a set, and decided to take a break and grab a bite to eat. I sat between Candace and Mumbles. No one ever sat between them but me. Candace smiled. She was already a good three sheets to the wind and it was only nine o'clock. Then again, she'd been pretty bombed around six when I set up for the night. She patted my knee. Fortunately the jeans I had on were a good barrier. "You are such a pretty girl, sweet pea. And so talented! Isn't she, Mumbles?"

Mumbles bobbed his head up and down slowly "Yep. Pretty."

I smiled at them both and then scanned the bar. "Thank you. Hey, where's Nick?"

Candace spun around on the red vinyl and pointed to a booth near the kitchen. "He's visiting with some old friends," she said.

Nick was seated across from a woman who, from where I sat, looked Hollywood pretty. She had a too-perfect, plastic quality about her, but whoever had done the work had done a good job. She sat next to a middle-aged, kinda handsome guy ... he was probably about fifty. Nick appeared a little bit uncomfortable, but he was having a drink with them and the conversation looked light and cordial to me. But there was something in his body language that I couldn't put my finger on, but I sensed his unease. Maybe it was what my mama used to term as my overactive imagination. I decided to get my own tacos.

Even with food in my belly, it just simply felt like it was one of those nights when things felt out of place and a little off. Candace excused herself to go to the bathroom when another woman who she seemed to recognize walked in. The woman was an attractive redhead—petite, probably close to Candace's age, but again, hard to tell age since guessing Candace's actual age was nearly impossible.

Candace glanced at me. "I'm going to the restroom to put some lipstick on."

Hmm. Now that was a first.

The redhead sat at the end of the bar. A few minutes later, I saw Nick come back behind the bar and head over to her. He kissed her on the cheek and they hugged. He looked happy to see her. I contemplated getting up to introduce myself when someone sat down next to me. Someone I had noticed in the bar before.

"Hi. I'm Jackson."

I turned to face the guy. He could frequently be found in a back booth with his laptop open, sipping a tall glass of iced tea. I'd seen him speak with Nick a few times but decided not to force an introduction ... partly because he was always so focused on his computer, and partly because of how intimidated I get around hot guys (and yes, he was hot).

"Hi," I said, looking into his brooding, dark eyes. Yeah, I know. I sound like the heroine of a romance novel. But what can I say? He had nice eyes. He also had deep brown, disheveled waves of hair ... very sexy. And, he was talking to me.

I started to stick my hand out and then thought better of it, "I'm Evie."

"I know. I asked Nick."

"Ah, so you know Nick?"

"Well, yeah. I love that guy. If I could only get him to star in my film project."

Film project? Nick? I shook my head. "Okay."

"I'm sorry. I get so excited sometimes. I never imagined I'd be hanging out with Nick Gordin."

I felt like I was missing something crucial but decided not to pursue it. "Nick's great. Thanks to him, I now have a steady job."

"You're an amazing singer. I love coming in to listen to you while I work." He nodded down at his ever-present laptop.

"Thank you. That's really sweet." I could feel the heat rise to my face big time. I hoped the dim lighting made it hard for anyone else to see. "Um, so tell me about your project."

"It's a documentary for my film class. I'm in a graduate program at the USC film school. My subject is childhood stars and what happened to them. Nick would be perfect for it. His story is so fascinating."

"It is?" I asked. I knew there was something more to Nick, and Jackson seemed to have a line on it.

"Oh, yeah."

Candace came back at that moment. "Excuse me. That's my seat."

He glanced up at Candace, "I'm sorry," then looked back to me. "Do you want to sit over there with me?" he asked, pointing to his usual booth. I started to say yes when I heard Nick calling my name.

"Evie, come meet a friend of mine." He beckoned me from the other end of the bar, where the redheaded woman sat.

I glanced back at Jackson. "Rain check?" I asked.

He nodded. "I actually have somewhere I need to be."

There were those brooding eyes again. Had I blown it? "Oh, okay."

He smiled, then (be still my beating heart!), "Rain check definitely."

I turned away as I felt the blush reappear and headed over to Nick and Red.

"Evie, this is, uh, well this is my good friend Rebecca Styles."

"Friend, huh?" Rebecca raised an eyebrow and started laughing. She faced me. "You can call me Becky, hon."

"I'm Evie."

Nick nodded slowly, "Beck is in town, maybe to stay, right?"

Becky took a quick sip of her drink before answering. "That's the plan. I'm looking for a place. I wanted to come home to be close to old friends. New York has been wonderful, but I needed a change of pace." She smiled widely at Nick.

Okay, clearly something was going on here, but once again, I was missing whatever it was. Not to be cliché and all, but you could slice the sexual tension with a knife. I looked back and forth between Nick and Becky.

"Hey, Beck, do you remember Bradley Verne?"

"Of course! You two still friends?"

"Yeah. That's him and his wife I was talking with. I don't think you've met her. They got married, you know, after..." He didn't finish his sentence, but Becky nodded as if she understood completely. "Want to say hello?"

"Sure." Becky smiled politely at me and picked up her glass of wine. The two of them headed back to the booth where the other couple sat.

I walked into the kitchen to fix dinner. On the way there, I couldn't help but notice Candace's glare fixed on a seemingly oblivious Becky. Things around the bar were getting awfully interesting.

CHAPTER FIVE

AS FOND AS I was of Nick, Candace, and Mumbles, I still had a major problem: the money (or lack thereof). I loved singing nightly at Nick's. I love to sing, period. And play the guitar. But fifty bucks a night (and that was on a good night) was not going to get me far. Cass and I were still holed up in that motel. It stank. It was loud. And I was way over it. However, choices were few and far between. I'd been on the apartment hunt every day in my spare time. Studio apartments in L.A. ran at least twelve hundred a month and most landlords wanted first and last month's rent (and this wasn't even in the nice parts of town). On top of that, most didn't rent to dog owners and if they did, they wanted at least a month's worth of cash for the deposit. You do the math. That five grand from Betty LaRue was looking like chump change.

Late one night, lying on the creaking, uncomfortable motel bed with Cass, I found myself in tears. Cass scooted closer to me and practically licked my hand off. When the tears didn't stop coming, she stood and licked my entire face dry (so to speak). I couldn't help but start laughing, which only wound Cass up even more as she twirled in a circle, her tail swinging back and forth wildly, smacking me in the face with each twirl.

"Easy, girl. Easy. Stop! Stop it!" I laughed even harder, and then a knock at the door sobered me up real quick.

Cass started barking and the knocking grew louder. Uh-oh.

"Just a minute," I yelled at the door and then hissed at Cass, "Stop, stop, shhh!"

"This is the manager. Open up the door! Do you have a dog in there?"

I tried to sound as innocent as possible. "No. No. It's just the TV."

"Open this door, or I'll call the cops!"

I closed my eyes and cringed. This was not looking good.

"Cass, get down," I whispered. "Down." She growled. Not at me, but at the door. I got her off the bed and locked her in the bathroom. I cracked the door open and there stood the manager—ugly, overweight, spectacled, and in a wife beater with his paunch exposed and hanging over ill-fitting sweats. Lovely.

"Hi!" I put on my best fake smile. "Is there a problem?"

He crossed his arms. "You have a dog here." A statement, not a question. Crap.

"No. It's the TV, Animal Planet."

"We don't get that channel. And the dog you don't have is scratching on the bathroom door. I'm not deaf. You need to get out."

"What?"

"No dogs. No cats. No birds. No lizards. No pets! Get."

"Now?"

"Did I stutter?"

The beginnings of panic unfurled in my chest, "I-I can put her in the van for the night."

"Nope. Get. Out. Bye-bye." He wiggled his pudgy fingers at me, and then accidentally dropped his keys. I bent down at the same time he did to grab them and my fingers grazed his. I yanked my hand back but it was too late. I saw the manager in a car with a tiny little girl. He looked much younger, a lot less weight on him, and he was happy. They were singing "Raindrops Keep Falling On My Head." Rain splattered against the windshield, and in an instant, something hit the car. It went black and then I saw the manager crying over the child. "No, Sara! No!" She was covered in blood and very still. I pulled my fingers back and stood up.

"You got ten minutes," he said.

"I'm sorry." It was all I could say.

He frowned. "I was going to charge you for the night as well and keep the cleaning deposit. I can't rent the room until it's fully cleaned and fumigated. Pets have fleas and I am running a nice place here. I can't allow someone to stay in this room after a dog has been in it."

"My dog does not have fleas." She probably did. I have, in fact, seen one or two on her, but seriously, this guy was not running the Ritz-Carlton by any stretch of the imagination. Motel 6 was a five-star by comparison.

"I said I was going to charge you, but you seem a bit down and out, so I won't. You still gotta go, though."

I nodded and shut the door softly. I knew if I had not touched him and saw what I had, he would have definitely charged me. In some ways it would've been worth it, even though I didn't have much left. It is not easy to see the suffering of others, especially when it involves the loss of a child. It's why I'm usually so careful not to touch people. Damn. But hopefully his pain had been eased some.

I sighed, and took Cass out of the bathroom. I quickly threw my things into my suitcase and we left the motel without a clue as to where we would go.

We drove around for thirty minutes with me in a daze and Cass curled up in the back seat. I finally decided the best idea would be to park in a residential area and get up early in the morning and move. I found a quiet, well-lit street, parked, and climbed in back with my dog. Was this how people wound up on the streets? I couldn't go back home. Not considering all the faith Betty had in me, and I didn't want to prove to my daddy I couldn't make it on my own. I also didn't want to wind up panhandling with Cass, looking sad and desperate. I could ask Nick for more money. I could ask him if I could work the day shift, but I knew that wouldn't work either. Nick ran the day shift, and it was rare that many patrons came in during the day. I knew Nick did not have the money to pay me more. I also knew I didn't want to give up singing. It was all I had, besides Cass, and she counted on me.

I put a blanket over the two of us and eventually slept, only to be woken by the early morning sun and the droning of a nearby lawn mower. Who mows their lawn at seven in the morning? It didn't matter. I needed to move before the neighbors wondered about the beat-up van with the homeless lady and her dog inside. Reality hit me then that we were living out of my van. Reality also hit that

I needed a shower. I was determined today was the day I got a second job and found a new place for Cass and me.

I washed up and put on some war paint inside a McDonald's restroom after getting a couple of Egg McMuffins. I put an old U2 cassette into my tape player. I needed to upgrade my sound system to an iPod, but the tape player still worked. I sang all the lyrics to "Beautiful Day" at the top of my lungs, and Cass howled along with me.

I had a full stomach, was sort of clean, and received an attitude adjustment from none other than Bono himself. I was ready to take on the day. Little did I know what was in store for me.

At eleven o' clock I received a phone call from Nordstrom. They needed a new MAC girl. For the record, MAC appears to be the best makeup in the world. Or maybe they just have the best marketing in the world. Because it seems everyone who is anyone wears MAC. I don't, because I can't afford it, but I thank my lucky stars Mama took such great pride in teaching me how to make up my face, hers, and everyone else's in Brady. This job had my name written all over it. I was going to get it if it killed me. I almost got the VW up to sixty on the freeway. It was shaking and rattling something fierce.

I walked in, trying to be as sophisticated as possible in my all-black ensemble, and do you know what? They hired me! That night I celebrated at Nick's with a glass of cheap Merlot and a hamburger.

Nick toasted me. "You're on your way, kid! And speaking of, I know a producer, one of the best, coming in next week to hear you."

"Really? Who?"

"Can't say, but I can tell you he's the man, and I told him you were terrific. He's excited to meet you."

"Great," I said, but wondered why Nick wouldn't tell me who the guy was. Why all the mystery? But that was Nick. Sort of a mystery himself.

Nick held up his beer and hollered, "Everyone..." Everyone consisted of Mumbles, Candace, and three other people I didn't know, "... cheers to Evie! She got a new job today, and she's going to be the next music sensation!"

Mumbles stood up and mumbled, "Evie, good deal, girl!"

"To Evie!" the others cheered.

Maybe this was the City of Angels of after all.

Cass and I offered to lock up that night, and although it felt sneaky, we slept in one of the booths inside the bar and I got ready for my first day of work the next morning in the bathroom. I knew Nick wouldn't open until ten, so I had time to get ready and get out. The problem was, I had no idea what to do with Cass. I decided to leave her in the van, parked in a shady spot, and crack the windows. I'd check on her at lunch.

So I started my new job at the Nordstrom on La Cienega at The Beverly Center. I liked it. I really did. But I was exhausted by the third day. Here I was, sleeping with my dog in a booth at Nick's every night, closing the bar for him, and trying hard to get out of there in the mornings before he came in. I checked on Cass during my breaks and took her out for quick walks. I hated leaving her in the van all day. I was still trying to find a place, but my hours at MAC and then at Nick's weren't too conducive to apartment hunting. I thought about asking Nick if Cass could stay with him during the day. But I didn't really want to impose, and then he'd know I was in need of a place. And honestly, I didn't want that.

At the end of the week, I was at my wit's end. Thankful I had only two more days until my day off. I was determined to take the first apartment I could find. Now that I had two steady jobs, I felt reasonably comfortable I could make it work.

I was finishing up for the day. The store would be closing in thirty minutes, which meant I would be running from the store to Nick's.

A young woman approached the counter. "Hi. I need a new look. I'm tired of being called cute. What can you do for me?"

"Well, we are getting ready to close." I really did not want to do a makeover. I always had to be careful about touching skin. Experiencing random people's traumas had a tendency to bring me down, so I exercised caution and did my best to use only tools to apply makeup for makeovers. I just wanted to get out of there, take care of Cass, and eat something before I set up at Nick's.

"I understand. But this is important. I want to look fabulous for a big party tonight." The young woman stared at me hopefully.

I eyed my boss who was watching from the behind the cash register and smiled. "Of course I can help."

Thirty minutes later, the young woman, named Brenda, looked like a movie star. Even my boss said she couldn't have done better. I gave Brenda a smoky look around the eyes to bring out the blue in them, and a dusting of soft pink across the cheeks, with just the right peachy-pink gloss on her lips for a pouty, kissable look. What I did not know as I rushed out the door, was that Brenda's new look would change my life and my lifestyle in less than twenty-four hours.

Next day while behind the counter, a guy approached me (scared me half to death, too, because he was all decked out in black, with slicked back hair, dark eyes—very Godfather- esque). He cleared his throat. "Are you Evie Preston?"

What I wanted to say was, "Who wants to know?" But I figured that wouldn't go over too well with my manager, so instead I replied, "Yes, how can I help you?"

He handed me a card with the name "Simone" written on it. I looked down at the card and then back up at him. "Simone?"

Mafia Man nodded and replied, "Yes. I'm Dwight Jenkins, and I represent Simone. You know, Simone, the singer?"

I took a step back, glancing around me. "Am I on one of those TV shows where y'all have hidden cameras? Do you mean the Simone?"

"No hidden cameras, I assure you. Yes, I'm referring to the pop star, mega sensation, Simone."

My head started spinning. Had she heard me playing at Nick's? Maybe Nick really did know people in high places, and maybe the producer guy who was coming to listen to me next week was her producer. Oh wow, would Betty LaRue be so proud, and my mama and daddy! How had I missed seeing Simone at Nick's? She had to have been in disguise. That's how those celebs do it when they want to go out—they go incognito.

"You made up her sister, Brenda, yesterday," Jenkins prompted.

"Brenda is Simone's sister?"

He nodded. "Simone was so impressed at how great Brenda looked, she wanted to meet you."

"Okay," I stuttered. "I have to sing tonight at this place called Nick's. I'm off tomorrow."

"I don't think you understand," he cut in. "She'd like to meet you now."

"I have a job here! I can't just leave."

Dwight Jenkins called my boss, Tish, over. "Miss Preston has a job interview with Simone. She's going with me."

"Wait a minute," I said. "I can't do that." And then his words made their way through the filters in my brain. "A job interview?"

"Simone would like you to be her personal makeup artist. The pay will be a bit more than what you're currently making here." He cocked an eyebrow.

"What? Is this for real?"

Tish came around the counter and put her arm around me. "You have to go. Something like this is a once in a lifetime opportunity. Do it, girl!"

I hugged her goodbye and followed Jenkins. He escorted me to a limo where I found Simone and Brenda waiting inside.

I was speechless as I sat down across from them. Jenkins climbed in the front with the chauffeur, and the car purred to life, smoothly pulling away from the mall. Simone smiled. "Thank you for coming."

As if I had a choice, right? I studied her in awe. She was a true beauty—long, blonde hair, big, blue eyes, a body men would love to ravish and women would kill for, and a voice that had venues around the country sold out months in advance. She was a cross between a younger Madonna and Mariah Carey, with a dash of Britney Spears. To be sitting across from her was mind blowing, and my stomach did this swirly, feel-like- I'm-gonna-puke thing that always happens to me when I get nervous.

"You are so genius," Simone said. She took Brenda's face in her hands and squeezed, bunching it up so she looked like a fat goldfish trying to breathe. "The hottest guy at this party last night hooked up with my sister. He wanted her, not me! And I was so working it, too. He didn't even look my way. Usually she looks kind of dorky. Cute, but dorky." She let go of Brenda's face and patted her cheeks gently.

Brenda rubbed her face. "Gee, thanks Sis."

"I asked her who did her face and she told me this chick at the MAC counter at Nordy's. I'm like, I so have to meet this woman! And, well, here we are. Is it your fucking lucky day or what?" Simone smiled, shiny, bleach-white teeth gleaming in the darkened limo.

"Well, thank you for the compliment." I wasn't sure what else to say. I mean, what do you say to someone with a planet-sized ego who has graced the covers of

Vogue, Rolling Stone, and Vanity Fair, won a handful of Grammy's, and talks like a truck driver? I almost had to pinch myself to be sure I wasn't dreaming, but then the car made a quick turn and Simone spilled her glass of champagne in my lap.

Without an apology, she said, "I need a new personal makeup artist. That last one was the shits. Oh, check this out..." She rolled down the privacy glass between us and the driver. "Harvey, take us over to Blake's place so I can show..." She glanced at me. "Hon, what the fuck is your name?"

"Evie."

"Right." She looked back at the driver. "So I can show Evie her new digs." She rolled the window back up.

"I'm confused. I thought this was a job interview," I said. Brenda poured me a glass of champagne, handing it to me. "Thanks, but I don't drink and definitely not before noon."

"First, confusion around my sister happens a lot," Brenda said.

Simone punched Brenda lightly in the arm. "Ha, ha, little sis thinks she's soooo fucking funny."

Brenda nodded. "And two..." She held up two fingers, "If you're hanging with us, which you will be, because big sis doesn't go far without her makeup and the one who puts it on her, you are going to have to learn to party like a rock star."

"Drink up." Simone clinked my glass. "Cheers. Here's to your new home."

I looked out the window and my jaw dropped. Literally. We'd pulled up to a large gate with a long, winding drive. I sucked back the champagne to calm my nerves. This simply could not be happening. "What do you mean?"

"Well, Edie," Simone started. "I'm pretty sure you don't live in a place like this…"

"It's Evie."

She waved a hand in my face. "My buddy Blake, this big producer guy, is in Europe for, like, a year or something, and he needs a house sitter. I volunteered Brenda, but she says she's afraid of the house and won't do it."

"Place is creepy." Brenda poured herself another glass of champagne.

"Shut up," Simone said. "So if you come on board as my makeup chick, you get to live in luxury, baby. This place is way cool."

I had to agree with her. Palm trees and an iron gate, with a retro, Spanish mission look going on and, from what I could tell, a view to die for. But what was the catch? I mean, was she serious? I could actually live here?

"Can I bring my dog?"

"You can bring fifty fucking dogs for all I care. What do you say, Edie? You in?"

Evie, Edie, makeup chick, whatever—I didn't give a damn what she wanted to call me. I was definitely in.

CHAPTER SIX

THREE WEEKS LATER, and I was kind of inclined to agree with Brenda regarding the house (mansion, villa, whatever it was). Blake's place was a little creepy. And any time I asked about Blake, the owner, I got the brushoff. The only thing Brenda had added one day when I was prepping to do Simone's makeup (Brenda was busy looting her sister's closet while Simone soaked in a tub of goat's milk and tuberose petals ... don't get me started) was that she'd heard the place was haunted.

"Haunted? Really? By who?" I asked.

Brenda shrugged. And then Simone walked in wearing a plush pink robe.

"What are you doing?!" She snatched a silky-looking shirt out of Brenda's hands. "Get the hell out of my fucking closet. Go buy your own clothes and leave Edie alone. And no more shit about her place being haunted." She turned to me, an exasperated look on her face. "You don't believe in that shit, do you?"

Here's the thing: I sort of do. When I was a kid, I saw a ghost. Or at least I think I did. I remember waking one night from a deep sleep to see a little girl, pale and, well, ghostly, pad silently past my open bedroom door. She held a candle, and the flame was the only thing with any kind of real color to it—a faint, yellow glow. She turned to face me and, with a smile, brought her free hand up to her face and shushed me with her finger. I wasn't scared, just surprised. I remembered wanting to talk to my mother about it, but never did. Fact is, ghosts and things that go bump in the night weren't exactly embraced with open arms in my household. And then, as I got older, a part of me began to wonder if maybe it had all been a dream.

Simone was looking at me expectantly. "Please tell me you don't believe in that crap. Brenda also thinks we're descended from space aliens." She walked past her sister and smacked her lightly on the top of her head. Brenda rolled her eyes.

"Um, no … not really," I stuttered.

Well, what did you expect me to say? Oh yes, Simone! Not only do I believe in ghosts, but I can also touch people, get a glimpse of their psychological baggage, and help them heal!

Speaking of Simone, when I did, on occasion, touch her face … there was nothing overly traumatic about her past that jumped out at me (aside from her fixation on an old magazine article that mentioned her slight weight gain). The only thing I did pick up from her was a deep, aching loneliness—surprising, because she was constantly surrounded by people. Nevertheless, it allowed me to feel some empathy for her, even though she was often incredibly obnoxious.

Whether or not the house was haunted, I had yet to experience anything frightening. I mean, how could I complain? I'd gone from living in my van and sleeping at the bar to staying at a seven-thousand-square-foot mansion overlooking Los Angeles. Simone was paying me good money, too. Oh, and I got to have

Cass with me—at the house, that is. Simone wouldn't allow my dog anywhere near her.

So the house was huge and it made me feel, well, uncomfortable. I figured eventually I would adjust to the size of the place. Even with Cass by my side, it was hard to get used to having all that space ... all those empty rooms ... to myself.

The house was tastefully decorated—all in whites, pale yellows, and light greens, with hardwood floors, and lots of bamboo and bougainvillea. There were a handful of Buddha statues and crosses scattered throughout (at least all my spiritual bases were covered, although my daddy would have had a heart attack seeing Jesus hanging with the Buddha, even if only in décor form). It was as if a fancy Mexican hotel lobby had mated with an Asian-themed resort spa.

There was also a boarded-up guesthouse on the back forty. Now, that place really creeped me out. It looked like a smaller version of the Amityville Horror house (yes, I managed to see that movie one night at a sleepover ... and I didn't sleep for about two weeks after that). The property was on two acres, and the guesthouse stood just above the slope of a gentle hill beneath a cluster of pepper trees.

Another thing I'd noticed was the random smell of marijuana. Not that I've ever smoked it, but given Brady's total lack of activities for teens, my high school years were heavily dotted with the pungent scent of weed: smuggled into football games beneath the bleachers, during lunch behind the library, and at informal gatherings in the parking lot of the local pizza joint. The only thing I could figure was maybe the neighbor on the hill below me liked to get high, and the breeze carried the scent up to the house now and then.

Cass absolutely loved our new place, but even she was wary of the guesthouse and tended to keep her distance. She immediately took to the swimming pool, and spent at least an hour or two a day swimming in circles and diving in to retrieve the toys I threw in for her. She was doing just that one afternoon when Simone called to say she didn't need me for the night. That was a first. In the few weeks I'd been working for her, she needed me pretty much night and day to do her makeup—do it Goth, do it like Garbo, do it like Gaga—you name it, Simone wanted it.

"Everything okay?" I asked.

"Yes," Simone sniffled. "I mean, no. I'm fucking sick! Me! I have a cold. I was going to tell you to bring me some soup, but Bren's getting it. She said I work you too hard." She paused for a moment, "Do you think I work you too hard?"

"Um ... no. I'm good."

"Okay. Oh! But I do have a photo shoot in the morning and I cannot look like death warmed over," she said in a congested- sounding voice. "And my nose looks like Rudolph the Red- Nosed fucking Reindeer!"

I cringed. Her constant use of the F-bomb was rapidly becoming my least favorite aspect of her personality. "I can fix that. Don't worry."

"Good. Be here by seven, and bring me a double-shot, skinny, pumpkin spice latte and don't let them give you any shit about how they only sell pumpkin spice lattes during the holidays. They have it and I want it. See you tomorrow!"

I placed the phone back on the cradle and sighed, looking over at Cass. "Early morning tomorrow, but I get tonight off." Cass wagged her tail in approval. "Let's go to Nick's!"

I grabbed my guitar, promising Cass some fish tacos once we got there. It didn't take much to convince her. She flew into the back of the VW and we headed toward La Cienega.

At Nick's, the usual crowd was there, including Becky, who had become a frequent flier, and one who constantly fawned over Nick. I had the impression Nick liked Becky fine, but Becky was way into Nick. Meanwhile, Candace seethed every time Becky came in.

Mumbles was on his forty-fifth gin and tonic, and Candace was happily nursing a "Candace Special," which as far as I can tell, has Midori and pineapple rum in it. At least that's what I put in when I made them for her and she hadn't complained yet. I shuddered to think about the state of her liver.

Becky, on the other hand, never strayed far from her chilled Chardonnay.

I noticed Jackson back in his corner booth, his laptop propped open on the table. He glanced up at me and waved briefly, his eyes almost immediately dropping back down to the screen in front of him. He was definitely distracted.

I thought it was kind of odd Jackson had never really made good on the rain check after our first conversation. In fact, as good-looking as the guy was, he was pretty moody. One night he'd be pleasant and sort of flirtatious. The next, he'd be cold and act like I wasn't there. I didn't know what to make of him. I had never been one to make the first move, and honestly, with him being so wishy-washy, I'd pretty much lost interest in him as a prospect. Not that I was prospecting. I had to steer away from hand-holding for a long time with someone and try to get to really know them before I took a good look at their most painful life experience. It made me shy of dating.

"Evie, g'see you. Got black eye." Mumbles pointed to his good eye.

Whoa! So he did. "How did you do that?" I asked, staring at the huge shiner spanning his eye.

"Oh, he fell off the stool last night. We missed you," Candace said.

I shook my head and sighed. "Someone really needs to check you two into rehab."

"Ouch! That hurts." Candace waved a hand in front of her face. "But know what, honey? You may be right, but what's the point? Ain't nobody out there who'd care one way or another."

"Oh, Candace, that's not true. I think you just like to be the victim."

"Damn girl. Don't talk to Auntie Candace that way! Be nice and pour me another Special." She lowered her voice suddenly and sidled over. "You know what, sweet pea? That boy over in the corner has it bad for you."

"He's weird," Mumbles mumbled. "Questions. Movie. Dunno 'bout him."

"Huh?" I said.

"He's not weird," Candace slurred. "He's an artist. A filmmaker. I think Nick is being an idiot for not helping him out."

"Creeps," Mumbles mumbled.

I was definitely getting interested in this conversation.

"Slow down you two. First you." I pointed at Candace while I stepped behind the bar to fix her a drink. "You think he likes me?" I tilted my head toward Jackson.

"Oh yeah. He has the hots, big time."

"Creep," Mumbles said a bit more clearly than usual.

I leaned in closer to him. "What's the problem, Mumbles?"

"Dunno. Feeling. Looks at you. Don't like it." He glared down into his glass.

"Oh, Mumbles, you're a softy."

"Youse a good kid. He's ... not right."

"Evie, honey, don't listen to him. He's an old drunk," Candace said.

"What are you?" Becky butted in from her seat a few stools down the bar.

Candace pulled herself upright and nearly launched herself at Becky. "You know what, bimbo? I've had about enough of you. In fact, I had enough of you twenty-five goddamned years ago."

Whoa! This was getting good.

Becky narrowed her eyes to angry slits, her mouth pressed into a thin line across her face. "I can say the same thing about you, you lush. And it's been almost thirty years!"

"Ladies, please!" Nick rushed out from the kitchen, his arms spread wide. "Can we please leave all of that in the past? Just let it go and let's move on."

"You mean like how we let Roger go?" Candace asked, her voice dripping with hostility.

Becky rolled her eyes and looked away, sullenly sipping her wine.

Nick leaned in close to Candace and lowered his voice. "I warned you, Candy. I have told you time and again to let that shit go. It's done and buried. I don't need any problems. You and I are friends now. All cool, right?" He glanced quickly over to where Jackson sat, his dark eyes trained on the entire scene. He looked the way a dog does when it's got an injured squirrel in its sights. For a split second, I understood Mumbles' comments about Jackson, and a shiver spun its way down my spine.

Candace sat back and crossed her arms. She eyed Nick for a long second and to me, it looked like a warning. I might just be a small-town girl from Brady, Texas, but even I could tell things were heating up good, as my mama would say. And that's when a really big dude walked in.

When Nick spotted him, he recoiled.

Big Guy didn't waste any time getting to the point. "Hey, you skinny, stupid fuck! We need to talk," he pointed a thick, meaty finger at Nick.

"Whoa..." I stepped out from behind the bar. I know I probably should have stayed put, but where I come from, that kind of talk is just plain rude. "You can't come in here talking to people like that. You need to leave."

He eyed me and started laughing. "She your bouncer, Nick? You're cute, sweetie. Stick around for a little while and maybe we can have a drink after I'm done chatting with your boss here. The name's Pietro SanGiacomo." He reached out to shake my hand. I quickly shoved my hands in my back pockets and kept them there.

I was about to fire out a not-very-cute response, when Nick stepped up next to me and laid a gentle hand on my shoulder. It just so happened I was wearing a tank top because of the hot weather. Which meant skin-to-skin contact ... and an unexpected glimpse into Nick's past. It only lasted a few seconds: a pool with a dead body and then Nick, sobbing.

I quickly stepped away from Nick's hand, even as he was saying, "Evie, it's okay." He turned back to the jerk. "Pietro, why don't we go in the kitchen and work this out."

Pietro drew his eyebrows down threateningly. "Yeah. Why don't we?"

We all turned to watch them go. I did not like this one bit. I was debating about whether or not to follow them when Becky reached out to grab my arm. I quickly moved out of her reach, before she could make contact. She looked at me in surprise and I mustered a weak smile. Frankly, I was not ready to see Becky's demons if she had them, and I was pretty sure she did.

"It's going to be fine. Nick has a problem with gambling. He gets in a little deep with the wrong people. If he needs it, I'll loan him the money." She took a last sip of her wine and sauntered into the kitchen.

A few minutes later, Becky, Pietro, and Nick came back out. Pietro left, Becky went back to her wine, Nick started cleaning glasses behind the bar, and Jackson sat in his corner looking creepy and intense. Mumbles, Candace, and I were total- ly confused.

After several minutes of uncomfortable silence, Nick put down his towel and gave me a piercing look. "Don't worry about all this. I do want you to be more careful, though. L.A. can be rough, and it's been known to eat young women like you for breakfast." For a minute I thought he was going to head back into the kitchen, but he suddenly seemed full of energy. "Hey, by the way, remember that dude I was telling you about, the music producer guy?"

I nodded. "The one who was supposed to come and hear me three weeks ago, then two weeks ago, and then last week?" I loved Nick and I knew he wanted the best for me, but this music producer thing was starting to wear thin.

"Now, Evie. Come on, you know these guys are busy. But he's for sure coming tonight. I'm sure of it. Now maybe you can dump that Slutone you work for."

"Her name's Simone."

"Whatever," he replied. "She's not good for you, kid, and she's not good people. Trust me."

I shrugged. "I can handle her, besides the job is easy..."

"Oh really? Being at someone's beck and call at all hours just so she can get some powder and lipstick slapped on her face? That chick has you right here." He held up his pinky and tapped it with his other pinky.

"Look. I know she's difficult." He eyed me. I held up my hand. "But the pay is great, and I have a place to live because of her, someplace I can keep my dog, too." Cass looked up from where she'd flopped herself down.

"Whatever." He fanned his hand over the meat on the grill. "Once this dude hears you sing, you can tell Slutone to go to hell."

"Nick," I warned. "Call her Simone, please. To be honest I haven't seen her act like a slut. She might use some strong language here and again ... well, all the time, but she doesn't sleep around."

"I'm sorry. I just don't like the way she treats you. Anyway, enough about her. Get your guitar ready and set up the mic. Prepare to become a superstar!"

Cass lifted her head and gave a sharp bark.

"Even she knows it," Nick said, pointing to my dog.

"Okay, okay, already. I'll be right back. Guitar is in the van." I headed out the back entrance to the VW. As I slid open the doors to grab my guitar, my cell rang. I looked at the number. Crap. It was Simone. I muted it and took out the guitar. The phone rang again. I gritted my teeth. Guilt washed over me as I stood looking at the number, ignoring it. Damn. Damn. Damn! What if something was really wrong?

Ugh. I flipped open the phone. "Hello?" I said meekly.

"Edie..." She still didn't always get my name right. "I need you to come now. I think I've taken too many Sudafeds. The lights are so bright and blurring and, oh my God! I'm dying. I know I'm dying."

"Okay. Um, well, where's Brenda?"

"That stupid bitch went to a party without me. I don't think I can forgive you for glamming her up. She thinks she's fucking Katy Perry now."

"Right."

"So I need you now!"

"Here's the thing ... I'm over at Nick's."

"That dive? Seriously, I don't get your love of that place. At all."

"I know, but Nick has this friend who is a record producer and he's coming to hear me sing tonight." I was trying hard to sound hopeful and not pathetic.

"Oh God, you're kidding, right? You're so fucking pathetic. Please. That guy doesn't know anyone worth anything. Look, you want an audition? I'll get you one over at Sony."

"Really?"

"Yeah. Sure. Now get your ass over here before I die!"

I looked back at Nick's place and then down at Cass, who stood there staring at me, and I swear if she were human, she'd have been shaking her head at me. "I know. I know," I said, gritting my teeth. Simone was right, I was pathetic.

I walked back into the front entrance, not wanting to face Nick in the kitchen. I caught Jackson staring at me and managed a smile. He waved but I didn't return it. Ever since Mumbles's comments earlier, I'd been feeling a bit uncomfortable about the guy.

I walked quickly over to Candace and turned her around on the barstool.

"Oh no, no more lectures. I'm not going to rehab. And after that little show here tonight, I ain't going nowhere. Even with her here." She pointed at Becky and glanced at Mumbles who sort of nodded. "Place is entertaining!"

Mumbles mumbled, "I got a black eye."

"Plus, I was sober once and it sucked," Candace interjected.

"Right. I don't want to lecture you," I replied. "Just tell Nick I had to go. It's an emergency and I'll try and be back as soon as I can."

"Emergecy?" Mumbles looked at me. "You got black eye?"

"Gotta go."

"Wait, hon," Becky said, trying to stop me. "Where are you going?"

"I just have to be somewhere."

Yes, I know—it was a crappy thing to do. I really believed Nick this time about the music guy, but I'd also been here long enough to realize his music mogul pal was likely past his prime, and, frankly, I couldn't take the chance of losing my job with Simone. Plus, she promised me an audition with Sony!

I ran out the door and got behind the wheel with Cass staring at me as if I was the devil incarnate. She can chastise like nobody's business. Only my father does a better job. We sped up La Cienega, then across and over to Wilshire. Hopefully, I could save Simone from her Sudafed overdose and become the next pop sensation.

CHAPTER SEVEN

SO MY RUSH TO SAVE Simone's life turned out to be a bust, except I became the new owner of a cat. Cass was so not pleased.

It went like this: I high-tailed it to the diva's house only to find her in her movie room watching one of the Ocean's Eleven movies.

"Hi," I said, standing awkwardly in the doorway. There were eight rows of plush movie theater-type seats in the screening room. She was in the middle seat of the middle row.

"Shhh! It's getting to the good part. Come watch it with me." She patted the seat next to hers.

"I've got Cass in the car, and you seem better."

"No." Simone shook her head and then, glared at me. "I am not better, Edie. I'm sick and I need you. I'd say bring your dog in, but I think I'm allergic to animals. Actually, you're gonna have to take my cat."

"What?" This was getting ridiculous. I sat down next to her.

"Yeah. You got to get my fucking cat out of here." She turned and stared back up at the screen. "Hey, who do you think is hotter? Clooney or Pitt? Damon has that weird lip thing, so he's out. I don't even know why I'm asking. They're like, way too fucking old, but I kind of like old guys. Oh, see what that Sudafed has done to me? I'm losing it. So, what do you think?"

"About what?" I was still mulling over the cat comment.

"The guys! God, are you high or something?"

"No. I'm just confused. What did you say about your cat?" I asked.

"Answer the question! Which guy do you think is better looking? Which one would you do, for God's sakes?" She pointed to the screen. "I've seen this movie twenty-seven times. Count that! Twenty-fucking-seven!" She paused for a moment, shooting a quick assessing glance my way. "Oh my God. I get it. You're gay! I know a chick you might like." She kept her blue eyes trained on the screen. "She's a gourmet chef who owns, like, six of my favorite restaurants. How cool would that be?"

"I'm not gay!" I shouted.

She flicked a hurt glance my way, "Hell, you don't have to bite my head off. What, do you have a problem with gay people?"

"No! I just—" Big sigh. "Can you tell me what you meant about your cat?"

"Fine, but pick a dude first. I'm going Clooney cause I think Angelina could kick my ass and who needs that. I mean now that they're all divorced and shit, I could easily get him, but I wouldn't want to become a step-mommy to that crew and piss of the Tomb Raider. Then, like all twenty-five bazillion of their fucking kids would jump me, and, well, you get my drift..." She tossed up her hands. "I think I could take on Clooney's wife. She doesn't look all that tough."

This was getting surreal. "Right. I actually think Matt Damon is good-looking."

She stopped staring at the screen to narrow her eyes at me. "You're a strange chick."

"Um, can you please explain the situation with your cat, because I'm not sure I heard you correctly."

Simone rolled her eyes. "It's not complicated. No wonder you're a makeup chick." She shook her head.

At that moment, I had a very clear vision of my fist punching into her cosmetically enhanced nose. I even briefly thought of quitting, but then the reality of what I now had and where I'd come from hit, and I shut my mouth.

"The cat. His name is McConaughey. Get it, after Matthew, who I had a little fun with one night, but then he had to shack up in his trailer and have babies with that Brazilian chick … Anyway, I'm totally allergic to McConaughey, and he has to get the fuck out of here." She wiggled her fingers.

"And you want me to take him?"

She pointed at me and winked. "Bingo. You're catching on."

"What do you want me to do with him?" I asked.

She shrugged. "I don't know. Take him to a shelter or something."

I sighed and shook my head. "Okay, where is he? I really do need to get home. If I have to be back here by seven, I should get some rest and so should you."

"Look at you, Mommy. Stay the night here. I have more than enough room. Obviously."

"No. I can't. I can't leave Cass in the van and I, uh, I always water the lawn at night to be, you know, environmentally conservative." I so did not want to be stuck overnight at Simone's place.

She gave me an odd look. "Whatever. Just hope I don't fucking kick the bucket tonight."

I shook my head. "I think you're okay. Drink lots of water and go to bed," I said, and then muttered under my breath, "and maybe you should wash your mouth out while you're at it."

"Oh sure, then I'll be pissing all night long. Wouldn't that be great? Hmmm. The cat. He's around here somewhere. He's an orange tabby with a weight problem."

"Would you, by chance, have a cat carrier?" I asked.

"Where the fuck do you think you are? Petsmart?"

"I'll figure it out," I said.

"See you in the a.m." She turned back to her movie and left me to make my escape.

I found McConaughey on the kitchen counter eating what looked to be the remnants of that evening's dinner—some kind of fish. Lucky cat. And Simone had not been kidding about the weight problem. He must have weighed at least twenty-five pounds. His name should have been Garfield. I eyed the plate of leftovers McConaughey was currently chowing down on ... it was pretty clear how he got so fat. Simone's cleaning service went home daily and she had drop-off delivery for her meals, which meant the leftovers sat out for the following morning's cleaning service to clean. If there were any left.

I sighed. "Okay, kitty. Looks like it's you and me and my dog." The cat eyed me suspiciously as he continued to lick the plate clean. "And I'm sorry, buddy, but as of this moment, you are on a diet." I already knew there was no way I could take the cat to a shelter. I was banking on Cass being cool with her new feline friend, considering my mother had two cats back home.

What I didn't expect was that Mac (I had to shorten the name. There was no way I could visualize Matthew McConaughey when I out to the fat cat) might have an issue with Cass.

The car drive home was interesting. Mac hissed and howled at Cass, who sat in the front seat, her chastising eyes boring into the side of my head.

I decided it best to drop Mac at the house and lock him in the laundry room while Cass and I went to the store to pick up necessary cat items—a litter box, for starters, and some diet food.

Finally, past our bedtimes, Cass and I walked through the front door of the mansion. She froze. Her ears pricked forward and the scruff of her neck stood on end.

"What is it, girl?" I whispered, noting a strange feeling in the room. I'd had that feeling before, but this time, it was front and center. The air felt dense, heavy. Really heavy. Almost like water. And again—that damn pot smell in the air! I took another step further inside and Cass let out a low growl. My fingers grew cold and a shiver went straight down my back. Suddenly, I felt a breeze pass through me, not over me, but through me. I shivered again. And then Cass dropped her guard and began sniffing me, the surrounding foyer, and family room beyond.

My sister's face suddenly surfaced in my mind. And then an eerie howl echoed up from the basement, startling me into action.

"Mac!" I ran down the back stairs with Cass in tow, to find one freaked out feline wedged behind the washing machine.

Getting an overweight cat from behind a stackable washer and dryer is no easy feat. How he got behind there in the first place, I have no clue, but after shoving, pushing, and inching the machinery forward for several minutes—and nearly slipping a disc in the process—Mac shimmied out and shot off through the laundry room and up the stairs. Cass and I ran after him, but he'd hidden himself in the depths of the house, and at that point, I was too exhausted to send out a search party for my overweight friend. He couldn't get out as far as I knew. I set out food, water, and a litter box and prayed he'd find them in case he had to do his thing. Then I headed to my room and to bed.

I thought sleep would come quickly. At least I'd hoped it would. But it didn't. Between thoughts of my sister, Simone, Mac, and the constant faint scent of marijuana floating through the halls, it was hard to fall asleep. But eventually I drifted off … or at least I assumed I had, because ever so slowly, the marijuana smell grew stronger, combining itself with the soft, familiar melody of Bob Marley's "Buffalo Soldier." It was almost as if Bob was right there in the room with me, next to my bed. As far as dreams went, this one was pretty nice. I mean, I never much cared for the smell of pot, and getting high was definitely not my thing. But I did like Bob Marley, and it was all so ... peaceful.

Then the dream changed—in a big way. How do I put this? I am not one for sex dreams. I don't have much sex, so dreaming about it isn't a regular occurrence in my life. But on those rare occasions when I do, I only have a vague sense that I've done it with someone. Usually it's someone famous like, well, Matt Damon. Sometimes it's someone ridiculous like the guy in line at the DMV (scary). Then I wake up and think, Huh. That was interesting. But this ... this was like insanely crazy, wild sex. It wasn't just wild though. It was kinky and dark and I felt violated. In the dream, I could see the man with me. He was blonde, with gold-colored skin and an eerie, blue-black glow surrounding him. He had hazel eyes that seemed oddly dark and, in all honesty, demonic. And they looked right through me. I felt panicky and afraid as my heart raced, pounding hard in my chest. I repeatedly tried to wake myself but I couldn't make it happen. Finally, Cass woke me with a loud, sharp bark. I flipped on the light to see her fur sticking straight up, her back hunched, and her eyes wild.

"Cass! What is it?!" I focused, trying to see if maybe Mac had come in the room and startled her. But there was no cat in sight. I calmly spoke to her until she settled down, and then I pulled the rumpled sheets and covers back up over me. I must have been really struggling in my sleep. I tucked the covers up around me. As I lay in the darkened room, waiting for sleep to arrive, I began to suspect Cass, Mac, and I were not the only beings at this house in the Hollywood Hills.

CHAPTER EIGHT

AT TEN PAST SEVEN the next morning, I could be found at Starbucks insisting to a barista she did indeed have everything needed to make a pumpkin spice latte in June. She, sadly, didn't agree. I tried pulling the, "I'm Simone's assistant, you know, the Simone" line. Her response?

"Right. Whoever you are, I can assure you we don't serve pumpkin spice lattes in June. How about hazelnut? That should make anyone happy."

"Oh, fine." I glanced at my watch, knowing there was going to be hell to pay. I'd overslept, probably the result of that disturbing sex dream combined with Mac waking me when he eventually found his way to my room and crashed on my pillow, cradling my head with his large body. Suffice it to say, it hadn't been the most restful of nights. I'd darted out of bed and then out of the house, leaving Cass and my new feline friend inside to sort things out.

And here I was, running behind schedule and without the requested pumpkin spice latte to sweeten the deal. I grabbed the hazelnut mocha or latte or whatever it was, and kicked the van into high gear—which means not high at all—making it to Simone's about twenty minutes late.

She greeted me at the door with a bright red nose, red- rimmed eyes, hair in a rat's nest, and hands on her hips. She wore a short, hot pink-colored silk robe with some kind of lace teddy underneath. Simone stared at me like I'd slapped her. She grabbed the hazelnut drink and took a sip. She spit it out. "What the fuck is this?!"

"I'm sorry, Simone. Look, the girl at the counter insisted she did not have pumpkin spice. I pleaded with her. I told her I was your assistant. I don't think she believed me."

She grabbed my arm. "Come on."

"What?"

"Did I stutter? Come on."

I followed her outside.

"Are your keys in this piece of shit?" She smacked her hand on the van.

"Yes."

"Get in."

Oh no. This was it. I had lost the only real paying job I'd ever had. She was sending me on my way. I had been fired. "I am really sorry. I am."

"Get. In. The. Van." She pointed at the driver's side, her slipper-clad foot tapping impatiently.

"Hey, you can fire me, but that means you don't get to order me around like this anymore."

"I'm not firing you, loser. We're going to Starbucks."

"I told you, she said..."

"I don't care what that idiot said," Simone said. "Now drive me to Starbucks."

We turned right off of Mullholland. "God, Edie, I can't believe you drive this tin can." She wiped her hands down her face tiredly.

"It's all I can really afford, and it gets me where I need to go. I'm saving my money."

"Saving your money? Why?"

"Uh, well, that's what most people do. They budget and save so one day they have nice things and can travel or afford to send their kids to college."

Simone shook her head. "Whatever. You don't even have kids."

We drove the rest of the way in silence until I pulled into the Starbucks parking lot. Simone grabbed the handle and threw the door open.

"What are you doing?" I asked.

"I am going to get my fucking pumpkin spice latte. You stay here." With that, she was out the door and marching into Starbucks wearing nothing but her pajamas.

I groaned, certain it wouldn't be long before the paparazzi showed up or someone whipped out a camera phone. All I knew was somehow this was going to end up my fault.

Less than five minutes later, she strolled out with two coffees in hand. She got into the van just as a crowd started gathering, handed me one of the cups, and said, "Let's get the fuck out of here."

I turned off of Sunset and floored it, as ordered. Once we'd reached cruising speed, I glanced over at Simone and asked, "What did you say in there?"

"Oh nothing much. Just let them know the next time my assistant comes in and asks for a pumpkin spice latte, they better fucking well give it to you. They gave me two. What do you think?" She motioned to the coffee.

"I think you should stop using the 'F' word."

"No, what do you think about the latte?" She rolled her eyes.

I took a sip. I wasn't really partial to super sweet coffee, and I really don't like pumpkin, but I figured now was not the time for honesty. "It's great."

She laughed. "You're a fucking liar!"

"No, I'm not." Then I started laughing, too. As obnoxious as Simone can be, there are times when she cracks me up.

"So you think I should stop using 'the F word,' huh?"

"Yes. It's just, well, it's not, um..." How to put this without ticking her off? "It just doesn't fit your image. You know, you're a songbird. You're glamorous. And I don't think vulgarity is really your style."

She nodded, pondering. "Hmmm. Okay."

"Really?"

She took a sip of her latte and swallowed, then looked over at me. "Fuck, no, Edie. The 'F' word is the only word I know that suits me to a T. Now take me home and put my makeup on."

I sighed. An hour and a half later, she looked gorgeous as usual, and she managed to increase the number of F-bombs, if that were even possible. My ears were numb, but the photographer and his crew didn't seem to notice. They told her how beautiful she was, what a great voice she had, and on and on. It made me nauseous.

As the photographer clicked away, my cell phone rang. It was Nick's cell number. Oh God. He had to be pretty irritated with me. Here I'd run out on him last night and hadn't even had the courtesy to call. What if that producer had stopped by? I was such a jerk. I picked up on the second ring.

"Hello? Hello? Nick? I am so sorry about last night." No response. Boy, he must be more upset than I thought. "Hello? Nick? Look, I am really sorry."

I paused, and that's when I heard a faint gurgling sound. What the heck? The hairs on the back of my neck prickled. Something was not right. "Nick? Is that you?"

"Help me." It was barely a whisper but I heard it loud and clear. I was certain it was Nick. And then the line disconnected.

I didn't tell Simone I was leaving. I just left. All I kept thinking was Nick was having a heart attack or a stroke. On my way to the bar, I decided to call 9-1-1 just in case. I relayed what had happened and the operator asked me if it was some kind of joke.

"Of course not! Why would I joke with you?"

"You wouldn't believe the pranks we get, lady. I'll send a unit to that address, but if this is a prank, you will find yourself in jail."

"Look, I know what I heard. Just send help."

I screeched to a stop in front of the bar. There were no police cars, no ambulances. Nothing. Not yet anyway. The bar wouldn't open for another hour, but the back door was unlocked. I ran inside, through the kitchen, calling Nick's name. No response. I scanned the booths. Nothing. I was just beginning to wonder if maybe he had called from home, when I stepped behind the bar. That's where I finally found him.

Dead, in a pool of blood.

I backed away, nearly stumbling as a scream caught in my throat. I hit something behind me. The scream let loose when I realized it wasn't something, but someone.

CHAPTER NINE

"HEY, EASY, EASY," a man's voice said. He turned me around, touching the bare skin of my arm, and I could just make out his LAPD uniform in the dim light.

I said something to him, but I don't know what, exactly. I was hysterical and frantic. I caught a quick flash of the officer as a kid with his mother who was passed out on a couch—a bottle of booze next to her. I shut the vision out quickly. My friend was dead and it seemed pretty clear from all the blood on the floor he'd been murdered. Shattered glass was everywhere behind the bar. It looked like a fight had taken place.

"I'm Officer Harris. Wait here." He sat me down in one of the booths.

My hands would not stop shaking. I wished I had Cass with me so I could bury my face in her fur.

I watched the officer walk around the bar and then disappear from sight as he knelt down behind it. Then I heard him on his radio, "I have a signal five at Fairfax and La Cienega. 527 La Cienega. Nick's Bar. Repeat, I have a signal five."

After Officer Harris called into the station, he came back and sat with me. "Can you answer some questions, miss?"

"Is he ... ?" I couldn't make myself say the word.

"Yes, ma'am, he is."

"Oh, my God! I can't ... I don't understand. How?" I dropped my face into my hands as a fresh wave of tears threatened to overtake me.

Officer Harris nodded sympathetically. "I'm sorry. It looks as if he sustained gun shot wounds. I take it he was a friend?"

I nodded. "Yes. My boss, too. I sang here in the evenings."

"Can you tell me his name?"

"Nick Gordin. He owns ... owned ... the bar. He, he..." I swallowed thickly, trying hard to keep from sobbing or throwing up. "He was a really good guy. He believed in me."

"I am sorry. Uh, did you say Nick Gordin?"

I nodded.

"As in the actor?"

I nodded again.

He looked slightly pained. Another fan, I guessed. "Can you tell me what happened?" he asked.

"I don't know." My eyes shot up to his face. "I found him like this ... I must have arrived only seconds before you." My hands still hadn't stopped shaking and I could hear the quiver in my voice.

"I understand. But can you tell me how you found him? You said you play music here in the evenings, but it's not quite ten o'clock in the morning. What were you doing here?"

I told him about the phone call from Nick.

"You were at work when you got the call?"

"Yes. I'm also a makeup artist."

"As a matter of procedure, I will need to verify your story. Where do you work?"

I had a sinking feeling in my stomach. Simone was not going to like this kind of publicity at all. "I work for Simone."

"Simone who?" he asked.

"Simone, the pop star," I mumbled.

"Excuse me?" he said.

"Simone. The singer."

"Really?"

I nodded.

"Okay. I'll need you to give me her contact info so I can verify where you were when all of this went down."

"Yes, of course."

An hour later, a Detective Franklin sat me down and asked the same series of questions I'd heard from Officer Harris. I told him everything I knew. He asked me about acquaintances, friends, enemies, bar regulars.

"There's Candace and Mumbles, and uh, Becky. But they would never hurt Nick."

Detective Franklin looked at me. "Do any of these people have a last name?"

"I'm sure they do but I don't know what they are. Except Becky. Her full name is Rebecca Styles. She was a really good friend of Nick's."

"Enemies?"

For some reason, Jackson's face popped into my mind. But I had bigger fish to fry. "This guy came here. His name was Pietro. I think his last name was like Santiago or San something." I snapped my fingers. "SanGiacomo. That's it. He looked like some sort of mafia guy, you know, like Tony Soprano. He yelled at Nick. Then Nick and Becky went into the kitchen with him. Becky said sometimes Nick gambled and owed money to the wrong people."

The detective jotted all of this down. "Pietro, huh? Damn."

"What?"

"It could be a mob hit, and if so, those are tough cases to close."

"Really? The mob?! I was kidding about the Tony Soprano thing."

Detective Franklin stood. "I've got your number and we will be in touch again. Thank you for your help. You're free to go now."

"But what about the bar?"

He shrugged. "I have no idea what the terms are on this place. Do you have a manager?"

I quickly said, "Yes. Me. I manage and sing." What in the hell was I doing? I was as much a manager of this place as Mumbles.

"And do makeup for Simone the pop singer?"

I nodded.

"Busy lady. I suppose in a few days you'll likely be able to reopen. If Mr. Gordin owned this place, he must have had a will of some sort. If you're the manager, I'm sure you'll be hearing from an attorney soon. Again, I am sorry, and thank you for being so cooperative."

I managed a weak smile and left. I don't remember the drive home at all. It felt like the day I realized my sister was gone. I felt the same guilt, too. When Hannah vanished, I was convinced it was my fault. And now I wondered, maybe if I had stayed at the bar the night before instead of rushing to Simone's aid, Nick would still be alive, too.

CHAPTER TEN

I SAT IN ONE of the lounge chairs by the pool and stared down at Hollywood and Los Angeles spread out below. I had my second beer in hand and a half-empty box of tissues on the table next to me. I hadn't stopped crying since I left the bar. The police had likely located Becky by now, but Mumbles and Candace ... probably not. They would be devastated.

Nick's murder had brought my sister's disappearance sixteen years ago to the forefront of my mind. I recalled it clearly as if it had happened yesterday. I remembered Hannah had been begging my parents for days to go to a concert up in Jacksonville, nearly two hours away. Of course Daddy said, "No way." And my mama had to back him up. Hannah was so upset.

She was almost sixteen and her best friend Karen could drive. There was a group of them going and I didn't see the harm in it. I encouraged her to go. Told her I'd cover for her. And that is what I did. After dinner, which in our house was promptly at 5:30 p.m. every night, my sister headed upstairs. I did the dishes and then told my folks Hannah and I were going to play a game of chess. I was banking on it that they would leave us alone. My parents tend to spend the evenings reading scripture unless it is a designated family night, which it wasn't. I went to bed, padded down the stairs to find my daddy asleep in his chair and my mother knitting a new sweater for him. I kissed her good night and told her Hannah had gone to bed already. She believed me.

When I woke at three in the morning to go to the bathroom, I went to the side of Hannah's bed to ask her how the concert was. She wasn't there. I panicked and woke my mother, who woke my father. The police were called. They found her bike only half a mile away up the road from the house. Her friends said she never made it to Riley's Diner where they'd agreed to meet. I have never copped to the fact I knew she had snuck out. The guilt eats at me daily.

I stood and poured the rest of the beer on the lawn next to the pool. Cass and Mac remained indoors, curled up tightly next to each other. Against all odds, they had become fast friends. I was kind of jealous, because it meant I only had a beer to provide comfort while they had each other.

As the sun slowly dipped towards the ocean and the sky turned a myriad of oranges, pinks, and reds, I decided to make myself a BLT. Suddenly, I had two loyal fans next to me in the kitchen. Behold, the magic of bacon! Mac walked a figure eight between my legs, and Cass twirled in circles as if she were dancing.

"Fine! I give in." I pointed the knife down towards Mac. "Don't think this means I've forgotten about your diet, mister." I shifted my gaze to Cass. "I see you're teaching Mac all your bad habits."

"Trust me. I don't think he needs her help," a male voice responded.

I jumped, nearly slicing off my thumb. I immediately changed my grip on the knife, holding it more like a weapon and less like something I'd just been using to slice tomatoes.

"Who's there?" My voice quivered, not nearly as threatening as I would have liked.

No one answered, but Cass started to growl and Mac stopped brushing against my legs.

"Hello?" I could hear the tremor in my voice. I did a quick search around the kitchen and nearby family room. Nothing. I went back to prepping my sandwich.

"I'm losing my mind. Maybe I should go home, back to Texas."

I turned on the stove and buttered the bread. And then I thought I heard sounds in the family room. I cautiously walked out of the kitchen, my animal entourage following closely behind. Again, nothing. The hair on my arms stood straight up but I reluctantly turned my back on the empty room and returned to the kitchen. A small billow of smoke curled up from the frying pan ... the bread! I shut off the stove, leaned my back against the counter with my head down, and started crying again.

And that's when it happened.

"No woman, no cry. Nooooo woman, nooo cry."

What in the hell?

"Little sister, don't shed no tears..."

Either I was dreaming, or Nick's murder had finally pushed me over the edge. Because when I looked up, Bob Marley stood in the middle of my kitchen, guitar in hand, singing.

Cass stared and Mac, the fat little traitor, moved between Bob's legs and started doing the figure eight thing there. Bob- frigging-Marley! In my kitchen!!

Bob was smiling, the smell of pot drifting in the air, and I was, quite frankly, shocked speechless.

And then (I know, right? As if Bob Marley in my kitchen weren't enough) ...

... a gorgeous specimen of a man wandered in and leaned back on the counter next to the dishwasher, just a few feet from where I stood with my mouth hanging open. The knife, which I'd been clasping for dear life, clattered to the floor with a sharp bang.

The guy was in soft, muted colors ... like he'd been digitally altered. Between dead-Bob Marley and Sexy Kitchen Guy, my brain was spinning, and all I could think was how much better Bob sounded live (no pun intended). As for Cass, well, she was completely mesmerized by the scene. We all stood there for a moment ... all of us, that is, except Mac, who continued to wind his way through Bob's legs. Suddenly, the sexy guy sort of floated over to my side. His edges sharpened and he got a lot brighter (think Technicolor). He reached out and gently wiped the damp tear trail off my cheek. I could feel the brush of his fingers on my skin ... but his touch was not like anything I'd ever felt before. Imagine soft, combed silk—feathery and sweet. It was both cold and warm at the same time and left a lingering imprint even after he removed his fingers from my face. He spoke in a hushed tone. "Bob is right, no more crying."

This man, ghost, being ... whatever he was, shimmered. He was steeped in a golden glow surrounded by the deepest indigo, and his eyes were the deep, purple color of a mountain at sunset. Yeah, I know. Hokey as hell, right? But seriously, his eyes were incredible-looking. He had dark hair that framed his face in thick waves. All I could think was—beautiful.

I tentatively reached out to touch him and then retracted my hand quickly. I could feel ... something. But it was simply a sensation—cool and then, slowly, growing warmer. I felt tingly—literally—all over my body. And I received no visuals at all.

Meanwhile, Bob was crooning "Positive Vibration" in the background, but his singing grew softer and started to fade out. I didn't want him to go. I mean, yes ... this was all incredibly insane, but it sure was beating the heck out of the pity party I'd been throwing myself only moments ago.

And then someone pounded on the French doors just off the kitchen and my two mystery guests vanished into thin air.

"Edie! Evie! Open the fucking door!"

Simone! I ran to the door, throwing it open. Cass started barking and Simone sidled in, scowling at Cass who growled and slunk away.

"Simone, what are you doing here?"

She ignored me and made a beeline for the fridge. "Are these the only beers you have? No Champagne? Wine? What the fuck?"

"Uh, yes."

She sighed, popped the top off a cold Heineken, took a deep swig, and turned to face me. "Okay Edie. What the fuck is going on?"

And that is when I saw him again. He was behind her, making a face, holding up two fingers over her head. I started to giggle nervously. She turned to see what I was looking at. He was gone.

Simone smoothed her hair down. "Seriously, are you okay?!"

I shook my head and muttered, "I wish I knew."

CHAPTER ELEVEN

"SO THIS IS REALLY what normal people do?" Simone asked.

We were sitting inside a Denny's on Sunset. She was in disguise, wearing a short black wig, torn jeans, and a yellow t-shirt with pink writing that read, Fuck You ... and the horse you rode in on. On the back was a cartoon woman on a horse flipping the bird. Classy.

After showing up at my place and drinking four beers, Simone insisted on doing something normal.

"Come on, Evie, let's go where the real people go. Let's do something real people do. Something normal. Where do you eat when you go out?"

I was still feeling off balance (go figure) with lingering tingling sensations running through my body.

"Uh, Denny's, I guess." Yeah, okay ... I realize Denny's isn't exactly gourmet cuisine, but where I come from, there aren't a lot of upscale family dining options. And it was the first thing that came to mind.

"Okay. Denny's it is." Then, right there in my kitchen, she stripped and yanked her disguise out of a big Michael Kors bag. She dropped the black, bobbed wig onto her head. "Call me Jill tonight. We can hang out ... you know, just like BFFs!"

"Right."

Now, at Denny's, Simone was stuffing her face with some fine diner cuisine, and I was still in shock from the day.

"This shit is good, Edie." She paused for a moment and then winked at me. "I just do that for fun, you know."

"What's that?"

"Call you Edie. I know your name. I just like messing with you."

I nodded. "Oh." At this point, nothing she said surprised me.

"Hey." She reached over and touched my shoulder; thankfully, I had on a light sweater, so no need to worry about uninvited visuals. "I know I threw a mini-tantrum earlier and I shouldn't have. I was a little surprised you took off this morning and then when the cops showed up and started asking questions about you, I was like, what?!" She took another bite out of her meal, peering at me closely. "You know the paparazzi will likely have a field day with this."

"I'm sorry." And I was. I knew she hated unwanted attention.

She shrugged. "I can handle those jackasses."

For a moment she actually seemed ... normal.

"So someone killed that guy? Nick?"

I closed my eyes, wishing I could forget the entire first half of the day. "Yes."

"That is super crazy. And you found him?"

"I did."

"God! What did he look like?"

I took a deep breath. "I don't know. Lots of blood and he was... he was dead."

She paused for a minute, staring down at her partially finished meal. "You know the house you live in? And my sister talking about how it's haunted and all…"

"Yes?" I asked, suddenly feeling very interested in where the conversation was going.

"Oh, you know … Brenda is such a wuss. She says the place is haunted because of what happened there. That's all. It's not haunted, but some shit did go down there." She shrugged.

Great. The hair on my arms stood to attention for the umpteenth time today. "What do you mean 'what happened there?'"

"I will only tell you on one condition…" She leaned across her plate, lowering her voice.

"What's that?"

"You gotta stay there. I promised Blake I had a responsible chick keeping an eye on the place."

"I'm not going anywhere, Simone."

"Jill!" She hissed, darting her eyes to the surrounding booths. "I am fucking Jill tonight!" That got a laugh out of me. "Oh, you know what I mean, Evie. Get your mind out of the gutter!"

I smiled. "Anyway, about the house. What happened?"

She sighed. "Back in the nineties, like '94 or something, someone was murdered there."

"What?!"

She nodded. "Yeah, this dude who played in a grunge band. Blake was their producer. They were supposed to be the next Nirvana or Pearl Jam, you know. The guy was a huge talent. I was like, only eight, so I don't know much, but anyway, he was the shit, I guess. And unlike Kurt Cobain, this guy was sexy hot. Then Blake had a party one night and a chick this singer-dude hooked up with went ballistic because he was hitting on some groupies. So she shot him right there, in front of everyone. Shot him dead!"

"Oh, my God!"

"Yeah. Anyway, sorry I didn't tell you, but like I said before, I don't believe in ghosts and all that shit." She took another big bite of her food, "God, this is really good. I'm getting this again next week when we come back."

"What?"

"Yeah, girlfriend. Standing date."

I shook my head. "Okay. Hey, what was the guy's name? The one who was shot?"

"Lucas Minx. Cool name, huh? Anyway, my sister thinks he haunts the place, but she's got issues." She brought her pointer finger to the side of her head and circled her fingers around her ear, making the crazy sign.

"Right." Apparently, so did I—have issues, that is.

"Anyway, I am sorry about your friend. I know you liked that guy. We all need friends." She looked down at her food.

"Yes, we do." Simone obviously needed a friend, and it appeared that I was the chosen one.

CHAPTER TWELVE

A FEW DAYS AFTER Nick's murder, the bar's future was still up in the air. I had been kept busy with Simone, who had a flurry of promotional things going on, including being photographed for feature pieces in InStyle and Bazaar. She even fielded a few paparazzi questions regarding Nick's murder, and I think someone snapped a photo of me in her Range Rover at one point. In any case, I began anticipating a story of some sort in The Enquirer and I'd already heard that TMZ was following us around, because what I discovered about Nick since his death was far juicier than I ever imagined.

The night after the murder and the outing to Denny's, I turned on the TV in the family room. I'd secretly been waiting for Lucas to show up again. After I got home the night before, I immediately googled Lucas Minx and found a photo of him— my ghost—in a Wikipedia article. He was beautiful when alive, that's for sure, but as a spirit, he was breathtaking. Then I found a clip of him on YouTube singing and playing guitar. His voice was like a combination of Eddie Vedder and Jack Johnson ... sexy, mellow, and powerful. It was surreal to hear him after having seen his ghost in my kitchen.

Anyway, while waiting for my next paranormal encounter and trying to keep my mind off of Nick's murder, Cass, Mac, and I sat in front of the TV eating dinner (tuna fish sandwiches, if you must know. And yes, I took the cat off the diet. He seemed so much happier). Entertainment Tonight came on with flashes of video footage of the bar, and photos of Nick as a kid when he starred in Next-Door Neighbors. And then Nancy O'Dell's voiceover began (and I quote), "Back in 1985 when Nick Gordin made the decision to leave show business for good, many speculated it was due to the untimely death of his good friend, Roger Hawks. Hawks, recently chosen to be the next James Bond, drowned during a party in the swimming pool at the vacation home of producer Warren Verne, where Gordin had been housesitting."

I could feel the goose bumps making their way down my arms. The vision I'd seen when Nick placed his hand on my shoulder the other night was of a dead man in a pool.

Nancy gazed sadly into the camera and shook her head. "We certainly hope Nick Gordin's murderer will be caught and brought to justice."

"Yes we do," agreed Mark Steines, nodding sincerely in his seat next to her. "Terrible, sad story, Nancy." Then his face lit up in a sly smile. "And now, let's talk about Angelina Jolie and Brad Pitt. They've been spotted together again, and some say they may be reconciling..."

I shook my head and stood up. I needed to get online and learn more about Nick and this Roger Hawks guy. Here he'd led me to believe he'd never been able to get any more acting gigs, but in reality, he'd made the decision not to continue with his career. And how awful to have a friend die at a party where he was housesitting!

Unfortunately, my attempts to go online proved fruitless. In spite of all the money floating around up here, the internet service wasn't the greatest. Drove me nuts. Instead, I hunkered down for a night of popcorn with my fur-covered friends and Pretty Woman playing on TNT. No ghosts. No good stories to uncover. Oh, well.

When I woke up the next morning on the couch, Mac at my head and Cass at my feet, I knew the day would be difficult. Nick's wake was today. I'd received a text from Becky yesterday saying Nick had been cremated after the coroner released his body. I wondered who'd given the consent. Maybe it had been in the will? Someone must have known his last wishes. I guessed it was Becky. They went back a while, but then again, so did Nick and Candace. I wondered if it was possible one or both of them had known Nick back in 1985? And hadn't Candace mentioned the name Roger during her tense standoff with Becky not too long ago?

As I got dressed, my mind reeling, I had that feeling again ... that I wasn't alone. I glanced around. Nothing. Cass lay curled up on the bed next to Mac, who was meticulously grooming himself.

"Hello?" I called out into the empty bedroom. Then, feeling vaguely silly, I said, "Lucas?" No response. I finished getting ready and left.

Maybe Lucas's visit with Bob was simply a one-time deal, like when I had seen the little girl when I was a kid. If so, I was disappointed. I mean what could be better than being sung to personally by the ghost of Bob Marley, and being haunted by a hot, dead guy? For the hundredth time in the last few days, I found myself wishing Simone hadn't shown up when she did. Her timing, as usual, was pretty damn horrible.

A half an hour later, and after a few days' absence, I was back at Nick's. I'd left Cass at home with Mac, although I'd contemplated bringing her. While some would have understood my bringing her, others might not have been okay with a dog at a memorial service.

It was strange being at the bar again. It felt different without Nick's constant presence. I hugged everyone I knew—Candace, Becky, Mumbles—but before I did so, I put a buffer in place in the form of long, black satin gloves so I wouldn't be forced to deal with painful visions. Yeah, I looked a bit like Jessica Rabbit, but it was better than having to deal with an onslaught of depressing life stories. Today was going to be hard enough.

I was a bit surprised to see Jackson there. He shook my hand, and gave me a quick kiss on the cheek. The kiss was just enough contact to force a vision of him as a young boy being beaten by a larger man. Oh dear. I quickly took a glove off, acting as if I needed to scratch the top of my hand. I then placed my hand over the top of his and squeezed for a second, sending him healing vibes. He glanced down at me and smiled.

"Tough day," I said, putting the glove back on.

"I can't believe he's gone," he replied, glancing curiously down at my gloved hands. "What's up with the gloves, if you don't mind my asking?"

"Umm ... eczema. It's a stress response." I quickly changed back to the earlier topic. "Did you talk with the police?"

He nodded. "Yeah, I did." He stopped for a minute and then moved closer, dropping his voice to a loud whisper. "The unofficial word on the street is it was a mob hit. They say no one will ever go to jail for his murder."

I brought my hands up to my mouth. "No! What do you mean?"

"The cops aren't exactly on this all hot and heavy. Look, they may act like it for the time being, but a mafia hit is one of those things that rarely gets looked into too deeply. Plus, the media hype will be gone by tomorrow."

I wrinkled up my nose in distaste ... kind of the way I do when I accidentally step in a pile of Cass's poop. "Yeah. The media hype. I had no idea Nick had been such a star."

Jackson crossed his arms. He held a beer in one hand. "Yeah. Kind of. I mean he was a big star as a kid. Then he got offered a role back in the mid-eighties for a show that was meant to compete with 21 Jump Street ... you know, the show that made Johnny Depp such a big star?"

"Oh, I don't know TV much. We weren't allowed to watch it when I was a kid. And I was born in '88, so a lot of this is before my time. Speaking of, you don't look any older than me."

"I'm twenty-six, but I grew up here in Tinseltown and this stuff has always fascinated me. Why do you think I wanted to do the documentary on Nick?"

"He really wasn't interested in that, was he?"

Jackson shook his head and I noticed his expression had gone a little sour.

"Nope. Not at all. So, maybe there was something to the theory that Nick was responsible for Roger Hawks's death back in the day." He shrugged. "Those two might know." He pointed first at Becky, who was talking with the attractive woman who'd been in the bar with the middle-aged, good-looking guy not long ago.

Becky had her usual glass of wine in hand and looked completely distraught. The glamorous woman looked casually bored, and her boyfriend or husband—whoever he was—had just sidled up to them and handed her a drink. He gave Becky a hug. I wondered who they were.

Jackson then pointed to Candace in her regular spot near Mumbles. They were hunched over the counter, nursing drinks. There were a couple of guys working behind the bar, and some waitresses passing around appetizers—I recognized none of them. I assume they were hired caterers. About sixty people were there and I had to wonder who was paying for it all. My guess was Becky. She appeared to be playing the grieving widow.

I wanted to ask Jackson what he meant with regards to Becky and Candace when the handsome, middle-aged man got up on the small stage.

"Hello! Hello, everyone. Good afternoon." The bar quieted down and the small crowd turned to face him. "First of all, I want to thank you for coming today. This is certainly not how I imagined my next visit to Nick's Place." He bowed his head momentarily. "But I know Nick would be honored and humbled to see all of you gathered here today in his honor."

Something shiny caught the corner of my eye across the room. I glanced over to see a big guy leaning against the wall. Actually "big" was a nice way of putting it ... he was seriously overweight. His hairy arms were crossed above his huge, sagging gut and a large, diamond-encrusted watch sparkled obnoxiously from his wrist. I had never seen him before, but then again, I hadn't seen most of the people in the bar today. There was something about him, though. Something not right. Fact is, he didn't look sad or solemn or contemplative. Just irritated.

I directed my attention back to the guy on the stage.

"For those of you who don't know me, I'm Bradley Verne. Nick was a good friend of mine. In fact, he was more than a friend. Nick was like a brother to me. I have many fond memories of Nick and me at my dad's place. We had so much fun as kids, and I feel fortunate to have had him in my life. My wife, Raquela, and I loved him dearly." His eyes caught those of the chic woman in the crowd who smiled and nodded. She then dabbed her dry eyes with a handkerchief.

So Bradley was the son of the guy Nick had housesat for. One more puzzle piece dropped into place. I looked back up at the small stage ... Bradley had tears in his eyes. Clearly he'd been close to Nick.

"I'm not looking forward to telling my father about Nick. They were quite close and Nick was family to us. Dad ... well, his health hasn't been great, and I'm worried this news won't help much." That was when the waterworks really started, and Bradley was unable to speak for several seconds. Finally, he stepped down and stood next to his wife who embraced him. "I'm sorry. We love you, Nick. Peace be with you, brother. If anyone else wants to share stories and memories about Nick, please step forward."

No one did, so I decided to go up. I hadn't known Nick for long but he'd been willing to take a chance on me.

"Hi. I'm Evie Preston, and I played music here in the evenings." I glanced at the small group of regulars and smiled. Candace waved and Becky smiled back, wiping her eyes. "Nick was a really good guy. I didn't know him that long. But he was the kind of person who really cared about others and he took friendship seriously. Thanks to Nick, I didn't have to turn around and head back home to Texas right after I got here. I know I will miss him dearly."

"Kind? Took friendship seriously?!" The voice was loud, male, and very unfriendly.

I peered out to see who was shouting. It was the fat guy with the flashy watch. He was covered in sweat and his face was turning an alarming shade of red.

"Let me tell you something about Nick Gordin, chica!"

Chica? Who was this guy and what was his deal? The low hiss of whispers slid across the room.

"Nick Gordin was a bum! He was supposed to be my partner. He stole my fish taco recipe and he was running with our idea of a franchise! He even had the loan docs all ready and I only just found out about it. Dropped me like a hot tamale! How's that for taking friendship seriously?!"

I couldn't speak, but Bradley and Jackson made their way over to him. There was a loud exchange with lots of colorful language, and then the large fellow was escorted out. But he managed to get the last word in when he yelled, "Karma is a bitch! Guy got what he deserved."

After his departure, an uncomfortable silence settled over the room. No one knew what to say following the outburst. Finally, Bradley stepped forward again.

"I am so sorry, everyone. That guy is a lunatic. I think Evie expressed what we all know and feel about Nick. Let's grab a drink and toast our friend!"

He kindly escorted me down from the tiny stage as I was still pretty shaky. "Thank you," I whispered.

"I am so sorry about that. You seem like such a nice young woman. Nick mentioned how much he believed in your talent."

"Really?"

Bradley nodded. "Yes. He was really fond of you. Here, let me get you a drink and introduce you to my wife."

"Thank you ... hey, who was that guy?"

Bradley grimaced and rolled his eyes. "That was George Hernandez, Nick's former partner. He's a jerk. I don't even know how he got in here today. Nick washed his hands of George about a year ago. Don't worry about him. He's loud, but he's harmless." Bradley went up to the bar and ordered drinks. He came back, handed me a glass, and then escorted me over to where his wife stood, handing her a drink as well.

Close up, I could see she had been nipped and tucked— tastefully—within an inch of her life. She had short, dark hair, clear blue eyes, and a killer body I am certain she paid a lot of money for. Her lips were large, but not obnoxious, and she smiled sincerely at me, her white teeth gleaming brightly in the dim lights of the bar.

She reached a free hand out. "Hi. I'm Raquela Verne. That was very nice of you, what you said, and I am so sorry about that a-hole, George."

"I'm grateful your husband stepped in when he did." I shook her hand, my gloves still on. "Nice to meet you. I'm Evie Preston."

Bradley smiled, placing an arm around his wife's tiny waist. "Raquela is my rock. She is always here for me, and with Nick being gone…" He started to cry again. Poor guy.

"Honey, you loved him. It's okay to be emotional." There were tears in her eyes as well. Real ones. "Come on, why don't we toast Nick?"

Bradley dabbed at his eyes again and cleared his throat, in an effort to get the attention of the bar.

"Before we toast," Bradley called out, "I want to let all of you know I will be doing what I can to keep the bar open." He turned to me in an aside. "I'm hoping you will stay on."

I nodded, surprised and pleased. "Great! Well then, here's to Nick."

Everyone raised their drinks. "To Nick!"

I said the words and I meant them, too. But my mind kept wandering. Was Nick's killer in the room? Or maybe George Hernandez was crazy enough to have murdered Nick? Didn't they say killers sometimes come back to the scene of the crime? I took a sip from my drink, looking around the room at all the people. Which, if any, of these folks had come back to gloat?

CHAPTER THIRTEEN

ONCE HOME, I MADE a determined effort to go online. It took some time, but finally, the service provider came through and I was able to Google Nick's name. Of course, there were articles about his murder. They all said the same thing: that the former child star had been killed in his bar on Monday morning.

But eventually, I found what I was looking for. It was an archived article from the 1985 edition of The Los Angeles Times. It showed a photo of a much younger Nick with Roger Hawks, and a photo of Warren Verne, Bradley's dad. The article read:

Last night at the estate of producer/director Warren Verne, actor Roger Hawks was found drowned in the swimming pool, just after 3:00 a.m. The evening before, actor Nick Gordin hosted a party for Hawks to celebrate Hawks' upcoming new role as the next James Bond. Verne, in Europe on location, was reported as saying, "I am devastated at the loss of such a talented young actor," upon receiving the news of Hawks' death.

Sources say Hawks was inebriated and some speculate drugs may have been involved. So far, there has been no comment from Nick Gordin.

As I delved deeper, the story got more interesting ... and troubling. There had been an investigation, because, as it turned out, Nick and Hawks argued that night. No one ever claimed to know what the argument was about. But my eyes popped when I read, Nick Gordin's fiancée, Barbara Dennison, claims Nick was with her when Hawks likely drowned.

"Oh boy!" Nick had been engaged? Had he also been married? Then divorced? What if they were still married? Barbara Dennison. I looked back at the screen. There was a photo of Nick and a pretty blonde woman. Something about her eyes reminded me of …

"No way! Candace!" Cass and Mac glanced over at me from the bed. I smacked my forehead lightly, "Of course! Candace told me her real name was Barbara."

"The plot thickens," said a voice from behind me.

Startled, I spun around in the desk chair. And there he was.

"Lucas." My voice cracked a little, not quite the come hither tone I was going for. Then again, how did one behave when a sexy ghost pops unannounced into your bedroom?

He grinned, "Ah, you know my name."

I nodded. He was even more gorgeous than I recalled. Lucas placed his hands on either side of my chair and drifted an inch closer. I could feel my heart racing, and hear the blood rushing through my ears. "What…" I shook my head. "How…"

He smiled. "You ask a lot of questions, Evie."

"You know my name." He knew my name!

"Yes, Cass told me."

"My dog spoke to you?" Curiouser and curiouser.

He shrugged, tilting his head to the side. "Not usually. I've been able to communicate with animals before, but they typically don't talk in words. Or at least, I haven't found one yet, until I met her." He pointed down at Cass. "She's a smart cookie ... she can carry on quite a conversation."

"Huh." I glanced down at Cass who looked back up at me innocently. "Who knew?" I shook my head.

He nodded, "But your cat, well ... he's no genius."

"He's not technically my cat."

"Try and tell him that. He's opinionated as hell."

"I think opinionated is a prerequisite for most felines. At least in my experience," I replied. And then I remembered I was chatting with a ghost. "Um, what are you exactly?"

"Exactly?" He gazed upwards and rubbed his chin. "Some would say I'm a ghost. Some might call me a soul, or a spirit, or even an energy or entity. I say I'm simply dead, but that's not technically true either. You can just call me Lucas." He grinned.

"Yeah, okay ... so what was up with Bob Marley in my kitchen yesterday? I mean, that was him, wasn't it? Or ... his spirit?"

"Sure was."

"This is insane. I mean, I think I saw a ghost once before. A little girl. She didn't look like you though, with the, the..." My hands fluttered in the air "The glow."

"The girl you saw was a ghost, but I'm not. Children don't typically return as spirits. They don't need to. A ghost is simply an energy imprint left behind ... like an echo of the person who used to be there. The soul or spirit of the child moved on. But I bet you've spent a long time after pretending you never saw her in the first place."

I nodded, thinking about my uber-religious family. "My father would have been horrified if I said I'd seen a ghost."

"He would have said you were making up stories."

"Or worse."

"You weren't. You saw what you saw. And then you closed yourself off to it. But looks like the timing is right for you to start seeing us again."

"What do you mean?" I asked.

He sat down at the edge of the bed. Cass wandered over and sat next to him. Mac followed Cass and soon they were both curled up next to Lucas. He frowned at Mac. "I'm not really a cat guy."

Um ... okay. "You were going to tell me what you meant about timing..."

"Right. You've heard of people who've seen spirits, right?" He patted the space next to him on the bed. "Come, sit."

I moved from the desk that also served as a vanity, and tentatively placed myself next to him on the bed.

"I can assure you I am very real, and," he flashed that sexy smile again, "I can teach you everything I know about being a spirit." He winked, and my toes curled.

Whoa, Nelly. Was I seriously lusting after a dead guy? My head was beginning to throb. Then I got a bright idea. "Can you tell me who murdered Nick?"

He shook his head sadly, "No."

"But why not? You're a spirit. You live on the other side. Don't you know things?"

"Yes and no, but we'll get to that. One thing at a time." He tilted his head and looked at me speculatively. "Aren't you at all interested to know why you can see me and other spirits now?"

"Wait, there are others?"

"You saw Bob."

"Yeah, okay. So I can see ghosts now? All the time?" I immediately wondered if I would be able to see Nick at the bar.

"Not all of us. Ghosts, as I said, are pure energy, an imprint that got left behind. They technically aren't here with you. Just an image … like a photo or video. When someone is emotionally connected to a person or place, the imprint might remain, but the spirit moves on. A ghost can't communicate with you or affect you in any way. A spirit can."

"I'm confused."

"Welcome to Spirit World 101, Beautiful."

I know I should have been weirded out by all of this, but the only thing I could focus on was that he'd called me beautiful. I seriously needed to get my priorities in order.

"I've been watching you," he said.

"You have?" I guess I should have been mildly disturbed but instead, I felt warm all over.

"Ever since you moved in. I've watched you play with Cass, scratch Mac behind the ears, make tuna sandwiches, watch old movies, cry ... lately you have been doing that a lot."

I shrugged. "Given the circumstances."

"I know. My favorite is when you play your guitar and sing."

I felt heat rise to my cheeks. "You've listened to me? You've heard me sing?"

"You're very good. More than good."

I couldn't respond for a few seconds. I have had people tell me I can sing and play guitar well, that I'm talented, but when Lucas said it ... it really meant something to me. For the very first time in over sixteen years, I felt truly recognized by another, uh, being.

"Thank you. That means a lot to me." I reached out to pet Cass. "Are you always here, then?"

"No. Not always."

"Where do you go?"

"I can't discuss that with you yet. Baby steps."

"Huh?"

"Things are, well, kind of complex on the other side. It can be a little overwhelming to people like you."

"People like me? You mean the living?"

He nodded.

"Jeez, I thought being alive was complicated enough. Now I get to look forward to a complicated afterlife too?"

Lucas laughed. "Well, when you put it that way ... but seriously, the reason you can see me and others like me is a part of you has opened up. It's your music. You have finally been able to begin truly exploring who you are as an artist and a musician, and that creative aspect has allowed you to see things you normally wouldn't."

"You're saying because I'm exploring and pursuing my music at a different level than before, like when I was home ... which, by the way, were you watching me back at home, in Texas?"

He laughed again. "No. I couldn't have gone to you. You had to come to me. To be honest, I didn't know you even existed until you walked through the front door. And I'm so happy you did."

Well now, what did one say to that?

"It's the music, Evie." He stood and came closer. His nearness put me on edge, in a good way.

"My music..." I stared into his eyes, my brain completely unable to recall what we'd just been speaking about.

"Earth to Evie..."

Now there was some irony. He reached out and his hands skimmed my face, fingers tracing my cheeks and sending little darts of electricity through my body. The color in his eyes deepened and I began to get an "incoming kiss" vibe. I closed my eyes ...

And then, my stupid phone rang. I opened my eyes. Just me and two pairs of animal eyes staring at me. There wasn't even a dent in the spot on the mattress next to me to show anyone had been sitting there.

"Lucas?" I called out.

The phone rang again.

"Dammit." I stood and grabbed it off of the desk. It was Simone. Of course.

"Yes?!" I shouted into the phone, surprising even myself.

Simone, oblivious as ever, didn't miss a beat.

"Evie, get your ass over to my house, pronto. Some fucking cop just came to talk to me about Nick Gordin again and I need you here! Now!"

CHAPTER FOURTEEN

I WAS NOT HAPPY about going over to Simone's. Lucas and I had been on the verge of—of something. How much worse could Simone's timing get? And why in the world did the cops want to talk to her again about Nick? It didn't make any sense. Or maybe it did. An awful thought crossed my mind. What if the police thought I was somehow responsible for Nick's murder? I had found Nick. He called me the morning he died. That had to be it. They were looking into time-lines, talking to other people who knew me, and trying to see if it all added up. I didn't like this one bit.

Eventually I calmed myself down and my mind drifted back to Lucas and the improbability of my being in lust with a spirit who lived (existed?) with me in the house where he'd been murdered almost twenty years ago. And, I'd only met him twice and only really spoken with him once. What was wrong with me?

On top of it all, thoughts of his murder suddenly brought my sister, Hannah, to mind. Thing is, I'd always suspected she'd been abducted and killed, even though her case was declared unsolved. I hated feeling that way, but I knew the only reason Hannah wouldn't have come back to us is if she were dead. I couldn't help but wonder, as I sped toward Simone's house, if Lucas might be able to help me find the answers to Hannah's disappearance. Then again, when I had asked him about Nick, he'd given me an emphatic "no." So maybe it didn't work that way on the other side. Damn.

I also liked the fact that when he "touched" me I couldn't see his traumas. I think the answer to that was twofold. He wasn't human, and I was certain his most traumatic experience was being shot to death. I didn't think I could heal a spirit. I didn't see how anyway. He was already dead.

Finally, after mulling things over way too much, I pulled up in front of Simone's mansion. I could hardly wait to see what she had in store for me this time.

I walked through the ginormous front door and into her all- white living room. She was seated on a white leather sofa, legs kicked up on a white, marble coffee table, with a white, silk pillow under her feet, and what appeared to be a fluffy, white cat in her lap. Yes. I did say cat. All the white combined with her white dressing gown made her beautifully coiffed head look as if it were floating, disembodied, in mid-air.

The thought of her floating head gave me a sudden fit of the giggles, which I quickly covered up with a fake coughing fit that rapidly turned into the real deal.

Simone glared at me in irritation. "Jesus, Evie, breathe much?" She gestured to a pitcher of water on the end table next to her. "Have some water. You look ridiculous."

If by ridiculous, she meant pissed, then yes, she was correct. "Excuse me, but I broke several speed limits to get here because of an emergency and this is how I find you? With that..." I pointed to the cat, "... in your lap?"

She smiled and made a kissy face at the contented-looking pile of fluff. Her voice took on a tone usually reserved for babies and small children. "Look at Edie, little man. She's growing a spine. And there is no way she could have broken any fucking speed limits in that piece of shit she drives."

I let out an aggrieved sigh.

"This is Clooney, by the way." Simone patted the spot next to her again, "Come say hello, Auntie Evie."

"I thought you were allergic to cats. Isn't that why Mac now lives with me?"

She shook her head. "Turns out I'm not allergic. I think that was a sinus infection. Anyway, I missed McConaughey, so I got Clooney here. He's a Persian."

"Nice. But why didn't you just ask for Mac back?"

"Cuz he's a fat slob and besides, I'm sure he likes you better. We sort of had this love-hate thing going on. But me and Clooney get along just perfectly."

I walked over and sat next to Simone and the new cat, who admittedly was cute. He stared up at me with sleepy blue eyes.

"What's the deal, Simone? I was in the middle of something."

She stopped petting the cat and her eyes widened. "Oh my God! You were having sex?!"

"No!"

"Evie! Who were you with? Wait. Let me guess. The photographer who was on the shoot the other day? He was eyeing you."

"He was gay, Simone."

"He was?"

"Yes."

"How did I miss that?"

"I don't have a clue. Especially since he wore pink Vans and couldn't stop talking about his new husband, Marcus."

"No shit?"

"Yes." That was Simone. Totally self-absorbed and in la-la land.

"Okay, then was it the lighting guy? He was cute. Really cute."

"I was not having sex with anyone. And the lighting guy is married. His wife is due to have their first baby any day now."

"How do you know these things and I don't?" Simone whined.

"Because I listen. You should try it some time."

"Ouch. You on the rag or something?"

I rolled my eyes. Seriously, I was not getting paid enough for this crap. "No. I just want to know what's going on. You called me, remember? You said to come right now, that the police wanted to talk to you about Nick."

"Oh yeah. That. So, here's the deal." She scooted closer and lowered her voice conspiratorially. "The cops were apparently going over Nick's phone records and my number showed up a few times."

"What?"

"Yeah. They wanted to know if you ever used my cell phone to call him."

"You told them no, right? I mean, I would never use your phone!"

She picked up a flute of champagne on the table and took a sip. "Want some?"

"No! I want to know you told the police I would never use your things without your explicit permission. Because it's the truth." I waited, expectantly.

"Actually, I told them you borrowed my phone a few times. With my permission, of course. And who you called was none of my business."

I felt my blood pressure rise. "You did what?! Why?"

She sighed heavily, suddenly unwilling to make eye contact with me. A hard knot began to form in my stomach. "Because I called him."

"You called Nick? Why?"

"Listen, I like you. You're the closest thing I've ever had to a friend. But you don't know how people can be. I grew up here ... and I have seen a lot of shit go down. I've seen a lot of people get strung along, ripped off, or beaten down by others. I know that guy, Nick, was giving you a line about his friend the music producer. I know he was stringing you along to get you to work late hours in that bar for no money, playing music to drunks and losers. I think you're better than that, so I called him a few times to tell him to fire you."

The blood drained from my face. "You—you are unbelievable."

"I'm sorry. But I want the best for you."

I couldn't even respond to that. I stood up from the couch and stared at her.

"You are so selfish. I can't always be at your beck and call. I am available to you most of the time. In fact, I even dropped everything to come and take care of you the night you supposedly overdosed on Sudafed. The night Nick's producer friend was coming in."

"According to Nick. Oh, you are so naïve."

"Yeah? Well what about you?"

She laughed bitterly. "Oh, I'm not naïve."

"I mean you promised me an audition at Sony. With a real producer."

She nodded. "I did. And I intend to make it happen. But first, I think you need to really understand what this life is like. Look, I can't even go to Denny's without dressing up like a washed- up Pat Benatar look-alike. The minute I take the wig off, there'd be a hundred tweens in my face wanting my autograph, and let's not even talk about their fucking insane, forty-year-old mothers. Then there's the paparazzi—" She sighed loudly.

"This is a lonely existence. It really is. Everyone wants something from you. You don't know who your friends are, if you even have any at all. Hell, my own sister wants to mooch off me constantly. Then you came along and you didn't want anything from me. Granted, I did give you a great place to live, but you didn't ask for it. You seem appreciative, and you're nice. Now, you want some-thing from me, like everyone else. I don't know why, but I thought we were friends and honestly, I was trying to protect you." A flash of hurt darted across her face and she quickly covered it up with another gulp of champagne. Although I wasn't a big drinker, that stuff sure was starting to look good right about now.

I tossed my arms up in the air and sighed. "Simone, we are friends. That's why I haven't bothered you about an audition. But where I come from, when you tell somebody you're going to do something for them, you do it. You're only as good as your word."

"What about Nick then? Was he a good guy?"

"Yes. I think he was. I think his intentions were good and for all I know, the producer came that night. I never did get a chance to follow back up with Nick about it." A stab of guilt shot through me. "I do believe Nick wanted the best for me too."

"So do I. I mean, I want the best for you, like I said. You're good peeps."

I wasn't sure I believed her. But I nodded anyway. "But why didn't you tell the cops this, instead of saying I borrowed your phone?"

"Duh. Because I don't need a scandal. If the cops thought I threatened the guy and the media caught wind of it, I'd be screwed. I don't need the paparazzi climbing up my ass any more than they already do."

The knot in my stomach was back again. "Wait a minute ... why would the police think you threatened Nick?"

"Because I did. I mean, I didn't mean it." Simone had a grim expression on her face.

"What?"

"And my sister heard me, and if she gets in one of her little snits and decides to tell that to the police, I could be in trouble. She hasn't connected any of it yet. She's in Hawaii for two weeks. But if she did, and I didn't keep doling out to her all the time, well, I could be front page on US Weekly or worse."

"What did you say to him? To Nick?"

She knocked back the rest of the champagne and poured herself another glass. "I told him I'd fucking kill him if he didn't let you go."

"You said that?! Oh my God." I turned to walk out.

Simone jumped up off the sofa, dropping Clooney unceremoniously on his rear. "Evie, please don't go! I'm sorry. I didn't mean it. I was only protecting you." She darted over and grabbed my arm—a shockwave of loneliness traveled through me and I shoved her hand away.

"You can't leave me. I need you. We have a shoot in the morning. You know, for my new video."

I turned the knob on the front door, determined to leave for good. But then I remembered exactly what would happen if I quit. I'd lose a much-needed salary, my only chance of ever singing for the Sony people, and most importantly, my home, which meant Lucas. I sighed.

Nevertheless, I decided to let Simone sweat it out for a while. I marched out the door without a word and headed back to my van.

CHAPTER FIFTEEN

I WAS THERE THE FIRST night the bar reopened, a week after Nick's death. As Bradley Verne promised, he did what he could to keep Nick's Place in business. His wife, Raquela, rectified the books and paid the bills. And they'd contacted the attorney in charge of Nick's affairs.

Becky was the new bartender, much to Candace's chagrin. But truth be told, Becky sure could mix a mean martini. And as for Candace, she could be found in her usual spot next to Mumbles. Honestly, it was as if nothing had changed. But of course, everything had.

I had yet to question Candace about her engagement to Nick. I wasn't sure how to bring it up. I mean, if Candace had wanted me to know about it, she would have told me herself. But after giving it a lot of thought, I decided to approach her that night after my final set.

As I prepped for my first song of the night, I recalled what Jackson had said about the cops losing interest when it came to murder investigations involving the mob, and I worried that Nick's murder would get the same treatment. My gut was telling me it wasn't the mob who'd killed Nick. Yeah, there was that nasty guy Pietro, and I intended to talk to Becky about what went down that evening when she and Nick ended up in the kitchen with him. But truthfully, the mob story just wasn't very convincing to me. And that's because I was becoming more and more certain Nick's murder had something to do with his past.

And of course, there was Simone. I continued to feel uncomfortable around her after she revealed her threat towards Nick. Which is why I wondered, briefly, if she could have possibly hired someone to kill him. She certainly couldn't have done it herself; she was at the photo shoot the morning I got the call from Nick. But there was one guy who hung around Simone from time to time. Dwight Jenkins, the guy who'd approached me at the counter at Nordy's and informed me of my "interview" with Simone.

See, Simone and Dwight seem to have this friend -with -benefits thing going on. They're very discrete about it. But I'd noticed a wink here, a meaningful look there, every so often when they though no one was looking. And then there was the night I walked out her front door to see Dwight speed up the drive in his sleek Audi. He told me he was bringing her take- out, even though he wasn't carrying any bags except for one from BevMo. I didn't trust the guy at all. And I think he would do anything for Simone. Even kill for her.

I managed to make it through the first set without any issues. I'd been worried how strange it would feel to be back at work without Nick's familiar, comforting presence. But once I started playing ... it all faded into the background, and I felt peaceful for the first time in weeks. I decided to take a breather and make myself a bite to eat in the kitchen. Sadly, Nick took his famous fish taco recipe with him to the grave ... but I knew the chicken and steak recipes by heart and promptly whipped up three for dinner.

Back out front in the bar, I noticed Jackson in his corner booth. He was typing fast and furious. I had some questions about his screenplay or documentary, whatever it was. I plopped down in his booth on the seat across from him. He looked up from the computer and smiled.

"Hey, Evie. How's it going?"

I shrugged. "I miss Nick."

"We all do."

I nodded, pointing down to the plate of tacos. Figured I might as well sweeten the deal a bit before I started asking questions. "Want one?"

Jackson eyed the tacos appreciatively. "Sure! Thanks." I scooted the plate across the table so he could grab a taco, and then leaned in close, clasping my hands together. I was pleased to see he was being Mister Nice Guy tonight.

"Can I ask you something?"

"Um ... yeah." He took a bite of the taco, moaning appreciatively.

"How well did you know Nick?"

He sat back against the booth, taco in hand, and didn't say anything for a few seconds. He took another bite and chewed thoughtfully. "I thought I told you all of that."

"Well sure, I mean ... I know you were doing a documentary and wanted him to be in it. But how did you guys meet?"

"I came in here one night and that was it." He dabbed at his mouth with a napkin and eyed my remaining two tacos enviously.

"But how did you find him?"

Jackson sighed and pointed to his closed laptop. "A good writer does his research."

"So, you targeted him."

"You make it sound so slimy. Yeah, I knew Nick owned this place, thanks to the powers of Google. And I've been a fan of Nick's because I'd watched Next-Door Neighbors a billion times as a kid. I didn't exactly have a great family life. TV was my best friend." He set his napkin down on the table and clasped his hands together. "Everything I've ever gotten was because I earned it, including getting into film school on a scholarship. Not too many people can say that. My mom was a single parent. I have three brothers and I'm the oldest, so guess who ran the family while mom was out? Me. And I still made it to USC. And I am going to have an awesome master's project when I'm finished, Nick or no Nick. Not that he planned to help me anyway."

I nodded. I couldn't help wonder if Jackson's mother had divorced his father due to the physical abuse I knew Jackson had suffered. I assumed the man I'd seen in the vision had been his father.

"I don't understand why he was so shy about being on camera. I mean, he'd obviously been in front of it for years as a kid and young adult."

Jackson leaned back and crossed his arms. "Secrets. Nick had secrets like everyone else, and he didn't want me to expose them."

"What kind of secrets?"

A smirk crossed his handsome face. "Who knows. But I'm uncovering them, and it's changing the entire storyline of my documentary. See, lies make for good entertainment."

"Lies?" I arched my brow in disbelief.

"There are tons in this bar. This place." He gestured at our surroundings. "It's built on lies. With this new angle, I don't need Nick anyway."

Jackson was really starting to irritate me. "That sounds a bit arrogant."

Again, he shrugged. "Maybe it is, but you know, it wasn't like Nick was super-warm and friendly to me. He didn't like me coming in here, trying to get the scoop on his life. But he couldn't do much about it either. It isn't like I was disruptive. I'm just doing my thing. And I pay, unlike those bums at the counter."

He did have a point. "Oh. Well, Nick gave me my first opportunity here in L.A., and I will always be grateful for that."

"More than he gave me."

I was feeling uncomfortable with the conversation, so I decided to finish up my meal in the kitchen and get ready for the next set.

"It was nice chatting with you, Jackson. Gotta get back to work now." He smiled at me, nodding as if we were the best of friends, which we definitely were not.

CHAPTER SIXTEEN

AFTER THE CONVERSATION with Jackson, I stood in the kitchen eating my now-cold tacos as quickly as possible. Becky was going in and out with food and gave me a little wave. It was kind of a busy night. Since Nick's death, the place had gotten some notoriety, so a few new faces had shown up.

"Hey, Becky, I don't mind helping out in here and tending bar. I can go back to playing when it quiets down some."

"Oh, honey, that would be helpful, if you don't mind."

"No problem."

"I can wait the tables and manage the kitchen, if you can tend bar," she said.

"You got it. Can I ask, how did you get elected to start running things?" I didn't say it in a mean way. I was simply curious.

She smiled. "I guess it was a natural fit, considering how close Nick and I were."

I wanted to ask how close that was, when we both heard a commotion coming from the bar.

"Probably Mumbles or the broad wanting another drink. Can you check it out? That table of kids from SC wants a mess of tacos," Becky said.

I nodded. Becky never referred to Candace by her name. She simply called her "the broad" while Candace called her "the bitch." Fun times.

I walked through the kitchen doors to find George Hernandez pounding his meaty fists on the bar. Mumbles sat with drooping shoulders, staring a hole into his drink. Candace had inched as far away from the large, angry man as she could. A few other patrons were watching and waiting to see what the crazy guy would do next. But thanks to the loud background noise and crowded tables, not everyone seemed aware a scene was brewing. I aimed to keep it that way.

I walked calmly to George and said, "Can I help you, sir?"

"I wanna talk to whoever is in charge here!" He bellowed, as if I were across the room instead of a foot or two away. His fleshy face was a deep crimson color and slick with sweat.

"That would be me," I said, straightening my five-foot-four frame as tall as it could go. No point dragging poor Becky into this, at least not yet.

"You? He left everything to you?"

"What do you mean?"

"What I mean is someone owes me. And if Nick left this place to you, I suggest you sell it and pay me back."

"Sir, I have no idea what you're talking about. But I'm going to have to ask you to leave."

"I bet you'd like me to leave." He moved closer to me, and I could smell his sour body odor mixed with cheap cologne.

Jackson suddenly appeared next to me. Now Jackson wasn't a huge guy, but at over six feet tall with a relatively fit build, something told me he could hold his own. Plus he was at least twenty years younger than this Hernandez character. Jackson clapped a hand over the big guy's shoulder. Hard.

"The lady asked you nicely to leave. I suggest you do so."

"You do, do you?" Hernandez said. He shook his shoulder, trying to knock Jackson's hand off. It didn't budge.

"I do. Unless, of course you would like to find out what it means to have your ass kicked by someone who is skilled in Krav Maga."

"What the hell is that?" Hernandez asked. I wondered as well. Whatever it was, I prayed Jackson wasn't bluffing.

"It means hand-to-hand combat. It's a form of street fighting in Israel, used by military forces around the world and in Special Forces like Israel's Mossad, the CIA, and the British SAS. I am quite adept in it."

I wasn't sure who looked more shocked by this admission. Me or the fat guy. It worked though. But not before he got the last word in.

"I suggest you get an attorney, lady. I plan to get the money back that Nick owed me." Then he turned and bolted out the door before Jackson could make good on his threat.

The room was silent. All eyes were focused on Jackson and me. I smiled and waved and went back behind the bar. Within a couple of minutes, everyone appeared to have lost interest. Jackson went back to his booth. I wanted to thank him, but by the time I'd poured a half a dozen beers and a handful of Jägermeister shots to the group of college kids, he was gone. I was pretty grateful to him for stepping in like that and resolved to thank him as soon as I was able.

Mumbles looked unsettled. I leaned towards him across the bar counter. "You okay, Mumbles?"

He looked up at me with his unpatched eye. It was tearing up. "Not same, Evie. No Nick. Not same. Bad people."

"Oh no, Mumbles. Don't let one bad seed ruin things. He's just an idiot and a bully. Of course it isn't the same without Nick. But we have to move on. We can do it together." I grabbed a paper napkin from behind the bar and wiped his eye.

"Are you crying? Goddammit, Mumbles! What the hell!" Candace scolded him.

I glared at her. "Now, come on, Candace. I would think you would have a little more compassion. I mean, you were once engaged to Nick!" So much for my delicate approach.

Mumbles stared at me and then looked at Candace who's normally blurry eyes snapped with anger. "Who told you that? That bitch?"

"No. I read it online." I quickly threw together a Candace Special and handed it to her. "There was a photo of you and Nick from an old newspaper clipping."

She pushed the drink away, spilling some of it over the side of the glass, and stood abruptly. "I don't want it. I have somewhere I need to be."

"At ten o'clock on a Thursday night? Really?" I didn't bother to mention she and Mumbles never seemed to have anywhere to go.

"Yes, really. Mumbles, you coming?!"

He didn't say anything at first. She started to stumble away. Mumbles slid off the bar stool. "Sorry, Evie. Gotta watch her. Bad on the street. Bad."

"I don't want the two of you on the streets! You both need to sober up first." I jogged after them. "Come on, Candace. I'm sorry if I offended you."

"You didn't, sweet pea. You didn't. Mumbles and I need a rest is all."

"On the streets?"

"We got a place. Don't worry about us."

One of the frat boys called out for more beer. I turned to see where the hollering was coming from, and when I turned back, Candace and Mumbles were gone. So much for a night of getting answers to my questions. If anything, I was more confused than ever.

.

CHAPTER SEVENTEEN

IT WAS AFTER TWO O'CLOCK when I finally headed home. And, thankfully, I had a day off from Simone tomorrow, which meant I did not have to get up at the crack of dawn, grab her pumpkin spice latte, and get to her place only to find her lounging with her cat, Clooney. She was having what she referred to as a "mental space vacation." I had no idea what exactly that entailed, and I did not plan to ask. She did not invite me. And I was okay with that.

I had been asking Becky and everyone else at the bar who might have been there the night before Nick's murder if anyone had noticed a new guy there—the producer. According to the regulars, no newbies had turned up. I hated to think maybe Nick had been stringing me along after all as Simone insisted. No matter what, though, in my heart I knew Nick had been a good guy who didn't deserve what he'd gotten, and I was driven to get some answers.

As I turned off Sunset and onto Laurel, I noticed a car behind me, following really close. After all that had happened recently, I was instantly on my guard. I turned right onto my street, and so did the car. I gunned the gas pedal, hoping to zip away. Yeah, that didn't work so well. I wasn't sure if I should just keep driving past my place and head back into town. The only plus was the automatic security gate at the entrance to the drive that wound up to the house. I figured I could open the gate, drive through, and block the drive until the gate closed behind me. Once inside, I'd set the alarm and have Cass there to protect me.

I clicked open the gate. The car was still right on my bumper. What if whoever it was jumped out and tried to open my car door? What if they had a gun? I double-checked the locks on my doors and waited. My heart was pounding. I inched the van through the gate and waited for it to close, keeping my eyes trained on my rearview mirror. Finally the gate locked shut and the car continued on. From what I could see in the dim light, it looked like some type of wagon. Maybe an older Volvo or Audi. I couldn't tell. I raced the van up the remainder of the driveway, anxious to get behind closed doors and snuggle up with Cass and Mac.

I bolted for the front door and unlocked it as quickly as I could. Before I had one foot inside, I knew something really weird was going on. I immediately forgot the car that had followed me.

I could not believe what I was seeing.

CHAPTER EIGHTEEN

NOW, IT'S ONE THING to see a ghost, um spirit. And it's another thing to run into the spirit of Bob Marley. But to walk into your home to find Bob Marley and the spirit of Janis Joplin on your sofa, smoking pot, while your overweight cat is lying on his back on the overstuffed chair opposite the sofa, seemingly stoned out of his mind, well, it's probably safe to say you have seen it all.

Bob looked up and smiled through the smoky haze. "Ah, Evie, thank you, sista, for lettin' us hang out here tonight."

Janis glanced up from where she sat strumming on her guitar and smiled at me. "Yeah. You're a cool chick. I like your pad."

"Uh, thank you." Mac opened one green eye and let out a soft, contented meow. He stretched a leg out and promptly went back to his happy little slumber. Cass thumped her tail but didn't move from her spot next to Janis.

"So, you guys been here long?" I know that sounded lame, but what the heck did you say to two famous spirits?

"Oh, you know, we don't be keeping track of the time here on dis side of tings," Bob said, his Jamaican accent melodic and soothing.

"Riiight."

Janis waved a hand at me. "No way, girl. There's no need for time and all that shit here. Come have a seat."

I decided I didn't have a choice, and it's not often you get to shoot the breeze with Janis Joplin and Bob Marley (even if they are dead). Speaking of which, "You guys are real, right? I mean, this isn't just one loooong hallucination I've been having ... is it?" Of course, asking your hallucinations if they are real or not is probably not going to clear things up much in the long run.

Bob laughed, his voice warm and smooth like chocolate. "Do you know I once said, 'I don't believe in death neither in flesh nor in spirit.' And that be the truth, Evie. It's all the same no matter where you be. And here," he gestured to me and Janis on the sofa, "... we are!" He laughed.

Well that certainly cleared things up for me. Now I knew how Alice felt trying to talk to that darned caterpillar. I plopped down next to Janis and reached over to pet Cass, who'd drifted off to sleep.

Janis took another hit off of her joint (I was still trying to figure out if the pot was real, and if so, where the heck did they get it?) and then blew a graceful plume of smoke into the air. "He's deep. Real deep. Just relax and enjoy the moment. Go with it."

"Is Lucas here, too?" As much as I wanted to get to know these two, and I definitely did, I was hoping he was here and just hadn't joined us yet.

"Nah. Lukie boy be off doin' some work," Bob said.

"Work? You work on the other side?" I asked. Well, so much for spending eternity lounging around playing harps.

Janis laughed. "Like Bob said, hon, there isn't much difference between here and there, and it really isn't so much the other side."

"So, are you still musicians?"

They nodded. "Among other things. We have projects," she said. Bob eyed her and shook his head. "But that's up to Lucas to discuss with you."

"Yes, indeed, and Lukie boy be needin' to get permission for his project."

"Permission? From who? What project? I'm confused." I didn't know if it was the exhaustion, the lingering smell of weed in the room, or the bizarre conversation I was having with two dead people, but I leaned back into the soft throw pillows and felt my eyes slowly close.

"It all be good, Evie girl. It all be good."

Bob started singing "One Love." Janis joined in with her raspy vocals. I was blissfully happy, and everything else floated away as I fell into a deep, peaceful sleep.

CHAPTER NINETEEN

I HAD NO CLUE what time it was, or how long I'd been asleep, but it was dark in the room and outside when I woke on the couch. There was a blanket over me, and my hand rested on Mac, who lay on top of my chest, all curled up. My other hand hung over the side of the couch, nestled deep in Cass's soft fur.

I remembered Bob and Janis, the conversation, the music, falling asleep. Had that been a dream? If so, who had put the blanket on me? I stretched out my legs and my feet bumped against something solid at the other end of the sofa. What the hell? I stared hard into the blackness until a faint, glowing form became visible.

"Bob? Janis?" I whispered.

"No. It's me, Lucas."

My heart skipped a beat.

"Lucas?"

He slid closer and the room brightened noticeably. At least it did around him. Cass lifted her head and then placed it back down again.

"How do you ... glow like that? Can all spirits do that?"

"It's actually called my Antarjyohi, my internal light. I come by it through those spirits who are in The Bodha."

"The Bodha?" Suddenly, the Twilight Zone theme song played in my head.

"I can't go into too much detail about all that yet. But maybe someday."

Okaaay. "Where were you earlier? When I came home, Janis Joplin and Bob Marley were here playing music and smoking weed. In my living room."

He laughed. "I know. I passed them on my way in."

"As in on your way in through the front door?"

"Kind of. When we visit here, we come through a portal. Whenever someone has a physical death somewhere, particularly in a place they lived or loved, a portal usually gets placed there."

"Go on." Seriously, Harry Potter had nothing on this. "Where is the portal here?"

"It usually only happens when a person dies suddenly, violently. I loved this place. I was staying here because Blake let me rent it until I found my own place. He's never here. Guy has so much cash and so many homes, who knows when he'll be back. Anyway, when I was killed here, a portal was created, and now I can come and go as I please. It's actually in the family room behind the kitchen. That's where I was shot."

"Not everyone can do that? Go through the portal, I mean?"

He shook his head. "No. There are many who are ready to move on when they die, and they go elsewhere. They don't need to come back here. They are content and at peace."

"Where do they go?" I had to ask.

"It depends," he said.

"On what?"

"Various things. Like the tiers. The tier you and I are on now is a grey one."

"Huh?" I was totally confused.

He ran a hand through his dark hair. "There are many levels of existence. We call them tiers. The human, or Earthbound tier, is grey due to the mixture of energies that exist here."

"So where do you go when you leave here? Another tier?"

"I can visit the Bodha if absolutely necessary."

"Oh now it's clear. As mud."

He ignored me. "Or I can turn my energy down to rest."

"You mean you sleep?"

"Sort of. I get drained on this tier, just like you get drained at the end of a trying day. I turn down my vibration and rest until I'm recharged."

"Do you go anywhere else?"

"I can go through the portals of spirits who have the same or very similar vibration as myself."

"Like Bob and Janis?" Finally, I understood why I was seeing more than just Lucas in the house.

"Yes. I can go to Nine Miles where Bob passed and sit in his living room where he grew up. I can go to The Landmark on Sunset and hang out with Janis. But that isn't really a place anyone likes to go."

"Wow. Can bad people—evil people—leave behind a portal?"

He lowered his voice to a soft whisper. "They can. And they do. They do it more often than the others."

A deep chill went through me. I stared at him. He reached out again and took my hand.

"It's one of the reasons I am here and why you are here. It's also why I was not here tonight when you came home."

"What do you mean?"

"The Black Tier and the Asat."

"The Black Tier? The Asat?" Lions and tigers and bears, oh my!

"Yes. The reason the Earthbound tier is grey has to do with the mixture of vibrations here, good—white—and bad—black. The black tier is home to the darkest of all the vibrations—the Asat. They are lost souls, the kind which can never move out of the black. As individual spirits, they are referred to as Asuras, as a collective whole, they are called the Asat. The Asat is opposite of the Bodha."

"Like heaven and hell? God and Satan?"

"Yes. I suppose you could say that if you want."

"But what does it have to do with you and me?"

"Because there is an Asura in the Black Tier who wants your vibration. You are special, and if the Black Tier can capture your vibration, it's a victory for them and a loss for the white. For each vibration such as yours who gets captured, the Black Tier gains strength on every level, meaning eventually there will be far more black than shades of grey or white, and the possibility of no other tiers to exist. You are what is referred to as a Govinda, someone who gives joy in the whole universe because of your gift."

"Oh come on. What gift? The only joy I give is to Cass ... and Mac, and that's only because I feed him."

"No. Not true. I'm here to make sure your vibration is not stolen. And you know what your gift is. The Bodha shared with me."

"What do you know?"

"I know you can heal people to a point. I know you can take their most painful experiences and place some light in them where there was once only darkness."

I didn't say anything.

"As you can imagine, those on the Black Tier don't like any vibration that can restore light in dark places, and that is what you do."

I swallowed hard.

He reached out and touched my hand. "Tell me. Tell me how you discovered the gift. It's important for me to know so I can help you. The Bodha only revealed you have the gift."

"Gift?!" I laughed.

"It is. Trust me. And it could save your soul."

I took another deep breath and tried hard to focus. He waited patiently. Finally, I unloaded the entire sad story about my sister.

Lucas never interrupted. He let me talk and feel the complex range of emotions the topic of Hannah always evoked. At home, we didn't talk about her. Ever.

So there was something incredibly freeing to finally, authentically, share the feelings I'd kept buried for so many years.

"After Hannah disappeared, um, I had this Uncle ... Uncle Wilson. He was kind of strange or, at the very least, quirky. According to my father, he had a demon in him. He was really into New Age stuff. He was my mother's brother and, unfortunately, not welcome in our home. My mama said Uncle Wilson had done a lot of studying with Native Americans of Cherokee descent. I think she would have liked to delve further into what he learned, but she'd never go against my dad's wishes."

Lucas nodded sympathetically.

"You know, I liked my uncle, and of course my mother loved him. But there were just some things my dad wouldn't budge on. Anyway, Uncle Wilson came to comfort my mom and me after Hannah disappeared. He and I walked along the path we think she took, and we stopped at the place the police said it all went down." The memory of that day weaved through my mind.

"My uncle stopped, took a deep breath, and began walking in circles. He didn't say anything. He walked like that for at least fifteen minutes. My eyes followed him, and then I began to scan the ground as if I, too, could find the answers to Hannah's disappearance. And that's when I spotted the feathers."

"The feathers?" Lucas asked.

I nodded. "Yes. I think they are the key to my, uh, gift. I picked them up. My uncle stopped walking. He took my hands in his and we both stared at the feathers for what seemed like ages. And then he spoke. 'Eagle,' he said. 'These are eagle feathers, Evie.'

"Then, he folded my hands carefully around the soft feathers and leaned in close, whispering, 'Keep these, okay? Don't lose them. Ever. I think they are meant for you.'"

"I was shocked and, of course, I wanted to know more about what he meant, but then my mom came over to us and he stopped talking. And ever since then, I've been able to ... to have visions about people. That was the last time I saw my uncle. He had a heart attack and died two years later. In any case, I kept the feathers and I have no plans to let them out of my possession."

Lucas nodded solemnly. "So how did you learn you had this gift?" He asked. He squeezed my hand again, reassuringly.

"I remember going back to school, and my teacher, Ms. Underwood, took my hand and told me how sorry she was about my sister's disappearance. In those few seconds, I saw a flash of Ms. Underwood and she was, she was ... being raped and beaten, and she was pretty young. At first I didn't understand what was going on. But she had always been such a sad person. After that day, though, she seemed to have new energy. She was happier and lighter. She seemed to enjoy teaching.

"I still didn't know if what I had seen had been real, but then I heard some of the ladies at my mother's beauty shop talking about her and how much better she had become in recent weeks. They mentioned the 'unfortunate incident' she had endured fifteen years earlier, and how they thought she'd never be happy again, and I knew. I mean I didn't know if I had healed her, but then more things like this started happening. I could touch someone, see horrible things, and then that person would either become easier for others to deal with, or happier and more confident. They changed somehow, and usually for the better. I still don't know what, if anything, the feathers have to do with it. But I keep them in my room on my desk, close to me like my uncle asked."

I glanced over at Lucas, feeling curious. "Do you know what the feathers mean?"

"No." He shook his head. "But I'm sure your uncle was correct, especially since after you found those feathers, your gift appeared. Let me see what I can find out on this side of the tier. Maybe I can get some answers for you."

"Really?"

"I will do what I can, but I have to tell you, I'm worried."

I scooted away from him just enough to look into his face. His expression was troubled. "What do you mean?"

"I don't know how else to put this, but your sister was taken from you. Hannah did not disappear. She was taken."

CHAPTER TWENTY

LUCAS AND I TALKED until almost sunup. Once he dropped the bombshell of the dark side wanting a piece of me, it was hard to focus on anything else. I didn't want to think about my sister, the feathers, my gift, or anything else I didn't understand, except, of course, Lucas himself—who I definitely didn't understand, but could not stop thinking about even if I tried.

After a little while and lots of subject changes, he made sure I was distracted. We talked about L.A., music, Cass (apparently my dog likes to quote the Buddha. Who knew?).

I looked at Cass, now at my feet. Lucas was gone. I don't know what time he left. I fell asleep with his hand in mine. When I woke with the sun blaring in through the large bay window off the family room, I was alone and somewhat dismayed. But there was Mac, who had finally gotten off my chest. He was sitting up at the end of the couch, staring at me intently. When he saw I was awake, he let out a truly annoyed meow.

"Hungry, are you?"

Cass did a twirl, and Mac leapt from the sofa, slowly jogging towards the kitchen, his large belly swaying. I couldn't help but laugh. I got up and followed the animals. Glancing at the oven clock, I was surprised to see it was almost eleven. I couldn't remember the last time I had woken up so late. Granted, I'd been up all night, but still.

I fed the "kids," showered, and found myself at a bit of a loss as to what to do with my day off. I had been on the go ever since getting both jobs.

No matter how hard I tried, I kept thinking about what Lucas said about the Black Tier, the Asuras, and the Asat, who seemed to think I was extra special. Murder was pretty dark and evil, right? Was that how the Black Tier got to people? Through horrible events? Loss of a loved one? I gulped. I couldn't help but wonder if they'd been after me since I was a kid ... since Hannah's disappearance? I'd have to ask Lucas when I saw him again, whenever that might be. I hoped it was soon. I thought about staying in the house all day and just relaxing with Cass and Mac, seeing who might show up through the portal, but I am not one to sit still. Mama used to tell people I had ADHD. But I doubt that's my issue. I just like to keep busy.

I decided there had been plenty of Black Tier stuff around me as of late, and I planned to tackle it head on. That George Hernandez guy was pretty nasty and had a big bone to pick with Nick, and now me. Becky had mentioned George had a Mexican restaurant down in Venice Beach, called Jorge's.

I liked Mexican food. So did Cass and Mac. I also enjoyed watching the nut jobs walk along the boardwalk. After Googling the restaurant, I rounded up the dog and the cat. I figured it was time for Mac to start doing ridealongs as well, and we headed out to have a little lunch and see if I couldn't get to the bottom of a few things.

CHAPTER TWENTY-ONE

MAC WASN'T SO SURE about the car ride and he let Cass and me know it, but by the time we got to Venice Beach, he'd mellowed out and was curled up next to Cass on a blanket in the back.

"All right, you two, I'll be back. Be good, and I promise I'll bring treats." Cass opened one eye, probably thinking something profound. I still couldn't fathom where she'd picked up the Buddhist stuff considering she spent most of her life in a strict Christian household. I gave her a quick pat on the head, and stepped out of the van into the Santa Monica sunshine.

I didn't have to walk too far before I located Jorge's Mexican Café. The place was small and quaint, brightly painted in oranges and blues. It looked pretty authentic, and the smells wafting throughout the fifteen-table place were amazing. The restaurant was nearly empty, though, and I wondered why.

A young, dark-haired hostess offered to seat me, and I followed her into the main dining area. There was a beautiful view of the beach and ocean, again … the place seemed like it should be packed with customers. But I soon discovered why there weren't many people there: The service was really slow. I waited a good ten minutes for a glass of water although there were only five other customers at three different tables. I was waiting patiently for the obligatory chips and salsa to arrive, my back to the front entrance, when I heard a familiar voice.

"George here?"

I did not want the speaker to see me, but I needed to confirm my suspicions. I turned my chair slightly, looking as discretely as possible towards the hostess stand. As suspected, there stood Pietro SanGiacomo, the guy who'd been at the bar screaming at Nick not so long ago. What was he doing here?

"He's upstairs in his office," the hostess replied.

I waited until Pietro went upstairs, and then I got up and left. The hostess called out after me, but I told her I had an emergency. Fortunately, Simone had left her disguise in my van after our most recent Denny's run. Cass flapped her tail when I opened the back door, and Mac gave a half-hearted meow.

"Sorry, guys. Just making a quick pit stop." I put on the wig and a pair of sunglasses, quickly changed into the t-shirt, and headed back to the restaurant. I needed to figure out how to get close to George's office. I walked inside and, thankfully, the hostess had her back to me and was walking towards the kitchen. I scanned the area, spotting the stairs to the second floor, close to the hostess stand, next to the restrooms. Pretending to search for the bathroom, I made my way up the steps.

The stairs creaked, and I cringed. There were only about two dozen steps. At the top were two doors, both closed—one to the left and one to the right. I heard men's voices coming from the door on the left. I snuck close and crouched down, figuring I could claim to be fixing my shoe if anyone stumbled across me, and listened in. Within just a few seconds, I heard Nick's name.

"Look, I didn't kill Nick!" It was George speaking. I could tell by his accent and booming voice.

"Maybe not, George. But you haven't exactly been keeping a low profile. You've been going around making a stink about that stupid fish taco recipe you said he stole and the money he owed you. I would shut the hell up if I were you."

"He did steal the recipe!" The sound of something slapping wood reverberated through the wall. I pictured George at his desk, banging it in frustration with his big hands. "And he and I had a deal! I loaned him a shitload of money to get things rolling with these restaurants because I didn't have the time to do it and he said he did. We agreed I'd be the silent partner, but then the asshole goes and gambles it away. I am entitled to getting my money back at the very least!"

"Oh come on, George. He didn't steal the recipe and you and I both know it. You're a damn drama queen, and if you're not careful, you could land yourself in jail. Let it go—the money, the recipe, the restaurants. All of it. We don't need the cops sniffing around. "

"But I didn't kill Nick! I have an alibi. I was with my wife, working from my home office. I'm only making noise to protect you."

"Protect me?" Pietro said. He sounded as perplexed as I felt.

"Yeah, man. I mean, we're partners and all. I think it's pretty obvious you killed that loser. I want to make sure my investment is protected. If that girl running the place doesn't give me my money back, and something happens to you, I am totally screwed. I'll lose this place and be back frying rolled tacos in some roach coach on the street."

"That's what I mean about the drama, George. And why do you think I killed Nick?"

"'Cause I figured you knew about him and Sofia. That he was screwing her."

The silence was thick and heavy on the other side of the door.

"What?" Pietro said, his voice cracking in surprise and anger.

"C'mon man, you must have known," George replied ... even though it was pretty clear to me Pietro hadn't. "He was screwing around with your little sister for months, and then he dumped her like a hot potato. I mean, I know if I found out some guy was doing my little sister and then broke her heart, I'd probably want to kill him, too!"

"I didn't kill him." Pietro's voice was lower now, more subdued. "Stop worrying about what Nick owed us. He's gone. Like I said, let it go. We got ourselves a decent side business. We don't need any trouble. Keep it on the down low, George. Down. Low."

George lowered his voice to a loud whisper, "Yeah, an illegal side business, and it scares me. I think we should get out while we can."

Oh boy. An illegal business? No wonder George sounded nervous. These two thugs were clearly up to more than making tacos and loan sharking. I wondered if their little side business could be connected to Nick's death.

Then again, it didn't matter what I believed, because suddenly, I heard someone coming up the stairs behind me. Before I had a chance to slip into the door on the right, the hostess spotted me and yelled, "Hey, this part of the restaurant is off limits! What are you doing?"

I realized I didn't have time to claim I'd lost my way to the bathroom. Time for Plan B! I bolted down the stairs as the door behind me opened. The hostess tried to block my way. Both George and Pietro yelled out. I could hear their heavy foot-steps breaking into a run. I pushed at the hostess. who fell back against the wall, and leapt down the few remaining steps, losing the black wig in the process. Lucky for me, I had been on the track team in high school and I was still pretty fast. I was out the front door in seconds, glancing behind me once to see Pietro hot on my trail. He may have recognized me, but at that point, there was nothing I could do about it. I had to get to my van. I darted into a surf shop, running straight through the racks of wet suits and boards and out a back door, nearly knocking down a very tan store employee. I was on the boardwalk, and as far as I could tell, no one had followed.

I kept up a decent pace until finally reaching the van. I threw the door open and leapt in, startling Mac and Cass. "Sorry, kids," I panted, completely out of breath. "No Mexican food today."

I fired up the VW and headed toward the freeway. I had no idea what to make of all I'd overheard, and worse yet, I kept worrying Pietro or George might come after me.

CHAPTER TWENTY-TWO

I MADE IT BACK HOME almost an hour later because I drove the long way and kept checking my rearview mirrors, hoping neither thug was after me. If either one had ID'd me, I was sure they'd be showing up at the bar for a confrontation, and I needed to figure out some kind of story.

I stopped off at In-N-Out Burger for lunch. The protein fix helped calm me, and I was almost back to normal when my cell phone rang, startling me.

"Hello?" My voice shook and I belatedly wondered if I should have let the call go straight to voice mail.

"Hey, Evie, listen." It was Simone, of course. "I changed my mind, and I'm not taking a mental health day after all. You and I are going to have a spa day instead!" She sounded thrilled at the prospect. I, on the other hand, groaned inwardly.

"Um, but it's my day off." Plus, a spa day after what I had just been through? No thanks.

"Yeah, and that's what you do on your day off. You go to the fucking spa and relax!"

"Well, I can't. I have plans."

"Really? What plans!?" Simone sounded heavily skeptical.

"I was going to watch a movie and relax, maybe hang out by the pool with Cass and Mac." Plus, I did want to do a bit more investigating and see if somehow I could figure out what George and Pietro were up to.

"Lame. Look, get your ass over here and come with me to the spa." She hung up.

I sighed, staring at the phone in my hand. Honestly, I only had myself to blame if I continued to jump every time she asked me to. But I didn't have the energy for a fight. Instead, I took Mac and Cass out of the van and into the house.

"Sorry guys. I'll be back later." I filled their water bowls and headed out the front door.

I groaned as I drove up to Simone's house. A silver Bentley limo was parked out front, and I had no doubt it was meant for the two of us. I hated going anywhere in that thing. It always felt so over the top. Frankly, the whole spa day thing felt over the top. I'd never been to a spa before. Well, I guess that isn't entirely true if you consider the "spa specials" my mom hosted on a monthly basis at her beauty salon. Something told me wherever we were going for the day would be nothing like my mother's salon.

I parked the van and went inside. As usual, Simone wasn't downstairs. She was lounging in her massive hot pink and silver bedroom suite. In the middle of the room stood a huge canopy bed with black velvet drapes held back by silver cords. The quilt was hot pink. At one end of the room stood a large fireplace (and seriously, who needs a fireplace in L.A.?!) with a retro-looking, black leather sofa situated in front of it. Big glass vases were scattered elegantly throughout the room and filled with pink roses and white calla lilies. The bedroom looked like what might happen if 1930s chic met Katy Perry (or Simone, for that matter). It always made me think of cotton candy and bubble gum. Of course, George Clooney (the cat), lounged elegantly in the middle of the bed.

Today, Simone was wearing a black kimono covered in pink flowers.

"Look what my sister sent me from Hawaii." She frowned down at the delicate robe. "Does she think I'm a fucking geisha?"

No Hello, how are you, Evie? Seriously, why did I even bother?

"She sent you one, too. It's in my bathroom. Paid for them with my fucking credit card, of course."

"But I don't need a kimono," I laughed, nervously. The last thing I wanted to wear to a spa was a fancy kimono. I am strictly a jeans and T-shirt kind of girl. It has to be a pretty special occasion to get me into anything else.

"Oh, give me a break. Just put it on. You'll hurt Brenda's feelings if you don't. And I promised her I'd send her a photo from your new iPhone."

"Excuse me?"

Simone took a brand new iPhone off her dresser and handed it to me.

"There. Now you can actually listen to music and text me and stuff. That old flip phone of yours was pitiful." I started to thank her. She held up a hand. "My accountant said I needed more write-offs. Now hurry up. Our first treatment is in forty minutes and I want to have a glass of champagne in the limo."

I looked up from the shiny new phone. "First treatment? How many treatments are there?"

She sighed heavily. "Jesus, what part of day don't you get? It's a spa day!"

"I need to be back by six though. I'm working at the bar tonight."

Hands on her hips, she shook her head and glared at me. "I don't get you and that place. Nick is dead. Why do you want keep going there?"

"To play my music." Seriously, how many times were we going to have this conversation before she stopped asking?

"Fine. I'll have you back by six before you turn into a fucking pumpkin or whatever. Now hurry up!"

I changed into the kimono. It was a pale, jade green with teal-colored leaves. Pretty, but I felt seriously underdressed. When I came out of Simone's bathroom, which was almost as big as my parents' house back in Brady, she clapped her hands like a schoolgirl and shrieked, "You look fabulous! Now let's go. We are going to have so much fun."

I wasn't holding my breath.

Twenty minutes later, we were ushered into the VIP room of the ultra-chic Moda Spa, where we had our own splash pool, Jacuzzi, sauna, and treatment room.

"This is for the special people." Simone winked at me.

I rolled my eyes. I mean, it's not like I didn't appreciate all of this. I did. But it felt so foreign and over-the-top, self-indulgent, I didn't know how I was going to relax. George and Pietro's conversation and the near run-in with them was still on my mind. God, I prayed Pietro hadn't recognized me.

I reclined in a padded lounge chair in front of the pool next to Simone who contentedly sipped the spa's signature drink. The place actually had a full bar, which seemed like an oxymoron to me considering that spas were supposed to be all about health and wellness. I mean, why bother advertising all those detoxifying treatments if you were going to encourage your clientele to get liquored up? Also, a full bar plus personal hot tubs and wading pools were a lawsuit waiting to happen. But hey, what do I know?

So here I was, me and my kimono, a captive audience for the next four hours with my on-again, off-again friend Simone. I decided now was as good a time as any to see what else I could learn about why Simone had contacted Nick. Her drink finished, I went in for the kill. "So, you and Dwight? What's the deal?"

"What do you mean, 'What's the deal?'" she asked.

"I mean with you and him? He worships you."

"Who doesn't?"

I knew better than to say, "not me." "Good point, but I think he has a thing for you."

Simone sat up and swung her legs over the side of the lounge chair. "We're screwing. That's it. He takes care of certain basic needs for me." She reached down and grabbed another fashion magazine.

Okay, I knew Simone's morals were questionable, but the casual way she said that took me by surprise. Where I come from, being sexually involved with another person wasn't treated quite as casually as, say, scratching an itch. Of course, I'm not so naïve to think everyone in my hometown only had sex with their spouses and strictly for the sake of procreating. But even the most illicit of affairs (and they most certainly happened in Brady) were built on more than base sexual need. Not for the first time, I found myself feeling sorry for Simone and her obvious lack of emotional connection with most of the people around her.

"Oh. So you don't love him?"

She laughed. "Are you kidding me? No. I don't love him. Love is for people like you."

"What do you mean?"

"Nice people. You're a nice person, the type of person all those sappy love songs I sing are written for. I'm a realist, and all I know is I have needs and love isn't one of them."

"Oh." I didn't have a clue what to say to that.

She frowned at me suddenly. "Why all the questions, Evie? About me and Dwight?"

"Just curious."

"Bullshit. What are you digging around for?"

I sighed. "Look, it's been bothering me … what you said about Nick and how you called and threatened him. And how you want me to cover up for you."

She laughed. "You think I could have killed your bartender friend?"

"No. But I think Dwight could have." There. I said it. "I mean, I think the guy would do anything for you. Don't you?"

She didn't respond right away. A handsome man popped his head into the room and said, "Miss Simone, we're ready for your massage."

She turned her hundred-watt smile on him. "So am I, Hank." She stood, letting her robe slip off into a silky puddle at her feet, revealing her naked body with a casualness I could never pull off. She turned back to me before leaving the room. "I think there are a lot of people who would kill for me, Evie. Including Dwight."

CHAPTER TWENTY-THREE

BY THE TIME WE LEFT the spa, I'd been plucked, rubbed, salted, waxed, and lymphatically drained. I had a very good idea how a car must feel going through one of those drive-thru car washes. As for Simone, by the time she'd finished with all her treatments, she was like Jell-O and could barely even say goodbye when the limo dropped us off at her house. Not that I knew what to say to her after our strange conversation in the private lounge. But truth be told, if someone murdered Nick on Simone's behalf, it was feeling less and less as if she'd actually asked them to do it. Which meant I wasn't any closer to finding out who had murdered Nick.

Back at Nick's, I played a set and then served a round of drinks. Becky was cooking in the back again. Candace's drink was the last one I poured. I slid it over to her and smiled.

"This one's on the house." I looked down, feeling uncomfortable and a little guilty. "Listen, I'm sorry about last night. I didn't mean to pry."

Candace reached over and patted my hand. "Oh honey, I'm the one who should be sorry. Thing is, I'm nothing more than a crazy drunk. You don't owe me an apology." She took a sip from her drink.

Mumbles sat two seats over, per usual, and glanced up at me. "Sorry, Evie," he mumbled.

I waved a hand at him. "Neither of you have anything to be sorry about."

"Listen, sugar, do you want to know the story?" Candace asked. "The story about me and Nick and what happened?"

I stared at her for a few seconds. This was certainly an about-face.

"Sure. Of course."

She sighed, downed her drink, and shoved the glass back towards me, a sure sign she wanted me to make her another. Truth be told, I didn't like feeding her addiction, but I also knew I couldn't stop her from chasing her demons.

"I met Nick on a set. This was back in the early eighties. He was getting ready to start shooting for a show about a group of young people attending a dance school. It was kind of a spin-off of Flashdance. Ever see it?"

I nodded. "It's one of the few I did see as a kid. My mom snuck me in." I smiled at the memory.

"Right. Anyway, I was auditioning for a part and we met. We fell madly in lust with each other." She giggled and her face took on a glow that for once wasn't fueled by alcohol. "Truth is, I loved him. It was ... immediate, like being hit by a car or something. I thought he loved me, too. I think there was a part of him that did. Anyway, I pushed him to get married. He finally proposed. But all along, I had a feeling there was someone else in his life." Tears sprung to her eyes.

I wondered if she meant Becky. Poor Candace. "I'm so sorry."

"Me, too. There was a party one night at Warren Verne's place. You've met his son, Bradley. Bradley and Nick have known each other since they were kids. Anyway, we were all at this party and Roger, who was a friend of ours, was there. The party was actually for him. He had just been chosen as the new James Bond." She took another sip of her drink. "Well, the bitch was there, too."

I lowered my voice. "Becky?"

Candace nodded. "Yes. She was supposedly Roger's date, but she was all over Nick and I became upset with him. Roger did too, because Nick seemed to be enjoying the attention."

The same Roger who had been found dead in Verne's pool.

"I went to bed drunk and stoned. We were all drunk and stoned. When I woke up, Nick was next to me, and Roger was in the pool, dead."

"But the article I read said you told police Nick had been with you all night. How do you know he was if you were passed out?"

Candace stared mournfully down at her drink, shoulders slumped forward. "I didn't know. I loved Nick, so I covered for him. But you want to know what I really think happened that night?"

I nodded in encouragement.

"I think Becky pushed Roger into that pool and the poor guy hit his head. I think Nick covered for her because she was the one Nick was screwing around with. I broke off the engagement, but I never stopped loving him."

"Is that why you come here?" And is that what I saw when I touched Nick's shoulder before he died? I could see him looking at a drowned man in a pool.

There was no Becky around, though. At least not in the brief flash I had seen. But by me simply receiving that small bit, I knew whatever had occurred that night had changed Nick forever.

"Yes. It's funny how things change. I didn't see Nick for almost twenty years, and then my life took a turn for the worse." She held up her drink. "Obviously. Four husbands. A daughter who won't speak to me. You know the story. When I came in here the first time, I really didn't know it was my Nick who owned it. Then I saw him, and strangely enough, we picked up as friends. We left the past behind, and we never talked about it since."

"Never?"

"Nope."

"Wow."

"Yep."

"So that's why you hate Becky?"

Candace regarded me wearily. "I don't hate her. I just don't like her." She shrugged. "And I don't trust her." She shook a finger at me, her eyes narrowing suspiciously.

I glanced up to see Bradley Verne walk in with his wife Raquela. I was eager to talk with him. If he had known Nick all of his life, or most of it, I was sure he might have some additional information to share. Maybe Raquela would as well. I didn't know how long they had been married, but it seemed as if it had been a while and that Raquela had also known Nick from the comments Bradley had made at Nick's wake.

They came over to the bar. Bradley looked a bit concerned. Raquela was dressed to the nines and had the most amazing diamond earrings on I had ever seen.

"Hi, how are things tonight?" Bradley asked.

"Not bad. How are you?"

"Oh, I'm okay. I had to tell my dad today about Nick. It was pretty upsetting. My father loved him like a son, you know. Every Monday, Nick would go visit him out at the home he's in."

"He did?" So that's what he did on Mondays. Interesting.

"Yes. My dad always looked forward to his visits."

"I'm sure." Poor man must have been devastated.

Raquela rubbed Bradley's back. "We will get through this. All of us." She sat down on one of the stools and ordered a glass of Cabernet. "How is business?" she asked.

I shrugged. "It's picked up some, actually. I think all of the press and such has caused people with morbid curiosities to come in. But I've also noticed an increase in the college crowd. Word has gotten out about the cheap and delicious tacos."

Bradley rubbed his face tiredly and then dropped into a seat next to Candace. "Hey, can I get a gin and tonic?"

"Sure thing." I poured Raquela's wine and made a drink for Bradley.

Becky came out of the kitchen about that time and set a plate of tacos in front of Candace and Mumbles.

"I didn't order this," Candace said, her voice surly.

"I know you didn't, but the two of you need to eat." She glanced at me, and then Bradley and Raquela. "Hello. How are you?"

He shrugged. "Told my dad today about Nick. Wasn't easy." "I suppose not," she said.

Becky was definitely not comfortable around Bradley or Raquela. Maybe it was because they seemed so far out of her league.

"I also received a call from Nick's attorney about this place," Bradley said.

"Oh?" Becky replied.

Bradley now had all of our attention.

"Yes. And there was a will. This place is designated to fall into the hands of a very specific person."

"Who?" I asked.

Everyone seemed to be listening intently.

"Nick's son."

"What?" I said. Everyone looked surprised. Everyone, that is, but Becky. "I didn't know he had a son."

"Yes. His name is Joshua. Joshua Styles." He looked at Becky.

Of course! Becky's last name was Styles.

"I guess I have a phone call to make," she said.

Raquela set her wine glass down and looked pointedly at Becky. "Yes. I suppose you do."

I reached out to touch Becky's arm and then pulled back, realizing there was no buffer between us. She was wearing short sleeves.

"Wait a minute. You and Nick?" I looked at her carefully. "You have a son together?"

"Yes, we do," she said.

CHAPTER TWENTY-FOUR

BECKY'S BOMBSHELL LEFT all of us speechless for several minutes after she headed back into the kitchen. I got pretty busy after that, pouring drinks. Bradley said he'd be back the following night to go over the specifics of Nick's will. I told him I had a few questions for him and wondered if he'd have time to meet with me privately.

"Between us, I've been delving a bit into what may have happened to Nick, or, you know, who may have killed him."

"You should be careful," Bradley said. "Nick knew some unsavory types. I wouldn't want anything to happen to you."

"Bradley is right," Raquela piped in. "I would let the police do the detecting. I am sure they will get to the bottom of it."

"Of course I can answer whatever you need, but I do think you should allow the police to deal with this," Bradley said, agreeing with his wife. "I can come over a little earlier if you'd like. Before it gets too busy. Raquela will be out of town so I have some free time." He frowned.

She smiled at him fondly. "Oh come on, darling, you know you love your free time. It's only one night."

"Where are you going?" I asked.

Raquela waved a hand at me. "Oh you know, a little spa getaway. Some of my gal pals and I do a day or two either in Santa Barbara or Napa. Tomorrow we're taking a jaunt down to Laguna Niguel and staying at The Ritz."

"Sounds nice," I said.

"It is lovely," she replied. "I'll be back in a few days with Bradley and see how everything is going."

"Have fun," I said. You know in spite of all her plastic surgery, big jewelry, and flashy clothes, Raquela seemed pretty decent.

"Sounds good. Thanks."

After they left, I didn't see much of Becky. She buzzed around taking food orders, prepping in the kitchen, and serving patrons. I took care of the drinks. I still had questions for her ... more than ever now. Thinking about Pietro made me anxious. I had not forgotten the possibility that he had recognized me and could show up any time. I had no clue what he and George were capable of, and I certainly hadn't ruled out murder.

The college crowd eventually showed up again and the place got packed. I only had time to play two sets. Candace and Mumbles drank themselves silly and didn't even say goodbye when they staggered out into the night.

I was busy clearing the last rounds when Becky walked through the kitchen door and waved. "I need to go home. I'm beat, and tonight was more than I bargained for. Do you mind locking up?"

"Sure, no problem ... hey, um, I was pretty surprised to find out you had a son with Nick."

She smiled. "Yes. So was Nick when I told him. He didn't know either until a year ago."

"Really?" Wow.

She nodded. "The thing is, I wasn't in Nick's life for many years, and a lot happened to us both back in the day. I knew Nick was pretty mixed up for a while there, and he once told me being a parent was not for him. So, I decided not to tell him when I found out I was pregnant. But there was no question about me keeping the baby." She smiled fondly, clearly recalling her son. "When I told Nick, he was pretty upset with me, but he understood why I'd done it. Truthfully, I had no idea he would give this place to Joshua."

I recalled Jackson mentioning how many stories were buried in this place. Boy, he hadn't been kidding. I wondered if he knew about Nick's son.

"Can I ask where he is? Joshua?"

A proud look came over her face. "He's in Africa. He works for the Red Cross."

"Did Nick ever meet him?"

"No." She glanced down at her hands, an uncomfortable look spreading across her face.

I was starting to feel like I might be prying but I couldn't stop myself.

"Um, does he even know about Nick? I mean, as a dad?"

"No!" she snapped, glaring at me. I took a step back and her expression instantly shifted to contrition. "Look, I'm sorry. I am not sure how I am going to handle all of this with my son. It really was unexpected."

"How do you think he'll take the news?"

"I don't know. How would you respond? I am sure it won't be an easy conversation." Her shoulders suddenly sagged, and she looked incredibly tired. "I have to go lie down and think things through. It's late. I'm sorry to leave you like this. You'll be okay, right?"

"I'll be fine, Becky. Don't worry about me. But I was also wondering real quick about something."

"Yes?"

I could tell she was becoming aggravated with me, but I figured I had her as a captive audience for the moment.

"When Pietro came here to see Nick and you went back into the kitchen with them, what happened?"

Her eyes narrowed like those of a bird of prey ready to dive in for the animal it's about to eat. "Why the inquisition?"

I shrugged. "I'm curious and concerned. The police don't exactly seem to be doing much investigating around who murdered our friend, and that Pietro character is a slimeball. I thought maybe he said or did something that night that could implicate him."

She shook her head. "I do care about who killed Nick, but you know what ... I am a bit uncomfortable putting my nose into business it doesn't belong in. The police have this handled. I think you should let them do their job and keep your questions to yourself." She stopped for a moment, rubbing her arms absentmindedly. "Jerks like Pietro SanGiacomo are not the kind of people you want to question. Do I think he could have murdered Nick? Yes. I think he's capable of doing something like that. But I'm no detective and neither are you. As for that night in the kitchen, Nick owed Pietro some money. It wasn't a ton. I had the money. I paid the debt. End of story. I have to go home now."

Becky left in a huff, and I was alone in the bar. I think I believed her story, but her hostility seemed surprising.

I had everything cleaned up and was ready to go ten minutes later. But my brain was buzzing like I'd drank two espressos, and I knew I wouldn't get any peace that night until I wrote everything down to see if I could answer a few of my own questions about Nick's murder.

I turned up all the lights and made myself a Shirley Temple. I even added a cherry. When my dad was in a good mood, he'd take us to Benny's, which was the best restaurant in Brady (and a Denny's knock-off). At Benny's, we could order anything we wanted. Hannah and I always got the same thing: Shirley Temples and cheesy grits with shrimp. After Hannah disappeared, we never went to Benny's again. But I always ordered Shirley Temples whenever I could.

I didn't have a notebook or any lined paper, so I tore a paper towel off of the towel dispenser in the ladies restroom. I sat down in Mumbles's seat. Of all the regulars at Nick's, he was the one who I felt most comfortable around. I figured maybe sitting in his chair would help me focus. I took out a pen and wrote down the reasons why people kill:

Revenge

Lust

Love (see lust above)

Greed

Money

Power

Sex (see lust above)

Then I thought about the various cast of characters

Candace

Becky

Jackson

Pietro

George

Mumbles (doubtful)

Bradley (?)

Simone (ugh, hated to think that)

Dwight via Simone

Why would Candace want to see Nick dead? Well, let's see ... he was the guy she was madly in love with almost thirty years ago. He cheated on her and she became an alcoholic. Revenge anyone?

Becky. She'd obviously loved Nick or thought she had. She'd been his lover when he was engaged to another woman. She had possibly been involved in covering up Roger's death. Becky had a son with Nick that she failed to tell him about for twenty-eight years. And now, here she was in the bar, serving patrons and acting like the grieving widow. What if Becky and her son had planned it? Came back into Nick's life, told him about his long lost son—off saving lives in Africa, how could he not leave that kid everything he owned—and rekindled the romance between them. And what if mom pulled the trigger out of ... yes ... revenge, rage, love, jealousy ... there were a plethora of reasons for Becky to want Nick six feet under. Not least of which was the opportunity to further provide for her only child, who may or may not actually be gallivanting around Africa giving vaccinations to children and teaching about safe sex.

Long sip from the Shirley Temple.

Sigh.

I needed some music to think by. I took out my new phone. Okay, I do have to give props to Simone for the gift. Pretty cool. I logged onto Pandora, and typed in "Ellie Goulding." "Lights" came on. Much better.

So, on to the next person on the list.

Jackson.

Now Jackson was just plain strange. He was a sexy, brooding weirdo who was totally obsessed with Nick. He wanted to script Nick's story and was pissed off Nick refused to provide him any personal information. He seemed to have a chip on his shoulder, and I frequently felt uncomfortable around him. Also, Mumbles didn't care for him much ... and Mumbles rarely took a dislike to anyone. And then there was that night when he rescued me from George Hernandez. Yeah, I was grateful to Jackson for stepping in when he did. But knowing he was some kind of black-belt Ninja definitely made me wonder about him. Could he be a charming psycho ... like Ted Bundy? It didn't take much to attract the attention of a sociopath. I mean, I now watched Dexter, and it seems to me those folks kill others mostly because they can.

I tapped the pen against my mouth, staring down at the next name on the list. Pietro SanGiacomo. Well that was pretty simple: money and anger. Nick owed him money. I wasn't sure how much, but I assumed it was substantial, although Becky claimed she paid him off. She did sound rather convincing, and the conversation I overheard between Pietro and George had shown Pietro wanted George to let it all go now that Nick was gone. Granted, he sounded pretty upset when George told him about his sister. So maybe Pietro had more motive than I thought. But he had sounded truly shocked when George made the big reveal to him. I wondered, did Becky know about Nick and his bed buddy? Was Becky's return the reason Nick had broken off whatever was going on between him and Sofia? Could Sofia, the mystery woman, have murdered Nick? I wouldn't even know how to track her down. It wasn't like I could ask Pietro for his sister's phone number.

As for George Hernandez—he of the bad temper—Nick supposedly stole his fish taco recipe and owed George money. And then George and Pietro had some illegal side gig going on. Could Nick have found out about that and threatened to call the cops if George didn't back off? Maybe George got tired of waiting for Nick to cough up his fair share of the earnings from their fizzled out partnership. In any case, he also seemed like a good candidate.

Then there was Bradley Verne. He'd known Nick since they were kids. Who knows what might have gone down back in the day? But I still felt he was my weakest suspect. Weak or not, he was definitely worth looking at. I had read enough books to know the least likely suspect often turns out to be the one who did it.

I sucked down the rest of my Shirley Temple and used the straw to fish out the cherry. "Fade Into You" by Mazzy Star came on. God, I love that song.

I thought suddenly of Lucas. Time to go home.

I walked around to the bar sink and dumped out the ice from my glass. "I wish I knew what happened here. I wish I knew what happened to you, Nick."

I rinsed out the glass and set it on the counter, walking back around to the stool to grab my sweater and sling my purse over my shoulder.

I moved towards the door. Suddenly, I felt an icy cold sensation pull at the back of my neck and yank on my long hair so forcefully, I thought it was being ripped out. I was momentarily paralyzed.

Now, you know me ... I am not one to swear. But every now and then, there is a time and a place for cussing. This was one of those times.

"Oh, shit! What the hell?!"

I forced my legs to move forward as the mysterious entity kept tugging on me from behind. I reached the door and quickly threw it open without bothering to shut off the lights. I locked the bar up from the outside and sprinted for my van parked across the street. Once inside, I started up the engine and peeled out of the lot.

Driving up La Cienega towards Sunset, all I could think was my father had been right in his assessment about this city. Maybe it was not a city of angels after all. Maybe, it was demon- filled and, like Lucas had warned the other night,

the dark side was out to get me.

CHAPTER TWENTY-FIVE

"TELL ME MORE about the portals and the tiers. How it all works." Lucas and I were in my bed—no, not like that. But I can dream, can't I? I was so happy when I came through the door and found him in my bedroom, especially considering what happened right before I left Nick's. It was scary enough when someone followed me home, but at least it had been a human. Whatever was in the bar with me this evening was most definitely not. Actually, when I think about it, I am not sure which is worse.

Anyway, Lucas was on my bed scratching Cass behind her ears. Mac was lying next to him. You know how in movies and books, animals are usually freaked out by the dead? Yeah, well, my two pets were definitely breaking the stereotype.

"But first I have to tell you, I found out something about the eagle feathers."

"You did? How?"

"It took some work, but I searched out a Native American spirit. Evie, I would like you to meet Hototo. It means 'he who whistles.' Hototo?" Lucas called out.

A Native American man of about twenty-five or so slowly came into sight in front of me at the foot of my bed. At first I didn't know what to say.

"Evie? Are you okay?" Lucas asked.

Oh sure. "Uh, yes." I smiled and nodded, sitting up and smoothing my shirt.

Hototo wore a pair of Levis and a light grey t-shirt. His hair was slicked back into a ponytail. He had the same purplish eyes as Lucas, only with a bit more gold flecks.

"Hello," Hototo said. "Lucas asked me to come and see if I could give you answers."

"Uh-huh." Smooth, Evie. Real smooth.

"He's told me about your gift and how you found the eagle feathers as a child."

"Okay." I couldn't help wonder what the guy must be thinking seeing Lucas and I lounging around on my bed. Awkward. Focus, Evie!

"Here is what I can tell you about the eagle feathers. They are sacred to most Native American tribes. No one is allowed to possess an eagle, alive or dead, or the feather from an eagle, unless they are of Native American blood."

"Oh! Well, as it turns out, I do have Native American blood in me. Cherokee." I found my voice. "On my mother's side."

"I know. You would not have received these if that wasn't true."

"Right."

"The feathers are used in powerful healing ceremonies," he added. "And even for shapeshifting."

"Whoa. Wait a minute. Shapeshifting?" Hototo laughed and looked at Lucas. "She's cute."

"Hey!" I said. He winked at me. "I will try to explain shapeshifting. It may help in the future with the eagle feathers."

Hototo sat down in my desk chair and wheeled it closer to the bed. "You see, shapeshifting is the transformation, mentally or physically, of one's self into an animal. Shapeshifters can regularly assume an animal or human form."

"Wait ... you mean, like werewolves?" Both of them looked at me in surprise. "Should I even bother asking if vampires exist?" I let out a nervous laugh.

"Yes, like werewolves, and no, vampires aren't real." Phew!

Hototo glanced over at Lucas before continuing. "There are two types of shapeshifting: changing your light body in the astral plane to a power animal, and changing your physical form on the Earth plane into a physical animal. My guess is your power animal is the eagle."

"Wait, you mean I can shapeshift?"

Hototo shrugged his shoulders casually. "Possibly."

This was only a tad overwhelming.

"Let me get back to the eagle for a moment. The white and black tipped feathers from the eagle," he continued, "were often used on the masks of the Pueblo Indians to give the appearance of white and black clouds. The bald and the golden eagle symbolize heroic nobility and divine spirit. The eagle is the messenger from heaven and the embodiment of the sun spirit. I think you are a messenger of healing. Your sister's disappearance was no coincidence, and you receiving the feathers wasn't one either. The feathers are helping protect you, and they may also help you find your sister Hannah."

Now I was really interested. "But how?"

"The feathers may carry memory in them for you to discover. They may guide you into seeing what happened to Hannah that night. I will try to track some of my ancestors and see if there is a way to access the memory. Or, if you learn to shift into your power animal at any time, then you may also find your answers."

"Okay then," I said, trying hard to swallow what Hototo had told me. I looked back at Lucas, who smiled and shrugged. Me turn into an eagle? Feathers with memories? And I thought Bob and Janis getting high in my family room was bizarre!

Hototo stood solemnly. "I must be going. I hope I helped," he said.

"Thank you." I think.

Lucas also thanked him, Hototo left, fading away until he'd disappeared entirely.

The first thing that came out of my mouth as I buried my head in my palms was, "Spirits and power animals, eagle feathers, shapeshifting? I mean, I've had my so-called gift now for sixteen years and still haven't gotten used to it. Now all of this. I can't wrap my brain around it. I thought he was supposed to help." I looked over at Lucas. "What happened to him anyway? How did he die?"

"Hunting accident. Shot by his brother."

"Oh." I didn't know what else to say. "That's awful."

Lucas nodded. "I know this is a lot to process, but I am here to help you. We can provide you with information, but we can't always give you answers. Those will often have to come from within you."

I glanced sideways at him. "I know, but to be honest, I don't know if I want your help even then. I mean, if you can't give me the answers, and I have to go on some scavenger-type hunt to get them, what's the use? It could take my entire life, and even then I might not find the answers. I think I was doing fine before all of ... all of this."

He sunk back onto a pillow and frowned.

"I'm sorry. It's just a lot."

"It is, but Evie, I've told you, you are a wanted woman, and I am here to ensure you can continue helping others using your gifts. The safer I keep you, the closer I get to leading a lighter, more peaceful existence myself. Will you work with me? Will you help find the answers?"

I sighed and then looked into those amazing eyes of his and uttered, "Yes. I don't think I have much of a choice."

"Okay. Let's start from the top. What more do you want to know? What will help you process all of this?" he asked.

I closed my eyes, and his fingers took hold of my hair as he twisted slowly, gently through it. Every part of my body, from my eyebrows to my toes, felt alive and zinging with energy. But I also felt drunk and lethargic, like I could drop into a deep sleep at any moment. "I want to know everything about your world."

I could feel him shift his position next to me. "My world is your world," he said, his deep voice doing funny things to my insides. How was it that in this short period of time I had real feelings for someone/something who wasn't exactly real? And, I sensed Lucas was feeling it too.

"What do you mean by that? You've said it before, but I don't understand."

"Okay, so the tiers, right?" He said, beginning to slowly massage my scalp.

"Uh-huh." Oh my. Earth to Evie's brain, come in brain ...

"I told you we live in various shades of grey, which range all the way from the black to the white. You know how color spectrums work?"

"Sure."

"The variations between colors are slight."

"How many tiers are there, then? And what makes one different from the next?"

"There are hundreds, with each variation being minutely closer to the white or closer to the black. It's all based on vibrations—the ones humans and spirits give off. But, there are truly only three vibrations that are extra strong. The white, the black, and the grey."

I laughed softly, "I guess all those old Westerns were right then." He looked down at me, questioning. "You know, the bad guy always wears the black hat, the good guy wears the white..."

He nodded earnestly, "Exactly! The white is all about the good things—love, joy, happiness. The black, well that's obvious. The grey represents choice and balance. Each of us in the Grey Tier has free will, but most other tiers do not. The grey is the equalizer."

"The Black Tier is obviously home to bad spirits." I said as a slight shiver hit me.

"Yes. Asuras who are governed by the Asat Order."

I wasn't sure I wanted to find out more, especially not after my experience tonight, but I needed to know. "Tell me, what does it mean that I am your project?"

He laid his head back on the pillow and let out a sigh, his breath (it's the only thing I can think to call it, even though I know he wasn't exactly breathing) swirling out of him in an indigo haze. He looked at me with those stormy eyes. His fingers reached out and grazed my forehead, my cheeks, and finally, my lips. I could feel myself melting into a puddle of molten Evie. "Let's not worry about it right now."

"But you said you would teach me. Tell me stuff."

"For now, I can only tell you what you need to know."

I sighed. "Okay. Can you tell me if there could be a portal at Nick's?"

"The bar?"

"Yes. You said portals are created when someone dies in violent ways or isn't ready to go."

"I did."

"I think maybe Nick left a portal, or one was created at the bar when he died."

"It's possible. But why do you think so?"

"I felt a presence there tonight when I closed up."

"A presence?" The aura, around him darkened suddenly and he frowned.

"Yes. Like I know when you're here, even before I see you. This was different though. I didn't feel warm and comforted. I felt cold and afraid and I wanted to get

out of there as quickly as possible. It also felt like something was pulling on me—
something strong."

Lucas didn't say anything for a moment or two, and I shifted uneasily on top
of the covers.

"What are you thinking?" I asked.

"I think I need to check it out. It could be a couple of things. It could be an
Asura from the Black Tier ... or, it could be Nick." A flare of hope lit in me. Would I
see Nick's spirit? But then I recalled how uncomfortable and frightened I'd felt.
How could it possibly be Nick? He'd never intentionally try to scare me. Lucas
nodded slowly as if sensing the direction of my thoughts. "He could be stuck
there, and you sensed what he felt prior to his death. His spirit, if it is him, is likely still in a state of simple energy, and he could be trying to warn you."

"A warning?" That was a lot better than the "being attacked by evil spirits"
scenario.

"And wait ... you could go there? To Nick's Place? But I thought you couldn't
go through portals built by spirits who contain a different vibration or exist on a
different tier."

"It isn't impossible, it's just ... complicated." He stood abruptly and began pacing around the room. If he'd been alive, I'd have said he seemed agitated. Clearly
the idea of something going down at Nick's was troubling him. "It depends where
I need to go. If I only have to travel a couple of tiers up or down to gather information, it's kind of like you traveling to another country. I have to obtain permission..."

"From the Bodha?"

He stopped pacing and dropped back down onto the bed. "Yes, and also from certain spirits within the tier I am going to. Each tier has its own hierarchy. And then, when I am in the other tiers, or going through portals I haven't been invited to come through, I have to follow specific rules that vary from tier to tier. If I don't abide by those rules, I am sent back out and forbidden to reenter." He reached out and grabbed my hand, as if it were the most natural and common thing for him to do. I tried to pretend it was no big deal for me either, but I was doing a massive happy dance on the inside. The best part was that every time he touched me, it felt good and there were no horrific visions.

"In any case," he continued, "I can't move too far away from this tier. If I need to move into a tier too many levels from this one, I take certain risks. I could be detained, like what might happen if you went to another country without a passport. But being detained in, say, the Black would be a whole lot worse than being detained in any country in your world."

"Worse how?" Focus on what he's saying, Evie. Must stop thinking about his hand.

"Worse in that 99.9% of the time a spirit is 'detained' in the Black, they never leave."

That caught my attention in a big way. "Hold on. So you don't even get a trial or hearing or a get out of jail free card? You're just trapped there? Forever?"

His fingers were gently making circles on the palm of my hand but he seemed worlds away. "Oh, there's always the obligatory trial. For example, when we pass from human form, we go through a sort of life review—it's like watching a short movie of your life, highlights and lowlights included—and finally there's a judgment. The White and the Black take into consideration who someone was, what they were like, how they treated others, how they treated themselves, and so on. Then the two sides convene and vote, and that determines where the spirit should fall within the tiers." He shrugged. "It's all very democratic."

"So what about you? How did you end up in the Grey Tier?"

"Me? Some spirits in the White found me worthy of a higher vibrational existence, and some in the Black disagreed. It was a tie, so to speak." He glanced down at his hand holding mine, a small smile on his face. "But I find I like it here in the Grey, especially lately." He shot a teasing glance in my direction. "And of course, I have a mission now."

"Me?"

"Kind of." He nodded. "By protecting you, I'm ensuring I don't end up in the Black."

This conversation was beginning to make me uncomfortable. I was bothered that Lucas's fate was, to some degree, in my hands. I also wondered how much his visits with me were motivated by what he needed to do to "earn his stripes." I mean, clearly he enjoyed my company, but I recalled how much of a player he'd been in life. It made me wonder, again, just how much someone's personality remained after death. I sighed and decided it was time to steer things back to the topic of Nick and the bar.

"What can you do to help me find out what happened to Nick? And I need to know what visited me tonight. I'd hate for that ... thing to try and harm someone else."

Lucas nodded and patted my hand. "Don't worry. I will do what I can to get more information."

"How?"

He waggled his eyebrows at me. "We have our ways." Then he snapped his fingers and a rose appeared. He handed it to me with a flourish. I wondered if he was going to start pulling coins out of my ears.

"What was that for?"

"Because I wanted you to have something beautiful. And I wanted to talk about something other than the tiers."

The butterflies in my stomach started line dancing. I tilted the rose towards my face, inhaling its sweet, intoxicating fragrance. The color was not like any I'd ever seen before ... red, pink, and purple striations with a shell-pink rim. And it glowed softly with the fragile warmth of a lit candle, just as he did.

"I need to go." He suddenly seemed uneasy.

"Why? Shouldn't you be here to protect me?" Okay, yes, I know that sounded very "damsel in distress," but I didn't want him to leave.

"You're okay for now. I've put a sort of barrier around you and the house that will last at least through the night."

"A barrier?"

"From anyone or anything seeking to cause you harm."

"How?"

He smiled. "You will learn about it in time. But I need to go now. I'll return. Promise."

And with those words Lucas, like Hototo, slid through an invisible door and quickly faded away.

CHAPTER TWENTY-SIX

AS A RESULT OF my wacky night, I woke up tired and wishing I had someone to talk to. I even picked up the phone twice to call my mother but kept changing my mind. Thing is, I was sure she'd hear something off in my voice and insist I come home. And what exactly did I plan to tell her anyway? "Hi, Mama. Yes, I'm fine. Oh, I've even met someone! You'd love him ... if only he weren't dead and haunting my house." In the end, I called Betty LaRue, who seemed happy to talk to me. But she couldn't really hear that well, which meant most of our conversation involved a lot of shouting and repetition. Finally I yelled that I'd write soon and hung up.

Tired or not, I had to get my butt in gear because Simone was going to be filming a new video and she had three "face" changes needed. I'd done a few sketches to outline her various looks, and I knew it was going to be a long day, especially since I planned to go to the bar again in the evening (but tonight I was leaving early ... no way was I going to be the last person out the door after what happened last night).

Simone's video was being filmed at a back lot in Studio City. I drove over bright and early, bringing the obligatory caffeinated beverages. She was in her trailer, waiting for the crew to set up. As I walked over to her trailer door, I spotted what appeared to be a large, glass box dotted with small holes and filled with butterflies. Next to that, a caged jaguar. The big cat stared at me as I opened the door. I'm a big animal lover, but there was something unnerving about its stare. Suddenly, I had a pretty good idea how it felt to be a gazelle in one of those nature programs.

I stepped into the trailer as quickly as I could, almost slamming the door behind me. "Hey," I said, sounding out of breath.

"Holy shit, Evie. Did you see that fucking tiger out there?"

"It's a jaguar." I placed her latte down on the table.

"Whatever." She opened up a prescription bottle and dropped a pill into her hand. "I need a Xanax. The director tells me the cat and I are going to be walking together through a field of fucking butterflies."

"Where's the field?" I asked. "It's all computer generated. I'll be using a green screen." She jerked her head back and swallowed the pill, and then stared at me. Her eyes slowly narrowed into slits. "There is something different about you. You're all, like, glowy and, I don't know ... you look happy." She sucked in some air, her eyes widening. "You got laid, didn't you!"

"No, Simone, I did not." Why did she always assume happy -looking people must be having sex?

She rubbed her chin thoughtfully, "Well, whatever it is, you definitely seem different. If I had to guess, I'd say it had to do with a man." She paused to gauge my reaction and then a sly smile spread across her face. "You like somebody, don't you? Who is he?! Please tell me he's not some loser from the bar."

Since when did self-absorbed Simone become so intuitive?

"There's nobody, Simone. I swear. I would tell you." I wasn't completely lying to her, right? It's not like Lucas was human or anything.

"You would tell me? You promise?"

"Yes," I lied.

"Really?"

"Yes. Now can we talk about something else?" Because this lying business was really making me uncomfortable.

She stood up from her chair and wrapped her arms around me.

"I'm so excited to finally have a real friend ... someone who would share secrets with me. Let's go to Denny's tonight! We can go have some of that fried steak shit. God, that stuff is good."

It was bad enough I was lying to her but now I had to turn her down too. Definitely not one of my more stellar days.

"Um, I can't. I have my other job."

She pulled away from me and frowned. "Oh yeah." And then a big smile broke across her face. "You know what I am going to do tonight?"

"No?"

"I am going to come to hear you sing."

"Really?" My stomach lurched. I wasn't sure how I felt about this.

"Really! I'll be in disguise, of course. Just remember to call me Stacy, okay?" She winked at me.

"Okay."

"Great! It's a date then." She rubbed her hands together excitedly. Honestly, you'd have thought we were heading off to an Oscar after-party. I worried how she might behave at the bar … clearly it was far beneath her standards. Simone tapped me on the shoulder, "Earth to Evie. Time for my butterfly face. My outfit is over there." She pointed to a few strips of turquoise- colored chiffon hanging on a closet door.

I walked over, brushing my fingers across the delicate bits of fabric. I turned back to her, lifting an eyebrow in disbelief. "This is what you're wearing? But there's nothing there!"

She shrugged. "I guess they'll put that sticky tape shit across my boobs." She sat herself down in a salon-style chair and gestured to the silver box that held all my makeup products. "Let's get started."

A couple of hours later, Simone looked like an extra from Avatar. Her face and body were covered in silver, turquoise, and purple, and her skin shimmered with a fine mist of metallic body glitter. The strips of turquoise chiffon were glued across her breasts and her privates, leaving the rest of her body exposed. While the costume guy was carefully applying her outfit, she leaned over to me and whispered, "I am so fucking glad I got a Brazilian at the spa the other day. Otherwise, can you imagine how awful it would be ungluing this shit from my crotch?"

Three hours later, Simone had the jaguar on a leash. They were walking across the set, a large green screen towering behind them while swarms of butterflies fluttered around the room. The jaguar's trainer was a French guy named Pierre (I know, right? Cliché-o-rama). He was rail thin with a scraggly mustache, a black turtle-neck, and black pants. At one point, he sidled up next to me and winked.

"Bonjour, ma petite. Isn't my Anastasia gorgeous?" I followed his eyes to the sleek bundle of muscles next to Simone. He kissed his fingers. "She is almost as beautiful as Simone and you."

I thought I might barf. Was this guy for real? "The cat is very beautiful," I said, trying to sound appreciative.

"Cat?!" He spat and moved away, glaring at me contemptuously. "She is more than just a cat, idiot!" Pierre turned on his heel and marched to the other side of the set, muttering to himself.

Honestly, the sooner I was done with today's job, the better. I leaned back against the wall, watching Simone stroll back and forth with Anastasia. She gazed around her, wide-eyed as if she was in awe of her surroundings. I was looking forward to seeing the final video once the CGI stuff was in place.

At one point, I made the mistake of glancing back over at Pierre. He stood sulking in a corner, giving me the evil eye. Seriously, some people were just creepy. I looked away, back towards Simone and the jaguar. And that's likely what saved my life. Because had I still been staring at Monsieur Freak, I most definitely wouldn't have seen Anastasia pull sharply away from Simone and begin running straight at me.

Simone screamed, and my life flashed before my eyes as death sprinted towards me in a lithe blur of yellow, brown, and black. My blood roared in my ears deafeningly.

From a distance I heard Pierre command, "Anastasia!" followed by a loud whistle. And just like that, the jaguar stopped in her tracks. Pierre walked quickly to her and led her back to her cage. He promptly returned, out of breath and with a contrite expression on his face.

"I am so sorry, Mademoiselle. I don't know what got into her. She must be tired. Please accept my apologies."

I couldn't speak. My hands were up around my neck, shaking. Simone was, if possible, more upset than me. She moved like a snake, fast and dangerous, and got right into Pierre's face.

"What the fuck was that?!" she screamed shrilly. "That—that fucking thing almost killed my friend!"

The animal trainer looked shocked ... either at Simone's accusation, or that she'd changed from a demure, ethereal beauty to screaming Amazon in seconds flat.

"But no!" he replied, his voice shaky. "Anastasia would not have killed her. She has no claws!"

"She has fucking teeth, you dumbass. I want you and your cat out of here!" Simone was still yelling loudly at the top of her lungs. Beyond her, I could see Anastasia in her cage, pacing in agitation, her eyes trained on me.

Dwight quickly appeared on the set. Where he had come from, I had no idea. I hadn't seen him the entire time we'd been there. He looked at me and quietly asked, "Are you okay, Evie?"

I nodded, finally finding my voice.

"Yes, I'm fine." I laid a hand on Simone's arm. "It was an accident, Simone. There's always a risk when working with wild animals, trained or otherwise."

Pierre darted a look at me and nodded. "Yes, yes. This is true. It's in the contract, clause eight."

Simone was still trying hard to relax. She shot Pierre a hostile glare, "You'd better shut it, buddy. If it were up to me, I'd have that animal euthanized." The trainer paled, his eyes darting nervously to Anastasia in her cage.

"It's okay, Simone. Really. But if you don't mind, can I go home?" My voice shook, sounding awkward. I took a deep breath and tried to focus. The perspiration beaded my forehead and ran a slick trail down my back. I felt off, and I needed to get out of there.

Simone put her arm around me. "Of course you can. You still going to the bar tonight?"

"Yes. I think so." She hugged me.

"I'll be there." She turned to the gathering crowd. "Let's pack this shit up!" she called out. "We'll be back tomorrow." She looked at Dwight. "And no more big cats! Got it?"

He nodded nervously.

"Fuck up like that again, and I'll fire you! Stupid idea, Dwight."

Simone turned on her heels, golden hair whipping around, and shook her finger at the director who was white as a sheet.

"Get me some hot chicks who can dance, a shitload of Cristal, a bunch of gold crap, and bring the fucking butterflies back, but not that cat." She pointed at

Anastasia, and even though the animal had lunged at me, I felt sorry for her. I was never entirely comfortable with wild animals being used like trained monkeys.

I started back towards the trailer to get my things when Pierre jogged up to me. "I am so sorry, Mademoiselle. Anastasia is a good girl, but sometimes ... well, she has a sense."

"A sense? She wanted to kill me!"

He smiled at me then, and in spite of all his apologies, goose bumps spread across my arms. He raised his eyebrows and lowered his voice to a bare whisper.

"Maybe you should be careful. My sweet kitty may not be the only one want who wants you dead."

CHAPTER TWENTY-SEVEN

THE SHAKING IN MY HANDS didn't stop until I got behind the bar at Nick's and mixed myself a Jack and Coke. I'm not a big drinker. But sometimes, well ... a Jack and Coke is exactly what the doctor ordered. It was the one drink I saw my mother make Daddy three days after the police showed up at the door, speaking in hushed tones. That was when I knew Hannah wasn't coming home. I can always tell when my dad misses my sister because he'll ask mom to make him the same drink—just one. I wondered if my father missed me, now, too. Honestly, I really hoped he wasn't completely disappointed in the choices I'd made so far.

Before heading to the bar, I'd gone home, feeling hopeful Lucas might be there. Or even Bob or Janis, but I was especially hoping for Lucas. But aside from the animals, the house was empty. Cass and Mac did what they could to comfort me.

Cass licked my hand while I sat on the sofa, a cup of hot tea cooling on the coffee table. I wondered what deep spiritual quote she might be sending my way. I had taken up looking up Buddhist quotes on the internet when time permitted. There were some good ones out there. I had even been able to memorize a few.

Perhaps Cass was thinking something like, "Even death is not to be feared by one who has lived wisely." Honestly though, I wasn't in the mood for quotes. Especially not from my dog. I rolled my eyes at her, grabbed my tea, and headed out to the patio.

She did not follow.

Mac did, though. He climbed into my lap on the lounge chair and made himself at home. Being a pretty straightforward cat, I'm pretty sure any quotes rolling around in his head were of the, "Give me some damn food," and "Your lap is comfy" variety. That worked for me.

I sat drinking my lukewarm tea, fat cat in my lap, as dusk set in. No Lucas. No Bob. No Janis. No Hototo, who I would have gladly accepted at this point. I thought more information about power animals and such could prove very interesting. But alas, no insight.

Eventually, when it got too dark to see clearly and those little, nasty black gnats that only come out at night appeared, I shifted Mac off of my lap and went inside. I gave my face a quick wash, threw on a blouse, and sat down at the vanity in the bedroom to dab a little makeup on. I kept the desk neat, with the bare essentials in cosmetics and the handful of eagle feathers, along with a small, semi-shrine for my sister.

I picked up one of the feathers and brushed it across my face, then set it down. Were the feathers the key to my abilities? Did they contain the memory of what happened to Hannah? Were they also the key to keeping me safe? I didn't know, but I figured they were at the very least a part of the solution. Would I ever find all of the answers? Probably not. But I'd take whatever I could get. I hoped Lucas could help me as he insisted he could. I hoped we would find out who murdered Nick and why, and I also hoped I would find answers surrounding Hannah's disappearance. I had no more time to ponder or be melancholy, so I finished my hair and makeup, fed my creatures, and headed out the door.

The bar felt a bit different than usual. For one thing, Gwen Stefani's voice was singing "I'm Just A Girl" through the speakers. It was loud, fierce, and beautiful, like Gwen herself (yes, I am a huge Gwen Stefani fan). For another, the lighting was different inside. The bulbs behind the bar had been switched over to green, and the bulbs on the customer side were light purple. Had I stumbled into some sort of eighties theme night?

That was about the time I fixed myself the Jack and Coke. Mumbles picked his head up from his Southern Comfort and 7-Up and gave me a knowing look. His unpatched green eye gleamed brightly.

"Things change, Evie," he mumbled. "Not always good. Lights kinda weird."

I had a dishtowel in my free hand and used it as a buffer between us while I reached my hand out and touched his aging hand through the towel. He didn't seem to mind. For some reason, I had been very cautious, even more so than with others, at touching either Candace or Mumbles. I really felt both of them had something deep and tragic inside of them that, for the time being, I was not pre-pared to see. And I'd become even more cautious after I had heard Mumbles's suf-ferings. Eventually, I would have to go there. But for now, I kept the buffers be-tween us. I noticed liver spots sprinkled amongst the wrinkles on Mumble's hand.

"True, Mumbles, it isn't always good. But you never know, sometimes it's for the best."

"I like your music. Better."

"Really? You like my music?"

He smiled and nodded. I leaned across the bar and lowered my voice. "Can I ask you something?"

He nodded again.

"Why are you here? You seem like a good person. How did you get to the point where you spend almost every night in a bar?"

One seat down, Candace cleared her throat loudly. "Oh, sweet pea, his story is boring. I doubt he wants to talk about it," she slurred.

"Let's give him a chance, okay, Candace?" I snapped, feeling frustrated and not a little protective of poor Mumbles. Candace was so controlling of him. I didn't quite understand their relationship.

Mumbles looked over at Candace and then back at me. "Lost my eye, Evie."

"I know. How?" I was starting to think I would find the answers to his personal tragedy without a physical touch.

Candace sighed, stirring her drink. "He was a stunt guy back in the day, and he lost it on the set." She leaned back in the bar stool and crossed her arms.

Mumbles nodded. "On a movie set."

"Really?" I was going to go out on a limb here, but didn't feel I had much to lose with my next question. "Were you on a movie set with Nick? Was it a movie he was making?" Neither said anything.

"What? Why so secretive?"

I felt an arm slide around my waist. I hadn't seen Jackson step behind the bar and sidle up to me. I'd been too intent on questioning Mumbles and Candace. He leaned down towards my ear, his nearness stirring up a confusing mixture of emotions.

"What they aren't telling you, Evie, is Mumbles here introduced Roger and Nick. Remember Roger? Some say Roger and Nick were the reason Mumbles lost his eye. He was Roger's stunt double. Back in the day, Mumbles was a pretty good looking guy, a real lady killer. I don't know the details, but rumor has it Nick and Roger coerced Mumbles, whose real name is Dale Sharp, by the way, into doing a stunt he wasn't prepared or conditioned for."

"That's a crock of shit!" Candace chimed in, clearly angry.

Mumbles didn't say a word, but I watched Bradley Verne, who had come in a few minutes before, walk up to the bar. Jackson pulled me in closer to him and I squirmed uncomfortably. He leaned into me and whispered, "It's all true, you little Daphne, you." He poked me in the ribs. Fortunately the buffer between us was our clothing.

"What?" I tried to pull away.

"Oh come on, like Daphne in Scooby-Doo? Everyone knows you're snooping around trying to figure out who killed Nick. Don't bother. You won't figure this one out." He shot a pointed look at Candace and Mumbles. "Too many people around here with too many secrets. I am sure they intend to keep them buried."

Bradley reached my side and tapped Jackson on the chest.

"Hey, man, I think maybe you've had too much to drink. Let me call you a cab." He reached into his pocket for his cell phone. "And let go of Evie. I think you're making her uncomfortable."

Jackson released me. "Am I making you uncomfortable?" From the look on his face, I couldn't tell if he gave a crap how I'd been feeling. He shot Bradley a nasty look. "And for your information, I don't drink anything but iced tea."

He was right about the tea. I had never seen him drink anything alcoholic, except at Nick's funeral when he'd had a beer. But Bradley had a point. Jackson was acting like he was on something.

Jackson backed away from me slowly, his arms in the air as if in surrender.

"Thing is, Daphne, I'd be way more concerned about one of these characters harming you. You don't have to be scared of me. I know the truth." He winked. Seriously, the guy was starting to creep me out, big time.

"You know, Jackson, maybe you should find a different watering hole to hang out in," Bradley said, moving in front of me protectively.

"I like it here. You just don't like me here. By the way, how's your dad, Brad? Oh and Candace, how about your little secret?"

Candace glared at him. "You're crazy."

"Ain't that the pot calling the kettle black? Every single one of you has something to hide." Then he looked right at me again. "Even you. It's just a matter of time before it all comes out."

I cringed. What the hell was this guy's problem?

Bradley moved forward menacingly.

"Time for you to go, Jackson. You're no longer welcome here."

I half worried Jackson would beat the crap out of Bradley. His threatening demeanor the night George came in was loud and clear in my mind.

"No problem. I've got everything I need to put out a fascinating documentary." Jackson slipped his laptop into an army-green backpack and slung it over his shoulder. He turned back, saluted me, and whistled his way out the door.

I was really getting tired of all the secrets and drama. In the silence following Jackson's departure, I finished my drink. I pondered what he'd said about Mumbles, Roger, and Nick. And then there was Candace ... and the snide remark about Bradley's father. What did Jackson know that the rest of us didn't?

"Good riddance," Candace said. "Pay him no mind, Evie." She waved a hand in front of her drink.

"Did you want to talk?"

I jumped, forgetting Bradley was still standing next to me.

"Sure. But where's Becky? Who'll tend the bar?" I said.

"No one's seen her tonight," Candace said.

"It's okay," Bradley said. "It's not that crowded, and everyone seems to have what they need for now. Let's sit over there." He pointed to the corner booth where Jackson always sat. "One of us can always jump up if need be."

"Okay." I poured myself a glass of water and followed Bradley.

"What a day," he said after plopping down on the bench seat.

"You okay?" I asked. He looked older and strained. He was clearly upset.

"It's my dad. He slipped into a coma today, and they don't expect him to come out of it."

"Oh no! I'm so sorry." I reached out to touch his hand, but then pulled back. "You said he's in a retirement home?"

"Yes. Platinum Partners. It's where the wealthy and wonderful go when they want the best of the best after retirement. Place is amazing and he's loved it for the past few years. But I think losing Nick has taken it out of him. I can't get a hold of my wife either to tell her. I left her a message on her cell. But when she has her 'girls' nights out, they go to the spa and out for drinks and, well, she'll call I'm sure once she gets the message." He sighed.

"She'll call. I'm sure of it. But you can talk to me for now if you want. I am terribly sorry about your dad. And it does sounds like Nick was a second son to him."

Bradley nodded, frowning. "Exactly. I have no idea what that ass Jackson was talking about."

I pursed my lips in distaste. "Yeah, Jackson obviously has some issues." I glanced around the room, making sure no one needed anything. Mumbles seemed to be slumping slowly onto the bar but otherwise, everything was in order.

"Did it bother you at all? That Nick and your dad were so close?"

He sat back and studied me for a second. "You are curious. You still looking into who might have killed him?"

I suddenly felt awkward. Truth be told, I was prying into things that were clearly not any of my business. "I'm sorry. I didn't mean to offend you. And yes, I can't seem to get it out of my mind."

He nodded. "It's okay. Honestly, it's refreshing to meet someone who really seems to care about others and wants to know what's going on." He smiled wryly. "You know, when I was younger, I was a real screwup. I did stupid things—partied too much, crashed cars, wound up in the tabloids a lot. I really hurt my dad, and I regret it every day. I can't blame him for feeling about Nick the way he did, the way he does. Nick was a good guy. He was pretty much on the straight and narrow. I mean he partied some like all of us, but he tried real hard to maintain himself and stay in line. I suppose I was bothered on some level, but with age comes maturity, and as I got off drugs and the party scene, I made amends with my dad. I also started cultivating a relationship with Nick because I owed him."

"Why is that?"

Bradley gazed over my shoulder, obviously lost in his memories.

"Because I had been an ass to him. When Roger Hawks died at my dad's place, I kind of stirred the pot with the tabloids, hinting maybe Nick was involved. Truthfully, there was no way I could have known if he was or wasn't. I was in Paris with some actress when Roger drowned. But my green-eyed monster got the best of me and caused Nick some problems. I think all that attention is why he became so reclusive and got out of show business altogether. My dad tried to talk him into making a comeback, but Nick refused."

I felt sad for Nick and wished things had happened differently for him. How hard it must have been to give up his career like that.

"Do you think Roger Hawks's death was an accident, or do you think he was pushed?"

"There has always been a lot of speculation about that night. But as for me ... well, I really believe it was an accident. Too much drinking. Roger was a known party animal, and he didn't always use his best judgment." He shook his head and chuckled softly. "Then again, none of us did back then." Bradley raised his arms into a broad stretch. "Why all the interest in Roger?"

I shrugged. "Jackson may be a jerk, but he hit the nail on the head when he said the people here have a lot of secrets. I guess it got me to thinking, maybe the mysteries surrounding Roger's death might have had something to do with Nick's murder."

He shook his head. "I don't think so."

"Who do you think might have killed Nick, then?" I asked.

He sighed. "I don't know. He did have some issues with gambling and borrowing money. And I heard he owed the wrong kind people a lot of cash. What gets me is how often my dad and I offered to give him a loan. Pride or foolishness kept him from accepting it. I keep wondering if I should have pushed Nick harder to accept our help." He rubbed his eyes again, clearly weary of the topic. "Then there's George Hernandez. What a hothead. I have no idea where he fits into the puzzle."

"Do you think Nick stole his recipe?"

Bradley laughed. "Does it matter if he did? Come on! Who would kill someone over a stolen fish taco recipe? As over the top as George seems, I can't imagine he'd be so stupid."

"Well, you know, there are a lot of idiots out there who have killed people for a lot less than that."

"I suppose," he said, shaking his head. He stood and stretched again, obviously ready to move on.

"Hey, thanks for talking with me, Bradley. And thanks for making Jackson leave. He kind of scares me." I shuddered, suddenly recalling my brush with death earlier in the day.

"Sure thing. Jackson seems to have some anger management issues. I wonder how closely the police have looked into him." He patted me on the shoulder. "Anyway, I suppose in a day or two, Becky's son will be here to take over and things will change. If I can help you in any way, you know, maybe get a gig somewhere else ... just let me know. I've got a few contacts here and there." He grinned widely, suddenly looking about ten years younger and very handsome.

"Wow, thanks! That would be nice."

"Hey, why don't I bartend tonight and you go play a set? It's not too crowded."

"Really? Thanks!" Bradley was easily turning out to be one of my favorite people at the bar.

"No problem."

I went to the kitchen and grabbed my guitar. I started setting up and as I sat down, Simone, aka Stacy, sauntered in with a red wig, ginormous sunglasses (seriously, what was the fascination with sunglasses at night?), knee-high leg warmers, a mini skirt, and a striped turtleneck. Subtle. She dropped into a nearby booth and scooted over to make room for Dwight. She'd obviously gotten over being mad at him. Simone lifted up her sunglasses and winked at me. I smiled wanly. It felt a bit odd to have her here listening to me, but I was glad she'd come all the same.

I started to play "Knockin' on Heaven's Door," and was just starting to mellow out, when I noticed a man who looked identical to Pierre the animal trainer in the back near the exit. Next to him stood a woman, also dressed in black. She had long pale hair and what appeared to be emerald green contact lenses ... because there's no way anyone had eyes that color in real life. The Pierre-clone's mouth turned up in a small, cryptic smile. I sucked in a deep breath and closed my eyes. When I opened them, he and the woman were gone.

What. The. Hell?

CHAPTER TWENTY-EIGHT

IN SPITE OF THE FACT that I might very well be losing my mind, by the third song of my set, I was starting to get into the groove. Apparently, I wasn't the only one. When I glanced at Simone while singing one of Adele's latest, she was visibly swaying to the music. I watched as she ordered another drink for herself and Dwight. A few minutes later, in the middle of my acoustic version of a La Roux song, she got up and grabbed Dwight's hand and they started dirty dancing. I knew things were going to go south pretty quickly. All it took was for Simone to completely lose what little inhibition she had and that wig would come off and her secret would be out. Nick's would turn into a madhouse of paparazzi, and fans would swarm. Not that this was a bad thing for the bar, of course, but it wouldn't go over well for Simone ... or me.

I decided it was time to take a break and get them both back into their seats.

Simone grinned broadly at me and gave me a hug. "Hey bestie, you are actually halfway decent!" She glanced at Dwight. "Isn't she?"

Dwight smiled. "Yeah, not bad, Evie."

The three of us sat down, and Simone leaned towards me excitedly. "I think I might really be able to help you. I'm going to call my producer tomorrow." She grabbed my hand and clasped it firmly in hers, her expression more sober. "Are you doing better? After that bullshit from earlier today?"

"Yeah, I'm okay now. Speaking of, I could have sworn I saw that Pierre guy in here with some blonde woman." I turned around and pointed to the back of the room. "Over there, near the back exit."

Simone peered sharply over my shoulder. "No. If I had, I would have seriously kicked his ass. I about fired Dwight after that stunt today. I mean, he needs to be more careful about who he hires for my videos. I don't think that guy is a good person. Him or his cat."

"I am sorry, and you both know I would never bring in anyone who I thought would harm you," Dwight said.

Simone waved her hand in his face. "Whatever. You're lucky I like you." She winked at him.

I was a little uneasy at her open flirting with Dwight. I nodded, noticing Bradley scrambling to fill an order. "Hey, I probably should get back behind the bar. Thanks for coming ... it really meant a lot to me."

"I had fun! And I can see why you like it here. It's cave-like and kind of seedy, but cool. This place has promise. Maybe I should buy it and turn it into something really special. Who owns it now?"

I chewed my lip. "I'm not really sure. Supposedly, Nick had a long lost son and he left this place to him. But I have yet to meet him."

I glanced back to the bar where Bradley seemed a bit overwhelmed. Come to think of it, I wasn't even sure he knew anything about bartending.

"When you find out, let me know," Simone said. "I'd be interested."

"Sure." I had no idea what Simone would do with a bar, but who was I to judge? "Look, I gotta run." I leaned over and gave her a quick hug.

"Okay chickadee, we're off. Pitbull invited us to his party tonight." She paused for a minute, "Hey, why don't you come with?"

"I can't. I need to work. You guys go have fun and tell me all about it tomorrow."

"All right. Later!" She turned and walked out the door, Dwight following like a lost puppy. Poor guy had it bad.

Simone's words about me being pretty good and talking to her producer played over and over in my mind. How cool would that be?

I walked back behind the bar and began pouring drinks. Not too long after, Bradley said he needed to head home, something about his dog having separation anxiety since his wife was away. He even mentioned, in all seriousness, that they had looked into hiring a dog psychologist. Oh my. I was growing to love L.A., but some of the comments I'd heard in Texas about flaky, wacky Californians had a grain of truth to them.

As I was mixing Tequila Sunrises for a couple of coeds, I noticed Mumbles watching me. I think he wanted to say something, and I moved down the bar to talk to him. Candace had vacated her seat and was likely in the restroom.

Before I reached Mumbles, however, Becky strolled in. She wasn't alone. I caught my breath as I locked eyes with the man at her side. As amazingly beautiful as Lucas was, the man with Becky was a serious rival as far as eye candy goes.

Unlike Lucas, this guy didn't glow or glide or seem on the verge of fading away. He was rugged, strikingly handsome, and very human. I felt my heartbeat speed up as I took him in. Light eyes (possibly blue but hard to tell from a distance), glossy brown hair, high cheekbones, and solidly built without looking overly bulky. Yum.

Becky and the young man reached the bar together.

"Evie, hi. This is my son, Joshua."

I wiped both hands on my jeans and reached across to shake his. His grasp was warm and firm, confident. In my moment of captivation, I'd broken my rule and caught a flash of Joshua knocking another man out hard in what looked to be a kitchen. Then I saw him seated in the back of a police car. I already knew too much.

"Nice to meet you," he said, in a deep, smooth voice. His eyes lightened a bit at my touch, and I knew whatever I'd seen in the vision had been lifted off him some.

"And you! Your mom said you work for the Red Cross in Africa. How was the flight home?" I found myself staring a little too long at his mouth. Seriously, what was wrong with me? I also found myself wondering about the vision.

Joshua nodded, smiling. "Yes, I was in Bangassou for the past few months inoculating women and children. The flight was long but," he glanced over at his mom affectionately, "I'm glad to be back home again." Becky reached over and hugged him.

I studied him for a few seconds, trying hard to spot Nick in his features. I wondered what Becky had told him about the bar.

"So, I guess this place is yours now?"

Joshua nodded. "That's what my mom tells me."

I decided against any mention of Nick. I had no idea what Becky had said and, frankly, it wasn't my place. Becky patted Joshua on his broad chest.

"Honey, I need to speak with Evie for a sec. Why don't you take a peek in the kitchen? I know how much you love to cook. Maybe we can turn this place into the restaurant of your dreams."

"Sure, Mom." He tossed a questioning glance at me and then walked towards the kitchen. We both watched him leave. I hoped my thoughts about how nice he looked from the back weren't obvious to Becky. As soon as he closed the doors behind him, Becky grabbed my arm and pulled me to the side. I was happy I'd chosen a long sleeved blouse.

"Listen, I know you are kind of, uh, how do I say this ... you aren't exactly so-phisticated."

What the—?

"Jeez, Becky. Why don't you tell me how you really feel?" Seriously, did everyone here think I was some sort of backwoods redneck?

Becky grimaced apologetically, "I'm sorry. It's just..." She chewed on her lip for a moment. "Well, sometimes you say things ... speak out of turn."

"Like asking him about being the owner of the bar?" If she hadn't wanted people asking awkward questions, perhaps she should have told him the whole story before bringing him to Nick's. But then again, what did a hick like me know?

"It's complicated. See, Joshua loves his work overseas. Coming home to all this has been—well, it's quite a change. And I would appreciate if you don't say anything about Nick." I waited a few seconds as my unsophisticated brain processed this information. Then I narrowed my eyes.

"Wait a minute, you mean you haven't told Joshua that Nick was his father?" She looked away and didn't answer. "So, what exactly did you tell him, Becky?"

"None of your business," she spat. "Stay away from my son and keep your mouth shut. In fact, I think you should start looking for another gig." My cheeks flushed and I felt myself becoming angry. I was suddenly gaining a deeper appreciation of Candace's dislike of Becky.

Luckily, Joshua reappeared and overheard some of his mother's tirade. "Wait a sec, Mom. Didn't you tell me what a fantastic singer and musician she is? Now you're asking her to leave?"

Becky turned to him, all smiles and innocence. She patted Joshua on the arm. "No, no, honey, it's just that she's so busy with her other job. I thought maybe it was getting to be too much for her."

He turned to me, one brow arched sexily. "Is it too much for you?"

I smiled and tilted my head slightly to the side. I'd learned a few tricks from Simone. "No. I'm good. I love singing here and helping out."

Joshua grinned broadly, his white teeth shining brightly against his tan skin. "Good! Grab your guitar and play. Something tells me I'm going to like you singing here."

I looked pointedly at Becky, who frowned, and I went to grab my guitar. Becky had another thing coming if she thought she could intimidate me so easily. She'd also shown me a side of herself I had only glimpsed once before. I could not help wondering which was the real Becky.

CHAPTER TWENTY-NINE

I CAN'T SAY I WAS unhappy to head home after the day I'd had. I didn't like the feeling in the pit of my stomach. I didn't like the way Becky treated me. I did like that her son was really hot, but then I felt guilty about my feelings, too. Whenever I started thinking about Joshua, my mind switched to Lucas and my heart beat a little bit faster. Fact is, I thought about Lucas more than I cared to admit. No man, alive or otherwise, had ever made me feel the way Lucas did. I didn't know if he'd visit tonight, but even though I was exhausted, I hoped he would. I didn't want to be alone.

I pressed down harder on the gas pedal and turned up the radio to Stevie Nicks singing "Edge of Seventeen." I sang along with her, trying to block thoughts of the day, the new guy, and Lucas out of my mind. As I rolled up the road to my house, I pushed the clicker to open the gate to the main entrance. A quick check in the rearview mirror showed an empty road behind me.

I still was feeling anxious about Pietro or George appearing on the scene. They had failed to show up at the bar, but if they found out where I lived ... I suppose going to George's place and eavesdropping had not been the smartest idea, and although I had learned some interesting things, I had more questions now than I did before I stood outside George's office.

When I opened the door to my place, I was greeted by Cass, Mac, and Lucas. They were all seated in the living room watching TV. I found myself smiling instantly.

"You're here," I said.

"I am. I told you I would be back."

"But you left in such a hurry last night, and I thought you were upset with me."

He shook his head. "No. But we need to talk."

I did not like the way that sounded. "Okay." I came over and sat down next to him. The glow around him was dimmer than usual. "When someone says 'we need to talk,' that usually isn't good."

He sighed. "I know I keep telling you our worlds are the same, but reality is, I am not completely of your world any longer no matter how badly I want to be."

I wasn't sure where this was going. "What are you trying to tell me?"

"Nothing." He waved a hand and the light surrounding it made a dizzying swirl around the room. He seemed almost angry. "I am here to distract you from falling into anything associated with the Black Tier, and to do so, we need to start with your friend's murder."

"Okay." God, I was so confused! "I've been looking into it already."

He groaned softly. "I was afraid you'd say that."

"I have to, Lucas! The police seem to think it was a mob hit, and they aren't all that interested in doing much to solve it. Nick deserves better than that."

"Then I have more work to do. I need to be sure you're protected."

"Why can't you just go with me wherever I go?"

He shook his head sadly. "You know I can't. I'm limited without permissions. My portal is here and my vibration will diminish if I leave this portal or anywhere I don't have permissions to be.

"So get permission," I said a bit angrily.

He closed his eyes and sighed. "It's not so easy. Even if I was with you every second, there is only so much power I have. I can be of more help to you from this side. I can keep the Black from getting to you, but at a human level, I can't do much. I need to find out who your guardian angel is and see what I can do to keep you further protected."

Say what? "My guardian angel? Really?"

"Really. Everyone has one. And many times, they're the last person you would expect. Some are born here with the knowledge of who and what they are. Some are sent here in another vessel."

"Like reincarnation?"

"No. Like if you died tonight and went through your review and ultimately met with the Bodha, they could script you. That means they would give you a script—a purpose—and you would be sent back to Earth to fulfill that purpose. Likely you would go somewhere you had never been, you would already be an adult, you would be given instructions on where you would work, live, how, why, all of it. And you'd be given details on who you were watching over."

"No kidding?"

"No kidding. This can also happen to people who cross over but want to come back. They aren't finished. The Bodha allows them return to wrap up unfinished business, but in return, they must become a guardian angel. They too, are given a script but it's different from being placed into another body."

"Let me get this straight ... someone like Simone could be my guardian angel?"

"As odd as that may seem, yes."

"Can you tell me who it is when you find out?"

"No. I can't. I would be breaking the trust between the Bodha and myself, and I am already on thin ice as it is." I wondered exactly what he meant by that comment. I hoped I hadn't somehow gotten him into trouble. "Since you are already investigating on this side of things, I think it's time you tell me what you know. Let me see if there is any way I can help."

I laid out the players. I told him about Becky and Joshua, conveniently leaving out the part about Joshua's good looks. I told him about Candace and Mumbles and the history between them. I laughed at the idea that George Hernandez could have offed Nick for stealing his fish taco recipe. It seemed crass, but it sounded ludicrous as I said it.

"Then there is this Pietro SanGiacomo character who seems like a mobster to me. I think he's a loan shark. Apparently Nick was screwing around with this guy's sister on top of owing him money, and then he dumped her. My guess is the guy wasn't pleased. Oh, and he and George Hernandez have some kind of illegal side business arrangement."

"What a tangled web." Lucas shook his head.

"Tell me about it. Then there is Bradley Verne. I like him. I mean, he seems like a decent, sincere person, but there is still something that bothers me about him. He and Nick have a long history, and I think I have only barely scratched the surface. They all have a past together. Candace, Becky, Bradley, and Nick." I went on to tell him about Roger and how he drowned in the pool at the Verne mansion.

"Roger Hawks?"

I nodded.

Lucas smiled.

"What?" I asked. "Why the smile?"

"I might be able to actually gain information directly from the source."

"What do you mean?"

"From Roger Hawks himself and what happened that night."

"So, you, uh, know him?"

Lucas shook his head. "No. But let me see what I can do. Seeing how he was once famous, died tragically—well, if he didn't wind up stuck in the Black Tier or glorified in the White, he may be closer than we think, and I may get access to his vibration."

"That would be great. If there is a link from that night, that could help us figure out who murdered Nick, then maybe Roger Hawks can give us some answers."

"I agree, but let's not get too far ahead of ourselves. I will likely have to jump through some hoops as it is."

"Right." I couldn't help but smile. Yes I was really attracted to Lucas, but it was also nice to have this kind of support. He wanted to help me.

"Anything else? Anyone else you've encountered who you think might have had it in for Nick?"

"I forgot to tell you about Jackson."

"Jackson?"

"Yeah." I gave him an abbreviated description of the strange man and his bizarre behavior.

"I don't like him at all," Lucas said, his voice low and gruff.

"Me neither. I should also tell you someone followed me home the other night. And then yesterday, I was almost attacked by a jaguar." Lucas looked incredulous until I told him about Pierre and how Anastasia tried to attack me. I even mentioned how I could have sworn I spotted Pierre back at the bar with some woman.

"This isn't good." He sounded angry. "That Pierre fellow, the jaguar, and the woman—who if I had to guess are one in the same—are from the Black and were sent to mess with you."

"Okay … but how can you tell?"

"Trust me. I can read the signs."

"But can you explain what's going on? I mean, who were those people?"

"First of all, they weren't people. Shapeshifters, most likely. And possibly a necromancer as well."

More shape shifter stuff? And now necromancers? "You mean as in someone who has been raised from the dead?" Lucas nodded. Oh boy! What in the hell had I gotten myself into?

"I have a very bad feeling about all of this, Lucas." And that, my friends, is what's known as an understatement.

"I know." His hand picked up mine. "But there is a reason why all of this is happening, and it's not just because of the Black. Remember, the White has influence too. Just as I have been sent here to protect and hopefully guide you, you've been brought here to find out who killed your friend, and maybe, solve the mystery of what happened to your sister."

I sucked in my breath and felt tears sting my eyes.

"Hey, hey, don't do that. I'm sorry. I thought that's what you wanted." His fingers brushed my cheeks wiping away the tears.

"No. Don't be." I looked up at him and he withdrew his fingers. "I want to know. I do want to know what happened to her."

"Okay. I will help you then. But I need to go."

"Again?" Here he had touched me and everything seemed so, I don't know, kind of like intimate. "Why? We're talking and hanging out and I like you here." I know I sounded whiny, but I did like him around.

"I like being here but I am not here to be your friend. I'm here because…"

"I'm your project."

He waited a minute to respond. When he did, he picked up my hand again, sending those fluttering feelings back down to my toes.

"I was kind of a bad boy in my day, when I was, you know, living. I lived and played hard. I had a lot of women. And now I'm here and I have to be honest, I want so badly to be there with you. Your world. Or here with you. My world. Do you know what I mean?"

"I think." My stomach sunk.

"If I were a real man again, I would have already pursued and seduced you and completely had my way with you."

Okay. Yep. Now my stomach really did sink. I found my voice, which sounded almost guttural when I spoke. "Well, how do you even know if you could have seduced me and had your way with me?" Jeez, I was flirting with a spirit!

He smiled. "I had some pretty good moves."

"Oh you did, did you?" Yes, I was flirting with a dead guy.

"I did."

"What were they?"

He looked into my eyes almost as if he could look through me, which maybe he could.

"Evie, I can't. I can't go there with you. I have some feelings that I shouldn't, and I want to help you. I want to protect you and you are my project, and..."

"Project! Oh, come on! I don't even know what that really means, Lucas!" I raised my voice. "This whole thing is crazy," I said my voice raised a couple of octaves as I felt lightheaded.

I noticed in those few seconds something different about the way his eyes looked—almost sad, and I regretted my words and actions. I sunk back into flirtation mode. I don't know what compelled me. I don't know what I was thinking, but dammit, I was completely and totally attracted to Lucas—his spirit— vibration, whatever the hell he wanted to call it.

"I mean can't you show me what your moves were? See if I would have fallen under your spell?"

He stood. "No I can't! You and me—no. We can't. You're a human and I'm not, and there are rules and ... I have to go." With those words, he was gone, and I was left speechless and in complete dismay.

CHAPTER THIRTY

IT WAS HARD TO CONCENTRATE the next day while doing Simone's makeup. Fortunately she didn't have much to do for the day. She was kind of a grump for some reason and didn't say much to me.

We were in her bedroom and she'd asked for a simple look.

"I want to go to a Starbucks and have coffee, but everyone wants a piece of me," she said.

I wanted to ask her about the record producer but could see she was sulky and when she gets like that, the world becomes even more about her than usual.

"I want my pumpkin spice latte and to be left alone, but I want to be around people."

"You can go in disguise," I suggested, brushing a peach color blush across her perfectly angled cheekbones.

She picked up one of my brushes and threw it across the room. "I don't want to go as someone else!"

"Sorry," I said, retrieving the brush. Clooney, who had been asleep on her bed, lifted his head up.

"No. I'm sorry. I'm, well, do you think I'm getting old?" she asked.

"No. Why?"

"The Hollywood Insider has an article about who they think will age well and who won't. I am on the 'won't' list." She pointed to the paper on her boudoir. I picked it up and read over the list.

"That's ridiculous," I said. "You're beautiful, and you will age like fine wine. I am sure of it." Not that I knew what fine wine really ages like, but the saying is out there so I gave it a shot. I flipped open the rag. "Why do you read this stuff in the first place?"

"I know. It's stupid."

"It is," I muttered as something caught my eye. An article about Nick, and it was written by Jackson Owens. What the hell? "I'll get rid of this for you. You look great. Do you want me to take you somewhere?"

"No." She sat there texting on her iPhone. "I guess it's silly for me to think I could ever go to a Starbucks as myself and sit there like a normal person. I only wanted to try and look pretty today." She frowned and went back to her phone. "I think I need to spend the rest of the day in the movie room watching Ocean's Eleven again. You can go," she muttered.

I was a little surprised she didn't insist I stay and watch with her, but as I pulled out of her front gates, I spotted Dwight's car winding up the street toward her house and knew she had other plans. He spotted me through the windshield and gave a wave. I waved back. I still really did not trust that guy.

But exploring my distrust toward Dwight at the moment didn't seem prudent. What did was reading the article Jackson had written.

Nick's was closed during the days now. Becky had made the decision to open the bar at four and no more lunch servings. I could understand the thought process. Nick's never did get much of a lunch crowd, and so I am sure Joshua and his mother were looking at it from a financial perspective. However, I did wonder what they planned to do with the place. In the back of my mind was Simone's mention of purchasing the bar.

There was a sandwich shop close by Nick's and I decided to stop in and grab a bite. I wished I had Cass with me, but I didn't want to take the time to go all the way home to read the article.

After ordering an iced tea and a turkey sandwich, I sat at a table outside and opened up The Hollywood Insider to Jackson's article, which was titled, "A Bar of Secrets: Finding Closure on the Death of Nick Gordin."

I gasped. What was Jackson up to?

After several weeks of the ongoing investigation into Nick Gordin's murder, it would appear the police don't have much interest in solving the case.

However, as a journalist, (I thought the guy was a screen writer) I decided to take a closer look at those who knew Nick Gordin best. And I discovered a nest of secrets at Nick's bar. Of course, I can't print actual names, but it won't be difficult for readers to put two and two together.

The regulars at Nick's are a peculiar bunch. They include a former wannabe starlet who was once engaged to Gordin and now goes by a different name. This woman is believed to know more about the night Roger Hawks died than she claims. Her sidekick may also know something. In fact, Hawks and Gordin cost him his right eye and his job as a stuntman.

A longtime friend of Gordin's, from one of the most prestigious Hollywood families, appears to be on the verge of bankruptcy. Wonder what that's all about and how it might tie into Gordin's death? Was he talking about Bradley Verne? He had to be.

Then there is the pretty, part-time bartender, part-time singer at Nick's who had high hopes of meeting a music producer through Gordin. Looks as though Gordin may have been holding out a carrot. I can't help wondering if someone was holding a grudge.

Why would he write such a thing? How could he even think of me as a suspect? I set my iced tea down, missing the table. The glass crashed to the ground, splintering everywhere. The cold tea splattered across the legs of my jeans.

"Oh no!"

A waitress came outside to help me.

"I'm so sorry," I said.

"Hey, it happens." She said, smiling and starting to clean up the mess.

I bent over to help when I heard my name. "Evie?"

I stood and saw Joshua. "Oh, hi!" I looked down at the waitress and then back at Joshua. I knew my cheeks were bright red.

"What are you doing here?" I blurted out and my cheeks burned even more. Wow. He was as good looking in the daylight as he was inside the bar. I, on the other hand, probably looked like a disaster. How embarrassing!

"My mom lives around the corner. I was taking Garbo here for a walk."

I looked down and saw a very cute bulldog on the end of a leash. "She's adorable! Is she yours?"

"My mom's, but she's taken a liking to me, and honestly, we needed to get out of the apartment. Living with my mom is stressing me out. And, it's only been a couple of days!" He laughed and it was warm and nice. "I'm not used to being cooped up with my mother."

"I'm sure. Africa vs. an L.A. apartment. Big difference."

"Definitely a change," he agreed.

The waitress smiled at Joshua, as taken with his good looks as every other female (and even a few males) in the nearby vicinity were. He smiled back. She shook her head, as if trying to clear it, and said she'd be right back with a fresh glass of iced tea. I thanked her and then was stumped for words as what to say next. I finally said, "Um, I'm having lunch. Want to join me?"

"Yeah sure. That would be nice. Come on, Garbo." They came through the small gate and sat down at the table with me. Garbo lay down at Joshua's feet.

I reached down to scratch her between her ears. "How old is she?"

"Only a year, but lazy already. But I think that comes with being a bulldog." He laughed again.

The waitress brought my tea and took Joshua's order.

"So, do you think you'll stay here long term or are you considering returning to Africa?"

He shrugged. "Hard to say. After you left and we closed up last night, my mom told me the truth."

"The truth?"

"I assume you already knew Nick was my father." He grimaced. "Actually, I suspect a few people already knew and she had to tell me, otherwise someone else would."

I didn't like secrets, and I didn't think it was right for her to keep something so huge from her son, so I was relieved she had done the right thing. She had redeemed herself in my eyes … for now.

"I did know, and I'm happy your mother told you. It was the right thing to do."

He nodded. "Yeah. I love my mom and all, but this whole thing has been difficult. I'm kind of upset with her. I mean, I know she kept secrets from me because she loves me, but the kind of secrets she kept … well, I'm a grown man, and I wish she had more confidence in how well I'd take these things."

"I think when it comes to family and friends—people you love—you have to find a way to forgive them, and your mom was only protecting you. I think that's how she sees it."

He nodded. "Maybe you're right." His green eyes sparkled as the overhead sun beat down on us.

"You don't have to like what she did, but you do have to forgive her. She's your mom and she's family. That's my two cents."

"I know. Not easy though, and now I really wish I knew who killed Nick, especially in light of who he was to me. I wish I'd known him." He stared at me intently. "What was he like?"

"He was a real decent guy. He was kind, and he loved to cook. He seemed to really care about people. As different as he was from my dad, I kind of saw him as a father figure."

The waitress brought our sandwiches, and in-between bites, we chatted further. He was incredibly easy to talk to. Which is why, not long after, I did something I probably shouldn't have. I invited him and Garbo over.

"Hey, you know, if she needs more exercise, why don't you bring her to my place and let her play with my dog Cass some time?"

"Really? That would be great. What are you doing until we open?"

"Nothing really. I was heading home after lunch."

My only real plan had been to finish reading the article Jackson had written, but I had to admit, Joshua's company was a bit more desirable at the moment, and frankly, after what I considered a flat-out rejection by Lucas, maybe having a human man visit me in my home would be a good thing.

He gazed off into the street. "I really don't want to go back to my mom's place."

"Well then, you can come with me, and if you can get a ride home from work, we can ride in together."

"Great!" He signaled to the waitress for the check. Once we'd taken care of the bill, he stood, unwinding Garbo's leash from the foot of his chair. "Come on, Garbo. It's playdate time!"

Once he said date, I started to second-guess my impulse to invite him over. What if Lucas showed up? What would he think? Then again, why did it even matter what he thought? The reality was, this guy was now my co-worker, my boss at the bar, and maybe he could be a friend, too. I am allowed friends. Even very good looking ones.

I was further embarrassed by my van. I would have thought I'd gotten over it after driving Simone around and having her berate me about what a piece of crap it was. But although Joshua didn't seem to mind at all, something about having him in my piece of crap van did make me feel a bit uneasy.

Back at my place, I took a good look around before letting Joshua too far into the house. No pot. No spirits. Just Cass and Mac. Happy to play with another dog, Cass bounced and twirled, taking off like a rocket along with Garbo, who, bless her heart, tried to keep up. Let's just say bulldogs aren't known for their speed or grace.

I took the paper with Jackson's article out of my purse and set it on the kitchen table while Joshua played outside with the dogs. I wanted it to dry out so I could turn the page and finish the article without tearing it. I grabbed two bottles of waters and some brownies I'd baked the day before. I glanced outside, and watching the dogs and Joshua put a smile on my face. As he bent over to hug

Cass, those stupid butterflies swarmed in my stomach. The same kind I got when Lucas was around.

And that was when I heard someone say my name. "Evie?"

I snapped around and Lucas was in my kitchen next to the fridge, just a few feet from me.

"Lucas! You startled me!" I lowered my voice to a loud whisper. The last thing I needed was my new boss thinking I was schizo or something.

"I'm sorry." He came closer. "Who's the guy?" He nodded toward Joshua playing with the dogs. Cass, sensing him inside with me, bolted towards the back door.

"He's a friend and my boss at the bar. His dog needed some exercise. I invited him over so Cass could play with a new friend."

I could see Joshua coming toward the house. I didn't want Lucas to leave, but I also didn't really want him there. It would be awkward, to say the least, especially since I wouldn't be able to even acknowledge Lucas while Joshua was in the house.

"He can't see me," he said, an amused look on his face. "A friend, huh?"

I nodded. "Yes. I can have friends."

"Sure you can. Look, I don't want to hang around and get in the way. I have some stuff to do anyway."

"When will you come back? I need to talk to you. Thing is…" I looked sheepishly at my feet. "I'm sorry about last night."

He waved a hand at me. "You don't need to apologize. I'm the sorry one. I crossed a line with you, and I know better."

I did not like what I was hearing.

"I don't know when I'll be back," he continued. "But don't worry. It won't be long. Just wanted to let you know I'm still working hard on getting information for you." He held up one of the eagle feathers from my desk and then was gone. No goodbye. Nothing.

I turned around and Joshua was striding into the kitchen. I tried to pull myself together. I wondered why Lucas had one of my feathers? He hadn't asked to take one. I knew, though, it had something to do with Hannah. I sighed, knowing now was not the time or the place for mulling over moody ghosts.

"Cass is awesome! I've never seen Garbo play like that. Ever!" Josh was smiling broadly and full of energy.

Cass and Garbo circled behind him, out of breath, and headed to the water bowl. Mac had been in hiding while Cass was busy with her play date. Now he came out from whatever hole he had slunk into and walked right up to Garbo, hissing and clawing at the poor girl. Then ran away.

"Mac!" I yelled, horrified, and then turned to Joshua. "I am so sorry!" Garbo whimpered. "He's a bit possessive about Cass."

"I can see that," Joshua said bending over to check on Garbo, chuckling to himself. "She's fine. Between you and me," he lowered his voice to a whisper, "she's kind of a baby."

I handed him a bottle of water and as I did, he spotted the paper on the counter.

"What's this?" he asked.

"I don't think you want to read that," I said. "It's garbage. I didn't even finish it." But it was too late. Joshua bent over the counter and stared intently at the paper for a few minutes. When he finished he looked up at me.

"I can't believe this. Who wrote this?" He looked at the paper again. "Jackson Owens? Who is this guy? I can't believe he mentioned I was in prison! And to write what he did about you! What an ass!"

"Jackson used to be a regular at the bar. He wanted to do a documentary on Nick, or so he said." I stood there shaking my head and then I jerked my eyes back over to Joshua. "Wait. What? You were in prison?" I immediately recalled the vision I had of him when we shook hands.

"You really didn't read all of it, did you?"

"No." But now I wished I had.

He handed the paper to me. I walked over to the table and sat down, my eyes rapidly scanning the page.

And now, the long lost son of Nick Gordin has returned from Africa where he has spent time trying to cleanse his past after spending five years in prison for the second-degree murder of one his mother's boyfriends. A mother, I might add, who stole Gordin from his fiancée thirty years ago and apparently forgot to tell her son for another thirty years who his daddy really was.

Like a game of Clue, there are plenty of potential suspects out there who might have had a hand in Nick's death. It's just a matter of putting the pieces together. Then again, maybe no one really cares what happened to a washed up actor who finished his days tending a dive bar.

I looked up and stared at Joshua for a few beats. "Murder?"

CHAPTER THIRTY-ONE

AFTER TOSSING JACKSON'S ARTICLE into a nearby recycling can, Joshua and I made our way out to the pool for some brownies and to wait for the dogs to catch a second wind. We both chewed the chocolaty goodness, not saying anything, until he finally broke the silence.

"I expect you're wondering what happened ... I mean, regarding the so-called murder and my time in prison."

I nodded, if a bit hesitantly. "Look, Joshua. It's not really any of my business. I am curious, but I don't expect you to give me the whole story."

He sighed heavily. "Yeah, well, the thing is, I don't want you to think I'm some sort of homicidal maniac, especially since we'll be working together and all." He took another swig of his water and gazed off into the distance.

"I was twenty and we were living in New York. I was going to NYU. I came home one night to see my mom and do some laundry," he sighed. "She was dating this guy I didn't like. He just didn't treat her right. Kind of verbally abusive and Mom always seemed upset when he was around. Anyway, he was there that night when I got there. And..." he closed his eyes, shaking his head as if trying to rid himself of the memory. "This guy was beating her. I lost it and I threw a few punches. One landed real hard, the guy went flying back, hit his head on a counter, and hemorrhaged." He paused, rubbing his face tiredly. "So yeah, I killed him."

"You were protecting your mom. And while I don't condone violence to stop violence, well, I can't say I would have done any different." I reached over and touched his hand, knowing full well I would see the same images I'd seen when we first met. I let my hand linger on his little longer than usual. He glanced over at me and smiled. I could tell some of the sadness had been erased. His eyes were brighter and his frown lifted. "Anyway, it was clearly an accident. I doubt you intended to kill the guy, right?"

Joshua nodded and continued his story. "That's why the jury decided on a manslaughter verdict. I went to prison for five years. When I got out, I volunteered for the Red Cross. No matter the reason, killing someone leaves a horrible stain on your soul. It never leaves you, and I needed to do something good. I needed to give back in a way that went above and beyond."

I nodded sympathetically. "I'm sorry that happened to you."

"You know what? As awful as that time was, I can say with certainty it made me a better man. I used to have quite a temper, and although that guy was beating my mom, I know now I could have managed the situation differently." He shrugged. "In any event, had I not killed that guy and ended up in prison for five years, I would never have gone to Africa, and I wouldn't trade that experience for anything."

"You miss it? Africa?"

He nodded, smiling wistfully. "I do, but I realize now it was probably time for me to rejoin the world here and think about my future, having a family, that sort of thing. I couldn't see raising a family in Africa. Too much upheaval and violence, at least where I was."

"What do you plan to do now? I mean, obviously you have the bar, but is that what you want?"

He cocked his head to the side, looking like a particularly handsome little boy. "I'm not really sure yet. I love to cook. I was even thinking about culinary school and maybe expanding the bar into a restaurant. The problem with that is capital. I don't have a way to fund it."

I almost mentioned Simone, but decided against it for the moment. She had the money to back something like that, but I didn't want to start throwing out a possible solution without the certainty she would follow through.

"Where there's a will, there's a way." I smiled.

Joshua smiled again and stretched sexily. "You are so different from most girls. Well," he lowered his voice to a conspiratorial stage whisper, "from most girls here in L.A."

I lowered my voice to match his. "That's because I'm not what I seem. I'm from Texas, remember?" We smiled at each other silently for a long moment and just as it was starting to feel awkward, I took a quick, nervous sip of water. "Fact is, most girls I've seen out here are beautiful and..."

"Superficial," he cut in.

I thought of Simone. "There are a few good eggs around."

He stood suddenly, and at first I thought he was going to reach out and touch my face, the way his hand lifted, but instead he balled up his fist and gently grazed his knuckles across my head, back and forth. It felt like I'd suddenly gained a big brother.

"You're a good egg."

I stood and laughed. "You don't know me that well!"

"I don't need to. I can tell."

Our eyes locked again and my stomach dropped into my toes. I don't know what would have happened had Cass not dived into the pool, followed by a less graceful Garbo. The combined force of the two dogs hitting the water resulted in a mighty splash that doused Joshua and I from head to toe. We both started laughing, and the moment we'd shared was broken.

Joshua picked at his wet t-shirt. "I guess, we should dry off and head to the bar. It's getting late."

"Yep." I grabbed the now-empty brownie platter and stepped back into my flip-flops. "Let me drop this stuff off in the kitchen, and I'll grab you a dry towel." I jerked my head around the side of the pool. "There's a full bathroom and changing room just over there if you need some privacy."

"Sounds good." Joshua picked up the empty water bottles and followed me into the kitchen. "Why don't you get a few extra towels and I can dry off these two mutts."

After getting Joshua and the dogs settled, I quickly changed clothes in my room and ran the dryer over my head. I found myself thinking about Lucas and couldn't help wondering when he'd be back and what he was up to. I liked Lucas. A lot. But Joshua was the real deal ... as in living.

When I walked back into the kitchen, I noticed Joshua had retrieved the paper with Jackson's article from the recycling bin. He didn't hear or see me come in, and I watched him carefully fold it and stuff it into his back pocket. I thought it was kind of odd, but decided against saying anything. Maybe he didn't want me reading the article again. Or he wanted to show it to his mom. Who knew.

In any case, Jackson was obviously a liar or, at the very least, prone to exaggeration. Look what he had written about me. Jerk!

I believed Joshua's story about his prison stint. I simply couldn't see him as a murderer. But I wondered, did he have a motive to kill Nick? As far as I knew, he'd only just found out Nick was his dad, and he'd literally stepped off the plane a few days ago, after Nick's murder. But then unless I'd been the one picking him up at the airport, I had no way to prove he hadn't been here in L.A. all along. And what if his anger issues hadn't been resolved? What if he'd suspected Nick was mistreating his mom and decided to take matters into his own hands?

I rolled my eyes. Come on, Evie. That's enough of that. Just because Jackson suspected everyone and their mother of killing Nick didn't mean I had to. And the thought of anyone thinking Joshua could hurt a fly was just ludicrous. Friend or boss, or both, I liked Joshua. He was easy to talk to and easy on the eyes.

CHAPTER THIRTY-TWO

THAT NIGHT AT THE BAR, I caught Joshua's eye a few times. And it appeared Becky had noticed. It wasn't as if we were openly flirting or anything, but during our afternoon together, we'd clearly begun a friendship, and it seemed Mama Bear was not too happy about it.

Every time Becky trained her eyes on me, she gave me a piercing look bordering on a fierce scowl. Protective much, Becky? Her expression reminded me of a story I'd read as a child about a mother dragon who almost reduced a nearby village to ashes in an effort to protect her young offspring from the local (and somewhat overzealous) knight. That thought led to shape shifters which then led to me envisioning Becky suddenly morphing into a huge dragon here in the bar (and would her clothes, like those of the Incredible Hulk, simply shred to pieces or vanish?). I started giggling to myself.

"What's so funny?" Joshua, who had sidled up next to me, gently nudged my ribs.

I startled and shot a guilty look at him. "Oh nothing. I was, uh, I was just thinking about something my mom told me about my dad." This lying thing was coming a bit too easy for me. My father's face popped into my head. He did not look happy.

"Got it." He was pouring a couple of drinks for last call. There weren't many patrons left. Even Candace and Mumbles had stumbled out a couple of hours earlier. They'd been acting a little bit strange lately. I wasn't sure if it was because of the changes to the bar or something else.

Becky had, thankfully, left as soon as the kitchen stopped serving. But not before shooting me a parting death glare and claiming she had a migraine. I can't say I was unhappy to see her go. It bothered me how her personality seemed to have turned on a dime. When she'd first come into the bar and Nick had made introductions, she'd acted like the two of us were buddy-buddy. But after Nick's death, something had changed. And her attitude towards me took an even bigger nosedive once Joshua arrived on the scene. Maybe she was one of those extremely overprotective mothers and saw me as a potential threat to her relationship with her son. In any case, I felt sorry for the future Mrs. Joshua Styles, whoever she was. And as far as I was concerned, I was certainly no threat.

Joshua handed me a round of drinks meant for a table of what looked like out-of-town, business types. I set their drinks down and, as I turned back to the bar, one of them patted me on the rear. I swung around to meet the flirtatious eyes of a handsome thirtysomething year old wearing a blue, button-down shirt, and a platinum wedding band on his ring finger.

"Excuse me?!" I was so not impressed.

He held up his open palms and smiled. "My friends and I were just commenting on what a pretty girl you are and how well you sing. You're also a wonderful waitress. I bet there are other things you do well, too." He looked around at his colleagues and the group laughed.

It's not often I lose my temper but when I do, watch out. I reached down, picked up his drink, and poured it down the front of his previously clean shirt. He stood quickly, knocking back his chair, eyes wide with surprise and anger.

"What the fuck?!"

I placed my drink tray on the floor next to me and rested my hands on either hip. "You're right, mister. I do lots of other things real well, like get rid of jerks like you. Get out of here. You and your friends are no longer welcome."

He shook his head and smiled again. This time, it wasn't very friendly. I glanced at the three other men with him and their expressions ranged from agitated to eager. Nasty Business Man took a step closer to me and threw a glance back at his colleagues.

"Looks like we have a feisty one, boys." He turned back to me, his eyes narrowed. "I like them feisty," he growled.

He picked up his chair from the floor and spun it around, then reached out and pushed me down into it. I struggled to get back up as the other men laughed and Mr. Nasty held me down by placing his hands on either side of my shoulders.

"Hey! What the hell?" Joshua yelled. "Get the hell away from her!" I could hear him come up behind me, and I noticed the other three men stand up. The man still holding me maintained his snarky grin. The blood began rushing through my ears and I could feel the pounding of my heart heavy against my chest— and that's when I heard it.

The soft but unmistakable click of a gun.

Anyone who grew up in Texas hill country, like myself, knows exactly what that sound is. The three men facing Joshua went pale, one of them dropping back into his chair like a rock.

"I said, get the hell away from her … now. Or your next trip home will be in a body bag."

The man facing me quickly yanked his hands off my shoulders and backed towards the table, away from Joshua and the gun.

"Hey man, no harm. We were just having some fun."

Joshua's calm, I-mean-business tone didn't waver in the slightest. "You have ten seconds to get your drunk asses out of my bar before I pull the trigger. And I better not see any of you in this establishment again."

The men grabbed their coats and moved quickly out of the bar. Joshua rushed over to me as I slumped against the back of the chair. I refused to start crying, but that had scared me pretty bad. I kept thinking back to Lucas's warning about the Black Tier wanting a piece of me. Could these guys be just another attempt to intimidate me, like Pierre and Anastasia? Thank goodness for Joshua and his gun.

CHAPTER THIRTY-THREE

JOSHUA'S HANDS WERE FIRMLY planted on his hips and he looked at me the way one might at a recalcitrant child. "For the last time, Evie, you don't need to stay. You've had a rough evening and I think you're entitled to an early night. I'll walk you to your car and close up."

"No, really, Joshua. I'm okay." I'm not certain who I was trying to reassure more—him or me, as my hands were still shaking from the encounter. "Doing some work might help. And I don't want to leave you here to do it all alone."

The truth was, a part of me didn't want to leave him all alone. He had intervened in what otherwise might have become an ugly situation, and I felt I owed him something. Also, I kept wondering if those men or whatever they were would be back for Joshua, or for me. I didn't know if I could prevent anything bad from happening, but if it did, Joshua wouldn't be alone— like Nick had been.

Like my sister had been.

"You sure?" he asked.

"Yeah, I'm sure."

He looked down at the carpeted floor for a moment. "I hope I didn't scare you even more, you know with..." He held up the gun, the dull gleam of black metal catching my eye and making me feel uneasy in spite of myself.

"Uh, no. But if you keep waving it around like that, I might change my mind."

He laughed suddenly. "Oh sure. Sorry!"

Joshua walked back behind the bar and took out a box, where he then placed the gun and locked it. I wondered if the gun had been there when Nick was alive.

After giving myself a few more minutes to regain my composure, I decided to go to the kitchen to make sure everything was squared away. More and more people were coming in to eat at Nick's—wanting the famous fish tacos. While I didn't have the recipe, it appeared Becky did. I guessed Nick must've shared it with her considering the nature of their relationship. But all those tacos made for a less-than-clean kitchen by the end of the day.

"I think I'll make sure the kitchen is clean and ready to go for tomorrow." I started for the door, when Joshua reached out and touched my arm—again the flash of him in the back of the police car. I pulled my arm away.

"I'm sorry. I didn't mean…" We shared an awkward few seconds between us as I'm sure my reaction caught him off guard. It wasn't as if he'd grabbed me hard or anything. "I was just going to say, I'll go with you. We can get it done together. The bar is clean now, so let's get the kitchen sorted out and I'll walk you to your car then."

"Okay." I nodded and smiled weakly at him, trying to soften the negative response I'd had to his touch.

We put away any food that'd been left out. Truth be told, Becky wasn't exactly the most detail-oriented person when it came to cleaning. I swept and wiped down the counters. Joshua mopped. We didn't say much while we worked, but his presence was comforting.

Joshua picked up a large box and headed towards the walk- in storage closet.

"Do you need help?" I asked.

"No, I'm fine. Well, maybe if you can get the door for me..."

"Sure." Happy to provide any assistance I could, I stepped behind him and swung open the door. The large closet was a bit disorganized and filled with bottles of liquor, plates, dried foods, canned goods—that sort of thing. I quickly stepped in, moving some items around to make room for the large box.

Suddenly, I felt something icy reach out and touch my neck. I whirled around and looked at Joshua. He stood behind me, still holding the box in his hands. He started to set it down in the newly cleared space as he did so, the door to the closet slammed shut behind us.

"What the ... ?" Joshua turned and tried to open the heavy door. Nothing. "That's weird."

I agreed, but then again, everything about my life had pretty much been what I would consider weird, especially lately. "Are we locked in here?"

"No." He laughed nervously, and I wasn't sure if I should believe him or not. "I may have left the back door open and the wind blew this one shut. It's just old and heavy." He pushed against it hard, putting all of his weight into his shoulder. The door didn't move.

Perspiration started to trickle down my neck and slink its way down my backside. What if those guys had come back? What if they'd locked us in here?

Joshua tried again and again. I came over and put my weight into the door as well. Nothing.

He shrugged. "I don't know what to say," he said. "We might be stuck here until tomorrow."

"What?! I have to get home to Mac and Cass." And what if Lucas showed up? What would he think if I didn't come home all night?

Joshua let out a deep breath. "Don't worry. I'll keep trying. Just let me sit down for a minute and think this through."

I nodded, telling myself to chill out. I knew I was tired and no doubt he was exhausted too. And, let's face it. If I was going to be trapped in a storage closet, one with a working light, lots of food, and alcohol was certainly better than nothing.

Joshua glanced around the small area and took down a set of dishtowels, spreading them out on the concrete floor. "Well, it's no sofa, but I guess it's better than cold cement."

I laughed, in spite of my anxiety. "I come from a hick town and I've sat my butt down on the hard ground more than once in my life. I think I can handle this. But I have to tell you, I'm not sure how my animals will fare through the night without me." Not, of course, that I'd have to worry about either of them starving to death ... especially not Mac.

"The good news is my mother will likely come looking for me if I'm not home in an hour. I may be almost thirty, but she treats me like I'm five."

I nodded, not wanting to say I'd noticed. "Wait, do you have your cell phone on you?"

He shook his head resignedly. "Left it on the bar. You?"

"Nope. In my purse in the kitchen."

"Worst case scenario then, we have to wait a couple of hours at the most before my mother figures out I'm MIA and comes on a rescue search." He waved his hand at the dishrags on the floor. "Seat?"

"Sure." It's not like I had any other options.

Joshua tore open the box he'd just set down and pulled out a bottle of wine. "Want some?"

"How do you plan to get the cork out?"

"I'm a bartender now, remember?" He took a corkscrew from the front pocket of his jeans.

I nodded. Kind of late for wine, but since we were stuck ...

"Are there any wine glasses in here?"

He reached up onto a shelf above him and took down a couple of Styrofoam cups. "No ... but beggars can't be choosers."

"They'll do just fine."

He opened the wine, poured us each a cup full, and sat down next to me, placing the bottle on the box next to him. "So, here we are."

"Yep."

"Pretty eventful night."

"You can say that," I said, taking a sip from my cup. Not bad, considering the circumstances.

He brought his cup up to his lips and took a long drink.

The silence between us was palpable.

"So, you know a bit about me," he said breaking the tension. "How about you? Tell me about yourself."

My shoulders and neck tightened. "Not much to tell." I shrugged. "I grew up in a small town in Texas. My mother owns the beauty shop there. It's actually called The Beauty Shoppe." He laughed at this. "My dad is the minister for Main Street Baptist Church."

"Really?" He looked at me curiously.

"Oh yeah. Really." I took another gulp of wine.

"I bet there were some rules in your house."

I nodded slowly. "There were, but my mom knows how to temper my father. They make a good team, and my dad loves us. There's no doubt."

"Must be hard to be away from them."

I swirled the wine gently in my cup. "Kind of, but I have a freedom here that I didn't at home. Don't get me wrong, I miss them, but it was time for me to make a name for myself."

He nodded and took another drink. "I know exactly where you're coming from. How about sisters, brothers ... you have any?"

I swallowed hard, not saying anything for a few seconds. I stared hard at the dishtowel beneath me. "I, uh, I do. Or I at least did." No matter how many years had passed, this part never got any easier. "My sister, Hannah, disappeared when I was twelve and she was fifteen."

I watched the color drain from Joshua's face. He touched the top of my free hand. "I am so sorry. I didn't mean to pry."

I shook my head. "It's a natural question. I'm not offended. It's a difficult subject and, let's face it, each of us has had some tough times in our lives." I polished off the wine and handed him my cup. He poured me another full cup and topped his off. "I just don't really like to talk about it."

He nodded sympathetically. "Of course not. Let's move on to something safe ... um, what kind of food do you like?"

This made us both laugh.

"I love food. Period. I love good Southern food, fish and chips—anything fattening."

"You are far from fat."

"I swim every day, now that I have a pool. And I do try to eat healthy, but I like to treat myself now and again."

"I hear that. In fact, I want to change up the menu here. I like the taco theme, but I want to add some things. I'd love to redo the place. It's a matter of money."

Simone's face popped into my head again. This might be the right time to mention her interest in investing in Nick's.

"You said something about that earlier." I rubbed my arms as it was getting chilly in the closet. "I might actually know someone who would be willing to help you."

"You cold?" he asked.

"No. Well, a little."

"Here." He started unbuttoning his long sleeved shirt.

Heat rose directly to my cheeks and dispersed itself all over my body. "Oh no! Don't do that. I don't want you to be cold, too."

"Don't be silly! I have a T-shirt underneath. I'll be fine."

He placed his shirt around my shoulders and I felt instantly more comfortable. "Thank you."

"No problem." He shifted himself into a more comfortable position and then peered at me interestedly. "You were saying you might know someone who could help me out?"

I nodded and took another sip. "Yes. So, you know I have a day job. I work for the pop star, Simone."

"Really? I mean I don't care for that kind of music much, but I know she's huge. What do you do for her?"

"I do her makeup."

"Women really have people do that? Does it pay well?"

"Men too, believe it or not. And yes, it pays very well, but I'm at her beck and call a good chunk of the time. Simone's okay though. A bit rough around the edges, but her heart is in the right place. Anyway, she was here not long ago, and she mentioned she'd be interested in buying the place."

He shook his head firmly. "No. I don't want to sell. At least I don't think I do."

"Maybe she could invest?"

Joshua pondered this for a minute. "Maybe, but she is so high profile, and I'm not sure I want that kind of publicity."

"Fair enough. But maybe she could be a silent investor. And she's not nearly as high maintenance as you might think." That's right, Evie. And there are snowballs in hell.

He rubbed his face thoughtfully. "Maybe. It might work. You really think she would be interested?"

"She's the one who said something to me. All I can do is talk to her."

"Okay. What do I have to lose?" He grinned and held his cup out towards me. "Shall we toast to my possible new business partner, Simone?"

I lifted my cup to meet his, "Cheers!" and quickly gulped the rest down. Now I had done it. Made a promise I wasn't sure I could keep. Simone was fickle and could have easily been talking out of her rear when she'd mentioned her interest in the bar.

A couple of hours later, and we had talked about Africa and his experiences there, how to make the best pot roast ever (we differed on this), our dogs, my cat, and life in general. I was beginning to think his mom had fallen asleep and not taken note that her son hadn't returned for the night.

"Who do you think might have killed Nick?" he asked at one point.

I gave him my take, leaving out his mother and the history surrounding her, Nick, and Candace.

"I wish I knew," he said.

"Me, too. He was a good man." I felt my tears well up at the thought of Nick. Clearly, I'd had far too much to drink.

"He must have been. He hired you."

I didn't know how to respond to that.

"Hey, can I ask if you have a boyfriend, or are you seeing anyone? I mean, I'm just curious. I'm not trying to, uh ... oh crap, maybe I've had too much wine."

I glanced over at the two empty bottles of wine next to me. "You think?"

He held up his now empty cup and turned it over, placing it on the floor. "Sorry. I don't mean to pry again."

"Don't worry about it. I mean, what the heck else are we supposed to do in here if not talk?" A searing vision of him leaning in to kiss me on the lips had me suddenly wishing I hadn't asked the question. Oh dear.

"Um, back to your question, I—"

Suddenly, the door to the storage closet opened with a sharp bang. There stood Becky. The look on her face went from shock to what I can only term as *What the eff?!* I stifled my laughter.

"You didn't come home, Joshua, so I came back here to see if there was a problem. You two just hanging out in here, drinking wine?" She crossed her arms, her eyes darting suspiciously from me to Joshua and back to me again.

Oh boy.

Joshua shot her a look of annoyance. "Yes, that's right, Mom. I like to invite my dates into the storage closet at work. There's nothing like a cold cement floor and wine in Styrofoam cups to make a lady feel special." He stood and brushed off his jeans, reaching a hand out to help me up. "We got locked in here, and I was hoping at some point you would notice I hadn't come home."

If anything, she looked more irritated than before. "I did. Let's go. Evie, you too." Her words were as clipped as her movements.

"I'm going to walk Evie to her car," Joshua said glancing back at his mother whose hands were now on her hips. If she could have come up with a good reason to stop him from helping me out, I'm certain she would have.

We made it to the van in a couple of minutes. He shoved his hands into his pockets and glanced back over his shoulder at where Becky still stood, watching us from the open back door of Nick's.

"Hey, sorry about her. She's been acting really strange. Anyway, uh, interesting evening." He smiled tentatively, looking even more handsome than he already was.

I smiled back "It was. Only next time, I think we should go out to a restaurant like normal friends, okay?" There, hopefully that removed some of the weirdness from the situation.

He laughed. "Okay. It's a date!"

Uh-oh. I swallowed and smiled again. "Yeah, well, I'll see you tomorrow. And thanks again for your help earlier tonight."

"My pleasure. Be safe! You okay to drive?"

"Yeah. I think you drank the lion's share, and we've had a few hours to sober up."

He winked at me. "I think I did drink the lion's share, but I had some great company."

For one awkward moment, I thought he might be leaning in to kiss me but he simply reached around to open my door. It didn't help that Becky chose that moment to squawk out his name from across the street. Joshua rolled his eyes and waited until I'd fired up the VW before making his way back to the bar and his overbearing mother.

Well, that was definitely an interesting night. I headed home, replaying the evening in my mind. The most prevalent question, aside from wondering where our conversation would have gone if Becky hadn't shown up when she did, was whether or not someone or something locked us in that storage closet? And, if so, why?

CHAPTER THIRTY-FOUR

CASS AND MAC WERE as happy to see me as I was them. I put the kettle on the stove to make some tea and then trudged upstairs to my room and switched out of my jeans and into sweats. I also put on a clean t-shirt. Mine still smelled of Joshua after wearing his long-sleeved shirt, and for a second, I thought about keeping it on (what can I say? He smelled good). But then I couldn't resist changing into something I hadn't spent the evening working and sweating in.

No sign of Lucas, or Bob, or Janis. They must've all been on another tier, recharging their vibrations, or whatever else spirits busied themselves doing. It was kind of disconcerting, considering this whole Black Tier out-to-get-me thing, and the night I'd had. But I felt relatively safe in the house. And Lucas had assured me he'd placed some kind of temporary barrier on the place to help protect me.

As I made my way back downstairs, the whistle of the kettle shrilled loudly. Then it stopped. And so did I. I closed my eyes for a second and sighed, wondering who had removed the kettle from the stove. I looked down at Cass, my canine barometer, and she didn't seem edgy at all, so I took that as a good sign. I continued my walk downstairs and stepped out of the hall and into the kitchen.

"Lucas," I said, spotting him next to the stove. He'd brought someone with him.

"Evie. This is Roger Hawks."

"Hi, Roger," I said, rather more calmly than I felt.

He nodded at me. "Hello. Nice to meet you."

Roger had classic movie-star good looks. His hair was light brown, and he had high cheekbones, a medium build, and the same luminescent eyes as Lucas (except Roger's were a deep, sea green).

Lucas nodded at me and then looked over at Roger who stood at his side, seeming nervous.

"Roger has never actually been back to this area of the Grey Tier. He hasn't wanted or needed to, so talking to a live human and coming through the portal is a little bit of a challenge for him. But he wanted to try and help when he heard about Nick."

Roger made a soft sound, like he was clearing his throat. "I, uh, I haven't felt or seen Nick's vibration at all, and I'm not sure what tier he might be on."

"Oh, okay." Yes, tonight was clearly my night for genius repartee. "So I guess Lucas has told you I've been trying to figure out Nick's murder on my own?"

Roger nodded slowly, as if he were underwater. I guess this must be what Lucas was referring to when he said it was a challenge for Roger to come here. "Yes. He did tell me that."

I forged ahead. "And your name has come up quite a bit. I mean, with what happened to you ... the night you died."

"Lucas mentioned that as well."

Roger was not only uneasy, he didn't seem to be much of a conversationalist. I decided it was time for a more blunt approach.

"Roger, were you murdered?"

If he seemed taken aback by my frankness, he didn't show it. He shook his head with that same slow movement. "Not intentionally, but I was killed at the hands of someone else."

"Do you know who did it?" I took in a deep breath of air and held it ... waiting, hoping for an affirmative response.

"Yes, I do." I waited patiently for an answer that seemed a very long time in coming. "It was my girlfriend at the time, who was also sleeping with Nick. We fought and she pushed me into the pool. I was drunk, and I hit my head on the corner tiles and, well, that was it." He shrugged.

"Your girlfriend? Rebecca Styles?" I had a sudden memory of Candace telling me her suspicions that Becky had been Roger's real killer. When you're right, well, you're right.

"The one and only. Becky killed me, right after she told me she was pregnant."

I shook my head in disbelief, my mouth slowly dropping open. If Becky had murdered Roger and gotten away with it all these years, would she have done it again? Had she killed Nick too? And while we were on the topic, was Nick really even Joshua's father?

CHAPTER THIRTY-FIVE

"THAT WAS NOT WHAT I expected," I said to Lucas, who was pacing the hardwood floors. Roger had gone back through the portal to the safety of whatever tier he vibrated on. I sat on the sofa, watching Lucas circling the room like a caged tiger. In the past, he'd sit next to me and we would talk, but after our last few encounters ... it seemed we weren't as cozy together as we'd once been.

"What do you mean?" He stopped, hands on hips, looked at me with those damn eyes of his. I felt another stab of sheer, piercing lust travel through me. Oh, hell. I was a hormonal wreck.

"I mean, I'm happy he knows what happened to him. Closure and all. But now I know, too, and there's nothing I can do about it."

"But now you know this Becky woman killed him, don't you think she could have also murdered Nick?" He started pacing again.

I tilted my head to the side, pondering the various possibilities in my head. "Maybe."

"I'd say more than maybe," he said.

"I don't know. You heard Roger. He said she didn't kill him on purpose."

"But she did kill him, and she's gotten away with it. For almost thirty years."

I took a sip from my tea, which was now cool, and worked up the courage to bring Joshua into the conversation. "So you know the guy who was here with the dog?"

He stopped pacing again and narrowed his eyes. "The one who kept staring at you when you weren't looking?"

"No, he wasn't. He was outside playing with the dogs! And while we're on the topic, how would you know he was staring unless you'd been spying on me?" I felt myself beginning to get annoyed. But Lucas seemed oblivious.

"Here let me show the hot girl with the dog that I, too, am a dog lover and there you have it..." He snapped his fingers, and red sparks shot into the air.

Whoa. My eyes narrowed, matching his. "There you have what?"

"Nothing." He muttered, starting to pace again.

Oh, for the love of... "What? You have what?"

He stopped, throwing his hands up into the air in a very human gesture. "You have sex and love and all of that! That guy is into you, that's all I am saying. And that's fine, because he's a human and he's alive and I'm not."

Oh. "Oh."

Lucas seemed to deflate suddenly and I felt a little sorry for him. "So, what do you want to tell me about this guy?"

"Well, for starters, we are not having sex." Where had that come from? Honestly, if my mouth weren't attached to my face, I'd have to wonder if it had a mind of its own.

Lucas' eyebrows shot up. "Okaaay. And if you were, well, that's none of my business. I am here to keep you safe and so far, that guy doesn't look as if he'd harm you. And like I said, it isn't so much the live humans I worry about with you."

I wanted to tell him about the men at the bar and how Joshua had stepped in to assist and then we got trapped in the storage closet, but instead, I said, "That guy who was here, the one who I am not having sex with, is Becky's son."

Lucas finally looked something other than frustrated. "That guy, what's his name?"

"Joshua."

"Joshua is Rebecca Styles son?"

"Yes." He appeared to be catching on. "And according to Becky, Nick was his father and Nick signed over his bar to Joshua in his will."

Lucas crossed his arms, deep in thought. "But Roger said this Becky was his girlfriend and she was pregnant."

"Bingo. So now I'm starting to wonder, who is Joshua's real father?"

"And now, you know what I'm thinking?" He shook a finger at me. "I'm thinking maybe this guy is not so good after all. He could easily be in cahoots with Mommy Dearest. Those two could've murdered Nick for the bar and whatever else he left behind."

I chewed my lip, pondering. "I don't know, Lucas. Could Becky have murdered Nick? Yes. But Joshua just returned from Africa volunteering for the Red Cross, so he's hardly a candidate for murder. And he honestly seemed surprised by the whole situation ... inheriting the bar, finding out Nick was his father... "I figured I would leave the part out about Joshua spending five years in jail for manslaughter.

"The Red Cross?" Lucas laughed.

"Yes." I crossed my arms, starting to feel annoyed again.

"Wow ... this guy is good. Why didn't I think of that line back in the day?"

I rolled my eyes and resisted tossing one of the sofa cushions at Lucas' head. Besides, it probably would have gone right through him. "Oh, please, I don't think he's trying to trick me."

"Then you are more naïve than I thought!"

Okay, enough. "Look, Lucas. Joshua saved me tonight," I snapped. "For someone who's trying to dupe me, or whatever it is you think he's doing, he's sure going to great lengths."

"What?!" Lucas stood incredibly still and an orange-yellow glow began to creep around the edges of his normal indigo aura. "What are you talking about?"

I sighed. And then told him the entire story, even the part about the storage closet. He didn't say anything for a long time.

"Lucas, you're making me really nervous."

"I think they were from the Black Tier. They were sent to mess with you." He sounded worried and confused. "This is all about your gift. But there is something more. They are after your vibration at a level I've not seen before."

"What do you mean, exactly?"

"First, it was Pierre and the jaguar."

"Anastasia." I shuddered, recalling my brush with death on Simone's music video set.

"And someone followed you home. Now this thing tonight. I've seen the Black Tier go after people before, people with healing gifts, or any kind of gift that promotes goodness in this world, but there is something bigger at work here, and I don't know what it is yet. It's as if they are trying to trip you up or something."

"Well, it didn't work."

Lucas looked at me solemnly, his mouth in a grim line. "Not yet, but they don't play fair. You realize that?"

"Yes, that's pretty clear," I said, nodding.

"Based on all you've told me, well, I need to visit the Bodha."

"Now?" I'm sorry to say I might have whined a bit.

"Yes," he said, walking over to me. It was the closest we'd been to all night.

"Could you wait?" I asked, pleadingly. Truth was, after my wild night and even with the protection in place on the house, I didn't feel entirely safe.

Lucas sighed, "Evie…"

"Just until I fall asleep, okay? That's all." He looked down at me for a minute, his face a mirror of the conflict going on in his head. And then he took my hand and gently tugged me off of the couch.

"Come on. Let's tuck you in."

CHAPTER THIRTY-SIX

LUCAS STAYED UNTIL I fell asleep. Of course, I don't know when he left, but he wasn't there the next day.

I was trying so hard to focus on the here and now—on humans and human interactions—but let's face it, it wasn't easy. My brain was on tiers, and black versus white, and all the bits and pieces in between. And on Lucas. However, after Roger's visit last night, I'd been able to fill in some key details of Nick's mysterious life. And now I had an additional mystery: Was Nick really Joshua's father? Or was Roger? And if Becky could accidentally kill Roger ... well, was it too much of a stretch to imagine she'd killed Nick in a fit of anger as well? Lastly, I felt obligated to tell someone, anyone, about Becky's involvement in Roger's death. But who? I mean, showing up at a local police station saying, "Hey, the ghost of Roger Hawks visited me last night at my house and told me his ex-girlfriend Becky Styles killed him. But it was mostly an accident." Yeah, that'd go over real well ... likely ending with me in seventy-two-hour hold at County General.

At the end of the day, Nick was still dead and his killer was on the loose. This needed to be my main focus for now. As for the past, it only mattered so much as it shed light on the current situation. So I hardened my resolve to focus on Nick's death and deal with the other stuff once I'd gotten answers about that.

But first, Simone.

Later that day, after making up Simone for a book signing event to promote a book she had not actually written (although her name was on the cover), she insisted we play dress-up and go out to eat.

Although Simone was kinda, sorta of on my list of suspects in a roundabout way via Dwight, I knew I needed to go back and investigate George Hernandez and Pietro SanGiacomo at Jorge's and I would need some back up. I was a bit nervous they'd recognized me from my earlier stint as a private investigator, which is why I figured having Simone along would be a good foil.

Simone and I were already in my van, driving down the road, when I nonchalantly said, "I was thinking we should eat somewhere else tonight. I mean, normal people do eat at other places besides Denny's, you know."

Simone looked at me suspiciously. Thing was, she loved Denny's and wasn't very open to branching out to other restaurants. "Like where?"

"Oh I don't know. How about Mexican? There's this nice little place in Venice Beach I know of but..." I frowned as if reconsidering.

"But what? Spit it out, Edie!"

"Well, maybe it's too much of a risk. You might be seen and..."

Simone interrupted me, "Venice Beach? Let's go."

Gotcha!

I parked on a side street about two blocks from Jorge's. I sighed and turned to Simone. I'd been trying to figure out how to use her in my evening antics. I figured the best way to do so was to be up front and see how she reacted.

"Okay, you know how you like to play dress-up on these outings? You look good tonight, by the way."

Simone smiled. "I am Debby tonight, and are you trying to hit on me, Evie? I mean, I have kissed a girl before. But I'm not that into it. For you though..." She closed her eyes and leaned towards me with puckered lips.

"Come on, Simone! I'm being serious here," I said, exasperated and not a little curious how she'd respond when I dropped the other shoe. I cleared my throat, "Tonight, I am also going incognito."

Simone's eyes popped open and her mouth made a little O of surprise. And then she grinned. "Really? How cool. But why?"

"We have a job to do," I said, reaching into the backseat for the duffle bag holding my wig and some other stuff.

"A job? What the fuck are you talking about?"

Here goes nothing. "The guy who owns this restaurant is, well, not a nice guy. He knew Nick, and he was out to get him because he claims Nick stole his fish taco recipe."

Simone frowned, and then laughed out loud. "You gotta be kidding me! That is so lame."

"It is, I agree. The thing is, this guy, George Hernandez, and this other guy, Pietro SanGiacomo, who is some kind of bookie and who also had it out for Nick, are involved in something shady together. I think they may have had Nick killed or, I don't know, I just need some answers and you get to help me."

Simone eyed me for a long minute. "Priceless," she muttered, shaking her head. "Should I start calling you Sherlock now?"

"Look, are you in or not?" I didn't want to spend the rest of the evening in my VW being insulted. I had a job to do.

"Yeah, okay. I'm in. But if this was the plan all along, why didn't you just spit it out in the first place? I mean, you didn't have to try and persuade me to go to this place instead of Denny's ... you could have just told me your plans."

"You're right, Simone. I'm sorry. I just ... I guess I thought I had to get you here first and you'd be more open to helping me out once we arrived."

Simone rolled her eyes but she was smiling too. "Whatever. So, what's the plan?"

"We go in. We eat. You be Debby and I'll be, uh, Chantal."

"Chantal?!" Simone barked out a laugh. "You do realize that's a total porn name, right?"

I didn't bother responding. "There's an office upstairs above the restaurant. When you're paying the bill, I am going to get up and act like I'm going to the bathroom. I need you to create some kind of distraction so no one sees me go up the stairs and into George's office. Give it about ten minutes, then head out to the van and wait for me."

We spent the next few minutes donning our disguises and once everything was in place, Debby and Chantal, two friends on the town, stepped out of a beat-up VW and made their way to Jorge's for dinner.

An hour or so and a margarita later, we were finishing up a tasty plate of tacos and enchiladas. I had not seen George or Pietro and figured it was a positive sign. The waitress (thankfully, not the same one from the last time I'd been here) dropped the check off at the table. I leaned across towards Simone.

"You still up for this?" I asked in a lowered voice.

"Hell, yes!"

Simone put the credit card in the bill folder and I waited until I noticed the waitress making her way back to our table before I got up to leave. As I headed toward the stairs, I heard Simone say, "You overcharged me!"

I quickly glanced around and headed up the stairs. So far so good. First, I'd try the office I had heard Pietro and George in before. Of course it was locked, but I had a trick up my sleeve, one I could thank my big sister, Hannah, for teaching me. I reached into my pocket and pulled out the necessary item ...

... and picked the lock with a little effort. I was in the office in under two minutes. I closed the door behind me, using the light on my phone to look around. George's office was large with a desk, file drawers, and an interesting looking printer. On the floor next to the printer lay an aluminum briefcase. I picked it up and opened it. My breath caught in my throat. It was filled with hundreds of hundred-dollar bills! I looked back over at the strange printing machine and put two and two together. These guys were laundering money!

Unfortunately, my great revelation came a little too late. Because the next thing I knew, there were footsteps outside the door and then it flew open.

It took all of ten seconds for George Hernandez to spot me, standing in the middle of his office like a deer in the headlights.

"What the hell?!" He shut the door behind him. I tried to sprint past him and make it to the door. But even though he was a big guy, he was surprisingly fast. George grabbed my arm, spun me around, placed a big, beefy hand over my mouth, and tossed me to the ground. My wig flew off and my head clanked hard against a metal file cabinet. On top of feeling dizzy, our skin-to-skin contact kept sending me disturbing visions of flames and George running from a house engulfed in flames.

Before my mind could register more, George had placed duct tape across my mouth and tied my hands and feet together. I was, to put it bluntly, trussed up like a rodeo calf. This was not good.

George eyed me carefully, echoing my thoughts, "Not good," he said. "This is not good."

You're telling me.

He dropped into a nearby armchair and stared at me glumly. "What were you doing here?" He wiped the perspiration from his brow. "What am I going to do? I can't let you go. Not now that you've seen this." He ripped the duct tape off, giving me a good idea why those poor ladies always winced in pain when my mom gave them a lip wax.

I cried out, tears springing to my eyes.

George darted a nervous glance back at the closed door, and hissed, "Shut up! What were you doing here?"

"I-I thought you killed Nick. I was trying to find something to incriminate you."

He threw up his hands angrily, "I didn't kill Nick!" He placed the duct tape back over my lips. "I may not be on the up-and- up, girly, but I'm no killer. That's why this is a problem." He sighed and took out his cell phone. Whoever he was calling, didn't answer. "I'll be back. I may not be a killer, but I know someone who is."

In the ominous silence of George's empty office, I frantically tried to come up with an escape plan. Simone had to come looking for me. Didn't she? Wouldn't she? I simply couldn't lie around, waiting for her. I had to do something.

My cell phone was in my pocket. I scooted as close as I could to the file cabinet and attempted to push the phone up and out of my pocket by rubbing against the cabinet's corner. It took a few tries, but it worked. The phone popped out onto the ground and I used my hip to slide it over a bit until I was sure I could reach it with my nose if I bent at the waist. Yeah, not the most glamorous situation but you use what you've got when the going gets tough. My nose kept hitting the utilities button but finally, the phone screen lit up. Thankfully, Simone was the last person I had dialed. I pressed the button and it began to ring. After three rings it went to voicemail. Shit.

I tried again and she finally picked up.

"Evie! Where the hell are you?"

I grunted as loudly as I could into the phone.

"Evie?! Where are you? Let's go!"

I grunted and groaned again, this time louder. Finally, she clued in.

"Oh no! Are you in trouble?"

"Mhhm-mmh." Hallelujah!

"Okay, are you still there? In that office?"

"Mhhm."

"Oh fuck! Okay, I'm coming in!" She hung up and I stared at the phone wondering if I should even try to call 9-1-1.

Five minutes later I heard a loud commotion downstairs. A minute after that, the office door swung open, and there stood Simone, in all her glory, and a very shocked looking restaurant hostess. Simone marched into the office as if it she owned it and knelt down beside me.

"Come on, Evie," she said calmly and began untying my hands. She tossed a glance back at the hostess. "Well, don't just stand there, moron. Go call the cops!"

As soon as she'd left the room and Simone pulled the duct tape off, I jumped dizzily to my feet and hissed, "We gotta get the hell out of here. Now!"

Simone nodded. "Roger that, girlfriend."

I took her arm and she guided me rapidly down the stairs, out the front door (we were lucky the hostess had her back to us or we'd have never made it), and to the van.

"I can't drive, Simone. I got knocked up pretty bad back there. My keys are in my purse." She loaded me into the passenger seat, found my keys, and we peeled out of the parking lot at lightning speed (for my VW, that is). I wondered, fleetingly, where George had gone.

We drove in silence for a good five minutes. Finally, she turned to me, her face questioning and concerned.

"What the hell happened back there?"

I filled her in on all the gory details. She giggled when I got to the part about me dialing her number with my nose. And then, after another pause, she said, "The cops are going to get involved. The only way to get that twit of a hostess out of my way was to take my wig off." She sighed. "Are you okay? What did he do to you?"

I rubbed my wrists. "I hit my head when he tackled me and then he elbowed me during the struggle. I'm sore but it could be a lot worse. I probably need some Tylenol and a good night's sleep." I peered at her in the darkened car. "I'm so sorry for getting you involved in this. Maybe we should call the cops and give our side of the story. I can emphasize how you saved me from a killer…"

"First of all, don't apologize. That's the most fun I've had in years. And secondly, we were never there. Okay? Never. Yeah, maybe we should tell the police the whole story, but when the cops arrive, they'll see what those guys were up to with the money laundering thing and they'll be all over that. The last thing they'll be interested in is a random Simone sighting. If I get involved and it's all over the media…" She shuddered dramatically. "I don't even want to think about it."

"But Simone, you used a credit card to pay for dinner." Yet another indication I hadn't thought this plan through nearly enough before we waltzed into Jorge's for dinner.

She shook her head. "Oh, that was Dwight's."

"But won't they connect anything?"

"No. I'll tell him to say it was stolen." The van wobbled dramatically as we sped up onto the freeway. "God, I don't know why you still drive around in this bucket of crap. I need to give you a raise so you can afford a decent car."

I shut my eyes and smiled. Normally, Simone's constant disparaging comments about the VW were annoying as hell. But I felt lucky to be in the van at all right now, considering how grim things were looking about thirty minutes ago.

Simone continued, "Anyway, like I told you before, I don't like the paparazzi and they love this kind of shit. So it's best if we play dumb. And who knows … once the cops are on the scene and they track down George and Pietro, maybe they'll confess to murdering Nick."

I nodded tiredly. "Maybe. But I don't think they killed him. At least, I'm pretty sure Hernandez didn't."

"Why's that?"

I recalled how reluctant George was to do much more than rough me up. "My gut. Hernandez could have easily killed me just now, but he didn't."

"He went to get someone to do it, though."

"True. But I still don't think he did it."

Fifteen minutes later, Simone pulled up to her place. "Do you want to come in? Or maybe I can have Dwight drop you off at the house and someone can bring your van over tomorrow?"

"I'm fine, thanks. I just want to go home. I think I'll be a bit sore tomorrow." I slowly stepped across the stickshift over to the driver's side.

"Okay. Well, thanks for the fun." She winked at me.

"Remember, mum's the word. And be careful."

I nodded, too tired to speak at this point.

Once I got home and greeted the animals, I made myself a cup of tea, took some Tylenol, and headed outside to look at the sparkling lights below. I was achy, but not too bad. I'd recover.

I couldn't help but wonder what happened when the cops finally arrived. Had they caught George? I sure hoped so. I was feeling a bit conflicted about not notifying the cops. It seemed, well, wrong not to give them my side of the story. But I was also loyal to Simone and didn't want to cause her additional problems.

As soon as I opened the patio door, Cass darted past me and made a beeline for the pool. She'd been cooped up inside with Mac while I was gone, so I figured she was eager to blow off some steam with a quick swim. She started barking, loudly.

"Cass! Just give me a sec, okay? I need to unwind a little." But she didn't stop. Instead, she got more insistent and ran back and forth from me to the pool a few times. Looked like I wasn't going to get a break tonight. I turned the pool lights on, hoping to find her ball in the water. Sometimes a toy was enough to distract her for a few minutes.

Instead, I found something else. Someone else. A scream caught in my throat as Cass continued barking maniacally. There was a body in my pool. And although it was face down, I recognized its clothes almost immediately. Jackson Owens.

CHAPTER THIRTY-SEVEN

AFTER CALLING THE POLICE, I went through the house, frantically calling out for Lucas. Cass was at my heels with Mac trotting more slowly behind. I had no idea if Lucas could hear me. Frankly, after tonight, we were going to have to establish some rules. Like how to reach him in the event that I came home to find a dead man in my swimming pool.

I thought about calling Simone. I needed someone to talk to. I was scared and my mind was running rampant with all kinds of crazy thoughts. But involving Simone would have consequences I wasn't sure I wanted to deal with.

The only level-headed person I could think to call was Joshua.

The police arrived only minutes before he did. They told him to remain in the kitchen while the police questioned me in the family room. I could see him peering around the corner, though. Still no sign of Lucas.

"So you came home and found Mr. Owens's body in the pool?"

"Yes." I glanced outside and could see people out there with a body bag. I turned away, not knowing if Jackson had already been taken out of the pool.

"And where were you this evening?"

Here we go. "With my boss."

The policeman raised his eyebrows. "Does your boss have a name?"

I sighed. "Yes. Simone."

"Simone what?"

"Simone. As in the Simone ."

The officer's eyebrows shot up almost to his hairline. "Huh. That is really interesting."

You don't know the half of it, buddy. "And it's really true."

Officer Eyebrows nodded. "We'll have to verify this with Ms. Simone. What were you doing with her?"

Now it was time for some fancy footwork. "We ate dinner together."

"Where?"

"At her place." Lie number one, fire away.

"Hey Hansen, come over here, I need you to check on something."

I groaned inwardly. "What? You don't believe me?"

The officer looked me in the eye. "Ma'am, there's a dead guy in your pool. At this point, everything you say needs to be verified."

Oh God, oh God. I could feel beads of sweat pooling in my armpits. What if Simone told them the truth about where we'd been tonight? How would that look to the police? Not so good. I needed to text her.

"Can I use the bathroom?"

He eyed me skeptically. "We aren't finished here."

"I'm not feeling so well. I'll be right back."

He sighed, shrugged, and agreed to let me pee. I darted to the nearest bathroom, closed and locked the door, and sent Simone a quick text: We ate dinner at your house. Then I put the phone on silent mode. I knew Simone would be confused by the message until the cops got there. I hoped she read it. And I hoped she didn't suddenly gain a conscience.

I left the bathroom and bumped into Joshua. "You okay?" He looked deeply concerned, as if he wanted to give me a hug.

I sniffed audibly, tears welling up in my eyes. "Not really."

Just then, Officer Eyebrows came up behind Joshua and cleared his throat. "Sorry, sir, but I have a few more questions for Miss Preston."

Joshua hesitated and then finally nodded, stepping back but staying closer than he had before.

The officer held a cell phone in his gloved hands. I could only assume it belonged to Jackson. "Did Mr. Owens ever threaten you?"

I shook my head. "No. I mean, he was kind of strange at times. But he never threatened to harm me." I explained to the officer how I'd known Jackson, and about his obsession with Nick. I gave him as much detail as I could. I also mentioned how he had been asked recently to stay out of the bar because of inappropriate behavior.

"Were you ever aware of him or anyone following you?"

I started to shake my head but then I remembered ...

"The other night, a week or so ago, someone did follow me home. I made it into my gate, but they slowed way down and even stopped until my gate closed. I couldn't see the driver, though."

The officer held up the cell phone with a photo showing a picture of the back of my van with the gate closing. "This your car?"

"Yes." I was shocked.

"This is Mr. Owens's phone. It would appear he's been watching you quite a bit." The officer scanned through several photos. They were all of me. Me in the bar. Me and Cass in the backyard playing. Me serving food or playing music. Me in my car.

"Looks like this guy had a real thing for you, Miss Preston."

"Oh my. I mean, I don't know what to say." I was beyond creeped out.

"And you weren't aware?"

"No! Not at all." The whole thing was troubling. Jackson had been following me, watching me, taking pictures of me. But why?

The other cop who had been given Simone's information came back.

"Story checks out. I just spoke with Simone and she says they had dinner at her place. But get this, some weirdo in Venice says Simone stormed into a Mexican joint tonight and rescued a girl who was tied up in the owner's office. Even better, our people discovered a money laundering shop set up in the restaurant. They arrested the owner as he was getting out of his car out back. Some dude named George Hernandez. He was with another dude. Pietro SanGiacomo. Looks like they could've been in cahoots together on the dirty money business."

"Any sign of said kidnapped victim and Simone?"

The other cop shook his head ... and then they shared a laugh.

"Hell of a story, right? Probably someone who works for her and thought it might make a good publicity stunt. Celebrities." He eyed me.

I shrugged. So, George went to get Pietro to kill me. Did that mean he'd killed Nick? "Like I said, we had dinner at her place. Simone hates the paparazzi and wouldn't be caught dead at a restaurant with less than four stars."

He nodded. "Right."

I tried not to be too obvious when I let out a sigh of relief.

The two officers moved to the other side of the room to consult with a third, more official-looking fellow. I watched, waited, caught Joshua's eye, and mustered a weak smile.

A few minutes later the lead officer came back.

"Thank you for your time, Miss Preston. We're almost finished up here and we'll be out of your hair soon. But from what the detectives can tell, we think Mr. Owens was stalking you. We don't know how he slipped and fell into the pool, but we assume he probably wasn't paying attention, hit his head on the edge, and drowned. That's for the coroner to figure out. We did find some medication in Mr. Owens' bag for a bipolar condition. There's a good chance he might have been off his meds, and that contributed to his erratic behavior. In any case, we appreciate your cooperation, and there's a chance we'll need to speak further with you in the next day or so. Anyway, I'll be in touch."

I nodded, trying to process all this new information about Jackson. Bipolar disorder? Now I didn't know if I should feel sorry for the guy or just be glad he wouldn't be stalking me anymore. "You don't think it was foul play?"

"Can't be sure, but from what we've assessed so far, it doesn't appear to be. To start with, we found only one set of tracks out there."

"Thank you again for all your help. Can I go see my friend now?"

For the first time that night, the officer seemed sympathetic. "Sure. You must be pretty tired after all this."

I found Joshua and he wrapped his arms around me.

"Oh, Evie, I am so sorry. Are you okay?"

I was about as far from okay as someone could possibly get. But I didn't think this was the time or the place to tell that to Joshua. "I'll be fine. I'm just so ... wow. I mean, Jackson was stalking me and they think he died accidentally."

"Are you serious? That's just insane. I'm so glad you're okay."

I looked up at him to thank him when something caught my eye.

No.

Someone.

It was Lucas, about three feet behind us, his arms crossed and an unhappy expression on his face.

CHAPTER THIRTY-EIGHT

"WHAT WAS I SUPPOSED to do?" I asked, not for the first time that night. "I called and called! It's not like I can reach you by phone!"

Lucas paced back and forth on my bedroom's hardwood floor. Cass's dark eyes followed his every move.

"Are you seeing that guy? Is he a boyfriend or something?"

I crossed my arms over my chest, having lost pretty much all patience with Lucas at this point. "No. I'm not. He's a friend. I told you that!"

"The way he was holding you and looking at you, I'd say he wants more than friendship."

I rolled my eyes in exasperation. "Really, Lucas? Is that all you have to say to me tonight? Because, newsflash: A dead man was found in my swimming pool, a man who'd apparently been stalking me for the last few weeks. And by the way, I wouldn't have had to call Joshua if you'd simply shown up when I needed you in the first place!"

Lucas stopped pacing and frowned, his voice calmer. "I tried to come as quickly as I could. But it's not as easy as simply hopping into a car and driving over. Sometimes, it takes time."

And then he moved next to me in the blink of an eye. "But I'm here now," he said, looking intently into my face.

All the anger in the room vanished, leaving behind tension of an entirely different sort. He stepped back from me and made a large sweeping motion around us with his arms. Suddenly, we were encapsulated in a giant bubble of color. Lucas moved towards me again and kept moving until the backs of my legs hit the bed behind me.

"I'm here now," Lucas repeated, this time in a husky voice that sent adrenaline running through me.

And then we were on the bed, surrounded by the softly glowing bubble.

Cass whined and slunk out of the room.

The lights in the room clicked off and the small cluster of candles on my vanity popped into flame. We stared at one another for a long moment. I was on my back with his weight pressing me firmly into the mattress. And then his hands began to unbutton my blouse, with the deftness of someone who'd done this many, many times before.

"Lucas, what are..." His mouth moved slowly downwards, and he began dropping kisses along my neck, and then my chest, until arriving at the top of my bra.

"Shhh, Evie. No questions."

He reached his hands behind me making short work of my bra. And then he began kissing my breasts, slowly, gently. It was heavenly ... and deliciously sinful, all at once.

Lucas continued to kiss his way further down my exposed torso, past my ribcage, over my stomach, to my hips, and then, after helping me wriggle out of my jeans and underpants, his hot mouth was between my legs doing incredible things. The bubble around us brightened into a full blaze of hot pink. I tried to grab the top of his head to pull him up, but he wouldn't budge. Eventually, I realized he was exactly where I wanted him. And then, I simply stopped thinking at all.

A few delicious minutes later, Lucas eased his way back up my body and brought a finger to my lips, our mouths only inches apart. I closed my eyes and inhaled. He smelled ... fantastic. Deep and wild, like a male ... but with an underlying note of something sweet ... vanilla? Cinnamon? And then he placed his mouth over mine and all thought flew out of my head.

I'd read some of the romances my mom kept at her salon. They always described how kisses tasted ... like honey or nectar ... blah, blah, blah. Not this kiss. Lucas tasted ... pure and sweet and salty. It was enduring and all encompassing.

Lucas stood up then and the tips of his fingers began to emit a pale, pinkish glow. He waved his hands around us, creating another large bubble. The rosy glow spread across the bed and above us. Lucas closed the circle and repeated the movement. In a few seconds, the large bubble's colors intensified. My curiosity piqued, I reached out to touch the softly curving walls.

"Luster," he said.

"Luster?" I stared up into his beautiful eyes.

"It's a form of protection ... and privacy. No being on any tier can see us, feel us, know us, or be with us in this moment. We are utterly invisible and safe for a period of time."

"I hope it's a long time," I said breathlessly.

"Not long enough," he responded. Then his hand reached around to the small of my back and he pulled me up close to him. There was nothing soft and ethereal about Lucas now. His fingers traveled to my hips. I shuddered.

He bent his head down and kissed my mouth again. My breath caught in my throat. Lucas was, quite simply, a work of art. I had never thought a man's body all that special. I mean, I love a nice body—you know—six-pack abs, nice muscle, shapely legs, etc. But I've never been rendered speechless at the sight of a nude male.

And then along came Lucas.

I'm embarrassed to say that I gawked like a schoolgirl. Lucas laughed and dropped back to his knees, crawling slowly, slowly over my body. The way he stared at me, like he wanted to eat me up, kicked my senses into overdrive.

I was completely lost in his touch—his hands, his lips, they were everywhere, leaving a searing trail of heat from my mouth to my belly and beyond. The second he entered me ... I felt my body ride wave after wave with him until the surrounding luster pulsed brighter and brighter and then seemed to burst out of us both in an explosion of deep fuchsia and purple. Then I allowed myself to fade into it, over and over again.

I don't know how long we made love. I do know when we were lying in each other's arms afterwards, Lucas lost some of his clarity. I couldn't see him as clearly and vibrantly as I had before, and the luster had lightened significantly.

"Why are you so much lighter now?" I finally asked.

"I allowed the feelings the Black Tier wanted me to feel get in the way. When I saw you being held by Joshua, my anger, jealousy, frustration—all took hold. Then, we made love, and again—a very human act—all of that diminished my vibration."

"Is it permanent?" I asked, afraid I had caused this change in him.

"No. But I will have to rest for a period."

"How will you do that?"

"I have to go through the portal and find space."

"Find space, like outer space?"

"No. Just simple space."

I propped myself up on one elbow, trying hard to understand what he meant. "Is it empty space?"

"It's nothing. I go there and there is nothing to distract me ... nothing for me to do ... but to be and to rest."

"No one else is there?"

"No. The space was created by the White Tier for this reason, for spirits to refocus and refresh themselves."

"I take it that no spirits from the Black Tier can go there."

He shook his head. "No, it's only open to grey and white spirits."

"Tell me, how do I find you again? I mean, like tonight … is there a way I can get you to hear me more quickly?"

He kissed the top of my head. "I'm sorry about tonight. I was on another tier, and I didn't hear you until just before I arrived." He dropped his head back onto the pillow with a frustrated sigh. "Usually, I make sure someone else is available for you—someone like Bob or Janis, who can come when you call. But today, well, I didn't and that was my mistake."

"What were you doing on another tier?"

He smiled. "I'll let you know when I can."

"I get tired of your secrets." I sighed, flopping my own head back down on the bed.

"I know. So when I am on another tier, it's very hard for me to sense you and it can take a while to reach me. If I have another spirit on watch, then they can help you and locate me a lot faster."

"Can I ask you, what's it like to be there?"

He turned his head towards me. "To be dead?"

I nodded.

"It's fascinating, actually. When you're born here, as a living human, you're born knowing certain things right off the bat. Things you don't even have to think about. You know how to breathe. Your heart knows how to beat. When I arrived there, I immediately understood what a portal was. I didn't know the laws around them, but I knew I had come through one and that they existed. I knew intrinsically about the various tiers. I knew the only tier one could not come back from without special intervention was the Black."

"Explain, please." I began making small circles on his chest, just below his collarbone.

"Okay. I am going to use you as an example, though."

I cringed. "I hate when you do that."

"I know, but I have my reasons."

"Fine." I batted my eyelashes. "Use me."

"I plan to." He laughed, his voice deepening a shade, and then grew serious. "But first, the thing with the Black Tier and the no return policy. In most instances, a spirit cannot return from there. It's a permanent situation."

I blew out a puff of air. "Eternity."

"Eternity," he repeated. "But remember, every human has free choice. You can choose to go one way or the other. Fact is, each of us is born carrying some darkness and some light inside of us. But some are born with more of one than the other."

"That doesn't seem fair."

"Well, on the surface, yeah, it seems like a raw deal. But I can tell you, the universe works hard to stay in balance, and everything really does happen for a reason."

"What reason is there to give a newborn baby less of a fighting chance to be a good person, a happy person? Who makes the rules?"

Lucas chuckled. "Well, that's the big question, isn't it, Love? Who indeed?" He reached over and grabbed my hand on his chest, squeezing it gently. "Just know this doesn't mean those who are born into the Grey Tier—those who have, as you called it, the raw deal are not automatically transferred to the Black Tier at the moment of death. They just have extra work to do in the Grey to get to the White. And then there are those with vibrations like yours..." I lifted my head and looked at him. "Your spirit can wind up in the Black if you're, well, tempted. Seduced."

"Really? Well, what do you call this?" I laughed, gesturing at the bed, and our naked limbs intertwined beneath the sheets.

Lucas barked out a laugh. "Good point." His smile faded. "But listen to me, because this is important." He propped himself up on his side, giving me a long, serious look. "A seducer can come in any form. They are all around you. They make you see things in a different way, they make you feel things in a different way, they make you want things in a different way."

"Like you."

He didn't respond immediately. "I guess, yes, like me. But I am not a seducer. It is not my goal to lead you into the Black Tier."

"How will they try to tempt me? I'm a pretty balanced, down to earth gal ... I'm not easily swayed by good looks and money."

Lucas planted a quick kiss on my cheek. "And that's what I like about you. But let's think for a minute. What do you love? What do you love more than anything in the world?"

I glanced up to the ceiling above, thinking. "Cass. My mom. My dad. Even Mac." I was a little bit afraid to say, you.

He nodded solemnly. "Yes. And the Black Tier could use all of them and then some. But what's your passion?"

"Music," I said without any hesitation at all.

"Ah." He tickled me under my chin. "Exactly."

"But how? How would they use my music?"

"A couple of ways, really. And when one tactic doesn't work, they'll try something else until it works. Let's say you played one of your songs at Nick's. You know, a song you wrote from the heart, one you feel really speaks to your soul."

"Oh, I can think of a few of those."

He nodded. "Okay, so let's say you're up there singing and playing this song and when you're finished, no one claps. Or maybe people even get up and leave while you're performing. And then someone with a review blog says Nick's would be an awesome dive bar if it weren't for the bad music."

I grimaced. "Ouch! That would hurt."

"And that's the exact response the Black Tier would be looking for. If you start to find pain in something that brings you so much joy, it leaves you open to their influence. Some less resilient people would simply give up. Give up their passion because of what others say, think, and feel."

"I could never do that."

"It happens all the time, though. You're stronger than that. But there are many out there who aren't, and that is exactly what the Black Tier wants. They feed off of unhappiness, off misery and depression and anger, and especially fear. You start giving up your joy, how can you spread joy to others? It might even diminish your gift to heal."

"Well, if that would never work on me, what else could?"

"Seduction. And if I were a betting man, I think that is exactly what the Black Tier would use on you. Remember, they could make you feel strong desires, and when humans want things, it can change them, and not always for the better. Your ego takes hold, and when the ego takes over, your vibration loses power." He shook his head and let out a deep sigh. "That's what happened to me. But fortunately, the Bodha saw enough good left to allow me to stay here in the Grey. And now, with you..."

"With me? What?" I was all ears.

"Well, I'll have an opportunity to shift tiers. If I handle this correctly."

"What do you mean handle this correctly?" I was beginning to feel less like Lucas' romantic interest and more like his project again. "Do you mean me? This situation?"

He glanced away. "In a sense."

"And ... wait a minute. You'll have the opportunity to shift tiers? Does that mean when your project is finished, you'll just move on? Poof? And I won't see you anymore?" If I could, I would have hit him with my pillow. Suddenly I realized how exposed I was on the bed and I wrapped the sheet tighter around me.

Lucas turned and grabbed me gently. "Evie, you should know you're more than a project to me." He let his eyes roam over my body, the bed, the luster shimmering around us. "This isn't exactly a perk I throw in to sweeten the deal." He smiled wryly.

But I was still not in the mood for jokes.

"Do you want to know what happens when a spirit gets to the White Tier?" His hand gently stroked the side of my cheek.

I didn't answer. But I nodded quickly.

He reached his hand up and pulled the luster down. It enveloped us tighter than before, like a cocoon.

"What I'm about to tell you is something that must be kept between you and I. Not all spirits, especially those from the Black Tier, knows what happens at the White level."

I nodded again, this time feeling more focused on what he was saying.

His voice lowered to a whisper. "The White Tier, or the Bodha, gives us two options. One is to remain on that tier, simply being and holding a light out to bring other spirits to us. But there is another choice. We are allowed five memories. We can choose anything from the Grey, any moment in time. It doesn't matter what it is. We can rotate those memories and relive them continuously. We can intertwine the memories and make new ones—new storylines so to speak. I would choose that option. The memories."

Lucas drew me closer to him, so close our mouths were almost touching.

"I only need one. One memory. I would ask to be here with you in this moment, Evie. For eternity."

CHAPTER THIRTY-NINE

"EVIE! YOU ARE GOING to get me unwanted publicity with your Nancy Drew crap."

I was at Simone's applying a fresh coat of paint on her face for an evening charity event. First off, I was shocked that she even knew who Nancy Drew was. I found it somewhat amusing. Simone was less than pleased at how last night turned out. I, on the other hand, couldn't have been happier. Thoughts of Lucas began to dance sensuously in my head.

"Evie!" Simone reached up and poked me hard. "What is going on with you? I don't think you've heard a thing I've said." She threw up her arms in exasperation, almost knocking the applicator brush out of my hand.

"Look," she said, her voice suddenly calmer, "I know you want to solve Nick's murder. I get he was your friend and you feel like the police aren't moving fast enough. But I need you to let the cops do their job, okay? I mean, did you even read the paper?"

I paused for a moment, staring at her. "Do you read the paper?" I was genuinely curious. Simone may be a talented gal but I'd never take her for the type who spends her time reading for fun.

"Yes, I do, as a matter of fact. I read three papers every day. The Wall Street Journal, The Los Angeles Times, and The New York Times. I get them all on my Kindle."

I reached down into my makeup kit to grab another brush. "So, what's this about the paper?"

Simone rolled her eyes heavenward. "About George Hernandez and Pietro SanGiacomo. Hernandez was arrested and he ratted out SanGiacomo. The cops are almost positive they had a hit out on your friend Nick." She reached across me to her dresser and pulled a sleek, black tablet computer off the top. "Here take a look." She turned it on, found what she was looking for, and handed it to me. "Read it."

My eyes quickly skimmed the article. "Okay … so it sounds like the police think they may be able to solve Nick's murder."

"So stop playing cops and robbers, Bestie. It's not safe for you, and it could be bad press for me." She clicked her newly polished nails on the sides of the antique vanity chair. "Besides, I have someone coming to listen to you next week. I'm taking you into the studio."

"Really?" My heart started thumping hard in my chest.

"Yes, really."

I squealed and gave her a quick hug.

"Watch the face, Chicken Little! I don't want to spend another hour in this chair getting touchups."

Chicken Little? Where she came up with this stuff I had no clue, but at the moment I didn't care! I jumped back, nodding eagerly. "Oh thank you, Simone. Thank you so much." I quickly sprayed some shimmer lightly across her perfectly angled cheeks. "Can I ask you one more favor?"

She rolled her eyes. "Only if we can go back to fucking Denny's soon."

"We can." Here goes nothing. "Um, I'd like you to come by Nick's place and meet somebody."

Simone's eyes widened and then she smiled slyly. "Look at you trying to set me up. That's sweet but I don't need any help."

I placed my hands on my hips. "Duh, Diva." I winked at her and she smiled. "No. It's not that." I started feeling nervous again. "Um, do you remember when you said you might be interested in buying the bar?"

"I was buzzed. I say lots of stupid shit when I've been drinking."

"Hear me out," I said. "The guy who owns it now, Joshua Styles, he's a good guy but cash flow is tight. He's an amazing chef and he's looking to fix the place up."

Her gaze narrowed perceptively. "You like him, don't you?"

"No! I mean, well, I like him as a friend but..."

"Is he hot?"

I didn't respond right away. "I guess you'll never know unless you come to the bar and see for yourself."

"Oh brother. Fine! I'll meet this guy you don't like and see what he has to offer."

I hugged her again, but with a little less enthusiasm. The fact is, I did like Joshua as a friend. And he was very easy on the eyes. And, of course, there was Lucas ... but who knew how long he'd be around? As for Simone, well, I had yet to meet a man who wasn't instantly bowled over by her good looks and star power. So while I really wanted to help Joshua, I was also a bit uncomfortable throwing Simone and him together. Which was pretty damn selfish of me, and I decided then and there to get over myself, pronto.

I finished her makeup and then helped Simone into her evening gown. It was long, beaded, and red, and silhouetted her figure beautifully. If I got to wear designer dresses like that all the time, I might be more interested in changing my jeans and t-shirt look. We walked out of her place together. Dwight was waiting for her in an expensive Italian suit by the front door. They stepped into the Bentley.

Simone rolled down her window and yelled, "See you tomorrow!"

I waved half-heartedly, knowing exactly how Cinderella must have felt watching her stepsisters going off to the ball. Only Simone was hardly an ugly stepsister.

As the limo's taillights faded down the drive, I opened the door to my van and drove off to my second job.

Once there, Becky greeted me with a cold shoulder. She refused to make eye contact at all.

Candace leaned towards me over the bar. "What crawled up her ass?"

I shrugged, knowing full well what Becky's problem was.

"Boy likes you," Mumbles chimed in.

"Aha!" Candace's face lit up and she pointed a gnarled finger at me. "That's it! Becky clearly doesn't like being replaced by another woman, especially when the man in question is her son." She lowered her voice a tad. "Watch out with her. As I well know, she has claws."

I didn't disagree. Instead, I turned to Mumbles and smiled.

"Mumbles, you think all the guys have eyes for me."

He smiled gently and his green eye lit up. "They do!"

"You're sweet, but wrong."

Candace knocked back another swig of her drink and wiped her mouth with the back of her hand. "Oh, I don't know. I think Mumbles is right about this one." Then she peered at me for a long moment. "I heard about Jackson. Was he really found dead in your pool?"

I'd been waiting for someone to bring Jackson up. According to Simone, there'd been a small article in the local section of the paper this morning. I hadn't wanted to read it. I guess since it was a more or less an open and shut case, the reporters weren't all that interested in the story. "He was. It was horrible."

"Told you. Bad guy," Mumbles mumbled.

I sighed. "You did, Mumbles. But I still feel bad he had to die at all. Apparently he suffered from manic depression or something like that, so who knows how much of what we saw of him in the bar was the real Jackson."

Candace stirred her drink with a finger. "Kind of bizarre he died the same way as Roger."

I stopped wiping down the bar and looked at her for a few seconds. "Yes. Yes I guess it is."

"What did the police say?" she asked.

"They think it was an accident. There were no signs of foul play and no tracks on the property other than Jackson's."

"That's what they said about Roger," she replied. "That it was an accident."

I glanced at Becky, who, mercifully, had her back turned to me while she worked at the other end of the bar. I kept thinking about what Roger had told me about his death. And then I spotted Joshua coming out of the kitchen, wearing a teal shirt that nearly matched his eyes. I could seriously get used to having him around to stare at all day.

"Hey! I didn't expect you in here tonight. Did you get any sleep? You look exhausted."

I frowned.

He chuckled, "You don't look bad, just tired."

I thought about Lucas and the time we'd spent together last night.

"I'm fine. And it actually helps me to be here around people." Everyone, that is, except Becky. "I like playing my music."

"We like having you here," Joshua said, smiling. "But no pressure. If you're tired and want to head home early, we'd all understand."

"I'm fine. Really. But thanks!" I was starting to get irritated by everyone insisting I needed taking care of. I was a big girl, after all. I grabbed my guitar and set up. My goal was to simply play my music for the rest of the night and go home when I was done. I didn't stop to help serve. I didn't stop to chat with anyone. I just played and sang.

CHAPTER FORTY

AS IT TURNED OUT, I ended up leaving the bar earlier than usual. I was tired after a few sets, but a good sort of tired. I felt replenished and renewed.

Although I spent much of my time on stage zoning out to my music or thinking about Lucas, I couldn't help pondering the situation with Jackson. Frankly, it was pretty freaky, especially with what Candace said. What if Jackson had been murdered like Roger had? What if the police had missed something?

I pushed it out of my mind, wondering for the umpteenth time if Lucas would be there when I got home tonight. I really wanted to see him again ... all of him. But part of me worried last night had been a one-time deal. I mean, wasn't sex technically sinful outside marriage? So how much worse was it that Lucas, a grey spirit trying to make it to the White Tier, had sex with a human? Well, even if last night was our one and only time, I wouldn't trade it in for anything in the world. And I knew I'd see Lucas again, since I was part of his big project.

All these thoughts of sex let me back to the wild, kinky dream I had when I first moved into the house. The one where I'd woken up feeling violated. The guy in that dream had blonde hair, very dark eyes, and frightened the heck out of me. Totally different from my experience with Lucas.

Oh boy, I really needed the distraction of my pets and mindless TV tonight. However, when I walked through the door, I quickly realized there was no way I was going to have the relief of late night TV to take me away from my troubles.

I had visitors again. Dead ones.

Bob was strumming "Careless Love" to a reggae beat, and Janis was following along in time with her raspy voice. They looked up and gave a nod as I walked through the foyer. The smell of pot was thick in the air. I couldn't help but wonder how the White Tier felt about pot ... if it was okay there, then I guess it couldn't be all that bad, could it?

"Evie!" Bob called out with a smile as the song ended. "Hey, pretty woman, come sing with us."

"Yeah, come jam with us, Evie," Janis said, patting the couch next to her.

Cass thumped her tail, happy to see me. Mac, of course, was on his back, once again stoned out of his mind. I am positive he loved these visits more than Cass or I did.

I sat down next to Janis.

"Bet you're wondering where Lukie boy is."

"Um, yeah." Then again, I thought I knew. He was getting "space" to recharge his batteries.

She cackled and I cringed, because even when laughing, she could hit the high note she was famous for. Something about the sound made me a bit uneasy.

"Of course you're wondering!"

Bob leaned his head on my shoulder, his heavy dreads draping down my back. "Don't be listening to her. She likes to tease."

Janis wiggled her bushy, strawberry blonde eyebrows at me. "I'm just having a little bit of fun. Lukie told us what happened here last night. That is some crazy shit, girl!"

For one intensely awkward moment, I thought she was referring to my time with Lucas in the bedroom.

Bob rubbed my shoulder with his head. "Leave off, Janis. That girl don't want to tink about dat body anymore."

Phew! "Yeah, it was definitely not what I was expecting to see when I got home."

Janis's raspy laughter stopped abruptly, and a look I can only describe as sly spread across her face. "Don't you want to know what happens next?" she asked in a low voice.

Bob pulled his head off my shoulder and cocked a brow at her, shaking his head just the tiniest bit. To me, it looked like a warning. But my curiosity was piqued.

"What do you mean, 'what happens next?'"

Janis leaned in closer. "With that guy. The one who drowned in your pool. Don't you want to know what happens to us when we go? How it all works?" she asked.

"Sure. But Lucas has already been telling me a lot of that stuff and, well, I guess I'll figure out the rest for myself one of these days."

"He done tell you 'bout the review and judgment?" Bob asked, cocking that brow in my direction and looking slightly amused. Clearly I was missing something here.

"He told me when we die, we go through a kind of trial or life review, and the Black Tier and White Tier are present and they vote."

Janis leaned her head forward and took another hit off her joint. She inhaled deeply, giving me a long look, and blew the smoke in a slow exhale. "Yeah, well that's all true. But wouldn't you like to see it for yourself? I mean, before it's your time to go?" She turned to Bob, "What do you say, Bobby?"

"Oh no. I doan know 'bout that." Bob shook his head, a look of alarm spreading across his face.

"Oh man, come on! It will be good for her to see. Let her get a real idea."

"What are you talking about?" I interrupted.

"The guy who died, you knew him." This was a statement, not a question.

I nodded. "Yes. He came into the bar where I work sometimes. His name was Jackson, Jackson Owens."

Janis looked down at her watch and then back over at Bob and me. "It's about time."

"For what?" I asked.

"His judgment. Want to go see it?"

Either Janis had taken one too many hits this evening, or the secondhand smoke was getting to me, because I was totally confused. "Huh? I mean, how could I possibly see Jackson's judging? He's dead, I'm not … end of story."

She grinned, showing her teeth. "Not so fast, little lady. Here's how it works. You become me for a little while and Bob will lead you through the portal and to the judging."

Say what? "Um, what happens to me?"

"I become you." Her eyebrows wiggled again, making her look more and more like a redheaded Groucho Marx. All she needed was a cigar and a moustache.

My eyes widened. "How do we do it?"

"What do you have that you hold dear? It should be something you've had for a long time, something of value."

I immediately thought of the eagle feathers on the dresser in my room. As if she'd read my mind, Janis brought her arms up and out, the same way Lucas had when he created the luster. But instead of the luster, there was a bright blue flash of light and then, one of my feathers appeared in her hand. Janis twirled it around for a moment. "Pretty, isn't it?" And then she reached down and grabbed her guitar, handing it to me. "I hang onto your feather and you take my guitar. That way you can come back."

"But, how did you do that? I mean, how did you even know about the feather at all? I didn't say anything."

She smiled and patted my knee. "Hey, there are some real perks to being on this side of things. One day, you'll see."

It was all very tempting. I'd been hearing so much about the tiers from Lucas … and the chance to go there, without having to take the usual path (which typically involved dying), definitely appealed to me. But there was one more thing …

"What will you do? I mean if we do this. What will you do here, in my body?"

"Be human again for a little while."

And there's the rub. I shook my head. "I don't know."

"Oh come on," she purred. "All I want to do is walk in your garden and smell the roses. Nothing more."

Bob cleared his throat nervously. "I doan know about this, Janis. What if..."

Janis cut him off. "Come on, Evie. Don't you want to take a walk on the wild side once in a while? Now's your chance!"

"Since you put it that way, I'll go," I said. "As long as you're sure I can come back."

"You can come right back," Janis said, smiling.

I looked at Bob for confirmation. He nodded slowly. "You can as long as no one knows the vibration is off."

"Her vibe won't be too far off. Hell, she's a singer! A musician, like us."

"She be pure, though." He shot Janis a pointed look.

"Oh come on, Bob! Don't be such a stick in the mud. I really want to walk and smell and breathe."

Bob tilted his head to the side in thought and then let out a deep sigh. "Okay then. You want to go, girl? Really?"

I did. I wanted to see what it was like through the portal. I nodded.

"You won't leave the house?" I asked Janis.

"Nope. Don't want to go anywhere special. Promise."

"Okay. How do we do this?"

She took my hand. The eagle feather was in her other hand and her guitar was strapped around my neck. "Sing with me. Close your eyes and we'll sing in pitch together."

She started singing "One Love." Bob started singing too. After a few minutes, my body felt like it was floating in a warm jacuzzi near one of the jets. Warm and drowsy.

Then it was over, and I was through the other side. Through the portal.

CHAPTER FORTY-ONE

BOB AND I STOOD on the edge of a cliff with a large door to our backs. The cliff was deep red and appeared to be suspended in mid-air. The sky had a soft, pastel yellow tint to it. Stretched out before us was a bridge, the kind I imagined you might see in the middle of a jungle somewhere—made of rope and wood. The kind that might make some people afraid to cross it. But for whatever reason, I wasn't scared.

There were doors lining both sides of the bridge and three large doors at the end, about a hundred or so yards away.

Bob took my hand. "We cross here."

I followed behind him, taking one step at a time. The bridge swayed a bit as I grabbed onto the sides of it. What I'd thought was rope wasn't rope at all but something soft and smooth, like silk, and very, very strong.

"What are all of the doors for?"

"Various tiers," he said, his dreadlocks swaying with the bridge. "This man we are going to see the judgment of will be told what door to go through when it's over. If he be lucky, he be going through the white door." He pointed ahead to a large, white door. "Not lucky, the black one. And if he need to straighten himself out, he go back through the grey. And if there be some confusion he might go through any one of the doors. It all depends how the judgment go."

The air in this space was still and silent. It felt serene … peaceful. Then I heard a bell. It rang clear and pure and seemed to come from all around us.

Bob glanced over his shoulder at me. "We need to be hurrying. The review beginning now."

We picked up our pace and walked straight to the middle door at the end of the bridge. It was painted a deep red, similar to the color of the cliff behind us. Bob opened it and we stepped through.

The place we entered reminded me of something from the Roman Empire. It was a large room with pillars and coliseum- type seating, and it was filled with spirits. I leaned over to Bob and whispered, "Does everyone come to these things?"

He replied in a hushed tone, "Nah. Be too many. Not everyone be needin' a trial tho. Those that do, then we be getting' a number so we know what trials to go to."

The afterlife was starting to sound a lot like jury duty to me. "And your number came up? And Janis'?"

He nodded. We sat. Down in the middle of the seating area, on a raised dais, were two enormous chairs. In one sat a young, handsome man in white, and in the other—you guessed it—a young, beautiful woman in black.

I leaned over to Bob again. "The Bodha?" I nodded toward the two spirits.

He shook his head. "Nah. Them be the messengers. No one sees the Bodha until they want to be seen, and the same with the Asat."

"The leaders of the Black Tier?"

Bob nodded as an older spirit in front of us turned around, bringing a finger to her mouth. She stared at me for several seconds and then turned back. For a moment, I wondered if she was surprised to see Janis Joplin seated behind her. But considering the number of famous people who were likely wandering around here, I doubted that was the case.

I took a good look around and noticed everyone in our section was dressed in various shades of grey.

A gavel rang out in the crowd, and suddenly I saw Jackson come in through the door Bob and I had entered. On either side of him stood what, I assumed, were two more representatives— one from each side. Jackson looked pretty confused. They sat him down in a chair and the trial began.

The man in white, representing the Bodha, spoke first. "We are here to review Mr. Jackson Owens's life. Mr. Owens, are you aware what has happened?"

Jackson shook his head slowly. "Is this a dream? Where am I?"

The young man in white gave Jackson a sympathetic look. "You are dead, Mr. Owens. And this is your life review, where a jury of your peers takes into account your life. Afterwards, we will vote, and the vote will determine where your spirit winds up. Do you understand?"

Jackson's eyes widened. "Is this Purgatory?" he asked.

The man laughed softly. "Oh no, dear boy. There is no Purgatory to speak of." The Bodha rep looked over at the Asat rep. "Are we ready to begin?"

The young woman in black nodded.

Everything around us went completely dark. Then, as if I were sitting in an IMAX theater, Jackson came into full view all around us, his life flashing by in segments. We saw him hit his dog when he was ten. We also witnessed him being beaten by a man I assumed was his father. We saw him walk an old lady across the street when he was a teenager but then he also stole from her purse when she wasn't looking. We saw him steal food from the local market. We saw him go to college, but it wasn't USC like he had said but a local state school. He watched re-runs of Nick's show and other TV shows, he yelled at his mother, he lived alone ... The review went on and on. Most disturbing to me was that not only could I see his life, I could also feel everything he felt.

And then I caught my breath. There he was with Nick—alone, just the two of them. Nick had the clothes I found his body in. And they were arguing. Punches were thrown. Nick went down behind the bar, and I was certain Jackson had murdered Nick. But then Nick got up, wiped the blood from his lip, and Jackson left. There was no sound to any of this. Just the visuals and the feelings.

Suddenly, I was on the screen. A wave of anger and lust swept over me. That was what he felt toward me. Jackson followed me. He took photos of me. And he had plans to hurt me. The night he had come to my house, he wanted to do very bad things to me. Then we saw Jackson falling into the pool and hitting his head on the side—and behind him was a shadow. The shadow became clearer on the screen. I caught my breath—it was that man! The one from my kinky sex dream! —and then he was gone. What the heck was going on?!

The minute the review stopped, the room erupted into agitated conversation. The Bodha rep yelled out, "Quiet down, everyone!"

Jackson looked pale. Granted, he was dead, but it was clear he hadn't been expecting any of this at all.

The young man in white stood and looked at the woman in black. "Mr. Owens was murdered by an Asura in your tier?!"

An enigmatic smile crept across the woman's face. "I cannot say if I recognize who that was or not."

"It is against the rules!" The Bodha rep said.

"Oh, come now, it is not as if you want Mr. Owens's vibration!"

"No, not as it is. But if he'd been allowed to live, he would've had the chance to change." The Bodha rep stood, his mouth in a grim line. "This will be taken up to the next level."

The young woman shrugged.

The Bodha rep turned toward Jackson. "Do you deny any of this to be true of your life, Mr. Owens?"

Jackson shook his head.

"Do you have anything to say? Any regrets about the things that happened in your life?"

A strange smile crossed his face. "No," he said.

The Bodha rep looked over to the Asat rep.

"I think this is an easy vote, and seeing how Mr. Owens was an Asat Order target, take him. But this is not over! You cannot steal vibrations before they are ready to go."

"We will gladly take him," she purred.

I took a closer look at the Asat rep on the stand. She seemed familiar. And then it dawned on me ... she was the woman I'd seen with Pierre that night at Nick's, when Simone and Dwight had come to listen to me play. And she was looking straight at me. Uh-oh.

Bob took my hand and pulled me to my feet. "Come on." I followed him quickly to the door. But the woman in black was there before us.

"Janis." she smiled. "Your vibration seems ... different."

"How would you be knowin that? She doan beat at the same vibe as you," Bob said, standing protectively in front of me.

"That's a matter of perspective," the woman replied.

The Bodha rep suddenly appeared in front of us. "What is the problem?" he asked, looking from me to Bob to the woman and back to me again.

Bob held his hands out, palms up. "No problem, brah. We be gettin' back to the Grey Tier now. Review be over."

The woman stepped forward. "A moment of your time, please." She sidled up to the young man in white. "Look at her. She's no spirit. She's human! The vibration is completely wrong."

They both turned to look back at Bob and me (but mostly me). And then the man in white reached out to touch my arm. "Janis, you need to go back to the

Grey Tier now." He eyed me pointedly and then turned back to the woman. "And you need to take your newest member and leave. This review is over. But please," he said a grimace spread across his face as if there were a bad taste in his mouth, "tell the Asat we know one of your kind murdered a human. I will take this up with the Bodha, and there will be consequences. Of that I am certain."

The Asat rep stared in hostile silence at the young man. "You cannot speak to me this way!"

The young man replied, "You don't want to start this here. This is not how it all begins or ends. Go back to your tier and do not anger the Bodha any more than you and your order already have, Anastasia."

Anastasia? I took another long look at the woman ... could she possibly be the jaguar who tried to attack me?

In a huff, she turned and walked back to where she'd left Jackson standing.

The representative for the Bodha turned to me then. "I don't know what is going on here. I don't know who brought you here ... however, I can wager a guess." He glanced at Bob, who just smiled. "But you are not allowed here. And if you ever come here again before you're allowed, the consequences will be grave."

He turned and walked away. Bob, still holding my hand, pulled me towards the open door and we crossed the bridge, back to the portal, without speaking. Within just a few minutes, we were back in my home.

And what I saw waiting for me in my living room made me want to go back through the portal door and never come back.

CHAPTER FORTY-TWO

JANIS-AS-EVIE WAS on my couch, crawling all over Joshua, who looked a bit uncomfortable but also happy. I cleared my throat. Of course Joshua couldn't hear me, but Janis could.

Bob laughed. "Oh boy. Well, doan say I didn't warn you."

"You think?" I stepped forward and cleared my throat again. "Janis!"

She turned around, a look of disappointment darting across her face. "Well, shit," she said.

"What?" Joshua asked.

"Get off of him, now, and switch back." I crossed my arms in front of my chest as authoritatively as possible in an effort to keep myself from strangling her. Not that it would've done a lot good, since she was dead already. "I am so angry with you!" Never thought I would be saying that to Janis Joplin, but I guess there's a first time for everything.

She glanced sheepishly at me and mouthed, "I'm sorry." Then glanced back over at Joshua. "I'm thirsty, you?" she asked.

He nodded, seeming rather dazed. "Yeah. Uh. Do you have any beer?"

"You got it." She winked at him and stood up, her hips swaying in a way they have never ever swayed when I was "in residence." She sashayed into the kitchen and I turned to follow, but not before I saw Joshua's eyes focus in on my retreating rear. Oh hell.

Once we were in the safety of the kitchen I hissed, "What are you doing?" Never mind there was no point whispering because Joshua couldn't hear me.

Janis leaned back into the counter, looking a lot more relaxed than I felt the situation warranted. "I was only having fun, and your boyfriend didn't seem to mind one bit."

"He's not my boyfriend!" I said.

She laughed, low and throaty. "He might be now."

This was so not happening. "What did you do with him?"

"Lighten up," she said, turning to the fridge to grab three beers. "Your generation is so fucking uptight. Mellow out." She reached around me for the bottle opener, popped the tops, and took a long, deep drink out of one of the bottles. "Ahhh. How I've missed beer." She nodded towards the other two bottles. "These are for you and loverboy out there. You look like you could use a drink."

Bob strolled into the kitchen, humming. "C'mon, J. We need to be leavin our girl alone. She had enough of our kind tonight."

Janis sighed and then drew my feather out of her (my) back pocket. I unstrapped her guitar from my back and handed it over. "Been fun," she said. She started singing "Piece of My Heart," and I joined in quietly. Janis shot me a frustrated look. "No girl, you gotta sing."

I belted out the song, and suddenly that warm feeling came over me. Then I was back in my body, and Janis and Bob had disappeared. I grabbed the two open beers and turned to leave the kitchen, almost bumping into Joshua, who stood just a few inches behind me. He looked very confused and not a little surprised.

"Whoa, Evie, was that you? You sounded almost exactly like Janis Joplin for a minute. My mom used to play her stuff all the time when I was a kid. I had no idea you had that kind of range! I mean, you've got a great voice as it is but that was pretty remarkable."

"Yeah." I handed one of the beers to him and took a long drink out of the other. We needed to drink these, fast, and I had to get him out of my place ASAP. I needed to think and process. What was he doing here anyway? It was after midnight!

"Look, uh, I am really sorry for being so ... grabby." Awkward.

He blushed, smiling. "I'm not. I mean it's not like anything happened between us. What are you sorry for?"

"I, well..." I took another sip of my liquid courage. "I'm not usually so assertive and I don't know what got into me."

He took a drink. "Honestly, I didn't mind the climbing, and you've been pretty stressed out lately. I think you're entitled to let loose once in a while."

"Yes." I nodded. "And it probably didn't help that I took an Ambien before you arrived." Lying might be a sin, but it seemed like I was a natural at it. "I've been feeling loopy for the past hour or two. Anyway ... You know what that famous golfer claimed Ambien did to him! Can't think of his name now, but made him a sex addict." Oh such the wrong thing to say! I took another sip of my beer. "I promise you as my boss and my friend that will never happen again."

Joshua reached out and took the beer out of my hand. "First of all, beer and Ambien do not mix. I'd say you've had enough, sweetheart." He set the bottle down on the counter and turned back to me. "Secondly, nothing happened. Remember? You dropped an earring behind the couch and when you went to look for it, you kind of stumbled and wound up in my lap. I wasn't thinking you were going all Tiger on me." He winked.

Seriously? Janis needed to update her moves. I mean, how obvious was that? Either Joshua was super naïve, or he was letting me off easy.

"Right." I feigned a deep yawn. "You know, I am kind of tired from that sleeping pill. Shall we call it a night?"

Joshua ran his hands through his hair. "Oh yeah, sure. Like I told you when I dropped in, I was only checking on you. You seemed pretty distracted tonight, so I called when I was closing and you didn't answer. I know it was late, but I was just worried."

I nodded, smiling up at him. "That's so nice of you, Joshua! I really appreciate it. I guess I have been a little distracted. And I'm sorry I didn't answer my phone. I didn't hear it."

"No worries at all. It was late. I'm sorry if I bothered you." He gave me a quick hug. "See you at work!"

I walked him to the front door and waved goodbye as he slowly walked down the driveway to his car parked on the other side of the gate. I locked the doors behind me and called out for Cass, who had gone into hiding along with Mac. She eventually crawled out of wherever she'd hidden herself and gave me a long, appraising look.

"Crazy night," I said.

Her eyes widened and then she wagged her tail. I figured she was glad to have me back to normal again.

I gave her a quick kiss on the top of her head. "You are so smart, and I am so not."

We traipsed back to my room where I fell onto my bed next to a dozing Mac. I wanted badly to close my eyes and go to sleep, but I couldn't. All I could think about was Jackson's review and the image of that man who pushed him into the pool, the same man I'd seen in that awful dream. Clearly he was part of the Asat, a spirit from the Black Tier. Had my so-called dream been real? If he could kill Jackson on my property, what was stopping him from coming into my house?

I reached over to scratch Cass's fur. I reminded myself Lucas said there was a protective barrier around the house, but for some reason, it wasn't making me feel all that safe.

I tried hard to think of nice things—the ocean, butterflies, hummingbirds (which I really like), cheesecake—and I finally drifted off to sleep. But those sweet visions didn't stick around for long. They were soon replaced by images of spirits dressed in grey, and jaguars ... and Joshua. But Lucas remained absent that night from my bedroom and my dreams.

CHAPTER FORTY-THREE

MY BRAIN WAS ON OVERDRIVE the next day. To sum it up...

...I was having sex with a spirit, after being raised in a pretty hardcore Christian home...

...I'd gone to the "other side" to see a man who'd been murdered in my pool and, without mincing words, ended up with a one-way ticket to hell ...

...My day boss was a pop star who I had become friends with ...

...My previous evening boss had been murdered and everyone around me seemed to be a possible suspect ...

...My new boss—the old boss's long-lost son ... I think— was so physically attractive and kindhearted but ...

...his mom was a major beyotch who had accidentally killed a famous movie star ....

...And lest I forget, not a day went by that I didn't think about my big sister who'd been missing for over sixteen years.

Oh yeah, and famous dead people visited me frequently, including pervy spirits from the dark side who wanted to nab my soul because I had the gift of healing, thanks to some eagle feathers I'd found on the ground near the location where my sister had been abducted.

Well, at least I couldn't ever say my life was boring.

After a little more feeling sorry for myself, I got dressed, brewed some coffee, and sat down to have breakfast while pondering all I'd discovered in the last few days. I got out a clean sheet of paper and started making a list. Cass was under my chair and Mac had remained in bed.

First I reread Jackson's article, having found it online. He'd obviously been there the day Nick had been murdered. He could have come back to the bar and killed Nick after their fight. But I'm pretty sure that would have been part of Jackson's review. Not, of course, that he needed more reasons to go to the Black Tier.

Obviously, Jackson was mentally unstable. But did that mean his entire article was bogus, the fantasy of a delusional young man with a bone to pick? I wasn't so sure about that. He'd skewed things, for sure. I mean, I believed Joshua when he explained about the guy he killed and his subsequent jail time. And knowing Joshua as I did, I couldn't fathom that he and Becky had been in cahoots and murdered Nick for his assets. That said, Becky was turning out to be a real piece of work and could have very likely offed Nick herself.

What if, after Nick and Jackson argued, Becky came in, caught him by surprise, and killed him? If Joshua was really Roger's son, Becky might have felt desperate enough to kill Nick in order to provide for her son and convince him to return home. And with Nick dead, there'd be no one to contest her claim that he was Joshua's father. Nick could've been weak and dazed from the fight with

Jackson and not able to defend himself. But as much as I didn't care for Becky, I still couldn't quite see it.

Candace was still on my list. She had old resentments, and alcohol can make people do crazy things. A memory could have triggered her, especially with Becky showing up on the scene. Maybe.

Pietro and George. That one just seemed too neat. Too much motive, and easy for the cops to place blame. They were bad guys, no doubt, but had they murdered Nick? I really did not think so. Even though I didn't doubt that they would've murdered me.

Simone and Dwight. Dwight maybe, but Simone was insistent that I was being paranoid, and I think she had something there. There was still something about Dwight, though, that bothered me. I knew if I wanted to get any answers from him, the only way would be to touch him.

Bradley Verne? He was a nice guy who appeared to think the world of Nick. But his dependency on Raquela was a little over the top. Could his childhood jealousy of his father's love for Nick cause him to go over the edge? And was there any truth to what Jackson mentioned in his article about bankruptcy?

Last on my list, but not least, was Mumbles. Frankly, I could never picture him hurting a fly. Then again, isn't that what they always say when the next-door neighbor goes postal? Hmmm.

I decided there were a few things to be done. First, I needed to confront Becky about Roger Hawks. Then I needed to do the same with Candace about her past and lay it on the line. After that, I needed to find out if Bradley Verne had filed bankruptcy. As for Dwight, he'd likely accompany Simone to our meeting at the bar this evening. So touching him was key. As for Mumbles ... I wasn't certain.

I was determined and, yes, a bit obsessed at this point. But I felt very, very close to solving the mystery of Nick's murder. It was time to catch a killer!

CHAPTER FORTY-FOUR

AS YOU KNOW, liquid courage is one of those things I am rarely dependent on, but lately I seemed to be breaking my own rules with disturbing frequency. I fixed myself a Jack and Coke as soon as I got to the bar.

Joshua came over and put a friendly arm around me. "I've noticed you don't usually drink much. I hope you aren't stressed out from last night. And..." he lowered his voice to a whisper, "I hope you laid off the Ambien." He gave me a friendly wink.

Candace's shot me a glance. I groaned inwardly. Clearly she'd heard the whole thing.

I smiled innocently at Joshua. "Not stressed out at all. And I really do appreciate you checking on me last night. Oh, as for the Ambien, I won't be going there again, that's for sure. I spent a big chunk of last night feeling completely out of it."

He nudged me gently with his elbow. "Got it. So why the drink?"

"Guess I just felt like it. And they're on the house ... right?" I grinned up at him. "I think I'll go back and see if your mom needs some help in the kitchen. Oh! And my friend, the one I told you about, will be by tonight."

"Great!" His eyes lit up. "I am looking forward to it."

I headed back to the kitchen to find Becky over the fryer. This was not a conversation I was looking forward to, but c'est la vie.

"Hi Becky," I said, thinking I would start this off as nice and easy as possible.

She glared at me, spatula in hand. "What do you want? I'm busy, in case you hadn't noticed."

Ah, yes. I could see this was going to go well. Not. "Oh, just checking in. We haven't spoken much lately."

She propped her hands on her hips, looking about as interested in talking to me as I was in talking to her. "About what?"

"First off, why have you gone from liking me to hating me?"

She dropped her arms and sighed. "I don't hate you. But I think you're too nosy for your own good, and you could get hurt. Also..." She chewed her lip for a moment. "Well, the truth is, I think you and my son don't make a good pair."

Although I was a little hurt by the remark, I laughed. "I hate to be the one to break it to you, Becky, but we aren't a pair."

She glanced at me skeptically. "I see the way he looks at you and how you look at him. I don't like it."

"We're friends, Becky. That's it."

She shrugged. "Keep your distance."

This wasn't going how I'd hoped. But the whiskey was starting to fan the flames of irritation, and I decided to throw caution to the wind.

"First off, last I checked, your son is an adult and perfectly capable of making his own choices regarding who he does, and does not, befriend. I'll keep my distance from Joshua when he asks me to." I glared at her, giving as good as I'd been getting lately. Her eyes widened a tad and I knew the arrow had hit home. But I wasn't finished with her yet.

"Secondly, I know what happened to Roger Hawks."

Becky sucked in a breath of air and an ugly flush spread across her face. "What?! What are you talking about?"

"I know he had an accident falling into the pool and hit his head. But I also know he fell because you pushed him ... after telling him you were pregnant."

Becky crossed her arms tightly in front of her chest, backing up to the stove behind her.

"You are out of your mind!"

I looked at her, long and hard. "Am I? I don't think so."

"You have no proof of anything! You're a crazy young woman, and I want you out of my bar!"

As much as I hated confrontations, this one was kind of fun. I tilted my head to one side, bringing a finger to the side of my chin. "Technically not your bar, but your son's. Whatever else you may have done, you're obviously a doting parent, and I'm sure it's been hard having Joshua away for so long. Killing Nick would bring your son back because he'd inherit the bar. Is that why you killed him?"

Her expression darkened with rage. "You're crazy! I did not kill Nick! I loved him!"

"Like you loved Roger Hawks?" Zing!

She slammed down the spatula and started towards me, hands fisted into tight balls. Had Joshua not walked through the kitchen door at that moment, I'm pretty certain we would have looked like a couple of crazed banshees bashing each other over the head.

"What's going on? I can hear you guys all the way out in the bar!" He looked from his mom to me.

Becky ran over to his side, pointing angrily at me. "She is trouble, Joshua! Trouble! Get rid of her!" She tore off her apron and stormed out of the kitchen, leaving Joshua staring at me, wide eyed.

"Uh ... so ... what was that all about?"

I bit my lower lip, hard. Then I shrugged. "She doesn't like me."

"I can see that." He sighed heavily. "She's never liked anyone I date."

"But we're not dating!"

He ran his hand through his hair in frustration. "Yeah, I know, but try and tell her that. She's like this with any woman who spends time with me, regardless of our relationship." He hooked his thumbs over his jean pockets and sighed again. "I'm sorry. I'll talk to her, see if I can't calm her down."

I nodded, feeling not a little guilty. After all, the reason Becky was so wound up was because I'd confronted her and made some pretty heavy accusations. Chances were slim to nil she'd be calming down any time soon. On top of it, I couldn't tell if she'd been lying or telling me the truth about Nick.

I walked over to Joshua and placed a hand on his arm. "Look, I'll manage the kitchen." Since it was pretty obvious we weren't going to see Becky again that evening.

He nodded. "Okay ... but people are going to want to hear you sing tonight."

"Who else do we have out there who can cook?"

He looked at me as if I were missing something obvious. "Uh, I can. Remember?" Duh. "You tend bar and play some sets. While you're playing, I'll tend bar and we'll close the kitchen. Simple solution."

"You sure?"

"Yes," he insisted.

"You're not getting rid of me?"

He laughed. "No way! Like I said, I'll handle my mother."

So Joshua took over the kitchen, and I went out to tend bar.

Candace was waiting for a new drink, and Mumbles continued to nurse the one in front of him. Candace leaned across the bar towards me.

"What happened in there? We heard raised voices, and then next thing I knew, the bitch stormed out like a Tasmanian devil on crack!" She could barely contain her glee at the apparent turn of events.

Oh what the hell ... I was on a roll, why stop now? "I accused her of murdering Roger Hawks and Nick."

Candace's eyes widened. Mumbles set down his drink for the first time that evening. "You did?" she said.

I nodded. "Look, I don't believe the theory that George and Pietro killed Nick. And I don't like to leave questions unanswered—especially when it concerns people I care about."

"That is noble of you, honey," she said. "I wouldn't put it past that woman. Never knew what happened to Roger, but I've always had my suspicions, and it sure is convenient that after Nick died, her kid now owns this place!"

I placed my elbows on the bar and rested my chin in my hands. "I agree, but I don't know if I'm completely convinced she did it."

Mumbles picked up his drink again and gazed into it as if he might find some answers in there. Candace raised clear eyes to me and cocked her head to the side. "If it wasn't Becky, who else could have done it?"

And here is where I really should've made some sort of noncommittal response and mixed myself another drink. Unfortunately, I didn't.

"Well, there's you."

"Me?" She laughed, her eyes wide and amused.

"And Mumbles."

He didn't even bother looking up, instead choosing to suck down the remainder of his drink.

"Oh, honey, you are priceless." Candace continue to chuckle to herself as she swirled her drink around slowly. "What makes you say that?"

"You loved Nick, for starters, and he hurt you. The way I see it, you've been pining away for him for years. And sometimes, people snap." I looked back at Mumbles. No reaction.

Candace's laughter stopped abruptly. "You do have a way with words, missy." She shook a finger at me. "I've never killed anyone, ever! Which is a lot more than the bitch can say. And Mumbles, well, he's as gentle as a goddamned kitten." From the looks of it, she appeared to be working herself into a fine state of agitation. She sat her glass down with a sharp rap and glared at me steadily.

"I suggest you get your head on straight and rethink this whole thing. This man here," she said, pointing at Mumbles. "He's your biggest fan, always looking out for you! And, I, well, I think of you like a daughter, but now you've royally pissed me off!"

Right about then I felt like a class-A heel. "I'm sorry, Candace, I was only looking at the facts and—"

"Your facts suck!" She slid off the bar stool and grabbed Mumbles by the hand. "Come on. We're going somewhere else tonight."

"Candace, wait."

She didn't turn back, but Mumbles did, and when I looked into his eye, I realized I'd crossed a line. He didn't look angry or sad, but he did look hurt. The last thing I ever wanted to do was hurt anyone. But it appeared I'd failed in more ways than one that evening.

CHAPTER FORTY-FIVE

YEAH, OKAY, SO I was making enemies fast. But the way I figured it, someone had to ask the tough questions ... because as far as I could tell, the cops had pretty much given up on Nick's case entirely. I hoped once the real killer was found, I'd be forgiven my behavior and things would get back to normal again.

After Candace and Mumbles left the building, I played a few sets to get my mind off all the drama I'd created. Finishing up and just before I was getting ready to go back to tend the bar, I noticed an older gentleman sitting in the back, in the spot Jackson used to hang out in. He looked distinguished— expensive dark suit, silver hair, nice jewelry, but not over the top. And he was wearing sunglasses. Why was it people in LA thought it was so chic to wear their sunglasses at night? Simone did it to help disguise her from the press. Maybe this guy was doing it for the same reason? And if so, who was he?

I was about ready to go ask him if he needed a drink, to try and get a read on him, when Simone came in with Dwight on her heels. She wore a long, red wig, reading glasses, a beret, torn jeans, and a baggy, white poet's blouse. Simone wiggled her fingers at me and walked up to the bar. I stepped around the counter as she leaned over and whispered, "Call me Alanis tonight."

Dwight smiled at her as she plopped onto a barstool. There was plenty of room now that Candace and Mumbles had fled.

She winked at me. "So, Evie, what do you think of my disguise?"

"It's, uh, poetry in motion."

She laughed, surprised, "Hey, that's pretty good!" And then she glanced around the bar.

"Where's the guy I'm supposed to meet?" she asked.

Oh, right. "He's in the kitchen cooking. Would you like a drink? Joshua should be out in a minute."

"Ooh, Joshua ... sexy." She glanced back over her shoulder at Dwight who was still standing. "Dude, sit the fuck down. You're making me nervous!" He dropped onto the stool next to her like a rock.

I rolled my eyes. Poor Dwight. "So, what do you guys want to drink?"

"I'll take a Long Island iced tea, and my driver here will have a regular one."

Dwight nodded. I fixed up the drinks and slid the boozy one over to Simone. Then I handed Dwight the iced tea. I made a point of touching his fingers when he took the glass from me.

At first, I got nothing. But then, boy did I get something. Something I never expected. It was a flash of light. Bright, crisp, and instant. I tried not to yank my hand away. Maybe he had been in an explosion? A fire? When I looked into his eyes, he smiled at me and seemed calm, relaxed. So maybe I had helped ease whatever pain Dwight had. The closest I'd had to that experience was when I touched Mumbles and got blasted with sound and pain ... yet my vision with Dwight was very, very different. Huh.

Just then, Joshua walked through the kitchen door and Simone's face lit up. I'd never seen her look like that before, and I immediately found myself regretting this whole deal.

"Hey, Evie, who are your friends?" Joshua asked, smiling politely at Simone and Dwight.

Dwight reached his hand out towards Joshua. "Dwight Jenkins." He had a slightly grim look on his face, and I wondered if he'd seen the same thing I just had on Simone's face.

Joshua clasped Dwight's hand and smiled politely, "Joshua Styles." They both turned to Simone, who leaned forward and reached out her hand.

"Tonight," she said in a low voice. "You can call me Alanis." She flashed her amazing smile at him and he smiled back in a way that clearly said he liked what he saw. I felt sick. And then I felt bad for feeling sick. Fact is, I had no right to feel this way at all. First, there was Lucas, and while I was attracted to Joshua, I'd made no effort to take things any further than friendship.

"Maybe we should go into the kitchen and talk in private," Joshua suggested.

My stomach flip-flopped again.

"That would be great," Simone replied. Then she turned to Dwight and touched his arm. "I'll be back."

He smiled smoothly at her but as soon as she turned to walk into the kitchen with Joshua, the smile dropped off his face completely. Hmmm.

"Great weather we've been having," I said. Yeah, I know ... lame. But at least I was trying.

Dwight nodded, looking distracted. "Yeah. So I hear you think I murdered your friend Nick."

It seemed I wasn't the only one who wanted to cut to the chase tonight. I held up a finger at him and quickly fixed myself a second drink. After taking a nice, long sip, I responded.

"Yep. I suppose I did." I sighed, thinking of all the folks I'd managed to upset this evening ... wondering if I would soon be adding Dwight to the list.

"Did?" He laughed. "You don't anymore?"

Another sigh, another long sip. "Honestly, Dwight, I have no idea what to believe lately." He shook his head and smiled at me, and for the very first time ever, Dwight didn't seem creepy or slimy. His smile was sincere and warm, and I found myself crack a semi-smile back. Or maybe it was simply the booze going to my head. I shot a suspicious look at the glass in my hand ... I was starting to see just how easy it was to slide into drinking. Was this how Candace and Mumbles got started?

"I didn't kill Nick," Dwight said, interrupting my thoughts. "But can I ask why you would even think that? Believe it or not, I'm a pretty passive kind of guy. I don't like violence. Not my thing. I'd prefer a Disney classic over a shoot 'em up any day."

Boy did I ever peg him wrong!

"You know, some of those Disney movies can be pretty violent. Look at Bambi, for instance. And, what about 101 Dalmatians? I mean, Cruela killing puppies for a coat?! What twisted and sick individual came up with that idea?"

He shook a finger at me, laughing. "I didn't know you had such a good sense of humor! I guess tonight's the night to learn some new things about each other, eh?" He winked and took another sip of his iced tea. "Enlighten me. Why would you think I murdered your friend?"

Guess it was time for Blunt Evie to come out and play again. "For Simone." He made a face. "You are into her. It's obvious! And she told me she threatened Nick because she thought he was stringing me along and using me. She can get a bit possessive about her people."

He nodded in agreement, sighing. "True. But her bark is a lot worse than her bite. She would never ask me, or anyone else for that matter, to kill someone. And even if she did, I'd never do it. As far as being into her, I am, but maybe not as much as you think. Simone isn't one of those women you can tie down. She's very special to me. But some day I want a wife and a family. That's not Simone's cup of tea, and even if it were, she wouldn't want to go down that path with me. We have some fun together but that's it."

Wow. I guess tonight really was a night of revelations. Just not the ones I expected.

"Really? Then how come you follow her around with that look on your face?" I made a sad, puppy dog face.

He smiled again. "Please tell me I don't look that bad." He tilted his head to the side. "Fact is, I worry about her. She may seem like she's a tough cookie and in charge, but actually, she's just a big softie on the inside and very vulnerable."

I laughed, thinking of the day when she'd given both Dwight and her director a major piece of her mind after the jaguar incident. "For someone so vulnerable, she sure has an interesting way of showing it!" I shook my head. "So you really didn't kill Nick?"

"Nope." He set his now-empty glass of tea down on the bar, glancing over at the door leading to the kitchen.

You know what? I believed him. Maybe it was the Jack Daniel's. Maybe it was the naiveté I brought with me from Brady. Or maybe I really didn't want to believe he would have killed Nick for Simone. In any case, he was now officially off my list of suspects.

A little while and another glass of iced tea later, Simone came out of the kitchen smiling and cheerful with Joshua, who beamed as if he'd won the lottery. In spite of my better intentions, I think I pretty much could have strangled her right then and there.

She sat back down at the bar and leaned over the counter. "We have a deal."

"You do?"

"Yes. Joshua and I are officially in business together."

"That's great," I said, trying so hard to sound sincere. Actually, it was great for Joshua and I felt pretty happy for him. But still ...

Dwight excused himself to the restroom and Simone asked for a glass of champagne. "We don't carry anything expensive," I cautioned her, knowing the brands she was used to drinking.

"That's all about to change." She reached across and grabbed my hand, squeezing it. "Isn't this so exciting!"

"Yes." I nodded as enthusiastically as I could, which was not very.

"Hey, ladies," Joshua interrupted. "I'm going to go take that group's order." He turned to Simone. "Thanks so much for meeting with me, and it was a pleasure doing business with you." He shook her hand, and she actually blushed! Would miracles never cease?

He walked away, and she abruptly turned to me and asked, "You and him?"

"What?"

"Are you and Joshua seeing each other, messing around, anything like that?"

"Um, no."

"You like him, though."

Here was my chance for total honesty. "Uh, no. Definitely not." I shook my head vehemently. Way to go, Evie.

"You sure? Because I wouldn't want to step on your toes." She stared after Joshua's retreating figure. "People like me, we don't fall in love. We just don't, and certainly not at first sight. But he is, I don't know … I've never seen or met anyone like him." She grabbed my hand again, tightly. "Now, are you sure you don't have a thing for him? Because when you talked about him the other day, I sensed something, and I can understand why. If you do, I'll back off, because I don't do that to my friends."

I found myself staring at her, not knowing what to say. I couldn't even get a handle on my own feelings, let alone describe them to someone else. I had to admit to myself there was something intriguing about Joshua ... and if Lucas hadn't been there, well, who knew? But at the end of the day, I didn't have any right to stand in the way of whatever might happen between Simone and Joshua simply because I wasn't sure about my own feelings.

Finally, I blurted out, "He's all yours. I'm seeing someone."

"What?" Her jaw dropped. "You are? Really?!" For a moment she looked hurt. "You promised you would tell me. Who is he?"

"It's, uh, it's long distance."

"Long distance? Like from back home?"

I paused a second. "Yes, actually, I guess you could say that."

Simone looked positively giddy at the news. "I'll fly him out here for you! I want to meet him!"

Oh, heck. "No, no. He's super busy with work and, well, we like it this way."

She cocked her head to the side, a confused look on her face. "I see. Well, what does he do?"

"He's a, he's a detective of sorts. Kind of a private eye, I guess."

"You guess?" Her look of confusion was rapidly shifting to one of skepticism. Uh-oh.

"Hey, tell me about your business deal?"

"No way! I'm much more interested in hearing about your guy."

Dwight returned about that time and Simone looked at him. "Evie has a boyfriend!"

"You do?" he asked, looking as surprised as Simone had been.

"From back home," Simone said.

I nodded again and forced a smile. "But it's very casual right now ... we're taking it slow."

"What's the lucky guy's name?" Dwight asked.

"Lucas," I blurted, relieved there was at least one truthful thing I could say in this conversation.

"Lucas?" Simone said, her brow furrowing. "Hey, isn't that the name of the rock star who was murdered at Blake's house?"

"Oh wow! I'd totally forgotten about that." So much for being honest.

I glanced back at Dwight who was watching me intently. "You should have him visit. We'd all love to meet him, I'm sure." And then he winked at me.

For a brief, unsettling moment, I had the distinct impression Dwight knew all about the real Lucas and me. But that was just ridiculous. So I began to wonder if he believed my boyfriend story at all ... or maybe he thought I'd made the whole thing up to cover up my feelings for Joshua to give Simone permission to pursue him. Of course, that was as far from the truth as it could get. Wasn't it?

CHAPTER FORTY-SIX

SIMONE, DWIGHT, AND MOST of the bar finally made their way to another port of
call, and I started cleaning up. Joshua was in the back wiping down the kitchen.
The only other person in the place was Sunglasses Man. And he didn't show any
signs of leaving.

I walked over to him and said, "Last call."

He took off his glasses (finally!) and looked up at me with light hazel eyes.
"Evie Preston." It was a statement.

"Yes?"

He took a business card out of his wallet and tossed it down on the table, nodding his head at it. "For you."

If this was a pickup line, the guy seriously needed to work on his moves. However, I picked the card up in spite of myself and quickly scanned it. One side simply read: Kane Richards: Executive Producer. On the top of the flip side, it read:
Kane Records. It took me a few seconds to process. But finally it clicked. Kane
Records was a major record label based in New York City.

"Nice to meet you, Mr. Richards." I rubbed my hand against my jeans, trying
to wipe off the sweat that had suddenly appeared. I didn't want to be rude and not
shake his hand, but... I shrugged. "My hands need washing."

He nodded. "Please call me Kane." He gestured to the seat across from his. "Have a seat." I did. Kane looked at me for a long moment. "I was a friend of Nick's. I'd been scheduled to come out to L.A. a couple of months ago and had to cancel. Nick and I tried to get together at least a few times a year. Anyway, he called me about you."

I felt elated and then very, very sad. Nick had been telling me the truth about his big-time producer friend.

"I cancelled my last trip." He shook his head. "Family matters. Wish I hadn't. I was so sorry to hear about Nick. He's been a good friend." Kane stared down at his hands, regret clearly etched across his face. "I was so disappointed I couldn't make his service. As I said, I've been dealing with some stuff at home. One of my kids got mixed up with the wrong crowd. That kind of thing." He waved a hand in front of his face. "Anyway, I had to come out on business this week, and I decided to stop in and see if you were still playing."

"I am."

"I'm grateful for that ... because you are as good as Nick promised."

I felt a happy blush spread across my cheeks. I was speechless.

"I'd like to have you come out to New York and speak with some of our people. I'm interested in doing what I can to help you launch a career."

"Seriously?" I could barely contain my smile.

He nodded. "As a heart attack."

"This is amazing! Yes! I'm in!" I resisted the sudden urge to launch myself across the table and hug him. I was that excited.

He grinned and clapped his hands together. "Great! Let me get your contact information and I'll be in touch. I'm heading off on vacation for a couple of weeks, but when I return, let's look at our schedules and see how we can make this work."

We both stood at the same time and he shook my hand. "I don't mind dirty hands." His grasp was firm and warm. But that's not all. Instantly, I received a vision of Kane and the blonde man from my bad dream. The man was threatening him in some way. I had no idea what it meant, but I removed my hand as if it were on fire.

Kane Richards looked at me with an odd expression. "Okay. We'll be talking soon."

"Yes," I uttered, not sure if I had even said the word out loud.

He left the bar soon after and Joshua waltzed out from the kitchen as if on cue.

He put an arm around me and pulled me into a half hug. "Thanks for introducing me to Simone. I'm going to have an amazing restaurant and bar, and ... Who knows? Your dreams could be next."

Yes, they could. But at what price?

CHAPTER FORTY-SEVEN

AFTER MAKING FAST WORK of closing up the bar, I made it home earlier than usual and Cass greeted me at the door with a wagging tail. I sighed. After a long, complicated night, there was nothing quite like a happy dog to ease tension. Mac padded up behind Cass and began meowing pitifully.

"My goodness, you guys act like you haven't been fed in weeks!"

I went to the cupboard and took out their food, emptying it into their respective bowls. Mac looked down at his bowl and then up at me with a you gotta be kidding me look.

"Sorry, big man, I have to put you back on a diet." I swear he rolled his eyes at me. "Okay. Fine. You can have a little cream on top."

I got the cream out of the fridge along with some lunch meat to top off Cass's meal. I started to grab a Coke, but decided the caffeine probably wasn't a great idea considering how late it was. I eyed the bottle of Chardonnay I kept in the fridge in case Simone dropped in. Frankly, I'd spent too much on that bottle of wine, but I knew if Simone did show up unexpectedly and I had cheap wine or, God forbid, no wine at all, I'd be screwed. I debated for a minute, weighing the pros and cons of opening the bottle now, and finally decided to live a little.

I was twisting the corkscrew down into the cork when one of the kitchen lights flickered. At first I got excited because I thought it meant Lucas might show up. He didn't, and the light went out. I popped out the cork, poured a glass of wine, and set it down, heading into the hallway to get a new bulb.

The house had originally been built in the thirties, which meant it was filled with several interesting nooks and crannies, like the row of four cupboards lining one side of the hall. Instead of opening from the side like most cabinet doors, these opened from the top by pulling the knobs down. I think at one time they were meant to hold kitchen and bath linens. They were about four-feet wide, a foot high, and a foot or so deep. Now they held items like light bulbs, extra candles, and a bunch of random stuff like a deck of cards, some jacks, and old, empty picture frames. There were also a handful of photos.

I grabbed a stack and idly flipped through them. The one common denominator they had was a handsome guy with grey-blue eyes and a healthy tan. He was between thirty-five and forty-five and could easily have been featured in one of those "Visit California!" ads I kept seeing everywhere. In the photos, he was always with one or several women, or what appeared to be a group of friends.

Strangely, I felt like I knew him. I began looking closer at the group photos and I gasped when I recognized Lucas's face. The picture had been shot in this very house in what appeared to be the kitchen (I could see the pool sparkling in the background). I studied the blonde guy again. Could this be Blake, the owner of the house? It seemed likely. This was his home, and he was in all of these photos. I wished I could ask Lucas. I really don't know why it mattered, other than the very strong sense I'd seen Blake before. I placed the stack of photos back into the cupboard and continued my search for a light bulb.

Finally, after a good five minutes, I located a box of bulbs and went back into the kitchen to fix the light. That finished, I decided to take my wine glass and head up to bed. Mac, who had finished his dinner in record time, jumped up on the bed and immediately curled up on my pillow. Cass, my little guard dog, was doing her post-dinner rounds. She'd come upstairs eventually.

I changed into a nightshirt and sat down in front of the vanity where I kept Hannah's feathers. I closed my eyes, thinking about her, wishing she would come through the portal to visit me. Or, even better, wishing she would come through the door—alive.

I could sense the light dim in the room. I opened my eyes and saw the candles on my desk were lit again and the flames fluttered gently.

Lucas!

He stood next to me, very close. I wanted to talk to him. Ask questions. Get answers.

But what he was doing made me forget about talking completely.

His hand grazed the back of my neck as he lifted the thick ponytail off my back and slowly loosened the tie. I closed my eyes at the wonderful feeling of his long fingers combing gently through my hair. A surge went through my body, moving like a wave from the middle of my spine up into my chest and out through my head. I could feel him bend close to my ear.

His fingers moved over my scalp and around to my collarbone while his other hand grazed my cheeks. He turned my chair around to face him. We stared at each other for a long, breathless moment.

"Lucas," I whispered. There was so much I wanted to say.

He picked me up, and my legs wrapped around him. I felt lightheaded with excitement, lust, need. He set me gently on the bed and raised both his arms straight up, whispering something. As before, the tips of his fingers began to emit a pale, pinkish glow. He waved his hands around us, creating the luster.

His dark hair shone brightly in the glow. Lucas moved in towards me, positioning his body over mine. He placed his hands over mine, clasping them tightly, pushing them into the mattress. I could feel his desire as much as my own. My back lifted into an arch and a soft moan escaped my lips. I desperately wanted him closer, wanted his body on mine.

He pulled one hand away and, agonizingly slowly, traced the outline of my lower lip with his finger, gazing into my eyes. The purple in his eyes deepened.

"I never needed anyone when I was alive. Not like this. But here I am. And I'm not supposed to feel this way," he said, shaking his head slightly, not taking his eyes from mine. "But you've done something to me, and I can't stop it. I don't know how."

I felt my pulse speed up. "You don't have to. Do you?"

He groaned. "There are rules. Rules I have to follow."

"But don't you ever get to have a day off from the rules?" I reached out and caressed his chest. It was like moving my hands through tropical water—warm, still, and peaceful, yet behind that calm was something bigger, something more powerful than I could comprehend. "Please break the rules again, Lucas. Just one more time. I need to feel you."

He bowed his head, lowering himself onto me. He dropped a slow kiss on my forehead. Then my cheeks, my eyelids, the tip of my nose, my chin ... so softly, so sweetly. His warm, smooth hands began to explore my body and I thought I would go out of my mind between the tender kisses and the feathery touches. Every brush against my skin fueled my ache, making me want more from him.

When he reached my toes, his lips kissing each one separately as his fingers grazed my legs, he rolled me onto my stomach where he worked his way back up, again kissing every inch of my skin and massaging every part of my body until he reached the top of my head, his fingers now intertwined in my hair, gently tugging on the strands. He gently removed my shirt and panties and his body moved closer to mine, his hands spreading my legs apart as his chest pressed against my back.

He kissed the nape of my neck, and I felt an intense rush of pleasure as he entered me. Together we moved like an ocean wave, ever so slowly at first. When I thought I couldn't take anymore, when I might scream with frustration, he picked up speed, taking us both further into a dizzying spiral of intensity. I felt his hands over mine again as he moved smoothly in and out. He was making it hard for me to think clearly. To think at all, really. My body responded instinctively to his as I gave myself completely to him.

Lucas—dead or alive—had captured every piece of me. Body, mind, heart, and soul.

CHAPTER FORTY-EIGHT

"LUCAS, WHAT WERE YOU like when you were alive?" I asked.

He leaned back against the pillow, closing his eyes. "You know, I was an un-happy person in life. I had a lot of ... issues." He turned his head slightly and smiled. "Hence the tie vote."

I nodded. When he mentioned the tie vote from his own review, I couldn't help wondering if he'd heard what had happened with Bob and me. If he knew I'd been at Jackson's review, he never brought it up so I figured the less said, the better. I didn't want to keep things from him, but I also didn't want to ruin the moment.

"But you were so young. You didn't even have a chance to turn things around."

He smiled. "Leave it to you to try and find the good in my former wastrel exis-tence. Truth is, I lied to people to get what I wanted. Especially to women. I ma-nipulated friends and family. I even stole if I thought it would benefit me. I was a very selfish man."

"Really?" I tried hard to picture the man with me in the way he described his former self. I couldn't do it.

"Really. And you know what?"

I shook my head.

"I realize now how absolutely worthless I was. I mean, I wasn't just hurting others ... I was hurting myself. I was so consumed by my ego, by my need to fill in the perceived emptiness, that I missed the wonder and beauty of what I had. My musical gift, my friends, my family, my life." He ran his hands through his hair. "It's true what they say—you have no idea what you've got until it's gone."

He paused for a moment and turned his deep gaze to me. The moment of silence stretched out until I began to wonder if it was my turn to speak.

"You know what else?" His voice was hushed and slightly husky. A frisson of heat ran down my spine and those damn butterflies began doing cartwheels again.

"Uh, what?" My voice sounded squeaky and Cass peered over at me from her perch next to Lucas. Real smooth, Evie, she seemed to be saying.

"I know why they want you so bad. The Black." I stared into his eyes, mesmerized. I seriously felt like I might be on the verge of a heart attack ... it was pounding so hard I was sure he could hear it loud and clear. He reached towards me again but this time, his fingers grazed my collarbone, stopping just above my heart. "They want you for the same reason I do."

I didn't know how to respond to that. "But you've already had me," I joked.

He smiled. "They want to consume you, and I have to be careful not to want that as well. It would only extinguish the gift you have. Truth is, we are not supposed to be doing what we're doing, and I'm finding it harder and harder not to want to be with you in this way."

"Is there any way around it? Is there any possible way of us being together, like this? I mean besides, besides..."

"You being dead?"

"Yes." I gulped.

"No. I don't think so." He kissed the top of my head. "And I don't want that. There are too many lives for you to touch and help. This is why there are a few things for me to do. It's why I've been gone. I've been trying to find who in the Black Tier has ordered that you be under attack."

I raised my eyebrows. "Attack?"

Lucas hugged me to him and sighed. "You are under attack, and they want you bad. But for the Black Tier to go after you so aggressively means there was a direct order from a vibration in the Asat."

He fell silent for a moment. "You should know ... I've also been trying to see if I can discover what happened to Hannah."

I didn't respond but felt my body tighten.

"Is there anything of hers you can give me that I can take? It may help. The eagle feathers are for you, really. They are a conduit for your gift. I need something personal of your sister's. I promise I'll bring it back."

"I do have something." I rolled onto my side and opened the drawer to my nightstand. Taking out a box, I opened it. Inside was a silver bracelet with Hannah's name written on it. I had one with my name on it as well. My parents had them made when we were born and they gave them to us on our respective tenth birthdays. I took it out and handed it to Lucas. "Will this work? She wore it to church on Sundays and for special occasions. I have one, too."

He held it up and smiled. "This is perfect." Lucas set it on the stand next to him. "You know, beautiful girl, I think the Black Tier is taking a risk with you, one that could result in a huge payoff for them. This is why putting all of these pieces together is so important. The stronger you become with the White vibration, the more power you receive, especially when you cross over. If, by the time you make the crossing, the Black has connected your vibration to their energy, then they win, and trust me, it is all about winning for them."

I snuggled deeper into his chest. "I don't want to talk about any of this right now. I only want to be here with you in this moment."

He gently rolled me onto my back and leaned over me. His eyes darkened, staring at my mouth. My pulse accelerated suddenly and all thoughts of the Black Tier, Nick, and my sister flew out of my head.

"Me too. Although we can't stay here forever, we do have now..." He paused, tilting his head down to place a long kiss between my breasts.

"I wish we had forever," I whispered, feeling his hands roam down past my hips to the sensitive spot between my thighs. I gasped and then moaned appreciatively.

"Shh. As I said we have now," he whispered in my ear.

I closed my eyes, not really caring who or what was after me ... just so long as Lucas didn't stop.

CHAPTER FORTY-NINE

LUCAS'S WORDS HAUNTED me the next day. He'd mentioned consequences for our relationship—if that is what you could call it. I'd never really had a true boyfriend, so I wasn't sure what I had with Lucas. We talked and shared. We laughed together. We made love. But there was that one issue: He was dead, and I was not.

When I woke, he was gone along with Hannah's bracelet. I could only hope it helped Lucas shed light on what had happened to her.

In an effort to distract myself, I began reviewing my ever- dwindling list of suspects in Nick's murder. Dwight was clearly no longer on the list, even though there was still something ... odd about him, something I couldn't quite put a finger on.

As for Pietro and George, I'd pretty much crossed them off as well. In any case, they were locked away, so if they had done it, they were exactly where they needed to be. But it seemed unlikely.

And then there was Candace, who was downright pissed off at me, and Becky, who made it pretty clear she wanted me gone, and Joshua, who I was convinced hadn't done a thing. Mumbles was Candace's sidekick and, as far as I could tell, he had zero motive, so I placed him on the back burner.

There was still one last person I needed to talk to: Bradley Verne.

I knew I would have to handle him differently than I had Candace and Becky—obviously. I scrolled through my phone list and pulled up his number. I was surprised when he answered my call on the first ring.

"This is Bradley Verne," he said.

"Oh hi, Bradley! This is Evie, from Nick's?" "Hey! How are you? My wife and I have been meaning to stop in for a visit, but I've been trying to get this new project off the ground and, well, that and the daily visits to my dad are really cutting into any free time I might have had."

"I understand. How is your father doing?"

He grew silent for a minute. "He's still in a coma. Truth be told, we don't expect him to be around much longer." His voice was thick with emotion.

"I am so sorry. I wish there was some way I could help."

"Thank you. I appreciate it."

I clicked over to speakerphone and set the iPhone on the counter. "Hey, I know you're busy, but I was wondering if you'd like to have lunch with me. Maybe today?"

"I would love to," he said, sounding genuinely disappointed. "But I have a full day today. I'm about to head over to see my dad, and I usually eat lunch there at the home." He paused for a moment. "But if you like, you could maybe meet me there and we could visit. I know it's not the ideal place for catching up, but you'd have a captive audience."

It wasn't exactly what I'd planned, but I sensed Bradley could use some support. I agreed to meet him at noon. But ...

"Will Raquela be joining you as well?" As nice as she seemed, I didn't really think I'd get very far with the whole Q&A thing if Bradley's wife was along for the ride.

"No. Not today. Usually she comes, but she's got a hair appointment this afternoon so it'll just be me and my dad."

"I'm sorry I won't get to see her, but I look forward to catching up with you!" We said our goodbyes and I hung up.

It was sheer luck Bradley had some time to meet with me today. Simone took another day off to visit the spa, and although she invited me to join her, I declined saying I needed some downtime at home. Actually, I did. But hopefully the meeting with Bradley would only take a few hours at most, and then I'd be back for a swim and dinner.

I kissed my little animal family goodbye. I promised Cass a dip in the pool when I came home.

"And as far as you go, fat cat..." I scratched Mac under his chin while he started his motor purring, "I may consider a kitty treat for you later."

I headed out in a surprisingly good mood considering everything that was going on. I had to attribute it to Lucas. When I thought about him, my entire body went all melty, and the images from the two nights I had spent with him made my cheeks burn and a smile spread across my face.

Platinum Partners, the retirement home where Warren Verne lived, was up the coast quite a ways, just past Malibu. I turned off the Pacific Coast Highway and took a long, windy road up into the hills. It struck me as a bit odd that a senior residence would be so isolated, until I reached the driveway. One look around, and I quickly realized this place was designed for privacy and catered to the golden years of those who had a lot of gold to spend.

Palm trees lined the gated drive and tropical foliage dotted the grounds. A circular drive looped gently around a massive water fountain where yellow chested birds dove in to drink and bathe. The view was worth every penny (I thought) and featured an endless expanse of deep, blue Pacific Ocean dotted by white-capped waves. Not a bad place to retire. Honestly, if I hadn't known better, I'd have thought I was pulling into a luxury hotel. It didn't help matters much when I spotted a valet sign. I felt very not-classy as I rolled up to a stop in my beat up VW van. My face burned as I stepped out of the van and handed my keys to the valet. He made a good show of pretending not to be fazed by the state of my car as he stepped up to me, clipboard in hand, and asked for my name.

"Evie Preston."

He jotted that down on a little claim ticket and stepped behind the valet podium to check his computer. "Welcome to Platinum Partners, Miss Preston. You are here for?"

"Warren Verne." I sure hoped Bradley had put my name down on the list.

Valet Guy clicked a few buttons on the keyboard and looked up, smiling. "And here you are, Miss Preston."

He stepped back around to my side, tore the claim ticket in half, handing me the bottom, and gamely stepped up into my van. I didn't stick around long enough to see if it started or not. But I did wonder, briefly, if I was expected to tip this guy. I only had two dollars in my purse, and something told me the valets here were used to getting a whole lot more.

I walked through the massive glass double doors at the front entrance and spotted Bradley right away. He was seated in the lobby, surrounded by yet more water features and amazing art. He popped up from a sleek leather sofa. "I'm so glad you came!"

I felt a small twinge of guilt at his words. I was glad to see him too, but my motives were far from pure. "Thank you for the invite. This place is incredible!"

He nodded tiredly. "It is, but as you can imagine, it can also be a very sad place." He gestured for me to join him as we began walking down a long hall. "We'll be going over to the critical care side."

Bradley escorted me through another set of double doors and back outside, where we strolled across a lovely rose garden in which several elderly people sat feeding birds, talking, and playing chess. Further off in the distance, on the other side of the garden, I spotted a fenced-in pool with what appeared to be waiters carrying trays, moving purposefully amongst the occupied lounge chairs. You could call this place what you liked, but as far as I was concerned, it was a five-star hotel for the over-55 crowd. Or at least that's what I thought until we stepped into another building that looked and felt much more like a hospital.

It was sterile and the smell of rubbing alcohol permeated the air. Bradley checked in at a nurse's station.

"Hello, Mr. Verne." A young, studly looking guy with a slight accent stood up from behind the desk. He wasn't my type, but I am certain I was in the minority. He had massive, broad shoulders, wavy golden hair, light blue eyes, the obligatory California tan, and a smile he had to have paid a hefty price for. He looked like his name should have been Sven. Golden Sven to be exact.

"Good afternoon, Dederick."

Or ... Dederick. Dutch maybe?

Bradley turned to me. "Dederick is my father's head nurse. He's been with us from the start. He's wonderful with him." He shifted his gaze back to the nurse. "How is Dad doing today?"

Dederick frowned, sympathetically. "The same, sir. I'm sorry."

Bradley sighed sadly. "I know you're doing what you can." He reached out to clap Dederick gently on the arm. "Thank you."

"I'll have Kristen take you down to your dad's room today, if that's okay. I have another patient who needs an IV bag changed and," he leaned over towards us, lowering his voice, "he's a bit cantankerous."

"Of course. No problem," Bradley said.

Dederick lifted a walkie talkie device to his mouth, speaking quietly into it. About thirty seconds later, a bright, attractive young woman with some major bounce in her step approached.

"Oh Mr. Verne!" she chirped. "So nice to see you." Her voice held more than a hint of a southern accent ... Georgia maybe? Alabama?

"You, too." He turned to me. "Evie, this is Kristen. Kristen just happens to be my dad's favorite nurse. Go figure."

We all shared a laugh and Kristen smiled cheerfully. Clearly Mr. Verne liked his women young and pretty.

Dederick cleared his throat gently. "If you'll excuse me, I need to check on that patient." He turned to go and then stopped momentarily. "Oh, and before I forget, Miss Preston, I'll need to take your purse and place it in one of our secure lockers. We don't allow bags of any sort into our critical care room, for security reasons."

"Oh okay. Sure." I handed him my purse. I wasn't exactly thrilled to have it away from my person but rules were rules.

"I'll be back at the nurse's station when you're finished and can retrieve it for you."

I nodded.

"Nice meeting," he said, smiling again.

"And you."

Dederick turned to leave, and we followed perky Kristen down the hall. She opened the door to a dimly lit room. In the middle was a narrow bed on wheels. Lying on the bed was a very thin and weathered elderly man. He was pale, almost grey, and hooked up to all sorts of machines. The only sound in the room was the repetitive pumping noise from one of the machines.

Bradley pulled up a seat for me and Kristen excused herself. Bradley didn't say anything for a few minutes. Finally he broke the silence.

"You know, he was always so disappointed in me. Always. I've been trying to please him since the day I was born. Or at least that's how it feels. I love him so much. I wanted to be like him. But he never really loved me. Not the way he did Nick."

"That must've been so hard for you." My parents may have been strict, but I never once felt like they didn't love me as much as they loved Hannah. I couldn't imagine how that must've made Bradley feel.

Bradley nodded, tearing up. "It was. It is. But I never held it against Nick. I mean, once I moved into adulthood and stopped being so focused on my own needs, I was able to get over the whole jealousy thing." He rubbed his face tiredly. "Truth is, I gave my dad so many reasons not to think highly of me. I got kicked out of expensive schools, partied like a rock star, dated all sorts of women, and even have a couple of illegitimate children my dad has graciously taken care of while also making sure the women didn't come back to take more from the family. Then, Raquela came along." He smiled softly. "I think marrying her is the only thing my dad has ever approved of. She set me on a good path, you know, and now I'm sure she's as disappointed in me as he'd be." Bradley sighed, placing his elbows on his knees and staring long and hard at the polished floor.

"Wait, what do you mean?" I asked.

"I had to file for bankruptcy. The article Jackson wrote—you must've seen it— it mentioned a well-to-do movie producer filing bankruptcy." He glanced back up at me sheepishly. "That guy was me. Is me. My last few movies have completely tanked, and I've made some poor business decisions. The last decent thing I did was pay off the bills on Nick's place. I'm so good at playing a rich guy but that's all it is—an act. It's embarrassing." He dropped his head into his hands looking as dejected as he sounded.

"I'm terribly sorry." And I was. Bradley really seemed like a decent guy. Sure, he'd made some mistakes in his life, but hadn't we all? A thought struck me. "Please don't take this the wrong way, but your father isn't doing well and ... he must have made provisions for you, something to ... to take care of you after he's gone."

Bradley sighed again, head still firmly planted in his hands. "Yes, I'm sure that's the case. But honestly, I don't have any more time to wait. The IRS is going to take our house and cars soon, and I don't have access to my father's money until after he's gone. And in reality..." He looked at me with tears falling openly down his face. "I'd rather my dad still be here, even like this. I know it's selfish, in a way, but I just wish he could hear me and feel how sorry I am for being a screwup." He stood, taking his father's limp hand in his, and leaned over the bed, sobbing.

It was pretty awkward and I really felt horrible for him. I knew I could have helped, even a small bit, by touching him. But it seemed like a huge invasion of his privacy and, well, sometimes the best way to deal with grief is to face it head on, as he was doing.

"I'm sorry. I really am." Bradley grabbed a tissue and blew his nose loudly. "Can you give me a minute? Then maybe we can go out to the garden and have lunch. I'm pretty hungry."

I nodded. "Sure. No problem. Take your time." I left the room, quietly closing the door behind me. Perky Kristen was standing outside and pounced on me the moment I stepped out into the hall.

"Everything okay, hon?"

"I'm fine. But, well, it's not an easy situation."

"Oh, I know, and poor Mr. Bradley, he comes here all the time, and it is always the same. He apologizes to his father and ends up leaving in tears. He was doing it when the old man was conscious, but nothing and no one ever seemed to make that old man happy but Mr. Bradley's friend Nick Gordin." She shook her head, tsking. "Terrible thing what happened to Nick," she said in a low voice. "Then when he got the news, Mr. Warren slipped into a coma and that was it. It is awfully nice of you to come and visit your grandpa, though!"

"Um, what?"

"Your grandfather, Mr. Warren."

I was just about to correct her when she continued, "Your dad told me you were away at school somewhere."

Wait. Bradley had a daughter? He had mentioned some illegitimate kids. I stayed silent, waiting to see what else she might reveal.

"Anyway, you coming out here to see the old man, especially the way he's treated your daddy, is so sweet. I suppose you know this, but Mr. Warren told me he was leaving the bulk of his money to Nick Gordin. Forty million dollars!" She placed her hands on her hips and shook her head. "And poor Mr. Bradley will get the remaining five million. It's just wrong, that's what it is. To treat his only son like so much trash."

Whoa.

Dederick came up behind us, startling me. His mouth pressed into a hard line.

"Kristen, what's going on? You know we don't discuss patient details with anyone!"

"Oh! But Miss Evie here is Mr. Verne's granddaughter." Dederick shot me a suspicious look. "No, she isn't. She's a friend of Mr. Bradley's."

Kristen brought a hand to her mouth. "Oh dear." She glanced over at me and then at Dederick. "I, um, I better be off. Nice to meet you, miss." She turned to go but not before Dederick requested her presence in his office when her shift ended.

I felt certain that Kristen's days were numbered at Platinum Partners. And I wished I could have helped her out ... because thanks to her slipup, I was certain I'd learned the motive for Nick's murder and I was certain I knew who the killer was. I calmly walked over to Dederick, who was again seated behind the desk at the nurse's station.

"Mr. Verne is having a really hard time in there with his dad. I've decided to take a rain check on our lunch and give him some much-needed downtime. Would you be able to pass along my regrets and let him know I'll call him later today?" Dederick nodded, but didn't say much. He retrieved my purse and I made a hasty exit, feeling his eyes on me all the way down the hall. I felt bad for ditching

Bradley in his time of need, but I wanted to make sure I was nowhere near

Bradley Verne, because I had no intention of following Nick to the grave.

CHAPTER FIFTY

MY HANDS WERE SHAKING as I dropped into the driver's seat of my van. I coasted out of the main entrance and pulled over further down the drive, away from potentially nosy valets. I knew I needed to talk to someone, and the only rational person I could think of, the only one who had a real stake in this, was Joshua.

I whipped out my phone and hit autodial. Joshua didn't answer, but I left him a message saying I thought I knew who'd murdered his dad. Yeah, it probably wasn't the greatest way to share the news, but it's not like I had a lot of options ... or time.

"I'll tell you about what I learned tonight and we can come up with a game plan." I hung up only to see a text arrive from Simone. Apparently she was having a business lunch with Joshua and things were going swimmingly. So much for her spa day. At least I now knew why I couldn't reach Joshua.

I texted her back, "Tell Joshua to check his messages after lunch." No point in ruining their little tête-á-tête.

Meanwhile, I had some time to kill before I was scheduled to work at the bar, and I needed to think all of this through.

I was pretty shaken by what Kristen told me. See, I liked Bradley. And, to a lesser degree, I liked his wife. But I also knew—and not just from listening to my dad on the pulpit— money and greed caused people to do evil things. Fact is, when you considered the resentment Bradley no doubt felt towards Nick and to his father, well, it sure seemed like he had some strong motive for murder. Sure, the guy would've gotten five million, and in my world, that is some serious cash. However, forty-five million was a heck of a lot more and, considering Bradley's bankruptcy and his obvious concern about failing his wife, well, it was a no-brainer.

But now came the hard part. As in, how to get proof.

As soon as I arrived back home, Bradley called. I decided to answer, trying hard to keep my voice as normal as possible.

"Hello?"

"Hi, Evie. It's Bradley Verne. Is everything okay? I came out of my father's room and Dederick said you'd decided to take a rain check on lunch." He paused for a moment. "I-I hope you weren't too uncomfortable with my waterworks."

"Hey, I'm sorry. Truth is, it seemed like you could use a break and I figured we could meet up for lunch another time when things weren't so, um, heavy. And as it turned out, I got a text from my other boss saying she needed me for a gig tonight. I wanted to tell you in person but you were so upset. I'm sorry."

"It's okay. I just wanted to make sure I hadn't scared you off."

Yes, you did! "No, not at all. Thanks for checking on me though." I paused, collecting my thoughts. "Hey, maybe you and Raquela can come by the bar tonight? Drinks are on me."

"You don't have to do that. Are you sure?" he asked.

"Yes, of course!" At this point, I wasn't sure if I should win an Oscar or receive a one-way ticket to hell. I'd never lied like this back home.

"Okay, sounds good. Let me check with Raquela and maybe we'll see you tonight."

"Great!" Oh God.

I hung up, confident he had no idea I was on to him. And now, I simply needed to figure out what I could do to rat him out.

I spent the rest of the day planning and trying to enjoy the typically awesome weather. Cass spent much of the day following me around with a ball in her mouth. Mac, on the other hand, was on his back on the sofa. It was nice having the place to myself, but this was also the longest I'd gone without seeing Janis and Bob. I couldn't help wondering if those two had gotten into trouble because of me and my visit to the other side.

Then again, I was still kind of miffed at Janis for her antics concerning Joshua. But now that Joshua seemed completely smitten with his new business partner, well, it didn't matter that much anymore.

Finally I'd had it with all the thinking and decided to play a game of fetch with Cass. We played hard. Cass even dove into the pool a few times. Just as it was clear she was getting tired, I tossed the ball one last time, extra hard. It shot over the pool and down the hill, towards the guesthouse. Cass and I watched it land in a dry patch of lawn with a thud. Then we looked at each other.

I shrugged. "Let's go. If you want it, you're coming with me."

We jogged down the hill together. The ball had rolled right up to the front door of the cottage. I moved towards the porch, the hair on my arms suddenly standing to attention. I glanced over at Cass, who'd lowered herself to a crouch, the fur along her back echoing my arm hair and standing straight up. She let out a low growl.

I should have turned away—it would've been the smart thing to do. But like one of those horror movie bimbos, I walked right up, reached out my hand, and turned the doorknob. To my surprise, it opened. The drapes were shut tight, making it dark inside. I flipped a light switch to the right of me, figuring if there was power in the house, there had to be power out here. I was right.

The house smelled musty and boxes were stacked all over. But it was actually kind of quaint, with hard wood floors and detailing around the windowsills and doors. The ceilings were high, with wood beams, making it feel larger than it was. I moved further inside, exploring, Cass following reluctantly.

The kitchen had a stove, a small island made of wood, and a colorful, if dated, tile backsplash in teal, yellow, and burnt orange. It was sort of retro-Spanish-looking to me.

Cass whined, clearly wanting to leave.

"It's okay," I whispered, not knowing why I was whispering.

On the other side of the kitchen was a small living room with an arched fire-place. It was covered in the same tiles as the kitchen back splash. I walked a bit further. There was a door that opened into a decent sized bedroom. The room was all white, minus the dust, with white linens on a rustic bed. The only color in the room came from a red, faded blanket at the foot of the bed. I moved closer, reaching out to touch the red blanket. And that's when I noticed something, a stain maybe, peeking out from one corner. I gingerly lifted the blanket up to reveal a few rust-colored blotches dotting the white cover beneath. It looked an awful lot like blood. I backed away quickly, releasing the blanket.

As I turned to go, a photo on the nightstand caught my eye. I walked over and picked it up. Cass increased her whining. I recognized one man, the guy who I had assumed was Blake, the owner. And there was Lucas, and a woman draped over him, a very beautiful, dark-haired woman. But it was the third man in the photo who captured my full attention. When I looked at him, my skin began to crawl and I dropped the photo to the ground, bolting out the door as fast as I could with Cass at my heels.

The man in the photo was none other than the man from my bizarre sex dream. The same man whose face had been splashed across the screen during Jackson's review—the one who'd pushed Jackson in the pool. And the same man who had shown up in the vision when I shook Kane Richards's hand. He was clearly alive in the photo ... but I was pretty sure he wasn't anymore.

CHAPTER FIFTY-ONE

ONCE INSIDE THE MAIN house, I screamed. Cass began to howl, and Mac rolled off the couch and strolled over to watch his two roomies go bonkers.

For the first time since I arrived, I felt the strong urge to go back to Texas. I was living in a haunted house. I was trying to solve a murder. I had freakishly strange friends and things were getting further and further out of hand.

But was going home the solution? If I went home, I would likely fade back into a shadow of my current self. Or, even worse, I would wind up working at the local Piggly Wiggly and married to someone named Billy Joe who chewed tobacco and swore worse than Simone.

After much mulling, I decided I much preferred L.A. crazy over small town crazy any day, and I'd simply have to deal with the ghosts and murders head on.

Once I calmed down, I took myself upstairs to shower and get ready for the night. It was a little after four o'clock. The long hot shower helped take me down a few notches.

I took a little extra time dressing and putting my makeup on. At one point, Cass started pacing the floor and then jogged out of the room. I heard her paws hit the stairs and travel down. She was as agitated as I'd been. Mac, of course, followed her.

I was putting on lip-gloss and getting ready to go down when I heard a whooshing sound from below, and then I heard what sounded like a heavy book hitting the floor. I started down the stairs calling for Cass, wondering what she and Mac had gotten into now. And I stopped as soon as I turned the corner into my kitchen.

Cass was there, but she was lying on the floor, whimpering, with blood oozing onto the tiles from somewhere on her body. I ran to her, horrified, bending down.

"Oh my God!" Then I looked up to see someone standing over me. Cass attempted to growl, and I felt a sharp blow to my face as what appeared to be an expensive high-heeled shoe connected with my jaw. I fell back onto the floor with a thud and stared in surprise at the two people above me. Raquela Verne and Nurse Dederick.

I moaned in pain, and Mac began meowing at a high pitch, until Raquela screamed, "Shut up!" and fired a small but deadly gun at him. Thankfully, Mac got away, and I hoped he'd hidden himself under a bed.

"Why?" I cried, looking up into Raquela Verne's wild eyes. "Why are you doing this to me?"

She sneered nastily down at me. "Because, you had to go and stick your nose where it didn't belong! And you're the only thing currently standing between me and forty-five million dollars! With Nick out of the way that money was to go back to my dipshit husband, and then it would all become mine—at least half of it would!" She began pacing the kitchen in agitation.

"Do you have any idea what it's like to be married to an insufferable, miserable prick like Bradley?! Fifteen years! Fifteen years of whining about his dad and Nick and all of that bullshit. Fifteen years of dealing with illegitimate children, none of whom I could give two shits about. And then I finally met someone wonderful." Her angry glare quickly morphed into a love-struck smile and she blew a kiss at Dederick. "A man who wasn't so wrapped up in his own pity party that he didn't have time for me. And then I find out that old bastard decided to leave the bulk of everything to that moron, Nick! Then Bradley tells me he has to file for bankruptcy. No way am I getting nothing after all I have put up with. So you have to go away, Evie! Such a shame, because you didn't even need to get involved in any of this. You could've lived your silly little life singing your silly little songs serving silly little drinks to those lushes! I've been watching you. Bradley told me all about your sleuthing. Then when he told me you two were having lunch today at the nursing home, I knew I needed to put an end to it all!"

I groaned slightly. I could see Dederick put an arm around her. Raquela handed him the weapon, probably deciding to let him do the "dirty" work. I can only assume he got my home address from my purse that morning at the nursing home.

"You're delusional, and so is your boyfriend," I muttered through a very sore mouth. "You realize you'll never get away with this."

That's when I heard Cass's moan, her breathing becoming more labored. And I don't know how it happened but I found the strength to sweep my legs out, hard, beneath Dederick's legs. He went down with a yelp, dropping the gun to the floor.

Raquela shouted angrily as she dove for the weapon. I kicked out again from my prone position on the floor. My wedge- heeled foot made contact with Dederick's face and he grunted in pain. I quickly propelled myself forward, along the floor, and made a grab for the gun.

"No one hurts my dog! No one!" I grabbed the gun with sweat-slicked hands and aimed it at Dederick, who was rolling on the floor, clutching his nose, which appeared to be bleeding profusely. Raquela, seeing I had her boyfriend in my sights, stopped in her tracks.

The three of us sat there silently, assessing the current turn of events. Just as I began to think I'd gotten the upper hand in things, Dederick shot his free hand out and roughly grabbed a fistful of Cass's fur. He yanked her towards him men- acingly. "Drop the gun or I'll break the dog's neck if I have to." He made as if to punch her with his fist and I cried out in anger and frustration.

And then Bob and Janis appeared right behind Raquela. Janis winked at me although I had no idea what the two of them planned to do. Janis raised her hands and a reddish light began to pulse out of them towards Raquela. She yelped, startled, and stumbled forward in surprise. Dederick turned to glance at her and it was the split second I needed to heave my sore body off the floor, grab Cass, and pull her away from him. Janis did the light thing again and almost knocked Raquela off her feet. Raquela turned behind her, an expression of fear and anger mingling on her face.

"What the fuck?!"

Neither of them were paying any attention to me as I slid further away with Cass in my arms.

"Who's there?" Dederick shouted, dashing from one side of the kitchen to the other. "We'll find you, no point hiding!"

I figured I needed to man up and fire the gun. Those two would only be distracted for so long. I'd never shot anyone in my life but I didn't think I had much choice, considering the alternative. Then I heard a shout, "Evie!"

Joshua bounded in through the patio door, almost colliding with Dederick. He grabbed the smaller man and made short work of him, with a little help from the nearby corner of the stove. Dederick dropped to the floor for the second time in minutes, but I seriously doubted he'd be getting up again anytime soon.

Raquela stared from Joshua to me with the gun and back again, an ugly look of panic flitting across her face. With a growl, she turned, probably to try and run, but Bob was there doing the same light thing from his hands as Janis had. He pushed Raquela straight into Joshua's arms. In a parody of an embrace, Joshua grabbed her and squeezed—hard. She struggled mightily, screaming obscenities, and I worried she'd knock him in the face with the crown of her head. I sprinted over (well, more like staggered) and dealt her a sharp blow across the head with the butt of the gun. She went instantly limp and Joshua dragged her away from the kitchen, presumably to tie her up.

For a few seconds, I simply stood there, panting. Bob and Janis had disappeared again. Cass was lying motionless on the floor, her breaths coming in shallow gasps. Dederick was ... gone. Oh, crap. I momentarily debated about trying to find him, but I didn't want to leave Cass, even for a second.

And that's how Joshua found me a few minutes later, cradling Cass in my arms and sobbing. He crouched down next to us.

"Shhh, Evie. It's going to be okay. Cass will be okay, I promise." He reached into his pocket and quickly dialed 9-1-1. His voice shook as he explained to the switchboard operator what had happened and gave them my address. Then he hung up and gently placed his arms around me.

I ached badly all over, and my sobbing grew heavier as I called out Cass's name, stroking her fur gently.

"Evie, I promise Cass will be okay. Paramedics are on the way. I will get her to the emergency vet hospital as soon as the authorities arrive."

I shook my head, wincing as a stab of pain shot through my neck. "No! Take her now. I'm fine."

"You're not fine. There's a killer running loose in the neighborhood, and I don't want to leave you here with that woman. Hang on, and I promise to do everything I can for Cass."

I choked back another sob. It hurt to cry. My rib cage was killing me. I closed my eyes and heard Cass whimper. My eyes shot open and, for the umpteenth time that day, I was shocked almost speechless. "Oh my God," I gasped.

"What?" Joshua said, looking at me and then at Cass in alarm.

About ten feet away from us stood Lucas—his colors drastically diminished. He had tears in his eyes and he was holding Hannah's bracelet up and in his hands. I started to call Lucas's name when the air shimmered behind him and two more figures appeared.

Pierre and Anastasia. I thought I might be sick.

"Evie, what is it? Are you okay?" Joshua kept asking me over and over.

Anastasia morphed into a jaguar and her mouth opened wide ... then wider still ... until it was a large, black hole ... grotesquely huge on her lithe body. She roared, and then, in a horrifying visual I will never forget, swallowed Lucas entirely. Pierre smiled. "See you in the Black Tier, Evie." Then they disappeared.

And I passed out.

CHAPTER FIFTY-TWO

I SPENT A NIGHT in the hospital being monitored. I had a couple of cracked ribs, a sprained ankle, and some ugly bruises. But I was alive. Dederick had, thankfully, been caught by the police and was now being charged with Nick's murder, along with attempted murder and assault. Raquela, as his sidekick, received the same charges, but I'd been told she'd likely get off easier since the evidence seemed strong she hadn't actually pulled the trigger on Nick that day in the bar. Nevertheless, the officers who came to take my statement assured me she'd be in jail for a very long time.

I felt horrible for Bradley, who had sent me a huge bouquet of roses and an apology. I didn't expect to see him for a while, as I suspected he had a lot to work out.

I could also not stop thinking about Lucas. It appeared he'd been taken by Pierre and Anastasia to the Black Tier. I also knew he had found Hannah or at least knew what had happened to her. What I did not know was if I would ever see him again. And that hurt much worse than any of the physical pain I'd been through in the last twenty-four hours.

I finally made it back home, with a little help from Simone, who had Dwight pick me up at the hospital and transport me home. Both Simone and Dwight had been adamant about me staying at her place, but thankfully, Joshua stepped in and offered to temporarily move in to care for Cass and me.

One week later, Joshua walked into my bedroom where I was napping with Cass. She lay on the bed near my feet, her fur partially shaved where she'd been shot, and a red, puckered line of stitches etched across her side. Joshua bent down next to her and gently gave her the twice-daily dose of antibiotics. She loathed them, but she opened her mouth nevertheless and swallowed stoically. She lifted her head and licked his face when it was over. He laughed.

"You're so good to her. You're good to me, too. Thank you." Joshua sat gently next to me on the bed. "I was thinking..." "Yes?"

He glanced down at his hands, looking momentarily uncomfortable. "I don't know if it's such a great idea ... you here ... alone."

"I have Cass and Mac here, and now that Simone had that new alarm installed, well I feel a whole lot safer."

He nodded thoughtfully. "True. But this is a big place, and you sometimes work late hours." He rubbed his neck. "The thing is, my mom is leaving."

Would miracles never cease? "Your mom's leaving?"

"Yeah. She wants to try to get back into acting and thinks she has a better chance on Broadway. She's leaving for New York in a week. Things between her and I have been ... tense, and we both think some space would be a good thing. I don't have a place right now, and you have that guesthouse." He turned and smiled winningly. "I won't bother you. Trust me, I'll let you have your privacy. I would be there, though ... just in case you needed me."

So Becky was leaving. I knew she'd caused Roger's death, but I also knew proving it was going to be next to impossible. And I wondered if she'd ever tell Joshua the real truth about his father, assuming it hadn't been Nick. The only thing that made me feel somewhat better was I knew Becky would face a review. If not now, then at the end of her life, and she'd have to atone for her bad choices just like the rest of us when we died. Hopefully, as she went forward into her future, her good deeds would outweigh the bad ones.

"What do you think?" Joshua asked me.

I realized I'd been silent for too long. "That place is a mess," I said, cautiously. "I've only been inside once. I can't imagine anything works."

He chuckled. "I worked for the Red Cross, remember? You can't imagine the places I've slept. Part of the job requirement was that I was able to make repairs ... not just to people but also to buildings, cars, you name it. I can fix that place up, no problem."

He was a good salesman. "One problem though. I don't own this place. I would have to talk to Simone."

"I know. I already did."

"What? Really?"

He nodded. "That girl really loves you. She stayed the entire night when you were at the hospital, in the chair next to your bed."

I had a vague memory of someone being there. But I was so hopped up on pain killers, I could barely remember my own name let alone notice someone else in the room with me. "She was?"

"She was, and she was very worried. When I mentioned the guesthouse to her and how I could be of help, she said—"

"Wait!" I held up a hand. "Let me guess. It involved the "f" word."

Joshua barked a laugh. "How did you know? Anyway, she called the guy who owns this place, and he didn't have a problem with me moving in. I think, maybe, he's hoping I might be able to make some repairs and upgrades to the property while I'm here."

For a minute, I didn't say anything. Joshua glanced down to scratch Mac who was purring loudly (the sneaky feline had crawled up onto Joshua's lap seconds after he sat on the bed).

Honestly, I wasn't sure about Joshua living here. I mean, I should've been happy my friends were concerned about me and wanted to be supportive. But what about my privacy and setting boundaries between Joshua and I? We were co-workers, after all. And there was his budding relationship with Simone. Then I remembered poor Cass nearly dead and me not too far behind.

"Yeah. Okay." Cass lifted her head and looked at us both. "On one condition." Cass closed her eyes.

"Sure. Name it."

"We need to come up with a list of house and property rules. I mean, set some basic boundaries and figure out who takes care of what on the property."

"Okay. Boundaries are good."

His head was still bent down looking at the top of Mac's head but I could tell he was smiling.

"And this is a trial thing. Two months. My mother gives her new hairdressers two months at her shop and if it doesn't work, if the hairdresser can't curl hair right or add an extension correctly, that's it."

Joshua smiled mischievously. "Pretty sure I can't do either of those things."

I rolled my eyes. "You know what I mean." I grimaced. "And you can't fire me if I kick you out!"

"Wouldn't that be weird, though? I mean, if I did something that warranted an eviction ... why would you want to continue working with me?"

I sighed. "Good point, but all the same. Deal?"

He reached out to shake my hand, grinning broadly. "Deal."

CHAPTER FIFTY-THREE

THREE DAYS LATER and still no Lucas. Kane Richards left a couple of messages about my coming to New York. I had not returned his calls. I still wasn't feeling great. But more importantly, I was deeply concerned about the vision I'd had when I shook Kane's hand. I had to find out who the evil dream guy was and how much of a threat he posed. I knew, sooner or later, I needed to make a decision about going to New York. I just wasn't ready yet.

I'd also begun having second thoughts about allowing Joshua to move into the guesthouse. The place gave me a bad feeling. I kept mulling over the photo of Creepy Dream Guy in the guesthouse bedroom and how Cass had been very reluctant to even step foot on the front porch. And then I recalled Lucas telling me about portals and how they could be found just about anywhere.

I stopped breathing as a sharp pain hit my stomach.

I knew where a portal was, possibly not the good kind.

I grabbed my crutches and hobbled down to the guesthouse. A U-Haul was parked in front.

I stormed through the front door. Simone stood there in short shorts and a tight tank top. Her hair was pulled back and her face bare of makeup. She was stacking dishes.

"Evie!" she squealed. "How the fuck are you?"

"Um, uh, what are you doing here?"

"Duh!" Her eyes widened. "I'm helping Joshua move in. I'm so happy he'll be here for you. Oh God, is he hot, or what!? I would love to hit that," she said lowering her voice. "I'm working on it." She winked at me. "And when you get better, I'm taking you over to meet the Sony guys. I told them we needed to reschedule. But I promise."

I closed my eyes and counted to three. "Where is Joshua?"

"In the truck."

"Okay. Um, it's nice you're helping out."

She came over and hugged me. "It's nice to see you on your feet. And look at me! No makeup! Hurry up and get better."

I think she meant it. In fact, I know she did. All of it. "You look great." And I meant it too. She did.

"I kind of like the au naturel thing, but I need you. I do!" she whined.

"I'll be back in no time. I have to go talk to Joshua now, though." I hobbled back outside to the U-Haul. I found him unloading a box.

"Um, hey."

Joshua turned, his brows furrowed in concern. "Evie! What are you doing out of bed? You need to be resting. I told you to call my cell if you needed me."

"I know, but I had to talk to you. Face to face."

"Okay." He wiped the sweat off his forehead and waited patiently.

"You can't move in here." Yes, I felt like an ass.

He laughed.

"No. I mean it."

The smile dropped off his face. "What? Why? It's not because of Garbo, is it? You said I could bring her."

This wasn't going to be easy. "Oh my gosh, no! I love dogs. You know that." I eyed Garbo sunning herself on the front porch. "It's just ... I don't know. There's something about this place, something ... not right."

He frowned and set the box on the ground, placing his hands on his hips and shaking his head. "We have a deal. Sixty day trial." He shot me a pleading look, "I have nowhere else to go."

"Go to Simone's," I snapped, instantly regretting it.

His head popped up and he glared at me. "Is that what this is about? She's being helpful. I can use all the friends I can get right now." He looked me up and down, his eyes lingering on my crutches. "You could too, for that matter."

I felt like a complete loser and didn't know what to say for a minute. I gave it one last try, "I'm sorry. Look, I'm tired and still recovering. But I keep feeling like you moving into this place is a mistake. It's not that I don't want you here ... it's just—"

He interrupted me, obviously having lost patience with the conversation. "We have a sixty day contract. If you want to kick me out when it's up, then fine. But can I get all my ducks in a row first?"

I nodded. Defeated in more ways than one. "Yes, of course."

I turned on my crutches and headed back to the main house. When I got to the top, I looked back down at the cottage. Simone came out and gave Joshua a hug and then grabbed another box, albeit a small one, out of the back of the truck. He looked up at that moment and caught my eyes. I mustered a smile. He turned away and headed back into the house.

I went inside my house and plopped on the couch next to Cass. I sighed heavily, "The only way I'm ever going to find out what happened to Hannah is to find a way through that portal."

Cass lifted her head and then started to lick my hand.

And the only way I was ever going to see Lucas again and possibly save him from living an eternity in the Black Tier was to find a way there. But I had no clue how that was going to happen. Lucas had been my teacher. He'd taught me all I knew about the tiers, the portals, and consequences ... everything. I closed my eyes. Two words came to mind.

Guardian angel.

That was the answer. I knew it. I had to find out who my guardian angel was. Once I did, I was positive that I would have the answers I needed.

The answers that would lead me back to Lucas.

Suggested Play List While Reading

Dead Celeb

Waiting on a Friend (Rolling Stones)

Rumor Has It (Adele)

Beautiful Day (U2)

Buffalo Soldier (Bob Marley and The Wailers)

Just a Girl (No Doubt)

No Woman No Cry (Bob Marley and The Wailers)

Positive Vibration (Bob Marley and The Wailers)

One Love (Bob Marley and The Wailers)

Lights (Ellie Goulding)

Fade Into You (Mazzy Starr)

Knockin' on Heaven's Door (Johnny Cash)

Edge of Seventeen (Stevie Nicks)

Careless Love (Janis Joplin)

Piece of My Heart (Janis Joplin)

The Dark Portal

Prologue

Sixteen Years Ago

Hannah Preston had made it outside her house without her parents noticing. Slivers of sunlight from the descending sun cast shadows through the trees in the side yard. Summer months held the daylight so much longer than the fall and winter. At that moment, Hannah wished the sun would hurry up and finish setting. She had somewhere to be and soon, but she also had to avoid getting caught.

She'd sworn her twelve-year-old kid sister Evie to secrecy.

Hannah jumped on her bike and pedaled as fast as she could, fingers crossed that her Daddy wouldn't look up from his Bible study. She was sure Mama was closing her eyes right about that moment, tuning Daddy out. Hannah knew. She'd seen it enough.

She raced down the dirt driveway. The light blue halter-top her best friend Karen had let her borrow stuck to her skin as the humidity spread across her body. She knew if her daddy saw her in the outfit she'd chosen to wear to the concert tonight, she'd be in so much trouble. Going to the concert in any outfit would've likely warranted house arrest for several months! Halter top and a pair of tight cropped jeans on top of that-yeah, Hannah was likely going to Hell.

But, she wanted to look extra special. Tommy McMahon would be driving all of them! Tommy was easily the hottest guy in Brady, and he had his own car—a black Camaro. And, Karen had said that he liked her! That meant she just had to look good. But the damn weather had already flattened the curls she'd put in her hair. She prayed the mascara she'd snuck from Mama's bathroom hadn't run.

Almost to the main street, she heard a car behind her. Maybe Tommy, Karen, and Robert, Karen's boyfriend, had come the back way and decided to pick her up out here instead of meeting at Riley's Diner like they'd originally planned. That would be great because she was sweating like a pig and knew that Tommy's car had air conditioning.

Hannah glanced behind her hoping to see Tommy's Camaro, but to her dismay noticed a silver Mercedes Benz. She did a double take because no one in Brady drove a Mercedes.

The car slowed down driving past her. All of the windows were dark, so she couldn't see inside, until the passenger window rolled down. Her stomach sank a little. She knew she should keep pedaling, but curiosity got to her. Who in the world drove a car like that through the back roads of Brady?

"Excuse me, Miss?" a man's voice came from inside the car.

Hannah glanced over but kept pedaling. Then, she stopped. So did the car.

The driver behind the wheel made Tommy McMahon look like chopped liver. The guy was probably around twenty, which, at fifteen, Hannah knew wouldn't exactly be a good thing in Daddy's eyes. Well, hell—riding her bicycle to meet up with her friends and traveling to Jacksonville to see The Backstreet Boys wouldn't exactly be approved of, so checking out the hot guy in the hot car seemed okay. Truth be told, none of this was okay.

She couldn't see the color of his eyes because he wore sunglasses—expensive ones. She knew that much. He was sure golden though—like he'd been on a tropical beach for the past month. He had blondish hair. Again, she couldn't really tell, given how dark it was in the car.

An unexpected breeze swept past her, cooling her for a moment. "Yes?" she asked.

"I'm turned around. I'm from Fort Worth, went to visit my aunt out here in the sticks and got off the freeway for gas. My sense of direction sucks. Can you tell me how to get back to the freeway?" He smiled widely.

She frowned. "Yeah. You just need to go to the main street, which is right up ahead and then make a right onto Third, and you'll see the signs to get you back to the freeway."

"Thank you. Just taking an evening ride, huh?"

She shook her head and smiled. "No. I'm actually meeting my friends up ahead at the diner. We're going to The Backstreet Boys concert."

"No way! Me too. My aunt wasn't happy that I didn't stay long. But..." He shrugged. "If I visited my aunt for the whole day, I'd never make the concert. Tough decision, huh?" he said sarcastically.

Hannah shrugged. "Yeah."

"I'm meeting some buddies there. I can give you a ride to your friends, if you want. It's pretty hot out. Don't want to mess up your pretty hair."

Hannah felt heat rise to her cheeks and thought about this for a few seconds. She was hot, and he was so cute, and he'd said that her hair was pretty. Plus, he seemed like a nice guy. He'd just come from visiting his aunt. And, he drove a Mercedes. That meant he wasn't a kidnapper or anything. Like how may kidnappers drive Mercedes? "What about my bike?"

"Take a look at the back of my trunk."

"Oh. You have a bike rack."

"Yep." He got out of his car. Her jaw dropped. The guy was even more gorgeous than she'd thought. He reminded her of Leonardo DiCaprio in Titanic. She'd seen the movie the last time she'd snuck out with her friends.

He picked up her bike with ease and reached his hand out. "Adram," he said. "Come on. It's too hot and sticky for someone as pretty as you to be out in it. You said it's just up the road, right? I can drop you there. No problem."

"Thanks." She hesitated before opening the car door. She could hear the warnings her parents had doled out about getting in a stranger's car. But this guy was not much older than she was. He looked harmless, and God, he was cute! "That's an interesting name. Adram. I'm Hannah," she said as she climbed in the passenger side of the car.

"It's short for Adramelech," he replied. "And I already knew your name, Hannah." He looked at her, locked the doors and smiled, pressing down on the accelerator.

Hannah's stomach sank, and not in a "I'm with a hot guy" way, but in a "Oh no, what's happening" way, as she reached over and tried to open the car door. Her hand burned like she'd touched fire itself and she yanked it back.

He turned to her and smiled wickedly, removing his sunglasses, as he rolled down the window and took a handful of feathers off the dash that she hadn't noticed before. He tossed the long white feathers out the window and laughed, the piercing sound hurting her ears. He turned to her then.

A scream caught in Hannah's throat. The eyes were black—soulless black, and she knew what the name Adramelech meant. It stirred in her memory: The Chancellor of Hell.

Her voice shaky, she said, "You aren't dropping me off with my friends, are you?"

He grabbed her hand, his fingers long, sharp nails digging into her small wrist. "No. I'm not. I'm taking you to meet some of mine."

Chapter One

Do you have any clue how hard it is to locate your guardian angel? Let me just say this, it is not easy. I mean, it isn't as if I can just walk up to someone on the street and say, "Um, hi, I'm Evie Preston and I was wondering if you might be my guardian angel?" I can see it now! The guy I would be asking would give me this quizzical look insinuating that I'm completely crazy, and yes, I agree it sounds ludicrous. But can you just imagine how the next part of this one-sided discussion might go? "See, I need to find my guardian angel because the dead guy who prefers to be called a spirit, and who I am head over heels in love with, has been taken by the Asat Order to the Black Tier, where he is certain to live an eternity of damnation and torture. If you're my guardian angel then you might have the answers on how I can find him, maybe bring him back here to the Grey Tier. Oh and on top of it, I really need to find him because I believe he knows what happened to my sister, who disappeared sixteen years ago."

Yeah, right; I'm pretty sure that would at the very least get me laughed at, and possibly thrown into jail for forty-eight hours on a 51/50, or worse, placed in an insane asylum. And once word reached my Southern Baptist minister father, he would be convinced I was possessed by the Devil himself. There'd be some holy water dousing then, I can assure you.

So you can see that I'm in some trouble. Not to mention severely depressed over this situation. If it had not been for my dog Cass (part coyote, half lab, German Shepherd and who knows what else) and my fat tabby cat Mac, as well as my complete diva of a boss, Simone, I think I would've crawled into a hole and cried myself into a stupor over the past couple of months.

"Evie! Get the fuck in here. I need your expertise." Speaking of my boss. She has, uh, how do I put this...um... She has a way with words.

I took my time. I have learned that even though Simone, who is one of the world's biggest pop stars, says jump, I have stopped considering how high. Nothing is as big an emergency as she thinks it is.

"What's up?" I made my way into her massive bedroom, which she'd recently redone. She'd gone from Vegas glam to a now subdued Zen state, which I liked a lot better. Instead of hot pinks and black, the room had been transformed into sages and a soft buttery color. It was quite bland for Simone, but I approved. I felt pretty certain that Joshua, my other boss and renter on the property for which I house-sat (long story), was developing what to me looked like a relationship with Simone—and was the reason for her sudden softening in many ways.

"About fucking time, Speed."

Except for one. Simone's mouth still needed a good douse of cleaning detergent—bleach came to mind. "Speed?"

"Yeah, Speed, like in the movie The Swan Princess. Speed was the turtle. You're as slow as a turtle."

I sighed and rolled my eyes. "And you are as obnoxious as a group of adolescent boys having a farting and burping contest."

"Good one. Nice comeback. Now, what the hell do you think of this?" She held up a spaghetti-strapped, teal chiffon floor-length number. "Or this..." She took the other dress off the back of the chair, holding up a deep V-neck, sleeveless, black floor-length dress, with a slit up the side of the leg.

"Wow! Okay, so the teal dress would make your eyes pop, but the black one is extremely hot. A little bit vampire-ish if I do say so, but still hot."

"Perfect! You said it's hot and that is what I'm going for. I am going to get Joshua into my bed tonight if it's the last thing I do!"

My stomach did this heavy dip thing that it does when things don't feel right, and trust me, my diva boss sleeping with my bartender boss didn't exactly feel right to me. I told myself it had nothing to do with the fact that I may have, a couple of months back, had a mild crush on Joshua. That was prior to Lucas' disappearance with the shape shifter and necromancer down the Dark Portal, and once Lucas went down that deep dark hole, I realized how strong my love for him was. So in reality, Simone having sex with Joshua should not have mattered one iota to me. Then why did my stomach sink, and why, every night, did I look to see if his light was on in the guest cottage?

I told myself it was because of my concern over the fact that the cottage he'd been occupying housed the Dark Portal. The same Dark Portal that the man, er, um, spirit who I had been sleeping with and fallen crazy in love for had likely been taken down.

"Soooo, have you thought any more about going to New York and auditioning for that guy...what's his name?"

Simone knew exactly what his name was. Kane Richards had been a friend of my former boss Nick at the bar where I sing. Nick had been brutally murdered, but prior to his death he had contacted Kane. I worked on finding out who had killed Nick because the police hadn't seemed super concerned. They'd pretty much chalked his murder up to a mob hit. I did find the killers, and in the process nearly got Cass and me killed. Justice had been served though. My friend could rest in peace now—I hoped. But, my tutorial in the spirit world by Lucas and friends over the past few months hadn't convinced me that anyone's soul ever really rests in peace.

Bad news was that the day I discovered who had murdered Nick, I also witnessed Lucas being taken from me. That has kind of solidified my beliefs in the ideas of "tortured souls."

It's a complicated story on so many fronts. Normally, people are people. We go to work. We have friends. We have partners. We laugh, love, get angry, sad, happy—all that. Well, my life, as I've mentioned, is crazy and some of those reasons I've already explained—like being in love with a spirit who was taken from me. But it's even deeper than that.

Not only am I in love with Lucas, but I am also considered his project on what is known as the Grey Tier. Lucas has explained how the spirit world works, and I'm still not up to speed, but I've been learning. The Grey Tier is the human tier. It's akin to a plane. Apparently there are hundreds of tiers and when we die, we can wind up anywhere along the spectrum depending on who we were and how we lived our lives here on Earth. The White Tier, or as close to it as a soul can get, is apparently where you want to be—to me, in my understanding of it all, it's like Heaven. Now, I'm not sure who all is there. My Daddy would tell you that Jesus and his cronies are all there, and some other good saints, but I can tell you that he wouldn't buy into this whole tier thing if his life depended on it.

I probably wouldn't either, if not for some of the experiences I've had, and not just with Lucas, but also Bob Marley and Janice Joplin. Bear with me. I see ghosts that vibrate at the same level that I apparently do, and since outside of doing makeup for the diva, my true and honest vibration is that of a musician. It makes some sense that if I'm going to hang out with dead people, they'd be musicians.

Trust me, no one was as shocked as me to come home to the mansion in Hollywood Hills (my housesitting job) and spot Bob and Janis jamming, smoking pot and hanging out on the couch with my stoned cat Mac. I really did almost call the looney bin myself and insist someone hightail it there and take me away. But, thankfully I didn't, because it appears I have a job to do. I guess the Bodha, who are the enlightened souls that reside at the White Tier, and the Asat order, who reside at the Black Tier, both want what I have for different reasons.

Unbeknownst to me for my entire life until Lucas told me, I am what is known as a Govinda, which means that I am someone who gives joy to the universe because of my "gift."

That so-called gift is that if I come into hand-to-hand contact with someone, I can see in my mind the most traumatic experience they've ever suffered through. If you've been physically abused and it scarred you for life—I can see it. If you've lost the most important person in your life and haven't ever been able to get over it at all—I've got your number. If your mom was a crack addict who neglected you —yeah, well, you get it. I get to see the worst in people's lives. The things that have harmed them the most, and trust me, I don't exactly consider that a gift, or even see how that brings joy to the universe.

I guess what does is the other part of my gift—that with the seeing of these horrific things and through my touch, I can in a way heal those painful memories and scars. Through my touch, I can lighten the load that someone has been carrying. It's almost as if I can blur the memory—make it kind of fuzzy for that person.

I'm careful about touching people. Very careful. Let me say that isn't so easy. You wouldn't believe how many times a day you actually touch people without meaning to. I stay as covert as possible. It's not that I don't want to help heal. It's just that it can be really draining. The sort of positive is that if I do touch someone and the memory goes through me, then that's it. If I touch them again, it doesn't matter. I've done my part. It's kind of like ripping off a Band-Aid for me and being okay with what I see someone has been through. Sometimes I take that chance, and sometimes I don't.

So, now my gift is out there and the Asat Order wants my soul so they can extinguish any kind of light in me—the kind of light I can spread to make the world (the Grey Tier) a better place. The Bodha wants to keep me safe, because let's face it, the Enlightened Ones want the best for everyone. The Asat Order, which is apparently run by dark souls called Asuras, they don't want good things for souls. It's your standard case of good versus evil.

Sort of.

Lucas was sent to help keep me safe from the Asuras; however, he revealed that he isn't my guardian angel—thus, my search.

"Hey, Speed, how long does it take you to answer a simple question?"

"What? I'm sorry. I'm a little bit distracted."

"No shit. Maybe I should start calling you Fucking Paris."

"What?" I shook my head, confused.

"Yeah. That bitch has ADD."

I shook my head again. "Sorry."

"Paris fucking Hilton. She has ADD. Have you ever hung out with her? It's like hanging out with a fly at Dog Beach—going from one pile of shit to the next."

"You are really strange, Simone. I don't have ADD. And, when have you ever been to Dog Beach?"

"Whatever, Paris. And watch your mouth. Strange isn't in my vocab. You can call me bizarre, eccentric, but strange is so boring. And, I just figured that flies like dog shit, and I know you take Tess to Dog Beach sometimes, so I knew you'd get my little analogy."

I sighed. "My dog's name is Cass."

"So?"

I rolled my eyes at her.

"So?" she asked again.

"So what?"

"New York. Are you going to meet with that dude? What's his name?"

"Kane Richards, and I don't know yet. There's a lot on my plate."

"Hmm," she said and picked up a champagne flute, walked over to the wine fridge in her room and took out a bottle of Veuve Clicquot, which she promptly opened and then poured herself a glass. She poured me one, too. I had known her long enough to know that she would insist I drink the bubbly, and it wasn't a fight that I wanted to have at the moment, so I took a sip.

She plopped back down on her sofa and stared outside. I'm sure she was contemplating her next words of manipulation. I knew that the last thing she wanted was for me to go to New York and meet with Kane Richards.

After Nick's death Kane shows up, hears me sing and offers to fly me to New York and audition. The caveat here is that Kane has some kind of connection to the Dark Portal. I know he does because an evil spirit from the dark side who had taken advantage of me and who had been stalking me until Lucas's disappearance showed up in a photo I found in the cottage where Joshua lives. I know this is all slightly confusing, so stay with me here...

The house that I housesit is owned by some big-time producer named Blake who I've never met. He is Simone's buddy and she has never said much about him. The thing is, I've found photos of this guy, Kane, Lucas, evil spirit guy (obviously before either one of them died, as well as a photo with evil spirit guy and Mr. Richards). Told you it was complicated. Oh, and on top of that, when I shook Kane Richards' hand back at Nick's bar, I saw something. And, it scared me. I saw evil spirit guy and Kane, and evil spirit guy was making some kind of threat that appeared to scare the heck out of Kane Richards. My hand had touched his so briefly that everything had been a little less vivid than usual for me.

All that revealed, I've been a bit hesitant to jump on the next US Airways flight headed to JFK. However, singing is my dream and I love it. Simone keeps promising me an audition with some bigwigs over at Sony, but that has yet to transpire.

"You know, you've had it tough lately. I mean with that bartender buddy of yours getting, you know…" She took her pointer finger and slid it across her throat. "…and then you nearly were killed by those psychos. Thank God you weren't because I have no idea who could ever take your place."

"I'm not sure how to take that, but thank you." It could go either way—take my place because she really did care, or take my place because she loves the way I can make her look.

"Yeah. Exactly. Anyway, you need a break, Bestie. I'm going to book that audition and see if we can't make you a fucking star like me."

I smiled but at the same time there was this part of me that really wasn't sure I wanted to be a star like Simone. I knew I wanted to play my guitar. I knew I wanted to share my music with others and hopefully entertain them. I just wasn't sure about all of the glitz and glamour and headaches that seemed to accompany that kind of success. "Yeah."

"Yeah? Yeah the fuck what? Yeah! Come on, Evie. Get pumped. Isn't this what you want? You've been begging me to get you an audition. Get psyched! I'm going to call my people in the morning and get this thing rolling. But even when you hit it, you have to do my makeup. No one else can touch my face! Only you."

"No problem." I laughed. The hard part about touching Simone wasn't that I'd never seen anything horrible in her past—no real trauma. What I got from her was a terrible, deep-seated loneliness and it sucked me straight in. Maybe, that kind of loneliness is the worst trauma of all. Every time I had an inkling to tell her to take her obnoxious self out of my life, I couldn't do it. I knew that deep down Simone was a lonely woman, and I also knew she really did consider me her best friend. Honestly, in the crazy world that surrounded me, being a BFF to a pop star (especially one who was human) didn't seem so ludicrous to me.

Simone stood, downed the champagne, dropped her silk pink robe and stepped into the tight-fitting black number. "Zip me up."

"Your wish is my command."

"Hmm. I hope Joshua says the same thing to me come the witching hour."

I had no response to that other than, "You look great. I think I'll head out now if you don't need me."

"Run along, Toto."

"Toto?"

"Wizard of Oz." She stared at me dumbfounded, or as if I was dumbfounded, which I sort of was.

"I know where Toto comes from, but why call me that?"

"Because you're as cute as Dorothy's doggie and I just watched the movie last night."

"You're weird. I mean bizarre."

"Yep. Now don't wait up. I'm thinking that Joshua will be more comfortable in his own place for the first time. He's a sensitive sort."

"I have no intention of waiting up. I'm headed to the bar, plan to play some music and when I go home, me, the cat and dog are going to sleep."

"Sounds like a plan." She winked at me, grabbed her velvet clutch purse and sauntered past me; a whiff of her gardenia perfume blew on by with her.

As I made my way down Simone's spiral staircase behind her, I knew my time was limited. I had known for a week now that she was taking Joshua to this big gala. I did not know of her seduction plans, though. As soon as I'd heard about the gala and Joshua's presence as Simone's arm candy, I made plans to go into the cottage and see if I could find a way into the portal, or at least gather some more information. I'd told a white lie about going to the bar because I needed to do some investigating. Problem now was, I knew that Simone would be vying for some "down time" with Joshua and would likely be angling to get him home sooner than I had originally bargained for. I'd have to work quickly.

Having this information didn't change my mind for a minute, though. I was going on a snooping venture. I wanted to get Lucas back. I wanted to find out what happened to Hannah. I also needed answers as to the identity of the evil spirit from the Black Tier who I knew was gunning for me.